Praise for #1 *New York Times* **bestselling author**

NORA ROBERTS

"Roberts' bestselling novels are some of the best in
the romance genre. They are thoughtfully plotted,
well-written stories featuring fascinating characters."
—*USA TODAY*

"A superb author...Ms. Roberts is an enormously gifted
writer whose incredible range and intensity guarantee the
very best of reading."
—*Rave Reviews*

"Characters that touch the heart, stories that intrigue,
romance that sizzles, Nora Roberts has mastered it all."
—*Rendezvous*

"Her stories have fueled the dreams
of twenty-five million readers."
—*Entertainment Weekly*

"Roberts is deservedly one of the best known
and most widely read of all romance writers."
—*Literary Journal*

"Roberts has a warm feel for her characters
and an eye for the evocative detail."
—*Chicago Tribune*

"When Roberts puts her expert fingers on the pulse
of romance, legions of fans feel the heartbeat."
—*Publishers Weekly*

Dear Reader,

Nobody likes being pushed out of their comfort zone, but as we see in these two classic stories from bestselling author Nora Roberts, sometimes a little adventure is exactly what we need to find what we've been looking for all along.

In *Impulse,* Rebecca Malone has always stuck to her finely tuned routine, but when a death in the family leaves her shaken, she decides to jettison the familiar and head to Greece on a whim. Her new, spontaneous outlook on life catches Stephen Nickdemus's attention the minute she walks into his restaurant. But as the two grow closer, Rebecca starts to panic. How can she tell the man she's falling for that she isn't the woman he believes her to be?

In *Lessons Learned,* we meet Juliet Trent, a driven publicist who refuses to let her personal and professional lives intersect. Enter Carlo Franconi, irresistible celebrity chef—and Juliet's new client. As a successful and independent businesswoman, Juliet knows she can't afford to be swept away by Carlo's charms, but she doesn't count on his determination...or her own desire to take a chance and enjoy the ride.

We hope these two stories inspire you to step outside your comfort zone and try something new. You never know what surprises life—and love—might have in store!

The Editors

Silhouette Books

NORA ROBERTS

Something New

Silhouette Books

Published by Silhouette Books

America's Publisher of Contemporary Romance

SILHOUETTE BOOKS

Recycling programs
for this product may
not exist in your area.

SOMETHING NEW

ISBN-13: 978-0-373-28182-4

Copyright © 2014 by Harlequin Books S.A.

The publisher acknowledges the copyright holder of the individual works as follows:

IMPULSE
Copyright © 1989 by Nora Roberts

LESSONS LEARNED
Copyright © 1986 by Nora Roberts

This edition published by arrangement with Harlequin Books S.A.

For questions and comments about the quality of this book, please contact us at CustomerService@Harlequin.com.

® and TM are trademarks of Harlequin Books S.A., used under license. Trademarks indicated with ® are registered in the United States Patent and Trademark Office, the Canadian Intellectual Property Office and in other countries.

Visit Silhouette Books at www.Harlequin.com

Printed in U.S.A.

CONTENTS

IMPULSE

Chapter 1

She knew it was crazy. That was what she liked best about it. It was crazy, ridiculous, impractical and totally out of character. And she was having the time of her life. From the balcony of her hotel suite Rebecca could see the sweep of the beach, the glorious blue of the Ionian Sea, blushed now with streaks of rose from the setting sun.

Corfu. Even the name sounded mysterious, exciting, glamorous. And she was here, really here. Practical, steady-as-a-rock Rebecca Malone, who had never traveled more than five hundred miles from Philadelphia, was in Greece. Not just in Greece, she thought with a grin, but on the exotic island of Corfu, in one of the most exclusive resorts in Europe.

First-class, she thought as she leaned out to let the

sweet breeze ruffle over her face. As long as it lasted, she was going first-class.

Her boss had thought she was suffering from temporary insanity. Edwin McDowell of McDowell, Jableki and Kline was never going to understand why a promising young CPA would resign from her position with one of the top accounting firms in Philadelphia. She'd made a good salary, she'd enjoyed excellent benefits, and she'd even had a small window in her office.

Friends and associates had wondered if she'd suffered a breakdown. After all, it wasn't normal, and it certainly wasn't Rebecca's style to quit a solid, well-paying job without the promise of a better one.

But she'd given her two weeks' notice, cleared out her desk and had cheerfully walked out into the world of the unemployed.

When she'd sold her condo and then in one frantic week, auctioned off every possession she owned—every stick of furniture, every pot and pan and appliance—they'd been certain she'd gone over the edge.

Rebecca had never felt saner.

She owned nothing that didn't fit in a suitcase. She no longer had any tax-deferred investments or retirement plans. She'd cashed in her certificates of deposit, and the home entertainment center she'd thought she couldn't live without was now gracing someone else's home.

It had been more than six weeks since she'd even looked at an adding machine.

For the first—and perhaps the only—time in her life, she was totally free. There were no responsibilities, no pressures, no hurried gulps of cold coffee. She hadn't packed an alarm clock. She no longer owned one. Crazy? No. Rebecca shook her head and laughed into the breeze. For as long as it lasted, she was going to grab life with both hands and see what it had to offer.

Aunt Jeannie's death had been her turning point. It had come so suddenly, so unexpectedly, leaving Rebecca without any family. Aunt Jeannie had worked hard for most of her sixty-five years, always punctual, always responsible. Her position as head librarian had been her whole life. She'd never missed a day, never failed to do her duty. Her bills had been paid on time. Her promises had always been kept.

More than once Rebecca had been told she took after her mother's older sister. She was twenty-four, but she was—had been—as solid and sturdy as her maiden aunt. Two months into retirement, two months after dear Aunt Jeannie began to make plans to travel, to enjoy the rewards she'd worked so hard to earn, she was gone.

After Rebecca's grief had come the anger, then the frustration, then slowly, the realization that she was traveling the same straight road. She worked, she slept, she fixed well-balanced meals that she ate alone. She had a small circle of friends who knew she could be counted on in a crisis. Rebecca would always find the best and most practical answer. Rebecca would never drop her own problems in your lap—because she didn't have any. Rebecca, bless her, was a port in any storm.

She hated it, and she'd begun to hate herself. She had to do something.

And she was doing it.

It wasn't running away as much as it was breaking free. All her life she'd done what was expected of her and tried to make as few waves as possible while doing it. All through school a crushing shyness had kept her more comfortable with her books than with other teenagers. In college a need to succeed and justify her aunt's faith had locked her tightly into her studies.

She had always been good with figures—logical, thorough, patient. It had been easy, perhaps too easy, to pour herself into that one area, because there, and really only there, had she felt confident.

Now she was going to discover Rebecca Malone. In the weeks or months of freedom she had, she wanted to learn everything there was to know about the woman within. Perhaps there wasn't a butterfly inside the cocoon she'd wrapped herself in so comfortably, but whatever she found—whoever she found—Rebecca hoped she would enjoy her, like her, perhaps even respect her.

When the money ran out, she'd get another job and go back to being plain, practical Rebecca. Until that time she was rich, rootless and ready for surprises.

She was also hungry.

Stephen saw her the moment she entered the restaurant. It wasn't that she was particularly striking. Beautiful women passed through the world every day and they usually warranted a glance. But there was something about the way this one walked, as if she were ready for anything, even looking forward to it. He stopped, and because business was slow at this hour he took a second, longer look.

She was tall for a woman, and more angular than slender. Her skin was pale, and that made him think she had only just arrived at the resort or was shy of the sun. The white sundress that left her shoulders and back bare accented the lack of color and gave dramatic contrast to her short cap of raven hair.

She paused, then seemed to take a deep breath. Stephen could almost hear her satisfied sigh. Then she smiled at the headwaiter, and followed him to her table, tossing her head back, so that her hair, which she wore arrow-straight, swung away from her chin.

A nice face, Stephen concluded. Bright, intelligent, eager. Especially the eyes. They were pale, an almost translucent gray. But there was nothing pale in their expression. She smiled at the waiter again, then laughed and looked around the restaurant. She looked as if she'd never been happier in her life.

She saw him. When Rebecca's gaze first skimmed over the man leaning against the bar, her automatic shyness kicked in and had her looking away. Attractive men had stared at her before—though it wasn't exactly a daily event. She'd never been able to handle it with the aplomb—or even cynicism—of most of her contemporaries. To cover her momentary embarrassment, she lifted her menu.

He hadn't meant to linger more than a few moments longer, but the impulse came suddenly. Stephen flicked a hand at the waiter and had him scurrying over, nodding quickly at Stephen's murmured request and hurrying off. When he returned it was to deliver a bottle of champagne to Rebecca's table.

"Compliments of Mr. Nickodemus."

"Oh." Rebecca followed the waiter's gaze over to the man by the bar. "Well, I—" She brought herself up short before she could stammer. A sophisticated woman wouldn't stutter over a gift of champagne, she reminded herself. She'd accept it graciously, with dignity. And maybe—if she wasn't a complete fool—she'd relax enough to flirt with the man who offered it.

Stephen watched the expressions pass across her face. Fascinating, he mused, and realized that the vague boredom he'd been feeling had vanished. When she lifted her head and smiled at him, he had no idea that her heart was pounding. He saw only a casual invitation, and he answered it.

He wasn't just attractive, Rebecca realized as he crossed to her table. He was gorgeous. Eye-popping, mouth-dropping gorgeous. She had an image of Apollo and ancient Greek warriors. Thick blond hair streaked by the sun fell over the collar of his shirt. Smooth, bronzed skin was marred—and somehow enhanced—by a faint scar under his jawline. A strong jaw, she thought. A strong face, with the darkest, deepest blue eyes she'd ever seen.

"Good evening, I'm Stephen Nickodemus." His voice wasn't accented, it was rounded, rich. He might have come from anywhere. Perhaps it was that, more than anything else, that intrigued her.

Lecturing herself on poise and image, she lifted her hand. "Hello. I'm Rebecca, Rebecca Malone." She felt a quick flutter when he brushed his lips over her knuckles. Feeling foolish, she drew her hand away and balled it in her lap. "Thank you for the champagne."

"It seemed to suit your mood." He studied her, wondering why he was getting such a mix of signals. "You are by yourself?"

"Yes." Perhaps it was a mistake to admit it, but if she

was going to live life to the fullest she had to take some risks. The restaurant wasn't crowded, but they were hardly alone. Take the plunge, she told herself, and tried another smile. "The least I can do is offer you a glass."

Stephen took the seat across from her, brushing the waiter aside to pour the wine himself. "You are American?"

"It shows."

"No. Actually, I thought you were French until you spoke."

"Did you?" That pleased her. "I've just come from Paris." She had to force herself not to touch her hair. She'd had it cut, with trepidation and delight, in a French salon.

Stephen touched his glass to hers. Her eyes bubbled with life as cheerfully as the wine. "Business?"

"No, just pleasure." What a marvelous word, she thought. *Pleasure.* "It's a wonderful city."

"Yes. Do you go often?"

Rebecca smiled into her glass. "Not often enough. Do you?"

"From time to time."

She nearly sighed at that. Imagine anyone speaking of going to Paris "from time to time." "I nearly stayed longer, but I'd promised myself Greece."

So she was alone, restless, and on the move. Perhaps that was why she had appealed to him, because he was, too. "Is Corfu your first stop?"

"Yes." She sipped at her drink. A part of her still believed it was all a dream. Greece, champagne, the man. "It's beautiful. Much more beautiful than I imagined it could be."

"It's your first trip, then?" He couldn't have said why that pleased him. "How long do you stay?"

"As long as I like." She grinned, savoring the feeling of freedom. "And you?"

He lifted his glass. "Longer, I think, than I had planned." When the waiter appeared at his side, Stephen handed over the menu, then spoke to him in soft, quick Greek. "If you don't object, I'd like to guide you through your first meal on the island."

The old Rebecca would have been too nervous to sit through a meal with a stranger. The new Rebecca took a second, deeper sip of champagne. "I'd love it. Thank you."

It was easy. Easy to sit, to laugh, to sample new and exotic tastes. She forgot that he was a stranger, forgot that the world she was living in now was only temporary. They didn't speak of anything important—only of Paris, and the weather, and the wine. Still, she was sure it was the most interesting conversation of her life. He looked at her when he spoke to her, looked at her as though he were delighted to spend an hour talking of nothing. The last man she'd had dinner with had wanted her to give him a discount when she did his taxes.

Stephen wasn't asking her for anything more than her company for dinner. When he looked at her it seemed unlikely that he'd care if she knew how to fill out Schedule C.

When he suggested a walk along the beach, she agreed without a qualm. What better way to end an evening than a walk in the moonlight?

"I was looking out at this from my window just before dinner." Rebecca stepped out of her shoes, then dangled them from her fingers as she walked. "I didn't think it could look more beautiful than it did at sunset."

"The sea changes, like a woman, in the light." He paused to touch a flame to the end of a slim cigar. "So men are drawn to her."

"Are you? Drawn to the sea?"

"I've spent my time on her. I fished in these waters as a boy."

She'd learned at dinner that he'd grown up traveling the islands with his father. "It must have been exciting, moving from place to place, seeing new things almost every day."

He shrugged. He'd never been sure whether the restlessness had been born in him or had been a product of his upbringing. "It had its moments."

"I love to travel." Laughing, she tossed her shoes aside, then stepped into the surf. The champagne was making her head swim and the moonlight felt as soft as rain. "I adore it." She laughed again when the spray washed up to dampen her skirts. The Ionian Sea. She was standing in it. "On a night like this I think I'll never go home."

She looked so vibrant, so alive, standing in the surf with her white skirts billowing. "Where's home?"

She glanced over her shoulder. The flirtatious look was totally unplanned and completely devastating. "I haven't decided. I want to swim." On impulse, she dived into the surf.

Stephen's heart stopped when she disappeared. He'd already kicked off his shoes and started forward when she rose up again. For a second time, his heart stopped. She was laughing, her face lifted to the moonlight.

Water cascaded from her hair, from her skin. The drops that clung to her were the only jewels she wore. Beautiful? No, she wasn't beautiful. She was electric.

"It's wonderful. Cool and soft and wonderful."

With a shake of his head, he stepped in far enough to take her hand and pull her toward shore. She was a little mad, perhaps, but engagingly so. "Are you always so impulsive?"

"I'm working on it. Aren't you?" She combed her hand through her dripping hair. "Or do you always send champagne to strange women?"

"Either way I answer that could be trouble. Here." He shrugged out of his jacket and draped it over her shoulders. Unframed, washed clean, her face glowed in the moonlight. There was a graceful kind of strength in it, to the sweep of cheekbone, the slightly pointed chin. Delicate—except for the eyes. One look there showed power, a power that was still. "You're irresistible, Rebecca."

She stared at him, confused all over again, as he gathered the neck of the jacket close around her throat. "I'm wet," she managed.

"And beautiful." With his hands still on the jacket, he brought her toward him. "And fascinating."

That made her laugh again. "I don't think so, but thanks. I'm glad you sent me the champagne and guided me through my first meal." Her nerves began to jangle. His eyes stayed on hers, journeying only once to her mouth, which was still damp from the sea. Their bodies were close, close enough to brush. Rebecca began to shiver, and she knew it had nothing to do with wet clothes and the breeze.

"I should go in…change my dress."

There was something about her. The impulsiveness, the easy flirtatiousness, hid an unmistakable innocence that baffled and attracted him. Whatever it was, he wanted more.

"I'll see you again."

"Yes." She prayed for her heartbeat to slow. "It's not a very big island."

He smiled at that, slowly. She felt, with a mixture of relief and regret, the relaxation of his hands. "Tomorrow. I have business early. I'll be done by eleven, if that suits you. I'll show you Corfu."

"All right." Better judgment and nerves be damned. She wanted to go with him. "I'll meet you in the lobby." Carefully, because she suddenly wasn't sure she could manage it, she stepped back. Moonlight silhouetted him against the sea. "Good night, Stephen."

She forgot to be sophisticated and dashed toward the hotel.

He watched her go. She puzzled him, puzzled him as no woman had since he'd been a boy and too young to understand that a woman was not meant to be understood. And he wanted her. That wasn't new, but the desire had come with surprising speed and surprising force.

Rebecca Malone might have started out as an impulse, but she was now a mystery. One he intended to solve. With a little laugh, he bent to scoop up the shoes she'd forgotten. He hadn't felt quite so alive in months.

Chapter 2

Stephen wasn't the kind of man who rearranged his schedule to spend the day with a woman. Especially a woman he barely knew. He was a wealthy man, but he was also a busy man, driven by both pride and ambition to maintain a high level of involvement in all his projects. He shouldered responsibility well and had learned to enjoy the benefits of hard work and dedication.

His time on Corfu wasn't free—or rather hadn't been planned as free. Mixing business and pleasure wasn't his style. He pursued both, separately, with utter concentration. Yet he found himself juggling appointments, meetings, conference calls, in order to have the afternoon open for Rebecca.

He supposed any man would want to get to know a woman who flirted easily over a champagne flute one moment and dived fully dressed into the sea the next.

"I've postponed your meeting with Theoharis until five-thirty this evening." Stephen's secretary scribbled on a notepad she had resting on her lap. "He will meet you for early cocktails in the suite. I've arranged for hors d'oeuvres and a bottle of ouzo."

"Always efficient, Elana."

She smiled and tucked a fall of dark hair behind her ear. "I try."

When Stephen rose to pace to the window, she folded her hands and waited. She had worked for him for five years, she admired his energy and his business acumen, and—fortunately for both of them—had long since gotten over an early crush. There was often speculation about their personal relationship, but though he could be friendly—even kind when it suited him—with Stephen, business was business.

"Contact Mithos in Athens. Have him telex that report by the end of the day. And I want to hear from Lereau by five, Paris time."

"Shall I call and give him a nudge?"

"If you think it's necessary." Restless, he dug his hands in his pockets. Where had this sudden discontent come from? he wondered. He was wealthy, successful, and free, as always, to move from place to place. As he stared out at the sea, he remembered the scent of Rebecca's skin. "Send flowers to Rebecca Malone's suite. Wildflowers, nothing formal. This afternoon."

Elana made a note, hoping she'd get a look at this Rebecca Malone before long. She had already heard through the grapevine that Stephen had had dinner with an American woman. "And the card?"

He wasn't a man for poetry. "Just my name."

"Anything else?"

"Yes." He turned and offered her a half smile. "Take some time off. Go to the beach."

Pad in hand, she rose. "I'll be sure to work it in. Enjoy your afternoon, Stephen."

He intended to. As she left him, Stephen glanced at his watch. It was fifteen minutes before eleven. There was work he could do to fill in the time, a quick call that could be made. Instead, he picked up Rebecca's shoes.

After three tries, Rebecca settled on an outfit. She didn't have an abundance of clothes, because she'd preferred to spend her funds on travel. But she had splurged here and there on her route through Europe. No tidy CPA suits, she thought as she tied a vivid fuchsia sash at the waist of her sapphire-colored cotton pants. No sensible shoes or pastel blouses. The last shock of color came from a primrose-hued blouse cut generously to layer over a skinny tank top in the same shade as the slacks.

The combination delighted her, if only because her firm had preferred quiet colors and clean lines.

She had no idea where she was going, and she didn't care.

It was a beautiful day, even though she'd awoken with a dull headache from the champagne, and the disorientation that went with it. A light, early breakfast on her terrace and a quick dip in the sea had cleared both away. She still had trouble believing that she could lounge through a morning as she pleased—and that she'd spent the evening with a man she'd just met.

Aunt Jeannie would have tut-tutted and reminded her of the dangers of being a woman alone. Some of her friends would have been shocked, others envious. But they would all have been astonished that steady Rebecca had strolled in the moonlight with a gorgeous man with a scar on his jawline and eyes like velvet.

If she hadn't had his jacket as proof, she might have thought she'd dreamed it. There had never been anything wrong with her imagination—just the application of it. Often she'd pictured herself in an exotic place with an exotic man, with moonlight and music. Imagined herself, she remembered. And then she'd turned on her calculator and gotten down to business.

But she hadn't dreamed this. She could still remember the giddy, half-terrified feeling that had swarmed through her when he'd gathered her close. When his mouth had been only an inch from hers and the sea and the champagne had roared in her head.

What if he had kissed her? What tastes would she have found? Rich, strong ones, she mused, almost able to savor them as she traced a fingertip over her lips. After just one evening she was absolutely certain there would be nothing lukewarm about Stephen Nickodemus. She wasn't nearly so certain about Rebecca.

She probably would have fumbled and blushed and stammered. With a shake of her head, she pulled a brush through her hair. Exciting men didn't tumble all over themselves to kiss neat, practical-minded women.

But he'd asked to see her again.

Rebecca wasn't certain whether she was disappointed or relieved that he hadn't pressed his advantage and kissed her. She'd been kissed before, held before, of course. But she had a feeling—a very definite feeling—that it wouldn't be the same with Stephen. He might make her want more, offer more, than she had with any other man.

Crossing bridges too soon, she decided as she checked the contents of her big straw bag. She wasn't going to have an affair with him, or with anyone. Even the new, improved Rebecca Malone wasn't the type for a casual affair. But maybe— She caught her lower lip between her teeth. If the time was right she might have a romance she'd remember long after she left Greece.

For now, she was ready, but it was much too early to go down. It would hardly make her look like a well-traveled woman of the world if she popped down to the lobby and paced for ten minutes. This was her fantasy, after all. She didn't want him to think she was inexperienced and overeager.

Only the knock on the door prevented her from changing her mind about her outfit one more time.

"Hello." Stephen studied her for a moment, unsmiling. He'd nearly been certain he'd exaggerated, but she was just as vibrant, just as exciting, in the morning as she had been in the moonlight. He held out her shoes. "I thought you might need these."

She laughed, remembering her impulsive dunk in the sea. "I didn't realize I'd left them on the beach. Come in a minute." With a neatness ingrained in her from childhood, she turned to take them to the bedroom closet. "I'm ready to go if you are."

Stephen lifted a brow. He preferred promptness, but he never expected it in anyone but a business associate. "I've got a Jeep waiting. Some of the roads are rough."

"Sounds great." Rebecca came out again, carrying her bag and a flat-brimmed straw hat. She handed Stephen his jacket, neatly folded. "I forgot to give this back to you last night." Should she offer to have it cleaned? she wondered when he only continued to look at her. Fiddling with the strap of her bag, she decided against it. "Does taking pictures bother you?"

"No, why?"

"Good, because I take lots of them. I can't seem to stop myself."

She wasn't kidding. As Stephen drove up into the hills, she took shots of everything. Sheep, tomato plants, olive groves and straggly sage. He stopped so that she could walk out near the edge of a cliff and look down at a small village huddled near the sea.

She wouldn't be able to capture it on film; she wasn't clever enough. But she knew she'd never forget that light, so pure, so clear, or the contrast between the orange tiled roofs and the low white-washed walls and the deep, dangerous blue of the water that flung itself against the weathered rock that rose into harsh crags. A stork, legs tucked, glided over the water, where fishing boats bobbed.

There were nets drying on the beach and children playing. Flowers bloomed and tangled where the wind had planted them, more spectacular than any planned arrangement could ever be.

"It's beautiful." Her throat tightened with emotion, and with a longing she couldn't have defined. "So calm. You imagine women baking black bread and the men coming home smelling of fish and the sea. It looks as though it hasn't changed in a hundred years."

"Very little." He glanced down himself, surprised and more than a little pleased that she would be touched by something so simple. "We cling to antiquity."

"I haven't seen the Acropolis yet, but I don't think it could be any more spectacular than this." She lifted her face, delighted by the way the wind whipped at it. Here, high above the sea, she absorbed everything—the salty, rough-edged bite of the wind, the clarity of color and sound, and the man beside her. Letting her camera dangle from its strap, she turned to him. "I haven't thanked you for taking the time to show me all of this."

He took her hand, not to raise it to his lips, just to hold it. It was a link he hadn't known he wanted. "I'm enjoying seeing the familiar through someone else's eyes. Your eyes."

Suddenly the edge of the cliff seemed too close, the sun too hot. Could he do that just by touching her? With an effort, Rebecca smiled, keeping her voice light. "If you ever come to Philadelphia, I'll do the same for you."

It was odd. She'd looked almost frightened for a moment. Fragile and frightened. Stephen had always carefully avoided women who were easily bruised. "I'll consider that a promise."

They continued to drive, over roads that jarred and climbed and twisted. She saw her first of the *agrimi*, the wild goat of Greece, and the rocky pastures dotted with sturdy sheep. And everywhere, rich and defiant, was the intense color of flowers.

He didn't complain when she asked him to stop so that she could snap pictures of tiny blue star blossoms that pushed their way through cracks in the rock. He listened to her delight as she framed a thick, thorny stem topped with a ragged yellow flower. It made him realize, and regret, that it had been years since he'd taken the time to look closely at the small, vital things that grew around him.

He looked now at Rebecca standing in the sunlight, her hat fluttering around her face and her laugh dancing on the air.

Often the road clung to cliffs that plunged dizzily into the sea. Rebecca, who was too timid to fight rush-hour traffic, found it exhilarating.

She felt almost like another person. She *was* another person, she thought, laughing as she held on to her hat to keep the wind from snatching it away.

"I love it!" she shouted over the wind and the noise of the engine. "It's wild and old and incredible. Like no place I've ever been."

Still laughing, she lifted her camera and snapped his picture as he drove. He wore sunglasses with amber lenses and had a cigar clamped between his teeth. The wind blew through his hair and chased the smoke behind them. He stopped the Jeep, took the camera and snapped a picture of her in turn.

"Hungry?"

She dragged her tousled hair back from her face. "Starving."

He leaned over to open her door. A current passed through her, sharp and electric, strong enough to make him pause with his arm across her body and his face close to hers. It was there again, he thought as he waited and watched. The awareness, ripe and seductive. And the innocence, as alluring as it was contradictory. In a test—a test for both of them—he lifted a hand to stroke her cheek. It was as soft as her scent.

"Are you afraid of me, Rebecca?"

"No." That was true; she was nearly sure of it. "Should I be?"

He didn't smile. Through the amber lenses she saw

that his eyes were very intense. "I'm not entirely sure." When he pulled away he heard her release an unsteady breath. He wasn't feeling completely steady himself. "We'll have to walk a little first."

Confused, her mind churning, she stepped out onto the dirt path. A woman on a simple date didn't tremble every time a man got close, Rebecca told herself as Stephen lifted the picnic basket out of the back. She was behaving like a teenager, not a grown woman.

Troubled by his own thoughts, Stephen stopped beside her. He hesitated, then held out a hand. It felt good, simply good, when she put hers in it.

They walked through an olive grove in a companionable silence while the sun streamed down on dusty leaves and rocky ground. There was no sound of the sea here, but when the wind was right she could hear the screech of a gull far away. The island was small, but here it seemed uninhabited.

"I haven't had a picnic in years." Rebecca spread the cloth. "And never in an olive grove." She glanced around, wanting to remember every leaf and pebble. "Are we trespassing?"

"No." Stephen took a bottle of white wine from the basket. Rebecca left him to it and started rummaging in search of food.

"Do you know the owner?"

"I'm the owner." He drew the cork with a gentle pop.

"Oh." She looked around again. It should have occurred to her that he would own something impressive, different, exciting. "It sounds romantic. Owning an olive grove."

He lifted a brow. He owned a number of them, but he had never thought of them as romantic. They were simply profitable. He offered her a glass, then tapped it with his own. "To romance, then."

She swept down her lashes, battling shyness. To Stephen, the gesture was only provocative. "I hope you're hungry," she began, knowing she was talking too fast. "It all looks wonderful." She took a quick sip of wine to ease her dry throat, then set it aside to finish unpacking the basket.

There were sweet black olives as big as a man's thumb, and there was a huge slab of sharp cheese. There were cold lamb and hunks of bread, and fruit so fresh it could have been just plucked from the stem.

Gradually she began to relax again.

"You've told me very little about yourself." Stephen topped off her wine and watched her bite into a ripe red plum. "I know little more than that you come from Philadelphia and enjoy traveling."

What could she tell him? A man like him was bound to be bored with the life story of the painfully ordinary Rebecca Malone. Lies had never come easily to her, so she skirted between fact and fiction. "There's little more. I grew up in Philadelphia. I lost both of my parents when I was a teenager, and I lived with my aunt Jeannie. She was very dear, and she made the loss bearable."

"It's painful." He flicked his lighter at the end of a cigar, remembering not only the pain, but also the fury he had felt when his father had died and left him orphaned at sixteen. "It steals childhood."

"Yes." So he understood that. It made her feel close to him, close and comfortable. "Maybe that's why I like to travel. Every time you see a new place you can be a child again."

"So you don't look for roots?"

She glanced at him then. He was leaning back against the trunk of a tree, smoking lazily, watching carefully. "I don't know what I'm looking for."

"Is there a man?"

She moved her shoulders, determined not to be embarrassed. "No."

He took her hand, drawing her closer. "No one?"

"No, I…" She wasn't certain what she would have said, but could say nothing at all when he turned her palm upward and pressed his lips to its center. She felt the fire burst there, in her hand, then race everywhere.

"You're very responsive, Rebecca." He lowered her hand but kept it in his. He could feel the heat, but he wasn't sure whether it had sprung to her skin or to his own. "If there's no one, the men in your Philadelphia must be very slow."

"I've been too…busy."

His lips curved at that. There was a tremor in her voice, and there was passion in her eyes. "Busy?"

"Yes." Afraid she'd make a fool of herself, she drew her hand back. "This was wonderful." Trying to calm herself, she pushed a hand through her hair. "You know what I need?"

"No. Tell me."

"Another picture." She sprang to her feet and, steadier, grinned. "A memento of my first picnic in an olive grove. Let's see…you can stand right over there. The sun's good in front of that tree, and I should be able to frame in that section of the grove."

Amused, Stephen tapped out his cigar. "How much more film do you have?"

"This is the last roll—but I have scads back at the hotel." She flicked him a quick laughing glance. "I warned you."

"So you did." Competent hands, he thought as he watched her focus and adjust. He hadn't realized he could be as attracted to competence as he was to beauty. She mumbled to herself, tossing her head back so that her hair swung, then settled. His stomach tightened without warning.

Good God, he wanted her. She'd done nothing to make him burn and strain this way. He couldn't accuse her of taunting or teasing, and yet...he felt taunted. He felt teased. For the first time in his life he felt totally seduced by a woman who had done nothing more than give him a few smiles and a little companionship.

Even now she was chattering away as she secured her camera to the limb of a tree. Talking easily, as though they were just friends, as though she felt nothing more than a light, unimportant affection. But he'd seen it. Stephen felt his blood heat as he remembered the quick flash of arousal he'd seen on her face. He'd see it again. And more.

"I'm going to set the timer," Rebecca went on, blissfully unaware of Stephen's thoughts. "All you have to do is stand there. Once I get this damn thing set, I'm going to run over so it'll take one of both—There." She interrupted herself, crossed her fingers and ran to Stephen's side in a dash. "Unless I messed up, it'll snap all by itself in—"

The rest of the words slid down her throat as he crushed her against him and captured her mouth.

Chapter 3

Heat. Light. Speed. Rebecca felt them, felt each separate, distinct sensation. Urgency. Demand. Impatience. She tasted them, as clearly as wild honey, on his lips. Though she'd never experienced it, she had known exactly what it would be like to be with him, mouth to mouth and need to need.

In an instant the world had narrowed from what could be seen and understood to a pure, seamless blanket of emotion. It cloaked her, not softly, not in comfort, but tightly, hotly, irresistibly. Caught between fear and delight, she lifted a hand to his cheek.

God, she was sweet. Even as he dragged her closer, aroused by the simplicity of her acceptance, he was struck by—disarmed by—her sweetness. There had been a hesitation, almost too brief to be measured, before her lips had parted beneath his. Parted, invited, accepted.

There was a sigh, so soft it could barely be heard, as she stroked her hands up his back to his shoulders. Curious, simple, generous. A man could drown in such sweetness, fall prisoner to such pliancy. And be saved by it. Beneath the patterned shade of the olive tree, she gave him more than passion. She gave him hope.

Charmed, he murmured some careless Greek phrase lovers might exchange. The words meant nothing to her, but the sound of them on the still air, the feel of them stroking across her lips…seduction. Glorious seduction.

Pleasure burst in her blood, in her head, in her heart, thousands of tiny bubbles of it, until she was straining against him.

The quiet explosion rocked him. It tightened his chest, fuddled his mind. She fitted into his arms as if she'd been born for him. As if, somehow, they had known each other before, loved before, hungered before. Something seemed to erupt between them, something molten, powerful, dangerous. But it wasn't new. It was ancient, a whispering echo of ageless passions.

She began to tremble. How could this be so right, so familiar? It wasn't possible to feel safe and threatened at the same time. But she did. She clung to him while a dim, floating image danced through her head. She had kissed him before. Just like this. As her mind spun, she heard her own mindless murmurs answer his. As freely, as inescapably as the sun poured light, response flowed from her. She couldn't stop it. Frightened by her sudden loss of control, she struggled against him, against herself.

He slipped his hands up to her shoulders, but not to free her, to look at her. To look at how their coming together had changed her. It had changed him. Passion had made her eyes heavy, seductive. Fear had clouded them. Her lips were full, softened and parted by his. Her breath shivered through them. Under his hands he could feel the heat of her skin and the quick, involuntary trembling of her muscles.

No pretense here, he decided as he studied her. He was holding both innocence and delight in his hands.

"Stephen, I—"

"Again."

Then his face filled her vision and she was lost.

Differently. Should she have known that one man could hold one woman in so many different ways? That one man could kiss one woman with such stunning variety? There was gentleness now, as familiar and as novel as the urgency. His lips persuaded rather than demanded. They savored instead of devouring. Her surrender came as quietly, and as unmistakably, as her earlier passion. The trembling stopped; the fear vanished. With a complete trust that surprised them both, she leaned against him, giving.

More aroused by her serenity than by the storm that had come before, Stephen pulled back. He had to, or what had begun would finish without either of them saying a word. As he swore and pulled out a cigar, Rebecca placed a hand on the olive tree for support.

Moments, she thought. It had been only moments, and yet she felt as though years had passed, racing backward or forward, perhaps spinning in circles. In a place like this, with a man like this, what difference did it make what year it was? What century?

Half-terrified, she lifted a hand to her lips. Despite her fear, they curved under her touch. She could still taste him. Still feel him. And nothing, nothing, would ever be quite the same again.

He stared out at the rough and dusty land he'd known as a boy, and beyond, to the stark, tumbling rocks where he and other wild things had climbed.

What was he doing with her? Furious with himself, he drew on the cigar. What was he feeling? It was new, and far from comfortable. And it was comfort he preferred, he reminded himself. Comfort and freedom. Bringing himself under control, he turned to her again, determined to treat what had happened as a man should—lightly.

She just stood there, with the sun and the shade falling over her. There was neither recrimination nor invitation in her eyes. She didn't flinch or step forward, but merely stood, watching him with the faintest of smiles, as if... As if, Stephen realized, she knew what questions he was asking himself—and the answers.

"It grows late."

She felt the ache and fought not to let it show on her face. "I guess you're right." She dragged a hand through her hair—it was the first sign of her agitation—then walked over to pick up her camera. "I should have a picture to remember all this by," she said, forcing brightness into her voice. Her breath caught when his fingers closed over her arm and whirled her around.

"Who are you?" he demanded. "What are you?"

"I don't know what you mean." The emotion burst out before she could stop it. "I don't know what you want."

With one jerk he had her tumbling against him. "You know what I want."

Her heart was in her throat, beating wildly. She found it strange that it was not fear but desire that she felt. She hadn't known she was capable of feeling a need that was so unreasonable, so reckless. It was almost purifying to experience it, and to see it mirrored in his eyes.

"It takes more than one afternoon." Didn't it? Her voice rose as she tried to convince herself. "It takes more than a picnic and a walk in the moonlight for me."

"One moment the temptress, the next the outraged innocent. Do you do it to intrigue me, Rebecca?" She shook her head, and his fingers tightened. "It works," he murmured. "You've hardly been out of my mind since I first saw you. I want to make love with you, here, in the sun."

Color flooded her face, not because she was embarrassed, but because she could imagine it, perfectly. And then what? Carefully she leveled her breathing. Whatever impulses she had followed, whatever bridges she had burned, she still needed answers.

"No." It cost her to go against her own needs and say it. "Not when I'm unsure and you're angry." She took a deep breath and kept her eyes on him. "You're hurting me, Stephen. I don't think you mean to."

Slowly he released her arm. He was angry, furious, but not at her refusal. The anger stemmed from the need she pulled from him, a need that had come too fast and too strong for him to channel. "We'll go back."

Rebecca merely nodded, then knelt to gather the remains of the picnic.

* * *

He was a busy man, much too busy to brood about a woman he barely knew and didn't understand at all. That was what Stephen told himself. He had reports to read, calls to make and paperwork—which he had both a talent and a distaste for—to deal with. A couple of simple kisses weren't enough to take a man's mind off his work.

But there hadn't been anything simple about them. Disgusted, Stephen pushed away from his desk and wandered to the terrace doors. He'd left them open because the breeze, and the fragrances it brought, helped him forget he was obligated to be inside.

For days he'd worked his way through his responsibilities, trying to ignore the nagging itch at the back of his mind—the itch that was Rebecca. There was no reason for him to stay on Corfu. He could have handled his business in Athens, or Crete, or in London, for that matter. Still, he'd made no plans to leave, though he'd also made no attempt to approach her.

She…concerned him, he decided. To be drawn to an attractive woman was as natural as breathing. To have the attraction cause discomfort, confusion, even annoyance was anything but natural. A taste of her hadn't been enough. Yet he hesitated.

She was…mysterious. Perhaps that was why he couldn't push her from his mind. On the surface she appeared to be an attractive, free-spirited woman who grabbed life with both hands. Yet there were undercurrents. The hints of innocence, of shyness. The sweetness. The complexity of her kept him wondering, thinking, imagining.

Perhaps that was her trick. Women had them…were entitled to them. It was a waste of time to begrudge them their illusions and their feminine magic. More than a waste of time, it was foolish, when a man could enjoy the benefits. But there was more, and somehow less, to Rebecca than innate feminine magic.

When he had kissed her, though it had been the first time, it had been like coming back to a lover, to a love, after a painful separation. When his lips had found hers, something had filled him. A heat, an impatience, a knowledge.

He knew her, knew more than her name and her background and the color of her eyes. He knew all of her. Yet he knew nothing.

Fantasies, he told himself. He didn't have time for them. Leaning a hip against the railing, he lit a cigar and watched the sea.

As always, it pulled at him, bringing back memories of a childhood that had been careless and too short. There were times, rare times, when he allowed himself to regret. Times when the sun was a white flash of heat and the water was blue and endless. His father had taught him a great deal. How to fish, how to see both beauty and excitement in new places, how to drink like a man.

Fifteen years, Stephen thought, a smile ghosting around his mouth. He still missed him, missed the companionship, the robust laughter. They had been friends, as well as parent and child, with a bond as easy, and as strong, as any Stephen had ever known. But his father had died as he would have wanted to, at sea and in his prime.

He would have taken one look at Rebecca, rolled his eyes, kissed his fingers and urged his son to enjoy. But Stephen wasn't the boy he had once been. He was more cautious, more aware of consequences. If a man dived into the sea, he should know the depth and the currents.

Then he saw her, coming from the sea. Water ran down her body, glistening in the strong sun, sparkling against skin that had warmed in the last few days to a dusky gold. As he looked, as he wanted, he felt his muscles clench, one by one, shoulders, stomach, thighs. Without his being aware, his fingers tightened, snapping the cigar in two. He hadn't known that desire could arouse a reaction so akin to anger.

She stopped, and though he knew she was unaware of him, she might easily have been posing. To taunt, to tease, to invite. As drops of water slid down her, she stretched, lifting her face skyward. Her skimpy suit rested low over her boyish hips, shifted enticingly over the subtle curve of her breasts. At that moment, she was totally absorbed in her own pleasure and as unselfconscious as any young animal standing in the sun. Nothing had ever been so alluring.

Then, slowly, seductively, she combed her fingers through her hair, smiling, as if she enjoyed the wet, silky feel of it. Watching her, he felt the air back up and clog in his lungs. He could have murdered her for it, for making him want so unreasonably what he did not yet understand.

She plucked a long, mannish T-shirt from a straw bag and, after tugging it on, strolled barefoot into the hotel.

He stood there, waiting for the need to pass. But it

built, layered with an ache that infuriated him and a longing that baffled him.

He should ignore her. Instinct warned him that if he didn't his life would never be the same. She was nothing more than a distraction, a momentary impulse he should resist. He should turn away, go back to work. He had commitments, obligations, and no time to waste on fantasies. With an oath, he tossed the broken cigar over the rail.

There were times, he thought, when a man had to trust in fate and dive in.

Chapter 4

Rebecca had hardly shut the door behind her before she turned back to answer the knock. The sun and the water had left her pleasantly tired, but all thoughts of a lazy catnap vanished when she saw Stephen.

He looked wonderful. Cool, a little windblown, intense. For days she'd wondered about him, wondered and wished. She felt her pulse skip and her lips curve just at the sight of him. With an effort, she kept her voice breezy.

"Hello. I wasn't sure you were still on the island."

It wasn't really a lie, she told herself. An offhand inquiry had assured her that Mr. Nickodemus hadn't checked out, but she hadn't actually seen him.

"I saw you come up from the beach."

"Oh." Unconsciously she tugged at the hem of her cover-up. To Stephen the small gesture was one more contradictory signal. "I can't seem to get enough of the sun and the sea. Would you like to come in?"

By way of an answer he stepped through and shut the door behind him. It made a very quiet, a very final sound. Rebecca's carefully built poise began to crumble. "I never thanked you for the flowers." She made a gesture indicating the vase near the window, then brought her hands back together and linked them in front of her. "They're still beautiful. I…I thought I might run into you, in the dining room, on the beach, or…" Her words trailed off when he lifted a hand to her hair.

"I've been busy." He watched her eyes, eyes that were as clear as rainwater, blur at the slight touch. "Business."

It was ridiculous, she knew, but she wasn't at all sure she could speak. "If you have to work, I doubt you could pick a more beautiful place."

He stepped closer. She smelled of the water and the sun. "You're enjoying the resort, and the island."

Her hand was in his now, caught lightly. It took only that to make her knees weak. "Yes, very much."

"Perhaps you'd like to see it from a different perspective." Deliberately, wanting to test them both, he lifted her hand to his lips. He grazed her knuckles—it was barely a whisper of contact—and felt the jolt. She felt it, and he could see that she did, so it couldn't just be his imagination. "Spend the day with me tomorrow on my boat."

"What?"

He smiled, delighted with her response. "Will you come with me?"

Anywhere. Astonished, she stepped back. "I haven't any plans."

"Good." He closed the distance between them again. Her hands fluttered up in flustered defense, then settled again when he made no attempt to touch her. "Then I'll make them for you. I'll come for you in the morning. Nine?"

A boat. He'd said something about a boat. Rebecca drew in a deep breath and tried to pull herself together. This wasn't like her—going off into daydreams, feeling weak-kneed, being flooded with waves of desire. And it felt wonderful.

"I'd like that." She gave him what she hoped was an easy woman-of-the-world smile.

"Until tomorrow, then." He started for the door, then turned, a hand on the knob. "Rebecca, don't forget your camera."

She waited until he'd closed the door before she spun in three quick circles.

When Stephen had said "boat," Rebecca had pictured a trim little cabin cruiser. Instead, she stepped onto the glossy mahogany deck of a streamlined hundred-foot yacht.

"You could live on this," Rebecca said, then wished she'd bitten her tongue. But he only laughed.

"I often do."

"Welcome aboard, sir," a white-uniformed man with a British accent said.

"Grady. This is my guest, Miss Malone."

"Ma'am." Grady's cool British reserve didn't flicker for an instant, but Rebecca felt herself being summed up.

"Cast off when you're ready." Stephen took Rebecca's arm. "Would you like a tour?"

"Yes." A yacht. She was on a yacht. It took all her willpower to keep her camera in the bag. "I'd love to see it all."

He took her below, through four elegantly appointed cabins. Her comment about living on board had been said impulsively, but she could see now that it could be done easily, even luxuriously.

Above there was a large glassed-in cabin in which one could stretch out comfortably, out of the sun, and watch the sea, whatever the weather. She had known that there were people who lived like this. Part of her job had been to research and calculate so that those who did paid the government as little as possible. But to be there, to see it, to be surrounded by it, was entirely different from adding figures on paper.

There was a masculine feel to the cabin, to the entire boat—leather, wood, muted colors. There were shelves filled with books and a fully stocked bar, as well as a stereo system.

"All the comforts of home," Rebecca murmured, but she'd noted that there were doors and panels that could be secured in case of rough weather. What would it be like to ride out a storm at sea, to watch the rain lash the windows and feel the deck heave?

She gave a quick gasp when she felt the floor move. Stephen took her arm again to steady her.

"We're under way." Curious, he turned her to face him. "Are you afraid of boats?"

"No." She could hardly admit that the biggest one she'd been on before this had been a two-passenger canoe at summer camp. "It just startled me." Under way, she thought as she prayed that her system would settle. It was such an exciting, adventurous word. "Can we go out on deck? I'd like to watch."

It was exciting. She felt it the moment the wind hit her face and rushed through her hair. At the rail, she leaned out, delighted to see the island shrink and the sea spread. Because she couldn't resist and he didn't laugh at her, she took half a dozen pictures as the boat sped away from land.

"It's better than flying," she decided. "You feel a part of it. Look." With a laugh, she pointed. "The birds are chasing us."

Stephen didn't bother to glance at the gulls that wheeled and called above the boat's wake. He preferred to watch the delight and excitement bloom on her face. "Do you always enjoy so completely?"

"Yes." She tossed her hair away from her face, only to have the wind rush it back again. With another laugh, she stretched back from the railing, her face lifted to the sun. "Oh, yes."

Irresistible. With his hands at her waist, he spun her toward him. It was like holding a live wire. The shock rippled from her to him, then back again. "Everything?" His fingers spread over her back and, with the slightest pressure, moved her forward until their thighs met.

"I don't know." Instinctively she braced her hands on his shoulders. "I haven't tried everything." But she wanted to. Held close, with the sound of the water and the wind, she wanted to. Without giving a thought to self-preservation, she leaned toward him.

He swore, lightly, under his breath. Rebecca jolted back as if he had shouted at her. Stephen caught her hand as he nodded to the steward, who had just approached with drinks. "Thank you, Victor. Just leave everything." His voice was smooth enough, but Rebecca felt the tension in his hand as he led her to a chair.

He probably thought she was a fool, she decided. All but tumbling into his arms every time he touched her. He was obviously a man of the world—and a kind man, she added as she sipped her mimosa. Not all powerful men spoke kindly to those who worked for them. Her lips curved, a little wryly, as she sipped again. She knew that firsthand.

His body was in turmoil. Stephen couldn't remember, even in his youth, having had a woman affect him so irrationally. He knew how to persuade, how to seduce—and always with finesse. But whenever he was around this woman for more than five minutes he felt like a stallion being spurred and curbed at the same time.

And he was fascinated. Fascinated by the ease with which she went into his arms, by the trust he saw when he looked down into her eyes. As he had in the olive grove, he found himself believing he'd looked into those eyes, those rainwater-clear eyes, a hundred times before.

Still churning, he took out a cigar. The thought was fanciful, but his desire was very real. If there couldn't be finesse, perhaps there could be candor.

"I want you, Rebecca."

She felt her heart stop, then start up again with slow, dull throbs. Carefully she took another sip, then cleared her throat. "I know." It amazed her, flattered her, terrified her.

She seemed so cool. He envied her. "Will you come with me, to my cabin?"

She looked at him then. Her heart and her head were giving very different answers. It sounded so easy, so… natural. If there was a man she could give herself to, wholly, he was with her now. Complications, what complications there were, were her own.

But no matter how far she had run from Philadelphia and her own strict upbringing, there were still lines she couldn't cross.

"I can't."

"Can't?" He lit his cigar, astonished that they were discussing making love as though it were as casual a choice as what dinner entrée to chose. "Or won't?"

She drew a breath. Her palms were damp on the glass, and she set it down. "Can't. I want to." Her eyes, huge and lake-pale, clung to his. "I very much want to, but…"

"But?"

"I know so little about you." She picked up her glass again because her empty hands tended to twist together. "Hardly more than your name, that you own an olive grove and like the sea. It's not enough."

"Then I'll tell you more."

She relaxed enough to smile. "I don't know what to ask."

He leaned back in his chair, the tension dissolving as quickly as it had built. She could do that to him with nothing more than a smile. He knew no one who could excite and solace with so little effort.

"Do you believe in fate, Rebecca? In something unexpected, even unlooked-for, often a small thing that completely and irrevocably changes one's life?"

She thought of her aunt's death and her own uncharacteristic decisions. "Yes. Yes, I do."

"Good." His gaze skimmed over her face, quickly,
then more leisurely. "I'd nearly forgotten that I believe
it, too. Then I saw you, sitting alone."

There were ways and ways to seduce, she was discovering. A look, a tone, could be every bit as devastating as a caress. She wanted him more in that moment
than she had ever known she could want anything. To
give herself time, and distance, she rose and walked
to the rail.

Even her silence aroused him. She had said she knew
too little about him. He knew even less of her. And he
didn't care. It was dangerous, possibly even destructive,
but he didn't care. As he watched her with the wind billowing her shirt and her hair he realized that he didn't
give a damn about where she had come from, where
she had been, what she had done.

When lightning strikes, it destroys, though it blazes
with power. Rising, he went to her and stood, as she
did, facing the sea.

"When I was young, very young," he began, "there
was another moment that changed things. My father was
a man for the water. He lived for it. Died for it." When
he went on it was almost as if he were speaking to himself now, remembering. Rebecca turned her head to look
at him. "I was ten or eleven. Everything was going well,
the nets were full. My father and I were walking along
the beach. He stopped, dipped his hand into the water,
made a fist and opened it. 'You can't hold it,' he said
to me. 'No matter how you try or how you love or how
you sweat.' Then he dug into the sand. It was wet and

clung together in his hand. 'But this,' he said, 'a man can hold.' We never spoke of it again. When my time came, I turned my back on the sea and held the land."

"It was right for you."

"Yes." He lifted a hand to catch at the ends of her hair. "It was right. Such big, quiet eyes you have, Rebecca," he murmured. "Have they seen enough, I wonder, to know what's right for you?"

"I guess I've been a little slow in starting to look." Her blood was pounding thickly. She would have stepped back, but he shifted so that she was trapped between him and the rail.

"You tremble when I touch you." He slid his hands up her arms, then down until their hands locked. "Have you any idea how exciting that is?"

Her chest tightened, diminishing her air even as the muscles in her legs went limp. "Stephen, I meant it when I said…" He brushed his lips gently over her temple. "I can't. I need to…" He feathered a kiss along her jawline, softly. "To think."

He felt her fingers go lax in his. She was suddenly fragile, outrageously vulnerable, irresistibly tempting. "When I kissed you the first time I gave you no choice." His lips trailed over her face, light as a whisper, circling, teasing, avoiding her mouth. "You have one now."

He was hardly touching her. A breath, a whisper, a mere promise of a touch. The slow, subtle passage of his lips over her skin couldn't have been called a kiss, could never have been called a demand. She had only to push away to end the torment. And the glory.

A choice? Had he told her she had a choice? "No,

I don't," she murmured as she turned to find his lips with hers.

No choice, no past, no future. Only now. She felt the present, with all its needs and hungers, well up inside her. The kiss was instantly hot, instantly desperate. His heart pounded fast and hard against hers, thunderous now, as he twisted a hand in her hair to pull her head back. To plunder. No one had ever taken her like this. No one had ever warned her that a touch of violence could be so exciting. Her gasp of surprise turned into a moan of pleasure as his tongue skimmed over hers.

He thought of lightning bolts again, thought of that flash of power and light. She was electric in his arms, sparking, sizzling. Her scent, as soft, as seductive, as a whisper, clouded his mind, even as the taste of her heightened his appetite.

She was all woman, she was every woman, and yet she was like no other. He could hear each quick catch of her breath above the roar of the motor. With her name on his lips, he pressed them to the vulnerable line of her throat, where the skin was heated from the sun and as delicate as water.

She might have slid bonelessly to the deck if his body hadn't pressed hers so firmly against the rail. In wonder, in panic, she felt his muscles turn to iron wherever they touched her. Never before had she felt so fragile, so at the mercy of her own desires. The sea was as calm as glass, but she felt herself tossed, tumbled, wrecked. With a sigh that was almost a sob, she wrapped her arms around him.

It was the defenselessness of the gesture that pulled him back from the edge. He must have been mad. For a moment he'd been close, much too close, to dragging her down to the deck without a thought to her wishes or to the consequences. With his eyes closed, he held her, feeling the erratic beat of her heart, hearing her shallow, shuddering breath.

Perhaps he was still mad, Stephen thought. Even as the ragged edges of desire eased, something deeper and far more dangerous bloomed.

He wanted her, in a way no man could safely want a woman. Forever.

Fate, he thought again as he stroked her hair. It seemed he was falling in love whether he wished it or not. A few hours with her and he felt more than he had ever imagined he could feel.

There had been a few times in his life when he had seen and desired on instinct alone. What he had seen and desired, he had taken. Just as he would take her. But when he took, he meant to keep.

Carefully he stepped back. "Maybe neither of us has a choice." He dipped his hands into his pockets. "And if I touch you again, here, now, I won't give you one."

Unable to pretend, knowing they were shaking, she pushed her hands through her hair. She didn't bother to disguise the tremor in her voice. She wouldn't have known how. "I won't want one." She saw his eyes darken quickly, dangerously, but she didn't know his hands were balled into fists, straining.

"You make it difficult for me."

A long, shuddering breath escaped her. No one had ever wanted her this way. Probably no one ever would again. "I'm sorry. I don't mean to."

"No." Deliberately he relaxed his hands. "I don't

think you do. That's one of the things about you I find most intriguing. I will have you, Rebecca." He saw something flicker in her eyes…. Excitement? Panic? A combination of the two, perhaps. "Because I'm sure of it, because I know you're sure of it, I'll do my best to give you a little more time."

Her natural humor worked through the sliver of unease she felt. "I'm not sure whether I should thank you politely or run like hell."

He grinned, surprising himself, then flicked a finger down her cheek. "I wouldn't advise running, *matia mou*. I'd only catch you."

She was sure of that, too. One look at his face, even with the smile that softened it, and she knew. Kind, yes, but with a steely underlying ruthlessness. "Then I'll go with the thank-you."

"You're welcome." Patience, he realized, would have to be developed. And quickly. "Would you like to swim? There's a bay. We're nearly there."

The water might, just might, cool her off. "I'd love it."

Chapter 5

The water was cool and mirror-clear. Rebecca lowered herself into it with a sigh of pure pleasure. Back in Philadelphia she would have been at her desk, calculator clicking, the jacket of her neat business suit carefully smoothed over the back of her chair. Her figures would always tally, her forms would always be properly filed.

The dependable, efficient Miss Malone.

Instead, she was swimming in a crystal-clear bay, letting the water cool and the sun heat. Ledgers and accounts were worlds away. Here, as close as a handspan, was a man who was teaching her everything she would ever want to know about needs, desires, and the fragility of the heart.

He couldn't know it, she thought. She doubted she'd ever have the courage to tell him that he was the only one who had ever made her tremble and burn. A man as physically aware as he would only be uncomfortable knowing he held an inexperienced woman in his arms.

The water lapped around her with a sound as quiet as her own sigh. But he didn't know, because when she was in his arms she didn't feel awkward and inexperienced. She felt beautiful, desirable and reckless.

With a laugh, Rebecca dipped under the surface to let the water, and the freedom, surround her. Who would have believed it?

"Does it always take so little to make you laugh?"

Rebecca ran a hand over her slicked-back hair. Stephen was treading water beside her, smoothly, hardly making a ripple. His skin was dark gold, glistening-wet. His hair was streaked by the sun and dampened by the water, which was almost exactly the color of his eyes. She had to suppress an urge to just reach out and touch.

"A secluded inlet, a beautiful sky, an interesting man." With another sigh, she kicked her legs up so that she could float. "It doesn't seem like so little to me." She studied the vague outline of the mountains, far out of reach. "I promised myself that no matter where I went, what I did, I'd never take anything for granted again."

There was something in the way she said it, some hint of sadness, that pulled at him. The urge to comfort wasn't completely foreign in him, but he hadn't had much practice at it. "Was there a man who hurt you?"

Her lips curved at that, but he couldn't know that she was laughing at herself. Naturally, she'd dated. They had been polite, cautious evenings, usually with little interest on either side. She'd been dull, or at least she had never worked up the nerve to spread her wings. Once or twice, when she'd felt a tug, she'd been too shy, too much the efficient Rebecca Malone, to do anything about it.

With him, everything was different. Because she loved him. She didn't know how, she didn't know why, but she loved him as much as any woman could love any man.

"No. There's no one." She closed her eyes, trusting the water to carry her. "When my parents died, it hurt. It hurt so badly that I suppose I pulled back from life. I thought it was important that I be a responsible adult, even though I wasn't nearly an adult yet."

Strange that she hadn't thought of it quite that way until she'd stopped being obsessively responsible. Stranger still was how easy it was to tell him what she'd never even acknowledged herself.

"My aunt Jeannie was kind and considerate and loving, but she'd forgotten what it was like to be a young girl. Suddenly I realized I'd missed being young, lazy, foolish, all the things everyone's entitled to be at least once. I decided to make up for it."

Her hair was spread out and drifting on the water. Her eyes were closed, and her face was sheened with water. Not beautiful, Stephen told himself. She was too angular for real beauty. But she was fascinating… in looks, in philosophy…more, in the open-armed way she embraced whatever crossed her path.

He found himself looking around the inlet as he hadn't bothered to look at anything in years. He could see the sun dancing on the surface, could see the ripples spreading and growing from the quiet motion of their bodies. Farther away was the narrow curving strip of white beach, deserted now, but for a few birds fluttering over the sand. It was quiet, almost unnaturally quiet, the only sound the soft, monotonous slap of water against sand. And he was relaxed, totally, mind and body. Perhaps he, too, had forgotten what it was like to be young and foolish.

On impulse he put a hand on her shoulder and pushed her under.

She came up sputtering, dragging wet hair out of her eyes. He grinned at her and calmly continued to tread water. "It was too easy."

She tilted her head, considering him and the distance between them. Challenge leaped into her eyes, sparked with amusement. "It won't be the next time."

His grin only widened. When he moved, he moved fast, streaking under and across the water like an eel. Rebecca had time for a quick squeal. Dragging in a deep breath, she kicked out. He caught her ankle, but she was ready. Unresisting, she let him pull her under. Then, instead of fighting her way back to the surface, she wrapped her arms around him and sent them both rolling in an underwater wrestling match. They were still tangled, her arms around him, her hands hooked over his shoulders, when they surfaced.

"We're even." She gasped for air and shook the water out of her eyes.

"How do you figure?"

"If we'd had a mat I'd have pinned you. Want to go for two out of three?"

"I might." He felt her legs tangle with his as she kicked out lazily. "But for now I prefer this."

He was going to kiss her again. She saw it in his eyes, felt it in the slight tensing of the arm that locked them torso to torso. She wasn't sure she was ready. More, she was afraid she was much too ready.

"Stephen?"

"Hmm?" His lips were a breath away from hers. Then he found himself underwater again, his arms empty. He should have been furious. He nearly was when he pushed to surface. She was shoulder-deep in the water, a few feet away. Her laughter rolled over him, young, delighted, unapologetic.

"It was too easy." She managed a startled "whoops" when he struck out after her. She might have made it— she had enough of a lead—but he swam as though he'd been born in the water. Still, she was agile, and she almost managed to dodge him, but her laughter betrayed her. She gulped in water, choked, then found herself hauled up into his arms in thigh-deep water.

"I like to win." Deciding it was useless to struggle, she pressed a hand to her heart and gasped for air. "It's a personality flaw. Sometimes I cheat at canasta."

"Canasta?" The last thing he could picture the slim, sexy bundle in his arms doing was spending a quiet evening playing cards.

"I can't help myself." Still breathless, she laid her head on his shoulder. "No willpower."

"I find myself having the same problem." With a careless toss, he sent her flying through the air. She hit the water bottom first.

"I guess I deserved that." She struggled to her feet, water raining off her. "I have to sit." Wading through the water, she headed for the gentle slope of beach. She lay, half in and half out of the water, not caring that the sand would cling to her hair and skin. When he dropped down beside her, she reached out a hand for his. "I don't know when I've had a nicer day."

He looked down to where her fingers linked with his. The gesture had been so easy, so natural. He wondered how it could both comfort and arouse. "It's hardly over."

"It seems like it could last forever." She wanted it to go on and on. Blue skies and easy laughter. Cool water and endless hours. There had been a time, not so long before, when the days had dragged into nights and the nights into days. "Did you ever want to run away?"

With her hand still in his, he lay back to watch a few scattered rags of clouds drift. How long had it been, he wondered, since he'd really watched the sky? "To where?"

"Anywhere. Away from the way things are, away from what you're afraid they'll always be." She closed her eyes and could see herself brewing that first cup of coffee at exactly 7:15, opening the first file at precisely 9:01. "To drop out of sight," she murmured, "and pop up somewhere else, anywhere else, as someone completely different."

"You can't change who you are."

"Oh, but you can." Her tone suddenly urgent, she rose on her elbow. "Sometimes you have to."

He reached up to touch the ends of her hair. "What are you running from?"

"Everything. I'm a coward."

He looked into her eyes. They were so clear, so full of enthusiasm. "I don't think so."

"But you don't know me." A flicker of regret, then uncertainty, ran across her face. "I'm not sure I want you to."

"Don't I?" His fingers tightened on her hair, keeping her still. "There are people and circumstances that don't take months or years before they're understood. I look at you and something fits into place, Rebecca. I don't know why, but it is. I know you." He tugged her down for the lightest, the briefest, of kisses. "And I like what I see."

"Do you?" She smiled. "Really?"

"Do you imagine I spend the day with a woman only because I want to sleep with her?" She shrugged, and though her blush was very faint, he noticed it and was amused by it. How many women, he wondered, could kiss a man into oblivion, then blush? "Being with you, Rebecca, is a difficult pleasure."

She chuckled and began to draw circles in the wet sand. What would he say, what would he think, if he knew what she was? Or, more accurately, what she wasn't? It didn't matter, she told herself. She couldn't let it spoil what there was between them.

"I think that's the most wonderful compliment I've ever had."

"Where have you been?" he murmured.

When she moved restlessly, he held her still. "Don't. I'm not going to touch you. Not yet."

"That's not the problem." With her eyes closed, she tilted her chin up and let the sun beat down on her face. "The problem is, I want you to touch me, so much it frightens me." Taking her time, she sat up, gathering her courage. She wanted to be honest, and she hoped she wouldn't sound like a fool. "Stephen, I don't sleep around. I need you to understand, because this is all happening so quickly. But it's not casual."

He lifted a hand to her chin and turned her to face him. His eyes were as blue as the water, and, to her, as unfathomable. "No, it's not." He made the decision quickly, though he had been turning the idea over in his mind all day. "I have to go to Athens tomorrow. Come with me, Rebecca."

"Athens?" she managed, staring at him.

"Business. A day, two at the most. I'd like you with me." And he was afraid, more than he cared to admit, that when he returned she might be gone.

"I..." What should she say? What was right?

"You told me you'd planned to go." He'd push if necessary. Now that the idea had taken root, Stephen had no intention of going anywhere without her.

"Yes, but I wouldn't want to be in the way while you're working."

"You'll be in my way whether you're here or there."

Her head came up at that, and the look she gave him was both shy and stunning. He stifled the need to take her again, to roll until she was beneath him on the sand. He'd said he'd give her time. Perhaps what he'd really meant was that he needed time himself.

"You'll have your own suite. No strings, Rebecca. Just your company."

"A day or two," she murmured.

"It's a simple matter to have your room held for you here for your return."

Her return. Not his. If he left Corfu tomorrow she would probably never see him again. He was offering her another day, perhaps two. Never take anything for granted, she remembered. Never again.

Athens, she thought. It was true that she had planned

to see it before she left Greece. But she would have gone alone. A few days before, that had been what she thought she wanted. The adventure of seeing new places, new people, on her own. Now the thought of going with him, of having him beside her when she first caught sight of the Acropolis, of having him want her with him, changed everything.

"I'd love to go with you." She rose quickly and dived into the water. She was in over her head.

Chapter 6

Athens was neither East nor West. It was spitted meat and spices roasting. It was tall buildings and modern shops. It was narrow, unpaved streets and clamorous bazaars. It had been the scene of revolution and brutality. It was ancient and civilized and passionate.

Rebecca quite simply fell in love at first sight.

She'd been seduced by Paris and charmed by London, but in Athens she lost her heart. She wanted to see everything at once, from sunrise to moonlight, and the heat-drenched afternoon between.

All that first morning, while Stephen was immersed in business meetings, she wandered. The hotel he'd chosen was lovely, but she was drawn to the streets and the people. Somehow she didn't feel like a visitor here. She felt like someone who had returned home after a long, long journey. Athens was waiting for her, ready to welcome her back.

Incredible. All her life she had accepted the parameters set for her. Now she was touring Old Athens, with its clicking worry beads and its open-fronted shops, where she could buy cheap plaster copies of monuments or elegant antiques.

She passed tavernas, but she was too excited to be tempted by the rich smells of coffee and baking. She heard the clear notes of a flute as she looked up and saw the Acropolis.

There was only one approach. Though it was still early, other tourists were making their way toward the ruins in twos and in groups. Rebecca let her camera hang by its strap. Despite the chattering around her, she felt alone, but beautifully so.

She would never be able to explain what it felt like to stand in the morning sun and look at something that had been built for the gods—something that had endured war and weather and time. It had been a place of worship. Even now, after centuries had passed, Rebecca felt the spiritual pull. Perhaps the goddess Athena, with her gleaming helmet and spear, still visited there.

Rebecca had been disappointed that Stephen couldn't join her on her first morning in Athens. Now she was glad to be alone—to sit and absorb and imagine without having to explain her thoughts.

How could she, after having seen so much, go back to so little? Sighing, she wandered through the temples. It wasn't just the awe she felt here, or the excitement she had felt in London and Paris, that had changed her.

It was Stephen and everything she'd felt, everything she'd wanted, since she'd met him.

Perhaps she would go back to Philadelphia, but she would never be the same person. Once you fell in love, completely, totally in love, nothing was ever the same.

She wished it could be simple, the way she imagined it was simple for so many other women. An attractive man, a physical tug. But with Stephen, as with Athens, she'd lost her heart. However implausible it seemed, she had recognized the man, as well as the city, as being part of her, as being for her. Desire, when tangled up with love, could never be simple.

But how could you be sure you were in love when it had never happened to you before? If she were home, at least she would have a friend to talk to. With a little laugh, Rebecca walked out into the sunlight. How many times had she been on the receiving end of a long, scattered conversation from a friend who had fallen in love—or thought she had. The excitement, the unhappiness, the thrills. Sometimes she'd been envious, and sometimes she'd been grateful not to have the complication in her own life. But always, always, she'd offered calm, practical, even soothing advice.

Oddly enough, she didn't seem to be able to do the same for herself.

All she could think of was the way her heart pounded when he touched her, how excitement, panic and anticipation fluttered through her every time he looked at her. When she was with him, her feelings and fantasies seemed reasonable. When she was with him, she could believe in fate, in the matching of soul to soul.

It wasn't enough. At least that was what she would

have told another woman. Attraction and passion weren't enough. Yet there was no explaining, even to herself, the sense of rightness she experienced whenever she was with him. If she were a fanciful person she would say it was as though she'd been waiting for him, waiting for the time and the place for him to come to her.

It sounded simple—if fate could be considered simple. Yet beneath all the pleasure and that sense of reunion was guilt. She couldn't shake it, and she knew she wouldn't be able to ignore it much longer. She wasn't the woman she had let him believe her to be. She wasn't the well-traveled at-loose-ends free spirit she pretended to be. No matter how many ties she'd cut, she was still Rebecca Malone. How would he feel about her once he knew how limited and dull her life had been?

How and when was she going to tell him?

A few more days, she promised herself as she began the walk back. It was selfish, perhaps it was even dangerous, but she wanted just a few more days.

It was midafternoon before she returned to the hotel. Ignoring the fact that she might be considered overeager, she went straight to Stephen's suite. She couldn't wait to see him, to tell him everything she'd seen, to show him everything she'd bought. Her easy smile faded a bit when his secretary Elana opened the door.

"Miss Malone." Gracious and self-confident, Elana waved her in. "Please sit down. I'll let Stephen know you're here."

"I don't want to interrupt." Rebecca shifted her bags, feeling gauche and foolish.

"Not at all. Have you just come in?"

"Yes, I..." For the first time, Rebecca noticed that her skin was damp and her hair tousled. In contrast, Elana was cool and perfectly groomed. "I really should go."

"Please." Elana urged Rebecca to a chair. "Let me get you a drink." With a half smile, Elana began to pour a tall glass of iced juice. She had expected Stephen's mystery lady to be smooth, controlled and stunning. It pleased her a great deal to find Rebecca wide-eyed, a little unsure, and clearly a great deal in love.

"Did you enjoy your morning?"

"Yes, very much." She accepted the glass and tried to relax. Jealousy, she realized, feeling herself flush at the realization. She couldn't remember ever having experienced the sensation before. Who wouldn't be jealous? she asked herself as she watched Elana walk to the phone. The Greek woman was gorgeous, self-contained, coolly efficient. Above all, she had a relationship with Stephen that Rebecca knew nothing about. How long has she known him? Rebecca wondered. And how well?

"Stephen's just finishing up some business," Elana said as she hung up the phone. With easy, economical moves, she poured herself a drink, then walked to the chair facing Rebecca. "What do you think of Athens?"

"I love it." Rebecca wished she'd taken the time to brush her hair and freshen her makeup. Lecturing herself, she sipped at her juice. "I'm not sure what I expected, but it's everything and more."

"Europeans see it as the East, Orientals see it as the West." Elana crossed her legs and settled back. It surprised her to realize that she was prepared to like Rebecca Malone. "What Athens is is Greek—and, more particularly, Athenian." She paused, studying Rebecca over the rim of her glass. "People often view Stephen in much the same way, and what he is is Stephen."

"How long have you worked for him?"

"Five years."

"You must know him well."

"Better than some. He's a demanding and generous employer and an interesting man. Fortunately, I like to travel and I enjoy my work."

Rebecca rubbed at a spot of dust on her slacks. "It never occurred to me that farming required so much traveling. I never realized how much was involved in growing olives."

Elana's brows rose in obvious surprise, but she continued smoothly when Rebecca glanced back at her. "Whatever Stephen does, he does thoroughly." She smiled to herself, satisfied. She hadn't been certain until now whether the American woman was attracted to Stephen or to his position. "Has Stephen explained to you about the dinner party this evening?"

"He said something about a small party here at the hotel. A business dinner."

"Men take these things more lightly than women." Feeling friendlier, Elena offered her first genuine smile. "It will be small, but quite extravagant." She watched as Rebecca automatically lifted a hand to her hair. "If you need anything—a dress, a salon—the hotel can accommodate you."

Rebecca thought of the casual sportswear she'd tossed into her bag before the impulsive trip to Athens. "I need everything."

With a quick, understanding laugh, Elana rose. "I'll make some calls for you."

"Thank you, but I don't want to interfere with your work."

"Seeing that you're comfortable is part of my work." They both glanced over when the door opened. "Stephen. You see, she hasn't run away." Taking her glass and her pad, she left them alone.

"You were gone a long time." He hated the fact that he'd begun to watch the clock and worry. He'd imagined her hurt or abducted. He'd begun to wonder if she would disappear from his life as quickly as she'd appeared in it. Now she was here, her eyes alive with pleasure, her clothes rumpled and her hair windblown.

"I guess I got caught up exploring." She started to rise, but before she could gain her feet he was pulling her out of the chair, seeking, finding her mouth with his.

His desperation whipped through her. His hunger incited her own. Without thought, without hesitation, she clung to him, answering, accepting. Already seduced, she murmured something, an incoherent sound that caught in her throat.

Good God, he thought, it wasn't possible, it wasn't sane, to want like this. Throughout the morning while all the facts and figures and demands of business had been hammering at him, he'd thought of her, of holding her, of tasting her, of being with her. When she had stayed away for so long he'd begun to imagine, then to fear, what his life would be like without her.

It wasn't going to happen. He scraped his teeth over her bottom lip, and she gasped and opened for him. He wouldn't let it happen. Where she came from, where she intended to go, no longer mattered. She belonged to him now. And, though he'd only begun to deal with it, he belonged to her.

But he needed some sanity, some logic. Fighting himself, Stephen drew her away from him. Her eyes remained closed, and her lips remained parted. A soft, sultry sound escaped them as her lashes fluttered upward.

"I..." She took a deep breath and let it out slowly. "I should go sightseeing more often."

Gradually he realized how hard his fingers were pressing into her arms. As if he were afraid she would slip away. Cursing himself, he relaxed. "I would have preferred to go with you."

"I understand you're busy. I'd have bored you silly, poking into every shop and staring at every column."

"No." If there was one thing he was certain of, it was that she would never bore him. "I'd like to have seen your first impression of Athens."

"It was like coming home," she told him, then hurried on because it sounded foolish. "I couldn't get enough." Laughing at herself, she gestured toward her bags. "Obviously. It's so different from anywhere I've ever been. At the Acropolis I couldn't even take any pictures, because I knew they couldn't capture the feeling. Then I walked along the streets and saw old men with *kom—konbou—*" She fumbled over the Greek and finally made a helpless gesture.

"Kombouloi," he murmured. "Worry beads."

"Yes, and I imagined how they might sit in those shadowy doorways watching the tourists go by, day after day, year after year." She sat, pleased to share her

impressions with him. "I saw a shop with all these cos-
tumes, lots of tinsel, and some really dreadful plaster
copies of the monuments."

He grinned and sat beside her. "How many did you
buy?"

"Three or four." She bent down to rattle through her
bags. "I bought you a present."

"A plaster statue of Athena?"

She glanced up, eyes laughing. "Almost. Then I
found this tiny antique shop in the old section. It was all
dim and dusty and irresistible. The owner had a handful of English phrases, and I had my phrase book. After
we'd confused each other completely, I bought this."

She drew out an S-shaped porcelain pipe decorated
with paintings of the wild mountain goats of Greece.
Attached to it was a long wooden stem, as smooth as
glass, tipped by a tarnished brass mouthpiece.

"I remembered the goats we'd seen on Corfu," she
explained as Stephen examined it. "I thought you might
like it, though I've never seen you smoke a pipe."

With a quiet laugh, he looked back at her, balanc-
ing the gift in both hands. "No, I don't—at least not of
this nature."

"Well, it's more ornamental than functional, I suppose. The man couldn't tell me much about it—at least
not that I could understand." She reached out to run
a finger along the edge of the bowl. "I've never seen
anything like it."

"I'm relieved to hear it." When she sent him a puzzled look, he leaned over to brush her lips with his.
"*Matia mou,* this is a hashish pipe."

"A hashish pipe?" She stared, first in shock, then

in fascination. "Really? I mean, did people actually use it?"

"Undoubtedly. Quite a number, I'd say, since it's at least a hundred and fifty years old."

"Imagine that." She pouted, imagining dark, smoky dens. "I guess it's not a very appropriate souvenir."

"On the contrary, whenever I see it I'll think of you."

She glanced up quickly, unsure, but the amusement in his eyes had her smiling again. "I should have bought you the plaster statue of Athena."

Taking her hands, he drew her to her feet. "I'm flattered that you bought me anything." She felt the subtle change as his fingers tightened on hers. "I want time with you, Rebecca. Hours of it. Days. There's too much I need to know." When she lowered her gaze, he caught her chin. "What are those secrets of yours?"

"Nothing that would interest you."

"You're wrong. Tomorrow I intend to find out all there is to know." He saw the quick flicker of unease in her eyes. Other men, he thought with an uncomfortable surge of jealousy. The hell with them. "No more evasions. I want you, all of you. Do you understand?"

"Yes, but—"

"Tomorrow." He cut her off, suddenly, completely, frustratingly Greek. "I have business that can't be avoided now. I'll come for you at seven."

"All right."

Tomorrow was years away, she told herself. She had time to decide what she would say, how she would say it. Before tomorrow came tonight. She would be everything she'd ever wanted to be, everything he wanted her to be.

"I'd better go." Before he could touch her again, she bent to gather her bags. "Stephen…" She paused at the door and turned to look at him as he stood in the middle of the room, comfortable with the wealth that surrounded him, confident with who and what he was. "You might be disappointed when you find out."

She left quickly, leaving him frowning after her.

Chapter 7

She was as nervous as a cat. Every time she looked in the mirror Rebecca wondered who the woman was who was staring back at her. It wasn't a stranger, but it was a very, very different Rebecca Malone.

Was it just the different hairstyle, poufed and frizzed and swept around her face? Could it be the dress, the glittery spill of aquamarine that left her arms and shoulders bare? No, it was more than that. More than makeup and clever stylists and glamorous clothes. It was in her eyes. How could she help but see it? How could anyone? The woman who looked back from the mirror was a woman in love.

What was she going to do about it? What could she do? she asked herself. She was still practical enough to accept that some things could never be changed. But was she bold enough, or strong enough, to take what she wanted and live with the consequences?

When she heard the knock on the door, Rebecca took a deep breath and picked up the useless compact-size evening bag she'd bought just that afternoon. It was all happening so fast. When she'd come back from Stephen's suite there had been a detailed message from Elana listing appointments—for a massage, a facial, hairstyling—along with the name of the manager of the hotel's most exclusive boutique. She hadn't had time to think, even for a minute, about her evening with Stephen. Or about any tomorrows.

Perhaps that was best, she decided as she pulled open the door. It was best not to think, not to analyze. It was best to accept and to act.

She looked like a siren, some disciple of Circe, with her windswept hair and a dress the color of seductive seas. Had he told himself she wasn't beautiful? Had he believed it? At that moment he was certain he'd never seen, never would see, a more exciting woman.

"You're amazing, Rebecca." He took her hand and drew her to him so that they stood in the doorway together. On the threshold.

"Why? Because I'm on time?"

"Because you're never what I expect." He brought her hand to his lips. "And always what I want."

Because she was speechless, she was glad when he closed the door at her back and led her to the elevators. He looked different from the man she had first met, the one who dressed with such casual elegance. Tonight there was a formality about him, and the sophistication she had sensed earlier was abundantly apparent in the ease with which he wore the black dinner jacket.

"The way you look," he told her, "it seems a shame to waste the evening on a business dinner."

"I'm looking forward to meeting some of your friends."

"Associates," he said with an odd smile. "When you've been poor—and don't intend to be poor again—you rarely make friends in business."

She frowned. This was a side of him, the business side, that she didn't know. Would he be ruthless? She looked at him, saw it, and accepted it. Yes, a man like Stephen would always be ruthless with what belonged to him. "But enemies?"

"The same rule, in business, applies to friends and enemies. My father taught me more than fishing, Rebecca. He also taught me that to succeed, to attain, you must learn not only how to trust, but how far."

"I've never been poor, but I imagine it's frightening."

"Strengthening." He took her hand again when the elevator doors opened. "We have different backgrounds, Rebecca, but, fortunately, we've come to the same place."

He had no idea *how* different. Trust. He had spoken of trust. She discovered she wanted to tell him, tell him everything. Tell him that she knew nothing of elegant parties and glamorous lifestyles. She was a fraud, and when he found out he might laugh at her and brush her aside. But she wanted him to know.

"Stephen, I want to—"

"Stephen. Once more you outdo us all in your choice of women."

"Dimitri."

Rebecca stopped, caught on the brink of confession. The man who faced her was classically handsome. His silver mane contrasted with bronzed skin lined by a half century of sun. He wore a mustache that swept majestically over gleaming teeth.

"It was kind of you to invite us here this evening, but it would be kinder still to introduce me to your lovely companion."

"Rebecca Malone, Dimitri Petropolis."

A diamond glittered on the hand he lifted to clasp Rebecca's. The hand itself was hard as rock. "A pleasure. Athens is already abuzz with talk of the woman who arrived with Stephen."

Certain he was joking, she smiled. "Then Athens must be in desperate need of news."

His eyes widened for a moment, then creased at the corners when he laughed. "I have no doubt you will provide an abundance of it."

Stephen slipped a hand under Rebecca's elbow. The look he sent Dimitri was very quick and very clear. They had competed over land, but there would be no competition over Rebecca.

"If you'll excuse us a moment, Dimitri, I'd like to get Rebecca some champagne."

"Of course." Amused—and challenged—Dimitri brushed at his mustache as he watched them walk away.

Rebecca had no way of knowing that to Stephen a small dinner party meant a hundred people. She sipped her first glass of wine, hoping she wouldn't embarrass them both by being foolishly shy and tongue-tied. In the past, whenever she had found herself in a crowd, she had always looked for the nearest corner to fade into. Not tonight, she promised herself, straightening her shoulders.

There were dozens of names to remember, but she filed them away as easily as she had always filed numbers. In the hour before dinner, while the guests mixed and mingled, she found herself at ease. The stomach flutters and hot blushes she'd often experienced at parties and functions simply didn't happen.

Perhaps she was the new Rebecca Malone after all.

She heard business discussed here and there. Most of it seemed to be hotel and resort business—talk of remodeling and expansions, mergers and takeovers. She found it odd that so many of the guests were in that trade, rather than prosperous farmers or olive growers.

Stephen came up behind her and murmured in her ear, "You look pleased with yourself."

"I am." He couldn't know that she was pleased to find herself at ease and comfortable in a party of strangers. "So many interesting people."

"Interesting." He brushed a finger over her wispy bangs. "I thought you might find it dull."

"Not at all." She took a last sip of champagne, then set the glass aside. Instantly a waiter was at her side, offering another. Stephen watched her smile her thanks.

"So you enjoy parties?"

"Sometimes. I'm enjoying this one, and having a chance to meet your associates."

Stephen glanced over her shoulder, summing up the looks and quiet murmurs. "They'll be talking about you for weeks to come."

She only laughed, turning in a slow circle. Around

her was the flash of jewels and the gleam of gold. The
sleek and the prosperous, the rich and the successful.
It pleased her that she'd found more to talk about than
tax shelters.

"I can't imagine they have so little on their minds.
This is such a gorgeous room."

She looked around the huge ballroom, with its
cream-and-rose walls, its glittering chandeliers and its
gleaming floors. There were alcoves for cozy love seats
and tall, thriving ornamental trees in huge copper pots.
The tables, arranged to give a sense of intimacy, were
already set with ivory cloths and slender tapers.

"It's really a beautiful hotel," she continued. "Everything about it runs so smoothly." She smiled up at
him. "I'm torn between the resort in Corfu and this."

"Thank you." When she gave him a blank look, he
tipped up her chin with his finger. "They're mine."

"Your what?"

"My hotels," he said simply, then led her to a table.

She spoke all through dinner, though for the first
fifteen minutes she had no idea what she said. There
were eight at Stephen's table, including Dimitri, who
had shifted name cards so that he could sit beside her.
She toyed with her seafood appetizer, chatted and wondered if she could have made a bigger fool out of herself.

He wasn't simply prosperous. He wasn't simply well-
off. There was enough accountant left in Rebecca to understand that when a man owned what Stephen owned
he was far, far more than comfortable.

What would he think of her when he found out what
she was? Trust? How could she ever expect him to trust
her now? She swallowed without tasting and managed

to smile. Would he think she was a gold digger, that she had set herself up to run into him?

No, that was ridiculous.

She forced herself to look over and saw that Stephen was watching her steadily. She picked up her fork with one hand and balled up the napkin in her lap with the other.

Why couldn't he be ordinary? she wondered. Someone vacationing, someone working at the resort? Why had she fallen in love with someone so far out of her reach?

"Have you left us?"

Rebecca jerked herself back to see Dimitri smiling at her. Flushing, she noticed that the next course had been served while she'd been daydreaming. "I'm sorry." With an effort she began to toy with the *salata Athenas*.

"A beautiful woman need never apologize for being lost in her own thoughts." He patted her hand, then let his fingers linger. He caught Stephen's dark look and smiled. If he didn't like the boy so much, he thought, he wouldn't get nearly so much pleasure from irritating him. "Tell me, how did you meet Stephen?"

"We met in Corfu." She thought of that first meal they had shared…quiet, relaxed, alone.

"Ah, soft nights and sunny days. You are vacationing?"

"Yes." Rebecca put more effort into her smile. If she stared into her salad she would only embarrass herself, and Stephen. "He was kind enough to show me some of the island."

"He knows it well, and many of the other islands of our country. There's something of the gypsy in him."

She had sensed that. Hadn't that been part of the attraction? Hadn't Rebecca just discovered the gypsy in
herself? "Have you know him long?"

"We have a long-standing business relationship.
Friendly rivals, you might say. When Stephen was
hardly more than a boy he accumulated an impressive
amount of land." He gestured expansively. "As you can
see, he used it wisely. I believe he has two hotels in
your country."

"Two? More?" Rebecca picked up her glass and took
a long swallow of wine.

"So you see, I had wondered if you had met in America and were old friends."

"No." Rebecca nodded weakly as the waiter removed
the salad and replaced it with moussaka. "We only just
met a few days ago."

"As always, Stephen moves quickly and stylishly."
Dimitri took her hand again, more than a little amused
by the frown he saw deepening in Stephen's eyes.
"Where is it in America you are from?"

"Philadelphia." Relax, she ordered herself. Relax and
enjoy. "That's in the Northeast."

It infuriated Stephen to watch her flirting so easily,
so effectively, with another man. She sat through course
after course, barely eating, all the while gifting Dimitri
with her shy smiles. Not once did she draw away when
the older man touched her hand or leaned close. From
where he sat, Stephen could catch a trace of her scent,
soft, subtle, maddening. He could hear her quiet laugh
when Dimitri murmured something in her ear.

Then she was standing with him, her hand caught in
his, as he led her to the dance floor.

Stephen sat there, battling back a jealousy he despised, and watched them move together to music made for lovers. Under the lights her dress clung, then swayed, then shifted. Her face was close, too damn close, to Dimitri's. He knew what it was like to hold her like that, to breathe in the scent of her skin and her hair. He knew what it was to feel her body brush against his, to feel the life, the passion, bubbling. He knew what it was to see her eyes blur, her lips part, to hear that quiet sigh.

He had often put his stamp on land, but never on a woman. He didn't believe in it. But only a fool sat idly by and allowed another man to enjoy what was his. With a muttered oath, Stephen rose, strode out onto the dance floor and laid a hand on Dimitri's shoulder.

"Ah, well." The older man gave a regretful sigh and stepped aside. "Until later."

Before she could respond, Rebecca was caught against Stephen. With a sigh of her own, she relaxed and matched her steps to his. Maybe it was like a dream, she told herself as she closed her eyes and let the music fill her head. But she was going to enjoy every moment until it was time to wake up.

She seemed to melt against him. Her fingers moved lightly through his hair as she rested her cheek against his. Was this the way she'd danced with Dimitri? Stephen wondered, then cursed himself. He was being a fool, but he couldn't seem to stop himself. Then again, he'd had to fight for everything else in his life. Why should his woman be any different?

He wanted to drag her off then and there, away from everyone, and find some dark, quiet place to love her.

"You're enjoying yourself?"

"Yes." She wouldn't think about what he was, not now. Soon enough the night would be over and tomorrow would have to be faced. While the music played and he held her, she would only think of what he meant to her. "Very much."

The dreamy tone of her voice almost undid him. "Apparently Dimitri entertained you well."

"Mmm. He's a very nice man."

"You moved easily from his arms to mine."

Something in his tone pried through the pleasure she felt. Carefully she drew back so that she could see his face. "I don't think I know what you mean."

"I believe you do."

She was tempted to laugh, but there was no humor in Stephen's eyes. Rebecca felt her stomach knot as it always did when she was faced with a confrontation. "If I do, then I'd have to think you ridiculous. Maybe we'd better go back to the table."

"So you can be with him?" Even as the words came out he realized the unfairness, even the foolishness, of them.

She stiffened, retreating as far as she could from anger. "I don't think this is the place for this kind of discussion."

"You're quite right." As furious with himself as he was with her, he pulled her from the dance floor.

Chapter 8

"Stop it." By the time he'd dragged her to the elevators, Rebecca had gotten over her first shock. "What's gotten into you?"

"I'm simply taking you to a more suitable place for our discussion." He pulled her into the elevator, then punched the button for their floor.

"You have guests," she began, but he sent her a look than made her feel like a fool. Falling back on dignity, she straightened her shoulders. "I prefer to be asked if I want to leave, not dragged around as though I were a pack mule."

Though her heart was pounding, she sailed past him when the doors opened, intending to breeze into her own rooms and slam the door in his face. In two steps he had her arm again. Rebecca found herself guided, none too gently, into Stephen's suite.

"I don't want to talk to you," she said, because she was certain her teeth would begin to chatter at any moment. She didn't argue well in the best of circumstances. Faced with Stephen's anger, she was certain she would lose.

He said nothing as he loosened his tie and the first two buttons of his shirt. He went to the bar and poured two brandies. He was being irrational and he knew it, but he seemed unable to control it. That was new, he decided. But there had been many new emotions in him since Rebecca.

Walking back to Rebecca, he set one snifter by her elbow. When he looked at her…he wanted to shout, to beg, to demand, to plead. As a result, his voice was clipped and hard.

"You came to Athens with me, not with Dimitri or any other man."

She didn't touch the snifter. She was certain her hands would shake so hard that it would slip out of her grip. "Is that a Greek custom?" It amazed her—and bolstered her confidence—to hear how calm her voice was. "Forbidding a woman to speak to another man?"

"Speak?" He could still see the way Dimitri had bent his head close to hers. Dimitri, who was smooth and practiced. Dimitri, whose background would very likely mirror Rebecca's. Old money, privileged childhoods, quiet society. "Do you allow every man who speaks to you to hold you, to touch you?"

She didn't blush. Instead, the color faded from her cheeks. She shook, not with fear but with fury. "What I do, and with whom I do it, is my business. Mine."

Very deliberately he lifted his snifter and drank. "No."

"If you think that because I came here with you you have the right to dictate to me you're wrong. I'm my own person, Stephen." It struck her even as she said it that it was true. She was her own person. Each decision she made was her own. Filled with a new sense of power, she stepped forward. "No one owns me, not you, not anyone. I won't be ordered, I won't be forced, I won't be pressured." With a flick of her skirts, she turned. He had her again quickly, his hands on both of her arms, his face close.

"You won't go back to him."

"You couldn't stop me if that was what I wanted." She tossed her head back challengingly. "But I have no intention of going back downstairs to Dimitri, or anyone else." She jerked her arms free. "You idiot. Why should I want to be with him when I'm in love with you?"

She stopped, her eyes wide with shock, her lips parted in surprise. Overwhelmed by a combination of humiliation and fury, she spun around. Then she was struggling against him. "Leave me alone! Oh, God, just leave me alone!"

"Do you think I could let you go now?" He caught her hair in his hand, dragging it back until her eyes met his. In them she saw triumph and desire. "I feel as though I've waited all my life to hear you say those words." He rained kisses over her face until her struggles ceased. "You drive me mad," he murmured. "Being with you, being without you."

"Please." Colors, shapes, lights were whirling in her head. "I need to think."

"No. Ask me for anything else, but not more time."

Gathering her close, he buried his face in her hair. "Do you think I make a fool of myself over every woman?"

"I don't know." She moaned when his lips trailed down her throat. Something wild and terrifying was happening inside her body. "I don't know you. You don't know me."

"Yes, I do." He pulled away just far enough to look down at her. "From the first moment I saw you, I knew you. Needed you. Wanted you."

It was true. She knew it, felt it, but she shook her head in denial. "It's not possible."

"I've loved you before, Rebecca, almost as much as I do now." He felt her go still. The color fled from her face again, but her eyes stayed steady on his.

"I don't want you to say what isn't real, what you're not sure of."

"Didn't you feel it, the first time I kissed you?" When he saw the acknowledgment in her eyes, his grip tightened. He could feel her heart thundering, racing to match the rhythm of his own. "Somehow you've come back to me, and I to you. No more questions," he said, before she could speak. "I need you tonight."

It was real. She felt the truth and the knowledge when his mouth found hers. If it was wrong to go blindly into need, then she would pay whatever price was asked. She could no longer deny him…or herself.

There was no gentleness in the embrace. It was as it had been the first time, lovers reunited, a hunger finally quenched. All heat and light. She gave more than she'd known she had. Her mouth was as avid as his, as seeking. Her murmurs were as desperate. Her hands didn't shake as they moved over him. They pressed, gripped, demanded. Greedy, she tugged the jacket from his shoulders.

Yes, he'd come back to her. If it was madness to believe it, then for tonight she'd be mad.

The taste of her, just the taste of her, was making his head swim and his blood boil. He nipped at her lip, then sucked until he heard her helpless whimper. He wanted her helpless. Something fierce and uncivilized inside him wanted her weak and pliant and defenseless. When she went limp in his arms he dived into her mouth and plundered. Her response tore at him, so sweet, so vulnerable, then suddenly so ardent.

Her hands, which had fluttered helplessly to her side, rose up again to pull at his shirt, to race under it to warmed flesh. She could only think of how right it felt to touch him, to press against him and wait for him to light new fires inside her.

With an oath, he swept her up into his arms and carried her to the bedroom.

The moon was waning and offered only the most delicate light. It fell in slants and shadows on the bed, dreamlike. But the vibrating of Rebecca's pulse told her this was no dream. There was the scent of jasmine from the sprigs in the vase beside the bed. It was a scent she would always remember, just as she would remember how dark and deep were the color of his eyes.

Needful, desperate, they tumbled onto the bed.

He wanted to take care with her. She seemed so small, so fragile. He wanted to show her how completely she filled his heart. But his body was on fire, and she was already moving like a whirlwind beneath him.

His mouth was everywhere, making her shudder and

arch and ache. Desires she'd never known sprang to life inside her and took control. Delirious, she obeyed them, reveled in them, then searched for more.

They rolled across the bed in a passionate war that would have two victors, touching, taking, discovering. Impatient, he peeled the dress from her, moaning as he found her breasts with his hands, his lips, his teeth. Unreasoning desire catapulted through him when he felt her soar.

Her body felt like a furnace, impossibly hot, impossibly strong. Sensations rammed into her, stealing her breath. Mindless and moaning, she writhed under him, open for any demand he might make, pulsing for any new knowledge he might offer.

Finally, finally, she knew what it was to love, to be loved, to be wanted beyond reason. Naked, she clung to him, awash in the power and the weakness, the glory and the terror.

He raced over her as if he already knew what would make her tremble, what would make her yearn. Never before had she been so aware, so in tune with another.

She made him feel like a god. He touched, and her skin vibrated under his hand. He tasted, and her flavor was like no other. She was moist, heated, and utterly willing. She seemed to explode beneath him, lost in pleasure, drugged by passion. No other woman had ever driven him so close to madness. Her head was thrown back, and one hand was flung out as her fingers dug into the sheets. Wanton, waiting, wild.

With her name on his lips, he drove into her. His breath caught. His mind spun. Her cry of pain and release echoed in his head, bringing him both triumph and guilt. His body went rigid as he fought to claw his way back. Then she seemed to close around him, body, heart, soul. As helpless as she, he crossed the line into madness and took her with him.

Chapter 9

Aftershocks of passion racked her. Stunned and confused, she lay in the shadowed light. Nothing had prepared her for this. No one had ever warned her that pleasure could be so huge or that need could be so jagged. If she had known... Rebecca closed her eyes and nearly laughed out loud. If she had known, she would have left everything behind years ago and searched the world for him.

Only him. She let out a quiet, calming sigh. Only him.

He was cursing himself, slowly, steadily, viciously. Innocent. Dear God. She'd been innocent, as fresh and untouched as spring, and he'd used her, hurt her, taken her.

Disgusted with himself, he sat up and reached for a cigar. He needed more than tobacco. He needed a drink, but he didn't trust his legs to carry him.

The flick of his lighter sounded like a gunshot. For an instant his face, hardened by anger and self-loathing, was illuminated.

"Why didn't you tell me?"

Still floating on an ocean of pleasure, she blinked her eyes open. "What?"

"Damn it, Rebecca, why didn't you tell me you hadn't been with a man before? That this—that I was your first?"

There was an edge of accusation in his voice. For the first time, she realized she was naked. Her cheeks grew hot as she fumbled for the sheet. One moment there was glory; the next, shame. "I didn't think of it."

"Didn't think of it?" His head whipped around. "Don't you think I had a right to know? Do you think this would have happened if I had known?"

She shook her head. It was true that she hadn't thought of it. It hadn't mattered. He was the first, the last, the only. But now it occurred to her that a man like him might not want to make love with an inexperienced woman. "I'm sorry." Her heart seemed to shrivel in her breast. "You said that you loved me, that you wanted me. The rest didn't seem to matter."

She'd cried out. He'd heard the shock and pain in her voice. And he hadn't been able to stop himself. Yes, he needed a drink. "It mattered," he tossed back as he rose and strode into the other room.

Alone, she let out a shuddering breath. Of course it mattered. Only a fool would have thought otherwise. He'd thought he was dealing with an experienced, emotionally mature woman who knew how to play the game. Words like *love* and *need* and *want* were interchangeable. Yes, he'd said he loved her, but to many love was physical and physical only.

She'd made a fool of herself and she'd infuriated him, and all because she'd begun a relationship built on illusions.

She'd knowingly taken the risk, Rebecca reminded herself as she climbed out of bed. Now she'd pay the price.

He was calmer when he started back to the bedroom. Calmer, though anger still bubbled inside him. First he would show her how it should have been, how it could be. Then they had to talk, rationally, coherently.

"Rebecca..." But when he looked at the bed it was empty.

She was wrapped in a robe and was hurling clothing into her suitcase when she heard him knock. With a shake of her head, she rubbed the tears from her cheeks and continued her frenzied packing. She wouldn't answer.... She wouldn't answer and be humiliated again.

"Rebecca." The moment of calm he'd achieved had vanished. Swearing through gritted teeth, he pounded on the door. "Rebecca, this is ridiculous. Open this door."

Ignoring him, she swept bottles and tubes of toiletries off the bureau and into her bag. He'd go away, she told herself, hardly aware that she'd begun to sob. He'd go away and then she'd leave, take a cab to the airport and catch the first plane to anywhere.

The sound of splintering wood had her rushing into the parlor in time to see the door give way.

She'd thought she'd seen fury before, but she'd been wrong. She saw it now as she stared into Stephen's face. Speechless, she looked from him to the broken door and back again.

Elana, tying the belt of her robe, rushed down the hall. "Stephen, what's happened? Is there a—"

He turned on her, hurling one short sentence in clipped Greek at her. Her eyes widened and she backed away, sending Rebecca a look that combined sympathy and envy.

"Do you think you have only to walk away from me?" He pushed the door back until it scraped against the battered jamb.

"I want—" Rebecca lifted a hand to her throat as if to push the words out. "I want to be alone."

"The hell with what you want." He started toward her, only to stop dead when she cringed and turned away. He'd forgotten what it was like to hurt, truly hurt, until that moment. "I asked you once if you were afraid of me. Now I see that you are." Searching for control, he dipped his hands into the pockets of the slacks he'd thrown on. She looked defenseless, terrified, and tears still streaked her cheeks. "I won't hurt you again. Will you sit?" When she shook her head, he bit off an oath. "I will."

"I know you're angry with me," she began when he'd settled into a chair. "I'll apologize if it'll do any good, but I do want to be alone."

His eyes had narrowed and focused. "You'll apologize? For what?"

"For…" What did he expect her to say? Humiliated, she crossed her arms and hugged her elbows. "For what happened…for not…explaining," she finished lamely.

"For whatever you like," she continued as the tears started again. "Just leave me alone."

"Sweet God." He rubbed a weary hand over his face. "I can think of nothing in my life I've handled as badly as this." He rose, but stopped again when she automatically retreated. "You don't want me to touch you." His voice had roughened. He had to swallow to clear his throat. "I won't, but I hope you'll listen."

"There's nothing more to say. I understand how you feel and why you feel it. I'd rather we just left it at that."

"I treated you inexcusably."

"I don't want an apology."

"Rebecca—"

"I don't." Her voice rose, stopping his words, stopping her tears. "It's my fault. It's been my fault all along. No, no, no!" she shouted when he took another step. "I don't want you to touch me. I couldn't bear it."

He sucked in his breath, then let it out slowly. "You twist the knife well."

But she was shaking her head and pacing the room now. "It didn't matter at first—at least I didn't think it would matter. I didn't know who you were or that I would fall in love with you. Now I've waited too long and ruined everything."

"What are you talking about?"

Perhaps it was best, best for both of them, to lay out the truth. "You said you knew me, but you don't, because I've done nothing but lie to you, right from the first moment."

Slowly, carefully, he lowered himself to the arm of a chair. "What have you lied to me about?"

"Everything." Her eyes were drenched with regret

when she looked at him. "Then, tonight… First I found out that you own hotels. *Own* them."

"It was hardly a secret. Why should it matter?"

"It wouldn't." She dropped her hands to her sides. "If I was what I'd pretended to be. After we'd made love and you—I realized that by pretending I'd let you have feelings for someone who didn't even exist."

"You're standing in front of me, Rebecca. You exist."

"No. Not the way you think, not the way I've let you think."

He prepared himself for the worst. "What have you done? Were you running away from America?"

"No. Yes." She had to laugh at that. "Yes, I was running." She gathered what composure she had left and folded her hands. "I did come from Philadelphia, as I told you. I've lived there all my life. Lived there, went to school there, worked there." She found a tissue in the pocket of her robe. "I'm an accountant."

He stared at her, one brow lifting, as she blew her nose. "I beg your pardon?"

"I said, I'm an accountant." She hurled the words at him, then whirled away to face the window. Stephen started to rise, then thought better of it.

"I find it difficult to imagine you tallying ledgers, Rebecca. If you'd sit down, maybe we could talk this through."

"Damn it, I said I'm an accountant. A CPA, specializing in corporate taxes. Up until a few weeks ago I worked for McDowell, Jableki and Kline in Philadelphia."

He spread his hands, taking it all in. "All right. What did you do? Embezzle?"

She tossed back her head and nearly exploded with laughter. If she said yes he'd probably be intrigued. But the time for intrigue was over. The time for the truth was now. "No. I've never done anything illegal in my life. I've never even had a parking ticket. I've never done anything at all out of the ordinary until a few weeks ago."

She began to pace again, too agitated to keep still. "I'd never traveled, never had a man send a bottle of champagne to my table, never walked along the beach in the moonlight, never had a lover."

He said nothing, not because he was angry or bored but because he was fascinated.

"I had a good job, my car was paid for, I had good, conservative investments that would have ensured me a comfortable retirement. In my circle of friends I'm known as dependable. If someone needs a sitter they know they can call Rebecca. If they need advice or someone to feed their fish while they're on vacation they don't have to worry. I was never late for work, never took five minutes extra for lunch."

"Commendable," he said, and earned a glare.

"Just the type of employee I imagine you'd like to hire."

He swallowed a chuckle. He'd been prepared for her to confess she had a husband, five husbands, a prison record. Instead she was telling him she was an accountant with an excellent work record. "I have no desire to hire you, Rebecca."

"Just as well." She turned away and started to prowl the room again. "You'd undoubtedly change your mind after I tell you the rest."

Stephen crossed his ankles and settled back. God, what a woman she was. "I'm anxious to hear it."

"My aunt died about three months ago, suddenly."

"I'm sorry." He would have gone to her then, but he could see she was far from ready. "I know how difficult it is to lose family."

"She was all I had left." Because she needed something to do, she pushed open the balcony doors. Warm, fragrant night air rushed in. "I couldn't believe she was gone. Just like that. No warning. Of course, I handled the funeral arrangements. No fuss, no frills. Just the way Aunt Jeannie would have wanted. She was a very economical woman, not only in finances but in dress, in speech, in manner. As long as I can remember, people compared me to her."

Stephen's brow lifted again as he studied the woman being buffeted by the breeze—the short red silk robe, the tousled hair.

"Soon after her death—I don't know if it was days or a week—something just snapped. I looked at myself, at my life, and I hated it." She dragged her hair back, only to have the wind catch it again. "I was a good employee, just like my aunt, a good credit risk, a dependable friend. Law-abiding, conservative and boring. Suddenly I could see myself ten, twenty, thirty years down the road, with nothing more than I had at that moment. I couldn't stand it."

She turned around. The breeze caught at the hem of her robe and sent it dancing around her legs. "I quit my job, and I sold everything."

"Sold?"

"Everything I owned—car, apartment, furniture,

books, absolutely everything. I turned all the cash into traveler's checks, even the small inheritance from my aunt. Thousands of dollars. I know it might not sound like a lot to you, but it was more than I'd ever imagined having at once."

"Wait." He held up a hand, wanting to be certain he understood everything. "You're telling me that you sold your possessions, *all* your possessions?"

She couldn't remember ever having felt more foolish, and she straightened her shoulders defensively. "Right down to my coffeepot."

"Amazing," he murmured.

"I bought new clothes, new luggage, and flew to London. First-class. I'd never been on a plane before in my life."

"You'd never flown, but took your first trip across the Atlantic."

She didn't hear the admiration in his voice, only the amusement. "I wanted to see something different. To *be* something different. I stayed at the Ritz and took pictures of the changing of the guard. I flew to Paris and had my hair cut." Self-consciously she lifted a hand to it.

Because he could see that she was overwrought, he was careful not to smile. "You flew to Paris for a haircut."

"I'd heard some women discussing this stylist, and I— Never mind." It was no use trying to explain that she'd gone to the same hairdresser, to the same shops, for years. The same everything. "Right after Paris, I came here," she went on. "I met you. Things happened. I let them happen." Tears threatened. She could only pray he didn't see them. "You were exciting, and attracted to me. Or attracted to who you thought I was. I'd never had a romance. No one had ever looked at me the way you did."

Once more he chose his words carefully. "Are you saying that being with me was different? An adventure, like flying to a Paris salon?"

She would never be able to explain what being with him had meant to her. "Apologies and explanations really don't make any difference now. But I am sorry, Stephen. I'm sorry for everything."

He didn't see the tears, but he heard the regret in her voice. His eyes narrowed. His muscles tensed. "Are you apologizing for making love with me, Rebecca?"

"I'm apologizing for whatever you like. I'd make it up to you if I could, but I don't know how, unless I jump out the window."

He paused, as if he were considering it. "I don't think this requires anything quite that drastic. Perhaps if you'd sit down calmly?"

She shook her head and stayed where she was. "I can't handle any more of this tonight, Stephen. I'm sorry. You've every right to be angry."

He rose, the familiar impatience building. But she was so pale, looked so fragile, sounded so weary. He hadn't treated her gently before. At least he could do so now.

"All right. Tomorrow, then, after you've rested." He started to go to her, then checked himself. It would take time to show her that there were other ways to love. Time to convince her that love was more, much more than an adventure. "I want you to know that I regret what happened tonight. But that, too, will wait until tomorrow." Though he wanted to touch a hand to her cheek, he kept it fisted in his pocket. "Get some rest."

She had thought her heart was already broken. Now it shattered. Not trusting her voice, she nodded.

He left her alone. The door scraped against the splintered jamb as he secured it. She supposed there might have been a woman somewhere who'd made a bigger fool of herself. At the moment, it didn't seem to matter.

At least there was something she could do for both of them. Disappear.

Chapter 10

It was her own fault, she supposed. There were at least half a dozen promising accounting positions in the want ads. Not one of them interested her. Rebecca circled them moodily. How could she be interested in dental plans and profit sharing? All she could think about, all she'd been able to think about for two weeks, was Stephen.

What had he thought when he'd found her gone? Relief? Perhaps a vague annoyance at business left unfinished? Pen in hand, Rebecca stared out of the window of the garden apartment she'd rented. In her fantasies she imagined him searching furiously for her, determined to find her, whatever the cost. Reality, she thought with a sigh, wasn't quite so romantic. He would have been relieved. Perhaps she wasn't sophisticated, but at least she'd stepped out of his life with no fuss.

Now it was time to get her own life in order.

First things first. She had an apartment, and the little square of lawn outside the glass doors was going to make her happy. That in itself was a challenge. Her old condo had been centrally located on the fifth floor of a fully maintained modern building.

This charming and older development was a good thirty miles from downtown, but she could hear the birds in the morning. She would be able to look out at old oaks and sweeping maples and flowers she would plant herself. Perhaps it wasn't as big a change as a flight to Paris, but for Rebecca it was a statement.

She'd bought some furniture. *Some* was the operative word. Thus far she'd picked out a bed, one antique table and a single chair.

Not logical, Rebecca thought with a faint smile. No proper and economical living room suite, no tidy curtains. Even the single set of towels she'd bought was frivolous. And exactly what she'd wanted. She would do what she'd secretly wanted to do for years—buy a piece here, a piece there. Not because it was a good buy or durable, but because she wanted it.

She wondered how many people would really understand the satisfaction of making decisions not because they were sensible but because they were desirable. She'd done it with her home, her wardrobe. Even with her hair, she thought, running a hand through it. Outward changes had led to inner changes. Or vice versa. Either way, she would never again be the woman she'd been before.

Or perhaps she would be the woman she'd always been but had refused to acknowledge.

Then why was she circling ads in the classifieds? Rebecca asked herself. Why was she sitting here on a beautiful morning planning a future she had no interest in? Perhaps it was true that she would never have the one thing, the one person, she really wanted. There would be no more picnics or walks in the moonlight or frantic nights in bed. Still, she had the memories, she had the moments, she had the dreams. There would be no regrets where Stephen was concerned. Not now, and not ever. And if she was now more the woman she had been with him, it had taken more than a change in hairstyle.

She was stronger. She was surer. She was freer. And she'd done it herself.

She could think of nothing she wanted less than to go back into someone else's firm, tallying figures, calculating profit and loss. So she wouldn't. Rebecca sank into the chair as the thought struck home.

She wouldn't. She wouldn't go job hunting, carrying her résumé, rinsing sweaty palms in the rest room, putting her career and life in someone else's hands again. She'd open her own firm. A small one, certainly. Personalized. Exclusive, she decided, savoring the word. Why not? She had the skill, the experience, and—finally—she had the courage.

It wouldn't be easy. In fact, it would be risky. The money she had left would have to go toward renting office space, equipment, a phone system, advertising. With a bubbling laugh, she sprang up and searched for a legal pad and a pencil. She had to make lists—not only of things to do but of people to call. She had enough contacts from her McDowell, Jableki and Kline days.

Maybe, just maybe, she could persuade some of her former clients to give her a try.

"Just a minute," she called out when she heard the knock on the door. She scribbled a reminder to look for file cabinets as she went to answer. She'd much rather have some good solid oak file cabinets than a living room sofa.

She knew better than to open the door without checking the security peephole, but she was much too involved with her plans to think about such things. When she opened the door, she found herself face-to-face with Stephen.

Even if she could have spoken, he wasn't in the mood to let her. "What in the hell do you think you're doing?" he demanded as he slammed the door behind him. "Do you deliberately try to drive me mad, or does it come naturally to you?"

"I—I don't—" But he was already yanking her against him. Whatever words she might have spoken dissolved into a moan against his lips. Her pad fell to the floor with a slap. Even as her arms came up around him he was thrusting her away.

"What kind of game are you playing, Rebecca?" When she just shook her head, he dug his hands into his pockets and paced the wide, nearly empty room. He was unshaven, disheveled and absolutely gorgeous. "It's taken me two weeks and a great deal of trouble to find you. I believe we'd agreed to talk again. I was surprised to discover you'd not only left Athens, but Europe." He swung back and pinned her with a look. "Why?"

Still reeling from his entrance, she struggled not to babble. "I thought it best that I leave."

"You thought?" He took a step toward her, his fury so palatable that she braced herself. "You thought it best," he repeated. "For whom?"

"For you. For both of us." She caught herself fiddling with the lapels of her robe and dropped her hands. "I knew you were angry with me for lying to you and that you regretted what had happened between us. I felt it would be better for both of us if I—"

"Ran away?"

Her chin came up fractionally. "Went away."

"You said you loved me."

She swallowed. "I know."

"Was that another lie?"

"Please don't." She turned away, but there was nowhere to go. "Stephen, I never expected to see you again. I'm trying to make some sense out of my life, to do things in a way that's not only right but makes me happy. In Greece, I guess, I did what made me happy, but I didn't think about what was right. The time with you was…"

"Was what?"

Dragging both hands through her hair, she turned to him again. It was as if the two weeks had never been. She was facing him again, trying to explain what she feared she could never explain. "It was the best thing that ever happened to me, the most important, the most unforgettable, the most precious. I'll always be grateful for those few days."

"Grateful." He wasn't sure whether to laugh or murder her. Stepping forward, he surprised them both by slipping his hands lightly around her throat. "For what?

For my giving you your first fling? A fast, anonymous romance with no consequences?"

"No." She lifted a hand to his wrist but made no attempt to struggle. "Did you come all this way to make me feel more guilty?"

"I came all this way because I finish what I begin. We'd far from finished, Rebecca."

"All right." Be calm, she told herself. When a man was this close to the edge, a woman's best defense was serenity. "If you'll let me go, we'll talk. Would you like some coffee?"

His fingers tightened reflexively, then slowly relaxed. "You've bought a new pot."

"Yes." Was that humor in his eyes? she wondered. "There's only one chair. Why don't you use it while I go into the kitchen?"

He took her arm. "I don't want coffee, or a chair, or a pleasant conversation."

It seemed serenity wouldn't work. "All right, Stephen. What do you want?"

"You. I'd thought I'd made that fairly obvious." When she frowned, he glanced around the apartment. "Now tell me, Rebecca, is this what you want? A handful of rooms to be alone in?"

"I want to make the best of the rest of my life. I've already apologized for deceiving you. I realize that—"

"Deceiving me." He held up a finger to stop her. "I've wanted to clear that point up myself. How did you deceive me?"

"By letting you think that I was something I'm not."

"You're not a beautiful, interesting woman? A passionate woman?" He lifted a brow as he studied her.

"Rebecca, I have too much pride to ever believe you could deceive me that completely."

He was confusing her—deliberately, she was sure. "I told you what I'd done."

"What you'd done," he agreed. "And how you'd done it." He brought his hand to her throat again, this time in a caress. His anger hadn't made her knees weak. She felt them tremble now at his tenderness. "Selling your possessions and flying to Paris for a new hairstyle. Quitting your job and grabbing life with both hands. You fascinate me." Her eyes stayed open wide when he brushed his lips over hers. "I think the time is nearly over when you'll be so easily flattered. It's almost a pity." He drew her closer, slowly, while his mouth touched hers. Relief coursed through him as he felt her melt and give. "Do you think it was your background that attracted me?"

"You were angry," she managed.

"Yes, angry at the idea that I had been part of your experiment. Furious," he added before he deepened the kiss. "Furious that I had been of only passing interest." She was heating in his arms, just as he remembered, just as he needed, softening, strengthening. "Shall I tell you how angry? Shall I tell you that for two weeks I couldn't work, couldn't think, couldn't function, because you were everywhere I looked and nowhere to be found?"

"I had to go." She was already tugging at his shirt to find the flesh beneath. To touch him again, just for a moment. To be touched by him. "When you said you regretted making love…" Her own words brought her back. Quickly she dropped her hands and stepped away.

He stared at her for a moment, then abruptly swore and began to pace. "I've never thought myself this big a fool. I hurt you that night in a much different way than I'd believed. Then I handled it with less finesse than I might the most unimportant business transaction." He paused, sighing. For the first time she saw clearly how incredibly weary he was.

"You're tired. Please, sit down. Let me fix you something."

He took a moment to press his fingers to his eyes. Again he wanted to laugh—while he strangled her. She was exactly what he needed, what he understood. Yet at the same time she baffled him.

"You weaken me, Rebecca, and bring out the fool I'd forgotten I could be. I'm surprised you allowed me to set foot into your home. You should have—" As quickly as the anger had come, it faded. As quickly as the tension had formed, it eased. Everything he'd needed to see was in her eyes. Carefully now, he drew a deep breath. A man wasn't always handed so many chances at happiness.

"Rebecca, I never regretted making love with you." He stopped her from turning with the lightest of touches on her shoulder. "I regretted only the way it happened. Too much need and too little care. I regret, I'll always regret, that for your first time there was fire but no warmth." He took her hands in his and brought them to his lips.

"It was beautiful."

"In its way." His fingers tightened on hers. Still so innocent, he thought. Still so generous. "It was not kind or patient or tender, as love should be the first time."

She felt hope rise in her heart again. "None of that mattered."

"It mattered, more than I can ever tell you. After, when you told me everything, it only mattered more. If I had done what my instincts told me to do that night you would never have left me. But I thought you needed time before you could bear to have me touch you again." Slowly, gently, he drew the tip of her finger into his mouth and watched her eyes cloud over. "Let me show you what I should have shown you then." With her hands locked in his, he looked into her eyes. "Do you want me?"

It was time for the truth. "Yes."

He lifted her into his arms and heard her breath catch. "Do you trust me?"

"Yes."

When he smiled, her heart turned over. "Rebecca, I must ask you one more thing."

"What is it?"

"Do you have a bed?"

She felt her cheeks heat even as she laughed. "In there."

She was trembling. It reminded him how careful he had to be, how precious this moment was to both of them. The sun washed over the bed, over them, as he lay beside her. And kissed her—only kissed her, softly, deeply, thoroughly, until her arms slipped from around him to fall bonelessly to her sides. She trembled still as he murmured to her, as his lips brushed over her cheeks, her throat.

He had shown her the desperation love could cause, the sharp-edged pleasure, the speed and the fury. Now he showed her that love could mean serenity and sweetness.

And she showed him.

He had thought to teach her, not to learn, to reassure her but not to be comforted. But he learned, and he was comforted. The need was there, as strong as it had been the first time. But strength was tempered with patience. As he slipped his hands down her robe to part it, to slide it away from her skin, he felt no need to hurry. He could delight in the way the sun slanted across her body, in the way her flesh warmed to his touch.

Her breath was as unsteady as her hands as she undressed him. But not from nerves. She understood that now. She felt strong and capable and certain. Anticipation made her tremble. Pleasure made her shudder. She gave a sigh that purred out of her lips as she arched against his seeking hands. Then he nipped lightly at her breast and she bounded from serenity to passion in one breathless leap.

Still he moved slowly, guiding her into a kind of heated torment she'd never experienced. Desire boiled in her, and his name sprang to her lips and her body coiled like a spring. Chaining down his own need, he set hers free and watched as she flew over the first peak.

"Only for me," he murmured as she went limp in his arms. "Only for me, Rebecca." With his own passions strapped, he slipped into her, determined to watch her build again. "Tell me you love me. Look at me and tell me."

She opened her eyes. She could barely breathe. Somehow the strength was pouring back into her, but so fast, so powerfully. Sensation rolled over sensation, impossibly. She moved with him, pressed center to center, heart to heart, but all she could see were his eyes, so dark, so blue, so intense. Perhaps she was drowning in them.

"I love you, Stephen."

Then she was falling, fathoms deep, into his eyes, into the sea. With her arms locked around him, she dragged him under with her.

He pulled her against him so that he could stroke her hair and wait for his pulse to level. She'd been innocent. But the surprise, the one he'd been dealing with for weeks, was that until Rebecca he'd been just as innocent. He'd known passion, but he'd never known intimacy, not the kind that reached the heart as fully as the body. And yet...

"We've been here before," he murmured. "Do you feel it, too?"

She linked her fingers with his. "I never believed in things like that until you. When I'm with you it's like remembering." She lifted her head to look at him. "I can't explain it."

"I love you, Rebecca, only more knowing who you are, why you are."

She touched a hand to his cheek. "I don't want you to say anything you don't really feel."

"How can a woman be so intelligent and still so stupid?" With a shake of his head, Stephen rolled on top of her. "A man doesn't travel thousands of miles for this, however delightful it may be. I love you, and though it annoyed me for quite some time I'm accustomed to it now."

"Annoyed you."

"Infuriated." He kissed her to cut off whatever retort she might make. "I'd seen myself remaining free for years to come. Then I met a woman who sold her coffeepot so she could take pictures of goats."

"I certainly have no intention of interfering with your plans."

"You already have." He smiled, holding her still when she tried to struggle away. "Marriage blocks off certain freedoms and opens others."

"Marriage?" She stopped struggling but turned her head to avoid another kiss.

"Soon." He nuzzled her neck. "Immediately."

"I never said I'd marry you."

"No, but you will." With his fingertips only, he began to arouse her. "I'm a very persuasive man."

"I need to think." But she was trembling again. "Stephen, marriage is very serious."

"Deadly. And I should warn you that I've already decided to murder any man you look at for more than twenty seconds."

"Really?" She turned her head back, prepared to be angry. But he was smiling. No one else had ever smiled at her in quite that way. "Really?"

"I can't let you go, Rebecca. Can't and won't. Come back with me. Marry me. Have children with me."

"Stephen—"

He laid a finger to her lips. "I know what I'm asking you. You've already started a new life, made new plans. We've had only days together, but I can make you happy. I can promise to love you for a lifetime, or however many lifetimes we have. You once dived into the sea on impulse. Dive with me now, Rebecca. I swear you won't regret it."

Gently she pressed her lips to his fingertip, then drew his hand away. "All my life I've wondered what I might find if I had the courage to look. I found you, Stephen." With a laugh she threw her arms around him. "When do you want to leave?"

* * * * *

LESSONS LEARNED

For Jill Gregory, aka The Baby,
one of my favorite roommates.

Chapter 1

So he was gorgeous. And rich…and talented. And sexy; you shouldn't forget that he was outrageously sexy.

It hardly mattered to Juliet. She was a professional, and to a professional, a job was a job. In this case, great looks and personality were bound to help, but that was business. Strictly business.

No, personally it didn't matter a bit. After all, she'd met a few gorgeous men in her life. She'd met a few rich ones too, and so forth, though she had to admit she'd never met a man with all those elusive qualities rolled up in one. She'd certainly never had the opportunity to work with one. Now she did.

The fact was, Carlo Franconi's looks, charm, reputation and skill were going to make her job a pleasure. So she was told. Still, with her office door closed, Juliet scowled down at the eight-by-ten glossy black-and-white publicity photo. It looked to her as though he'd be more trouble than pleasure.

Carlo grinned cockily up at her, dark, almond-shaped eyes amused and appreciative. She wondered if the photographer had been a woman. His full thick hair was appealingly disheveled with a bit of curl along the nape of his neck and over his ears. Not too much— just enough to disarm. The strong facial bones, jauntily curved mouth, straight nose and expressive brows combined to create a face destined to sabotage any woman's common sense. Gift or cultivated talent, Juliet wasn't certain, but she'd have to use it to her advantage. Author tours could be murder.

A cookbook. Juliet tried, and failed, not to sigh. Carlo Franconi's *The Italian Way,* was, whether she liked it or not, her biggest assignment to date. Business was business.

She loved her job as publicist and was content for the moment with Trinity Press, the publisher she currently worked for, after a half-dozen job changes and upward jumps since the start of her career. At twenty-eight, the ambition she'd started with as a receptionist nearly ten years before had eased very little. She'd worked, studied, hustled and sweated for her own office and position. She had them, but she wasn't ready to relax.

In two years, by her calculations, she'd be ready to make the next jump: her own public relations firm. Naturally, she'd have to start out small, but it was building the business that was exciting. The contacts and experience she gained in her twenties would help her solidify her ambitions in her thirties. Juliet was content with that.

One of the first things she'd learned in public relations was that an account was an account, whether it was a big blockbuster bestseller already slated to be a big blockbuster film or a slim volume of poetry that would barely earn out its advance. Part of the challenge, and the fun, was finding the right promotional hook.

Now, she had a cookbook and a slick Italian chef. Franconi, she thought wryly, had a track record—with women and in publishing. The first was a matter of hot interest to the society and gossip sections of the international press. It wasn't necessary to cook to be aware of Franconi's name. The second was the reason he was being pampered on the road with a publicist.

His first two cookbooks had been solid bestsellers. For good reason, Juliet admitted. It was true she couldn't fry an egg without creating a gooey inedible glob, but she recognized quality and style. Franconi could make linguini sound like a dish to be prepared while wearing black lace. He turned a simple spaghetti dish into an erotic event.

Sex. Juliet tipped back in her chair and wiggled her stockinged toes. That's what he had. That's just what they'd use. Before the twenty-one-day author tour was finished, she'll have made Carlo Franconi the world's sexiest cook. Any red-blooded American woman would fantasize about him preparing an intimate dinner for two. Candlelight, pasta and romance.

One last study of his publicity shot and the charmingly crooked grin assured her he could handle it.

In the meantime, there was a bit more groundwork to cover. Creating a schedule was a pleasure, adhering to one a challenge. She thrived on both.

Juliet lifted the phone, noticed with resignation that she'd broken another nail, then buzzed her assistant. "Terry, get me Diane Maxwell. She's program coordinator on the *Simpson Show* in L.A."

"Going for the big guns?"

Juliet gave a quick, unprofessional grin. "Yeah." She replaced the phone and started making hurried notes. No reason not to start at the top, she told herself. That way, if you fell on your face, at least the trip would be worth it.

As she waited, she looked around her office. Not the top, but a good ways from the bottom. At least she had a window. Juliet could still shudder thinking of some of the walled-in cubicles she'd worked in. Now, twenty stories below, New York rushed, bumped, pushed and shoved its way through another day. Juliet Trent had learned how to do the same thing after moving from the relatively easygoing suburb of Harrisburg, Pennsylvania.

She might've grown up in a polite little neighborhood where only a stranger drove over twenty-five miles per hour and everyone kept the grass clipped close to their side of the chain-link fences, but Juliet had acclimated easily. The truth was she liked the pace, the energy and the "I dare you" tone of New York. She'd never go back to the bee-humming, hedge-clipping quiet of suburbia where everyone knew who you were, what you did and how you did it. She preferred the anonymity and the individuality of crowds.

Perhaps her mother had molded herself into the perfect suburban wife, but not Juliet. She was an eighties woman, independent, self-sufficient and moving up.

There was an apartment in the west Seventies that she'd furnished, slowly, meticulously and, most important, personally. Juliet had enough patience to move step by step as long as the result was perfect. She had a career she could be proud of and an office she was gradually altering to suit her own tastes. Leaving her mark wasn't something she took lightly. It had taken her four months to choose the right plants for her work space, from the four-foot split-leaf philodendron to the delicate white-blossomed African violet.

She'd had to make do with the beige carpet, but the six-foot Dali print on the wall opposite her window added life and energy. The narrow-beveled mirror gave an illusion of space and a touch of elegance. She had her eye on a big, gaudy Oriental urn that would be perfect for a spray of equally gaudy peacock feathers. If she waited a bit longer, the price might come down from exorbitant to ridiculous. Then she'd buy it.

Juliet might put on a very practical front to everyone, including herself, but she couldn't resist a sale. As a result, her bank balance wasn't as hefty as her bedroom closet. She wasn't frivolous. No, she would have been appalled to hear the word applied to her. Her wardrobe was organized, well tended and suitable. Perhaps twenty pairs of shoes could be considered excessive, but Juliet rationalized that she was often on her feet ten hours a day and deserved the luxury. In any case, she'd earned them, from the sturdy sneakers, the practical black pumps to the strappy evening sandals. She'd earned them with innumerable long meetings, countless waits in airports and endless hours on the phone. She'd earned them on author tours, where the luck of the draw could have you dealing with the brilliant, the funny, the inept, the boring or the rude. Whatever she had to deal with, the results had to be the same. Media, media and more media.

She'd learned how to deal with the press, from the *New York Times* reporter to the stringer on the small-town weekly. She knew how to charm the staff of talk shows, from the accepted masters to the nervous imitators. Learning had been an adventure, and since she'd allowed herself very few in her personal life, professional success was all the sweeter.

When the intercom buzzed, she caught her tongue between her teeth. Now, she was going to apply everything she'd learned and land Franconi on the top-rated talk show in the States.

Once she did, she thought as she pressed the button, he'd better make the most of it. Or she'd slit his sexy throat with his own chef's knife.

"Ah, *mi amore. Squisito.*" Carlo's voice was a low purr designed to accelerate the blood pressure. The bedroom voice wasn't something he'd had to develop, but something he'd been born with. Carlo had always thought a man who didn't use God-given gifts was less than a fool. *"Bellisimo,"* he murmured and his eyes were dark and dreamy with anticipation.

It was hot, almost steamy, but he preferred the heat. Cold slowed down the blood. The sun coming through the window had taken on the subtle gold texture with tints of red that spoke of the end of the day and hinted at the pleasures of night. The room was rich with scent so he breathed it in. A man was missing a great deal of life if he didn't use and appreciate all of his senses. Carlo believed in missing nothing.

He watched his love of the moment with a connoisseur's eye. He'd caress, whisper to, flatter—it never mattered to him if it took moments or hours to get what he wanted. As long as he got what he wanted. To Carlo, the process, the anticipation, the moves themselves were equally as satisfying as the result. Like a dance, he'd always thought. Like a song. An aria from *The Marriage of Figaro* played in the background while he seduced.

Carlo believed in setting the scene because life was a play not simply to be enjoyed, but to be relished.

"Bellisimo," he whispered and bent nearer what he adored. The clam sauce simmered erotically as he stirred it. Slowly, savoring the moment, Carlo lifted the spoon to his lips and with his eyes half-closed, tasted. The sound of pleasure came from low in his throat. *"Squisito."*

He moved from the sauce to give the same loving attention to his *zabaglione*. He believed there wasn't a woman alive who could resist the taste of that rich, creamy custard with the zing of wine. As usual, it was a woman he was expecting.

The kitchen was as much a den of pleasure to him as the bedroom. It wasn't an accident that he was one of the most respected and admired chefs in the world, or that he was one of the most engaging lovers. Carlo considered it a matter of destiny. His kitchen was cleverly arranged, as meticulously laid out for the seduction of sauces and spices as his bedroom was for the seduction of women. Yes, Carlo Franconi believed life was to be relished. Every drop of it.

When the knock on the front door reverberated through the high-ceilinged rooms of his home, he murmured to his pasta before he removed his apron. As he went to answer, he rolled down the silk sleeves of his shirt but didn't stop for adjustments in any of the antique mirrors that lined the walls. He wasn't so much vain, as confident.

He opened the door to a tall, stately woman with honey-toned skin and dark glossy eyes. Carlo's heart moved as it did whenever he saw her. *"Mi amore."* Taking her hand, he pressed his mouth to the palm, while his eyes smiled into hers. *"Bella. Molto bella."*

She stood in the evening light for a moment, dark, lovely, with a smile only for him. Only a fool wouldn't have known he'd welcomed dozens of women in just this way. She wasn't a fool. But she loved him.

"You're a scoundrel, Carlo." The woman reached out to touch his hair. It was dark and thick and difficult to resist. "Is this the way you greet your mother?"

"This is the way—" he kissed her hand again "—I greet a beautiful woman." Then he wrapped both arms around her and kissed her cheeks. "This is the way I greet my mother. It's a fortunate man who can do both."

Gina Franconi laughed as she returned her son's hug. "To you, all women are beautiful."

"But only one is my mother." With his arm around her waist, he led her inside.

Gina approved, as always, the fact that his home was spotless, if a bit too exotic for her taste. She often wondered how the poor maid managed to keep the ornately carved archways dusted and polished and the hundreds of windowpanes unstreaked. Because she was a woman who'd spent fifteen years of her life cleaning other people's homes and forty cleaning her own, she thought of such things.

She studied one of his new acquisitions, a three-foot ivory owl with a small rodent captured in one claw. A good wife, Gina mused, would guide her son's tastes toward less eccentric paths.

"An aperitif, Mama?" Carlo walked over to a tall smoked-glass cabinet and drew out a slim black bottle. "You should try this," he told her as he chose two small glasses and poured. "A friend sent it to me."

Gina set aside her red snakeskin bag and accepted the glass. The first sip was hot, potent, smooth as a lover's kiss and just as intoxicating. She lifted a brow as she took the second sip. "Excellent."

"Yes, it is. Anna has excellent taste."

Anna, she thought, with more amusement than exasperation. She'd learned years before that it didn't do any good to be exasperated with a man, especially if you loved him. "Are all your friends women, Carlo?"

"No." He held his glass up, twirling it. "But this one was. She sent me this as a wedding present."

"A—"

"Her wedding," Carlo said with a grin. "She wanted a husband, and though I couldn't accommodate her, we parted friends." He held up the bottle as proof.

"Did you have it analyzed before you drank any?" Gina asked dryly.

He touched the rim of his glass to hers. "A clever man turns all former lovers into friends, Mama."

"You've always been clever." With a small movement

of her shoulders she sipped again and sat down. "I hear you're seeing the French actress."

"As always, your hearing's excellent."

As if it interested her, Gina studied the hue of the liqueur in her glass. "She is, of course, beautiful."

"Of course."

"I don't think she'll give me grandchildren."

Carlo laughed and sat beside her. "You have six grandchildren and another coming, Mama. Don't be greedy."

"But none from my son. My only son," she reminded him with a tap of her finger on his shoulder. "Still, I haven't given you up yet."

"Perhaps if I could find a woman like you."

She shot him back arrogant look for arrogant look. "Impossible, *caro*."

His feeling exactly, Carlo thought as he guided her into talk about his four sisters and their families. When he looked at this sleek, lovely woman, it was difficult to think of her as the mother who'd raised him, almost single-handedly. She'd worked, and though she'd been known to storm and rage, she'd never complained. Her clothes had been carefully mended, her floors meticulously scrubbed while his father had spent endless months at sea.

When he concentrated, and he rarely did, Carlo could recall an impression of a dark, wiry man with a black mustache and an easy grin. The impression didn't bring on resentment or even regret. His father had been a seaman before his parents had married, and a seaman he'd remained. Carlo's belief in meeting your destiny was unwavering. But while his feelings for his father were ambivalent, his feelings for his mother were set and strong.

She'd supported each of her children's ambitions, and when Carlo had earned a scholarship to the Sorbonne in Paris and the opportunity to pursue his interest in haute cuisine, she'd let him go. Ultimately, she'd supplemented the meager income he could earn between studies with part of the insurance money she'd received when her husband had been lost in the sea he'd loved.

Six years before, Carlo had been able to pay her back in his own way. The dress shop he'd bought for her birthday had been a lifelong dream for both of them. For him, it was a way of seeing his mother happy at last. For Gina it was a way to begin again.

He'd grown up in a big, boisterous, emotional family. It gave him pleasure to look back and remember. A man who grows up in a family of women learns to understand them, appreciate them, admire them. Carlo knew about women's dreams, their vanities, their insecurities. He never took a lover he didn't have affection for as well as desire. If there was only desire, he knew there'd be no friendship at the end, only resentment. Even now, the comfortable affair he was having with the French actress was ending. She'd be starting a film in a few weeks, and he'd be going on tour in America. That, Carlo thought with some regret, would be that.

"Carlo, you go to America soon?"

"Hmm. Yes." He wondered if she'd read his mind, knowing women were capable of doing so. "Two weeks."

"You'll do me a favor?"

"Of course."

"Then notice for me what the professional American woman is wearing. I'm thinking of adding some things to the shop. The Americans are so clever and practical."

"Not too practical, I hope." He swirled his drink. "My publicist is a Ms. Trent." Tipping back his glass, he accepted the heat and the punch. "I'll promise you to study every aspect of her wardrobe."

She gave his quick grin a steady look. "You're so good to me, Carlo."

"But of course, Mama. Now I'm going to feed you like a queen."

Carlo had no idea what Juliet Trent looked like, but put himself in the hands of fate. What he did know, from the letters he'd received from her, was that Juliet Trent was the type of American his mother had described. Practical and clever. Excellent qualities in a publicist.

Physically was another matter. But again, as his mother had said, Carlo could always find beauty in a woman. Perhaps he did prefer, in his personal life, a woman with a lovely shell, but he knew how to dig beneath to find inner beauty. It was something that made life interesting as well as aesthetically pleasing.

Still, as he stepped off the plane into the terminal in L.A., he had his hand on the elbow of a stunning redhead.

Juliet did know what he looked like, and she first saw him, shoulder to shoulder with a luxuriously built woman in pencil-thin heels. Though he carried a bulky leather case in one hand, and a flight bag over his shoulder, he escorted the redhead through the gate as though they were walking into a ballroom. Or a bedroom.

Juliet took a quick assessment of the well-tailored slacks, the unstructured jacket and open-collared shirt. The well-heeled traveler. There was a chunk of gold and diamond on his finger that should've looked ostentatious and vulgar. Somehow it looked as casual and breezy as the rest of him. She felt formal and sticky.

She'd been in L.A. since the evening before, giving herself time to see personally to all the tiny details. Carlo Franconi would have nothing to do but be charming, answer questions and sign his cookbook.

As she watched him kiss the redhead's knuckles, Juliet thought he'd be signing plenty of them. After all, didn't women do the majority of cookbook buying? Carefully smoothing away a sarcastic smirk, Juliet rose. The redhead was sending one last wistful look over her shoulder as she walked away.

"Mr. Franconi?"

Carlo turned away from the woman who'd proven to be a pleasant traveling companion on the long flight from New York. His first look at Juliet brought a quick flutter of interest and a subtle tug of desire he often felt with a woman. It was a tug he could either control or let loose, as was appropriate. This time, he savored it.

She didn't have merely a lovely face, but an interesting one. Her skin was very pale, which should have made her seem fragile, but the wide, strong cheekbones undid the air of fragility and gave her face an intriguing diamond shape. Her eyes were large, heavily lashed and artfully accented with a smoky shadow that only made the cool green shade of the irises seem cooler. Her mouth was only lightly touched with a peach-colored gloss. It had a full, eye-drawing shape that needed no artifice. He gathered she was wise enough to know it.

Her hair was caught somewhere between brown and blond so that its shade was soft, natural and subtle. She wore it long enough in the back to be pinned up in a chignon when she wished, and short enough on the top and sides so that she could style it from fussy to practical as the occasion, and her whim, demanded. At the moment, it was loose and casual, but not windblown. She'd stopped in the ladies' room for a quick check just after the incoming flight had been announced.

"I'm Juliet Trent," she told him when she felt he'd stared long enough. "Welcome to California." As he took the hand she offered, she realized she should've expected him to kiss it rather than shake. Still, she stiffened, hardly more than an instant, but she saw by the lift of brow, he'd felt it.

"A beautiful woman makes a man welcome anywhere."

His voice was incredible—the cream that rose to the top and then flowed over something rich. She told herself it only pleased her because it would record well and took his statement literally. Thinking of the redhead, she gave him an easy, not entirely friendly smile. "Then you must have had a pleasant flight."

His native language might have been Italian, but Carlo understood nuances in any tongue. He grinned at her. "Very pleasant."

"And tiring," she said remembering her position. "Your luggage should be in by now." Again, she glanced at the large case he carried. "Can I take that for you?"

His brow lifted at the idea of a man dumping his

burden on a woman. Equality, to Carlo, never crossed the border into manners. "No, this is something I always carry myself."

Indicating the way, she fell into step beside him. "It's a half-hour ride to the Beverly Wilshire, but after you've settled in, you can rest all afternoon. I'd like to go over tomorrow's schedule with you this evening."

He liked the way she walked. Though she wasn't tall, she moved in long, unhurried strides that made the red side-pleated skirt she wore shift over her hips. "Over dinner?"

She sent him a quick sidelong look. "If you like."

She'd be at his disposal, Juliet reminded herself, for the next three weeks. Without appearing to think about it, she skirted around a barrel-chested man hefting a bulging garment bag and a briefcase. Yes, he liked the way she walked, Carlo thought again. She was a woman who could take care of herself without a great deal of fuss.

"At seven? You have a talk show in the morning that starts at seven-thirty so we'd best make it an early evening."

Seven-thirty A.M. Carlo thought, only briefly, about jet lag and time changes. "So, you put me to work quickly."

"That's what I'm here for, Mr. Franconi." Juliet said it cheerfully as she stepped up to the slowly moving baggage belt. "You have your stubs?"

An organized woman, he thought as he reached into the inside pocket of his loose-fitting buff-colored jacket. In silence, he handed them to her, then hefted a pullman and a garment bag from the belt himself.

Gucci, she observed. So he had taste as well as money. Juliet handed the stubs to a skycap and waited while Carlo's luggage was loaded onto the pushcart. "I think you'll be pleased with what we have for you, Mr. Franconi." She walked through the automatic doors and signaled for her limo. "I know you've always worked with Jim Collins in the past on your tours in the States; he sends his best."

"Does Jim like his executive position?"

"Apparently."

Though Carlo expected her to climb into the limo first, she stepped back. With a bow to women professionals, Carlo ducked inside and took his seat. "Do you like yours, Ms. Trent?"

She took the seat across from him then sent him a straight-shooting, level look. Juliet could have no idea how much he admired it. "Yes, I do."

Carlo stretched out his legs—legs his mother had once said that had refused to stop growing long after it was necessary. He'd have preferred driving himself, particularly after the long, long flight from Rome where someone else had been at the controls. But if he couldn't, the plush laziness of the limo was the next best thing. Reaching over, he switched on the stereo so that Mozart poured out, quiet but vibrant. If he'd been driving, it would've been rock, loud and rambunctious.

"You've read my book, Ms. Trent?"

"Yes, of course. I couldn't set up publicity and promotion for an unknown product." She sat back. It was easy to do her job when she could speak the simple truth. "I was impressed with the attention to detail and the clear directions. It seemed a very friendly book, rather than simply a kitchen tool."

"Hmm." He noticed her stockings were very pale pink and had a tiny line of dots up one side. It would interest his mother that the practical American business-woman could enjoy the frivolous. It interested him that Juliet Trent could. "Have you tried any of the recipes?"

"No, I don't cook."

"You don't…" His lazy interest came to attention. "At all?"

She had to smile. He looked so sincerely shocked.

As he watched the perfect mouth curve, he had to put the next tug of desire in check.

"When you're a failure at something, Mr. Franconi, you leave it to someone else."

"I could teach you." The idea intrigued him. He never offered his expertise lightly.

"To cook?" She laughed, relaxing enough to let her heel slip out of her shoe as she swung her foot. "I don't think so."

"I'm an excellent teacher," he said with a slow smile.

Again, she gave him the calm, gunslinger look. "I don't doubt it. I, on the other hand, am a poor student."

"Your age?" When her look narrowed, he smiled charmingly. "A rude question when a woman's reached a certain stage. You haven't."

"Twenty-eight," she said so coolly his smile became a grin.

"You look younger, but your eyes are older. I'd find it a pleasure to give you a few lessons, Ms. Trent."

She believed him. She, too, understood nuances. "A pity our schedule won't permit it."

He shrugged easily and glanced out the window. But the L.A. freeway didn't interest him. "You put Philadelphia in the schedule as I requested?"

"We'll have a full day there before we fly up to Boston. Then we'll finish up in New York."

"Good. I have a friend there. I haven't seen her in nearly a year."

Juliet was certain he had—friends—everywhere.

"You've been to Los Angeles before?" he asked her.

"Yes. Several times on business."

"I've yet to come here for pleasure myself. What do you think of it?"

As he had, she glanced out the window without interest. "I prefer New York."

"Why?"

"More grit, less gloss."

He liked her answer, and her phrasing. Because of it, he studied her more closely. "Have you ever been to Rome?"

"No." He thought he heard just a trace of wistfulness in her voice. "I haven't been to Europe at all."

"When you do, come to Rome. It was built on grit."

Her mind drifted a bit as she thought of it, and her smile remained. "I think of fountains and marble and cathedrals."

"You'll find them—and more." She had a face exquisite enough to be carved in marble, he thought. A voice quiet and smooth enough for cathedrals. "Rome rose and fell and clawed its way back up again. An intelligent woman understands such things. A romantic woman understands the fountains."

She glanced out again as the limo pulled up in front of the hotel. "I'm afraid I'm not very romantic."

"A woman named Juliet hasn't a choice."

"My mother's selection," she pointed out. "Not mine."

"You don't look for Romeo?"

Juliet gathered her briefcase. "No, Mr. Franconi. I don't."

He stepped out ahead of her and offered his hand. When Juliet stood on the curb, he didn't move back to give her room. Instead, he experimented with the sensation of bodies brushing, lightly, even politely on a public street. Her gaze came up to his, not wary but direct.

He felt it, the pull. Not the tug that was impersonal and for any woman, but the pull that went straight to the gut and was for one woman. So he'd have to taste her mouth. After all, he was a man compelled to judge a great deal by taste. But he could also bide his time. Some creations took a long time and had complicated preparations to perfect. Like Juliet, he insisted on perfection.

"Some women," he murmured, "never need to look, only to evade and avoid and select."

"Some women," she said just as quietly, "choose not to select at all." Deliberately, she turned her back on him to pay off the driver. "I've already checked you in, Mr. Franconi," she said over her shoulder as she handed his key to the waiting bellboy. "I'm just across the hall from your suite."

Without looking at him, Juliet followed the bellboy into the hotel and to the elevators. "If it suits you, I'll make reservations here in the hotel for dinner at seven. You can just tap on my door when you're ready." With a quick check of her watch she calculated the time difference and figured she could make three calls to New York and one to Dallas before office hours were over farther east. "If you need anything, you've only to order it and charge it to the room."

She stepped from the elevator, unzipping her purse and pulling out her own room key as she walked. "I'm sure you'll find your suite suitable."

He watched her brisk, economic movements. "I'm sure I will."

"Seven o'clock then." She was already pushing her key into the lock as the bellboy opened the first door to the suite across the hall. As she did, her mind was already on the calls she'd make the moment she'd shed her jacket and shoes.

"Juliet."

She paused, her hair swinging back as she looked over her shoulder at Carlo. He held her there, a moment longer, in silence. "Don't change your scent," he murmured. "Sex without flowers, femininity without vulnerability. It suits you."

While she continued to stare over her shoulder, he disappeared inside the suite. The bellboy began his polite introductions to the accommodations of the suite. Something Carlo said caused him to break off and laugh.

Juliet turned her key with more strength than necessary, pushed open her door, then closed it again with the length of her body. For a minute, she just leaned there, waiting for her system to level.

Professional training had prevented her from stammering and fumbling and making a fool of herself. Professional training had helped her to keep her nerves just at the border where they could be controlled and concealed. Still, under the training, there was a woman. Control had cost her. Juliet was dead certain there wasn't a woman alive who would be totally unaffected by Carlo Franconi. It wasn't balm for her ego to admit she was simply part of a large, varied group.

He'd never know it, she told herself, but her pulse had been behaving badly since he'd first taken her hand. It was still behaving badly. Stupid, she told herself and threw her bag down on a chair. Then she thought it best if she followed it. Her legs weren't steady yet. Juliet let out a long, deep breath. She'd just have to wait until they were.

So he was gorgeous. And rich…and talented. And outrageously sexy. She'd already known that, hadn't she? The trouble was, she wasn't sure how to handle him. Not nearly as sure as she had to be.

Chapter 2

She was a woman who thrived on tight scheduling, minute details and small crises. These were the things that kept you alert, sharp and interested. If her job had been simple, there wouldn't have been much fun to it.

She was also a woman who liked long, lazy baths in mountains of bubbles and big, big beds. These were the things that kept you sane. Juliet felt she'd earned the second after she'd dealt with the first.

While Carlo amused himself in his own way, Juliet spent an hour and a half on the phone, then another hour revising and fine-tuning the next day's itinerary. A print interview had come through and had to be shuffled in. She shuffled. Another paper was sending a reporter and photographer to the book signing. Their names had to be noted and remembered. Juliet noted, circled and committed to memory. The way things were shaping up, they'd be lucky to manage a two-hour breather the next day. Nothing could've pleased her more.

By the time she'd closed her thick, leather-bound notebook, she was more than ready for the tub. The bed, unfortunately, would have to wait. Ten o'clock, she promised herself. By ten, she'd be in bed, snuggled in, curled up and unconscious.

She soaked, designating precisely forty-five minutes for her personal time. In the bath, she didn't plot or plan or estimate. She clicked off the busy, business end of her brain and enjoyed.

Relaxing—it took the first ten minutes to accomplish that completely. Dreaming—she could pretend the white, standard-size tub was luxurious, large and lush. Black marble perhaps and big enough for two. It was a secret ambition of Juliet's to own one like it eventually. The symbol, she felt, of ultimate success. She'd have bristled if anyone had called her goal romantic. Practical, she'd insist. When you worked hard, you needed a place to unwind. This was hers.

Her robe hung on the back of the door—jade green, teasingly brief and silk. Not a luxury as far as she was concerned, but a necessity. When you often had only short snatches to relax, you needed all the help you could get. She considered the robe as much an aid in keeping pace as the bottles of vitamins that lined the counter by the sink. When she traveled, she always took them.

After she'd relaxed and dreamed a bit, she could appreciate soft, hot water against her skin, silky bubbles hissing, steam rising rich with scent.

He'd told her not to change her scent.

Juliet scowled as she felt the muscles in her shoulders tense. Oh no. Deliberately she picked up the tiny cake of hotel soap and rubbed it up and down her arms. Oh no, she wouldn't let Carlo Franconi intrude on her personal time. That was rule number one.

He'd purposely tried to unravel her. He'd succeeded. Yes, he had succeeded, Juliet admitted with a stubborn nod. But that was over now. She wouldn't let it happen again. Her job was to promote his book, not his ego. To promote, she'd go above and beyond the call of duty with her time, her energy and her skill, but not with her emotions.

Franconi wasn't flying back to Rome in three weeks with a smug smile on his face unless it was professionally generated. That instant knife-sharp attraction would be dealt with. Priorities, Juliet mused, were the order of the day. He could add all the American conquests to his list he chose—as long as she wasn't among them.

In any case, he didn't seriously interest her. It was simply that basic, primal urge. Certainly there wasn't any intellect involved. She preferred a different kind of man—steady rather than flashy, sincere rather than charming. That was the kind of man a woman of common sense looked for when the time was right. Juliet judged the time would be right in about three years. By then, she'd have established the structure for her own firm. She'd be financially independent and creatively content. Yes, in three years she'd be ready to think about a serious relationship. That would fit her schedule nicely.

Settled, she decided, and closed her eyes. It was a

nice, comfortable word. But the hot water, bubbles and steam didn't relax her any longer. A bit resentful, she released the plug and stood up to let the water drain off her. The wide mirror above the counter and sink was fogged, but only lightly. Through the mist she could see Juliet Trent.

Odd, she thought, how pale and soft and vulnerable a naked woman could look. In her mind, she was strong, practical, even tough. But she could see, in the damp, misty mirror, the fragility, even the wistfulness.

Erotic? Juliet frowned a bit as she told herself she shouldn't be disappointed that her body had been built on slim, practical lines rather than round and lush ones. She should be grateful that her long legs got her where she was going and her narrow hips helped keep her silhouette in a business suit trim and efficient. Erotic would never be a career plus.

Without makeup, her face looked too young, too trusting. Without careful grooming, her hair looked too wild, too passionate.

Fragile, young, passionate. Juliet shook her head. Not qualities for a professional woman. It was fortunate that clothes and cosmetics could play down or play up certain aspects. Grabbing a towel, she wrapped it around herself, then taking another she wiped the steam from the mirror. No more mists, she thought. To succeed you had to see clearly.

With a glance at the tubes and bottles on the counter she began to create the professional Ms. Trent.

Because she hated quiet hotel rooms, Juliet switched on the television as she started to dress. The old Bogart– Bacall movie pleased her and was more relaxing than a dozen bubble baths. She listened to the well-known dialogue while she drew on her smoke-colored stockings. She watched the shimmering restrained passion as she adjusted the straps of a sheer black teddy. While the plot twisted and turned, she zipped on the narrow black dress and knotted the long strand of pearls under her breasts.

Caught up, she sat on the edge of the bed, running a brush through her hair as she watched. She was smiling, absorbed, distracted, but it would've shocked her if anyone had said she was romantic.

When the knock sounded at her door, she glanced at her watch. 7:05. She'd lost fifteen minutes dawdling. To make up for it, Juliet had her shoes on, her earrings clipped and her bag and notebook at hand in twelve seconds flat. She went to the door ready with a greeting and an apology.

A rose. Just one, the color of a young girl's blush. When Carlo handed it to her, she didn't have anything to say at all. Carlo, however, had no problem.

"Bella." He had her hand to his lips before she'd thought to counter the move. "Some women look severe or cold in black. Others…" His survey was long and male, but his smile made it gallant rather than calculating. "In others it simply enhances their femininity. I'm disturbing you?"

"No, no, of course not. I was just—"

"Ah, I know this movie."

Without waiting for an invitation, he breezed past her into the room. The standard, single hotel room didn't seem so impersonal any longer. How could it?

He brought life, energy, passion into the air as if it were his mission.

"Yes, I've seen it many times." The two strong faces dominated the screen. Bogart's, creased, heavy-eyed, weary—Bacall's, smooth, steamy and challenging. *"Passione,"* he murmured and made the word seem like honey to be tasted. Incredibly, Juliet found herself swallowing. "A man and a woman can bring many things to each other, but without passion, everything else is tame. *Sì?"*

Juliet recovered herself. Franconi wasn't a man to discuss passion with. The subject wouldn't remain academic for long. "Perhaps." She adjusted her evening bag and her notebook. But she didn't put the rose down. "We've a lot to discuss over dinner, Mr. Franconi. We'd best get started."

With his thumbs still hooked in the pockets of his taupe slacks, he turned his head. Juliet figured hundreds of women had trusted that smile. She wouldn't. With a careless flick, he turned off the television. "Yes, it's time we started."

What did he think of her? Carlo asked himself the question and let the answer come in snatches, twined through the evening.

Lovely. He didn't consider his affection for beautiful women a weakness. He was grateful that Juliet didn't find the need to play down or turn her natural beauty into severity, nor did she exploit it until it was artificial. She'd found a pleasing balance. He could admire that.

She was ambitious, but he admired that as well.

Beautiful women without ambition lost his interest quickly.

She didn't trust him. That amused him. As he drank his second glass of Beaujolais, he decided her wariness was a compliment. In his estimation, a woman like Juliet would only be wary of a man if she were attracted in some way.

If he were honest, and he was, he'd admit that most women were attracted to him. It seemed only fair, as he was attracted to them. Short, tall, plump, thin, old or young, he found women a fascination, a delight, an amusement. He respected them, perhaps only as a man who had grown up surrounded by women could do. But respect didn't mean he couldn't enjoy.

He was going to enjoy Juliet.

"*Hello, L.A.* is on first tomorrow." Juliet ran down her notes while Carlo nibbled on pâté. "It's the top-rated morning talk show on the coast, not just in L.A. Liz Marks hosts. She's very personable—not too bubbly. Los Angeles doesn't want bubbly at 8:00 A.M."

"Thank God."

"In any case, she has a copy of the book. It's important that you get the title in a couple of times if she doesn't. You have the full twenty minutes, so it shouldn't be a problem. You'll be autographing at Books, Incorporated on Wilshire Boulevard between one and three." Hastily, she made herself a note to contact the store in the morning for a last check. "You'll want to plug that, but I'll remind you just before airtime. Of course, you'll want to mention that you're beginning a twenty-one-day tour of the country here in California."

"Mmm-hmm. The pâté is quite passable. Would you like some?"

"No, thanks. Just go ahead." She checked off her list and reached for her wine without looking at him. The restaurant was quiet and elegant, but it didn't matter. If they'd been in a loud crowded bar on the Strip, she'd still have gone on with her notes. "Right after the morning show, we go to a radio spot. Then we'll have brunch with a reporter from the *Times*. You've already had an article in the *Trib*. I've got a clipping for you. You'd want to mention your other two books, but concentrate on the new one. It wouldn't hurt to bring up some of the major cities we'll hit. Denver, Dallas, Chicago, New York. Then there's the autographing, a spot on the evening news and dinner with two book reps. The next day—"

"One day at a time," he said easily. "I'll be less likely to snarl at you."

"All right." She closed her notebook and sipped at her wine again. "After all, it's my job to see to the details, yours to sign books and be charming."

He touched his glass to hers. "Then neither of us should have a problem. Being charming is my life."

Was he laughing at himself, she wondered, or at her? "From what I've seen, you excel at it."

"A gift, *cara*." Those dark, deep-set eyes were amused and exciting. "Unlike a skill that's developed and trained."

So, he was laughing at both of them, she realized. It would be both difficult and wise not to like him for it.

When her steak was served, Juliet glanced at it. Carlo, however, studied his veal as though it were a fine old painting. No, Juliet realized after a moment, he studied it as though it were a young, beautiful woman.

"Appearances," he told her, "in food, as in people, are essential." He was smiling at her when he cut into the veal. "And, as in people, they can be deceiving."

Juliet watched him sample the first bite, slowly, his eyes half-closed. She felt an odd chill at the base of her spine. He'd sample a woman the same way, she was certain. Slowly.

"Pleasant," he said after a moment. "No more, no less."

She couldn't prevent the quick smirk as she cut into her steak. "Yours is better of course."

He moved his shoulders. A statement of arrogance. "Of course. Like comparing a pretty young girl with a beautiful woman." When she glanced up he was holding out his fork. Over it, his eyes studied her. "Taste," he invited and the simple word made her blood shiver. "Nothing should ever go untasted, Juliet."

She shrugged, letting him feed her the tiny bite of veal. It was spicy, just bordering on rich and hot on her tongue. "It's good."

"Good, *sì*. Nothing Franconi prepares is ever merely good. Good, I'd pour into the garbage, feed to the dogs in the alley." She laughed, delighting him. "If something isn't special, then it's ordinary."

"True enough." Without realizing it, she slipped out of her shoes. "But then, I suppose I've always looked at food as a basic necessity."

"Necessity?" Carlo shook his head. Though he'd heard such sentiment before, he still considered it a sacrilege. "Oh, *madonna,* you have much to learn. When one knows how to eat, how to appreciate, it's second only to making love. Scents, textures, tastes. To eat only to fill your stomach? Barbaric."

"Sorry." Juliet took another bite of steak. It was tender and cooked well. But it was only a piece of meat. She'd never have considered it sensual or romantic, but simply filling. "Is that why you became a cook? Because you think food's sexy?"

He winced. "Chef, *cara mia.*"

She grinned, showing him for the first time a streak of humor and mischief. "What's the difference?"

"What's the difference between a plow horse and a thoroughbred? Plaster and porcelain?"

Enjoying herself, she touched her tongue to the rim of her glass. "Some might say dollar signs."

"No, no, no, my love. Money is only a result, not a cause. A cook makes hamburgers in a greasy kitchen that smells of onions behind a counter where people squeeze plastic bottles of ketchup. A chef creates…" He gestured, a circle of a hand. "An experience."

She lifted her glass and swept her lashes down, but she didn't hide the smile. "I see."

Though he could be offended by a look when he chose, and be ruthless with the offender, Carlo liked her style. "You're amused. But you haven't tasted Franconi." He waited until her eyes, both wry and wary, lifted to him. "Yet."

He had a talent for turning the simplest statement into something erotic, she observed. It would be a challenge to skirt around him without giving way. "But you haven't told me why you became a chef."

"I can't paint or sculpt. I haven't the patience or the

talent to compose sonnets. There are other ways to create, to embrace art."

She saw, with surprise mixed with respect, that he was quite serious. "But paintings, sculpture and poetry remain centuries after they've been created. If you make a soufflé, it's here, then it's gone."

"Then the challenge is to make it again, and again. Art needn't be put behind glass or bronzed, Juliet, merely appreciated. I have a friend…" He thought of Summer Lyndon—no, Summer Cocharan now. "She makes pastries like an angel. When you eat one, you're a king."

"Then is cooking magic or art?"

"Both. Like love. And I think you, Juliet Trent, eat much too little."

She met his look as he'd hoped she would. "I don't believe in overindulgence, Mr. Franconi. It leads to carelessness."

"To indulgence then." He lifted his glass. The smile was back, charming and dangerous. "Carefully."

Anything and everything could go wrong. You had to expect it, anticipate it and avoid it. Juliet knew just how much could be botched in a twenty-minute, live interview at 7:30 A.M. on a Monday. You hoped for the best and made do with the not too bad. Even she didn't expect perfection on the first day of a tour.

It wasn't easy to explain why she was annoyed when she got it.

The morning spot went beautifully. There was no other way to describe it, Juliet decided as she watched Liz Marks talk and laugh with Carlo after the camera stopped taping. If a shrewd operator could be called a natural, Carlo was indeed a natural. During the interview, he'd subtly and completely dominated the show while charmingly blinding his host to it. Twice he'd made the ten-year veteran of morning talk shows giggle like a girl. Once, once, Juliet remembered with astonishment, she'd seen the woman blush.

Yeah. She shifted the strap of her heavy briefcase on her arm. Franconi was a natural. It was bound to make her job easier. She yawned and cursed him.

Juliet always slept well in hotel rooms. *Always.* Except for last night. She might've been able to convince someone else that too much coffee and first-day jitters had kept her awake. But she knew better. She could drink a pot of coffee at ten and fall asleep on command at eleven. Her system was very disciplined. Except for last night.

She'd nearly dreamed of him. If she hadn't shaken herself awake at 2:00 A.M., she would have dreamed of him. That was no way to begin a very important, very long author tour. She told herself now if she had to choose between some silly fantasies and honest fatigue, she'd take the fatigue.

Stifling another yawn, Juliet checked her watch. Liz had her arm tucked through Carlo's and looked as though she'd keep it there unless someone pried her loose. With a sigh, Juliet decided she'd have to be the crowbar.

"Ms. Marks, it was a wonderful show." As she crossed over, Juliet deliberately held out her hand. With obvious reluctance, Liz disengaged herself from Carlo and accepted it.

"Thank you, Miss…"

"Trent," Juliet supplied without a waver.

"Juliet is my publicist," Carlo told Liz, though the two women had been introduced less than an hour earlier. "She guards my schedule."

"Yes, and I'm afraid I'll have to rush Mr. Franconi along. He has a radio spot in a half hour."

"If you must." Juliet was easily dismissed as Liz turned back to Carlo. "You have a delightful way of starting the morning. A pity you won't be in town longer."

"A pity," Carlo agreed and kissed Liz's fingers. Like an old movie, Juliet thought impatiently. All they needed were violins.

"Thank you again, Ms. Marks." Juliet used her most diplomatic smile as she took Carlo's arm and began to lead him out of the studio. After all, she'd very likely need Liz Marks again. "We're in a bit of a hurry," she muttered as they worked their way back to the reception area. The taping was over and she had other fish to fry. "This radio show's one of the top-rated in the city. Since it leans heavily on top forties and classic rock, its audience, at this time of day, falls mainly in the eighteen to thirty-five range. Excellent buying power. That gives us a nice mix with the audience from this morning's show which is generally in the twenty-five to fifty, primarily female category."

Listening with all apparent respect, Carlo reached the waiting limo first and opened the door himself. "You consider this important?"

"Of course." Because she was distracted by what she thought was a foolish question, Juliet climbed into the limo ahead of him. "We've a solid schedule in L.A." And she didn't see the point in mentioning there were some cities on the tour where they wouldn't be quite so busy. "A morning talk show with a good reputation, a popular radio show, two print interviews, two quick spots on the evening news and the *Simpson Show*." She said the last with a hint of relish. The *Simpson Show* offset what she was doing to the budget with limos.

"So you're pleased."

"Yes, of course." Digging into her briefcase, she took out her folder to recheck the name of her contact at the radio station.

"Then why do you look so annoyed?"

"I don't know what you're talking about."

"You get a line right…here," he said as he ran a fingertip between her eyebrows. At the touch, Juliet jerked back before she could stop herself. Carlo only cocked his head, watching her. "You may smile and speak in a quiet, polite voice, but that line gives you away."

"I was very pleased with the taping," she said again.

"But?"

All right, she thought, he was asking for it. "Perhaps it annoys me to see a woman making a fool of herself." Juliet stuffed the folder back into her briefcase. "Liz Marks is married, you know."

"Wedding rings are things I try to be immediately aware of," he said with a shrug. "Your instructions were to be charming, weren't they?"

"Perhaps *charm* has a different meaning in Italy."

"As I said, you must come to Rome."

"I suppose you enjoy having women drooling all over you."

He smiled at her, easy, attractive, innocent. "But of course."

A gurgle of laughter bubbled in her throat but she swallowed it. She wouldn't be charmed. "You'll have to deal with some men on this tour as well."

"I promise not to kiss Simpson's fingers."

This time the laughter escaped. For a moment, she relaxed with it, let it come. Carlo saw, too briefly, the youth and energy beneath the discipline. He'd like to have kept her like that longer—laughing, at ease with him, and with herself. It would be a challenge, he mused, to find the right sequence of buttons to push to bring laughter to her eyes more often. He liked challenges—particularly when there was a woman connected to them.

"Juliet." Her name flowed off his tongue in a way only the European male had mastered. "You mustn't worry. Your tidily married Liz only enjoyed a mild flirtation with a man she'll more than than likely never see again. Harmless. Perhaps because of it, she'll find more romance with her husband tonight."

Juliet eyed him a moment in her straight-on, nononsense manner. "You think quite of lot of yourself, don't you?"

He grinned, not sure if he was relieved or if he regretted the fact that he'd never met anyone like her before. "No more than is warranted, *cara.* Anyone who has character leaves a mark on another. Would you like to leave the world without making a ripple?"

No. No, that was one thing she was determined not to do. She sat back determined to hold her own. "I suppose some of us insist on leaving more ripples than others."

He nodded. "I don't like to do anything in a small way."

"Be careful, Mr. Franconi, or you'll begin to believe your own image."

The limo had stopped, but before Juliet could scoot toward the door, Carlo had her hand. When she looked at him this time, she didn't see the affable, amorous Italian chef, but a man of power. A man, she realized, who was well aware of how far it could take him.

She didn't move, but wondered how many other women had seen the steel beneath the silk.

"I don't need imagery, Juliet." His voice was soft, charming, beautiful. She heard the razor-blade cut beneath it. "Franconi is Franconi. Take me for what you see, or go to the devil."

Smoothly, he climbed from the limo ahead of her, turned and took her hand, drawing her out with him. It was a move that was polite, respectful, even ordinary. It was a move, Juliet realized, that expressed their positions. Man to woman. The moment she stood on the curb, she removed her hand.

With two shows and a business brunch under their belts, Juliet left Carlo in the bookstore, already swamped with women crowded in line for a glimpse at and a few words with Carlo Franconi. They'd handled the reporter and photographer already, and a man like Franconi wouldn't need her help with a crowd of women. Armed with change and her credit card, she went to find a pay phone.

For the first forty-five minutes, she spoke with her assistant in New York, filling her pad with times, dates and names while L.A. traffic whisked by outside the phone booth. As a bead of sweat trickled down her back, she wondered if she'd chosen the hottest corner in the city.

Denver still didn't look as promising as she'd hoped, but Dallas... Juliet caught her bottom lip between her teeth as she wrote. Dallas was going to be fabulous. She might need to double her daily dose of vitamins to get through that twenty-four-hour stretch, but it would be fabulous.

After breaking her connection with New York, Juliet dialed her first contact in San Francisco. Ten minutes later, she was clenching her teeth. No, her contact at the department store couldn't help coming down with a virus. She was sorry, genuinely sorry he was ill. But did he have to get sick without leaving someone behind with a couple of working brain cells?

The young girl with the squeaky voice knew about the cooking demonstration. Yes, she knew all about it and wasn't it going to be fun? Extension cords? Oh my, she really didn't know a thing about that. Maybe she could ask someone in maintenance. A table—chairs? Well golly, she supposed she could get something, if it was really necessary.

Juliet was reaching in her bag for her purse-size container of aspirin before it was over. The way it looked now, she'd have to get to the department store at least two hours before the demonstration to make sure everything was taken care of. That meant juggling the schedule.

After completing her calls, Juliet left the corner phone booth, aspirin in hand, and headed back to the bookstore, hoping they could give her a glass of water and a quiet corner.

No one noticed her. If she'd just crawled in from the desert on her belly, no one would have noticed her. The small, rather elegant bookstore was choked with laughter. No bookseller stood behind the counter. There was a magnet in the left-hand corner of the room. Its name was Franconi.

It wasn't just women this time, Juliet noticed with interest. There were men sprinkled in the crowd. Some of them might have been dragged along by their wives, but they were having a time of it now. It looked like a cocktail party, minus the cigarette smoke and empty glasses.

She couldn't even see him, Juliet realized as she worked her way toward the back of the store. He was surrounded, enveloped. Jingling the aspirin in her hand, she was glad she could find a little corner by herself. Perhaps he got all the glory, she mused. But she wouldn't trade places with him.

Glancing at her watch, she noted he had another hour and wondered whether he could dwindle the crowd down in that amount of time. She wished vaguely for a stool, dropped the aspirin in the pocket of her skirt and began to browse.

"Fabulous, isn't he?" Juliet heard someone murmur on the other side of a book rack.

"God, yes. I'm so glad you talked me into coming."

"What're friends for?"

"I thought I'd be bored to death. I feel like a kid at a rock concert. He's got such…"

"Style," the other voice supplied. "If a man like that ever walked into my life, he wouldn't walk out again."

Curious, Juliet walked around the stacks. She wasn't sure what she expected—young housewives, college students. What she saw were two attractive women in their thirties, both dressed in sleek professional suits.

"I've got to get back to the office." One woman checked a trim little Rolex watch. "I've got a meeting at three."

"I've got to get back to the courthouse."

Both women tucked their autographed books into leather briefcases.

"How come none of the men I date can kiss my hand without making it seem like a staged move in a one-act play?"

"Style. It all has to do with style."

With this observation, or complaint, the two women disappeared into the crowd.

At three-fifteen, he was still signing, but the crowd had thinned enough that Juliet could see him. Style, she was forced to agree, he had. No one who came up to his table, book in hand, was given a quick signature, practiced smile and brush-off. He talked to them. Enjoyed them, Juliet corrected, whether it was a grandmother who smelled of lavender or a young woman with a toddler on her hip. How did he know the right thing to say to each one of them, she wondered, that made them leave the table with a laugh or a smile or a sigh?

First day of the tour, she reminded herself. She wondered if he could manage to keep himself up to this level for three weeks. Time would tell, she decided and calculated she could give him another fifteen minutes before she began to ease him out the door.

Even with the half-hour extension, it wasn't easy. Juliet began to see the pattern she was certain would set the pace of the tour. Carlo would charm and delight, and she would play the less attractive role of drill sergeant. That's what she was paid for, Juliet reminded herself as she began to smile, chat and urge people toward the door. By four there were only a handful of stragglers. With apologies and an iron grip, Juliet disengaged Carlo.

"That went very well," she began, nudging him onto the street. "One of the booksellers told me they'd nearly sold out. Makes you wonder how much pasta's going to be cooked in L.A. tonight. Consider this just one more triumph today."

"Grazie."

"Prego. However, we won't always have the leeway to run an hour over," she told him as the door of the limo shut behind her. "It would help if you try to keep an eye on the time and pick up the pace say half an hour before finishing time. You've got an hour and fifteen minutes before airtime—"

"Fine." Pushing a button, Carlo instructed the driver to cruise.

"But—"

"Even I need to unwind," he told her, then opened up a small built-in cabinet to reveal the bar. "Cognac," he decided and poured two glasses without asking. "You've had two hours to window-shop and browse." Leaning back, he stretched out his legs.

Juliet thought of the hour and a half she'd spent on the phone, then the time involved in easing customers along. She'd been on her feet for two and a half hours straight, but she said nothing. The cognac went down smooth and warm.

"The spot on the news should run four, four and a half minutes. It doesn't seem like much time, but you'd be surprised how much you can cram in. Be sure to mention the book title, and the autographing and demonstration at the college tomorrow afternoon. The sensual aspect of food, cooking and eating's a great angle. If you'll—"

"Would you care to do the interview for me?" he asked so politely she glanced up.

So, he could be cranky, she mused. "You handle interviews beautifully, Mr. Franconi, but—"

"Carlo." Before she could open her notebook, he had his hand on her wrist. "It's Carlo, and put the damn notes away for ten minutes. Tell me, my very organized Juliet Trent, why are we here together?"

She started to move her hand but his grip was firmer than she'd thought. For the second time, she got the full impression of power, strength and determination. "To publicize your book."

"Today went well, *sì?*"

"Yes, so far—"

"Today went well," he said again and began to annoy her with the frequency of his interruptions.

"I'll go on this local news show, talk for a few minutes, then have this necessary business dinner when I would much rather have a bottle of wine and a steak in my room. With you. Alone. Then I could see you without your proper little business suit and your proper little business manner."

She wouldn't permit herself to shudder. She wouldn't

permit herself to react in any way. "Business is what we're here for. It's all I'm interested in."

"That may be." His agreement was much too easy. In direct contrast, he moved his hand to the back of her neck, gently, but not so gently she could move aside. "But we have an hour before business begins again. Don't lecture me on timetables."

The limo smelled of leather, she realized all at once. Of leather and wealth and Carlo. As casually as possible, she sipped from her glass. "Timetables, as you pointed out yourself this morning, are part of my job."

"You have an hour off," he told her, lifting a brow before she could speak. "So relax. Your feet hurt, so take your shoes off and drink your cognac." He set down his own drink, then moved her briefcase to the floor so there was nothing between them. "Relax," he said again but wasn't displeased that she'd stiffened. "I don't intend to make love with you in the back of a car. This time." He smiled as temper flared in her eyes because he'd seen doubt and excitement as well. "One day, one day soon, I'll find the proper moment for that, the proper place, the proper mood."

He leaned closer, so that he could just feel her breath flutter on his lips. She'd swipe at him now, he knew, if he took the next step. He might enjoy the battle. The color that ran along her cheekbones hadn't come from a tube or pot, but from passion. The look in her eyes was very close to a dare. She expected him to move an inch closer, to press her back against the seat with his mouth firm on hers. She was waiting for him, poised, ready.

He smiled while his lips did no more than hover until he knew the tension in her had built to match the tension in him. He let his gaze shift down to her mouth so that he could imagine the taste, the texture, the sweetness. Her chin stayed lifted even as he brushed a thumb over it.

He didn't care to do the expected. In a long, easy move, he leaned back, crossed his feet at the ankles and closed his eyes.

"Take off your shoes," he said again. "My schedule and yours should merge very well."

Then, to her astonishment, he was asleep. Not feigning it, she realized, but sound asleep, as if he'd just flicked a switch.

With a click, she set her half-full glass down and folded her arms. Angry, she thought. Damn right she was angry because he hadn't kissed her. Not because she wanted him to, she told herself as she stared out the tinted window. But because he'd denied her the opportunity to show her claws.

She was beginning to think she'd love drawing some Italian blood.

Chapter 3

Their bags were packed and in the limo. As a precaution, Juliet had given Carlo's room a quick, last-minute going-over to make sure he hadn't left anything behind. She still remembered being on the road with a mystery writer who'd forgotten his toothbrush eight times on an eight-city tour. A quick look was simpler than a late-night search for a drugstore.

Checkout at the hotel had gone quickly and without any last-minute hitches. To her relief, the charges on Carlo's room bill had been light and reasonable. Her road budget might just hold. With a minimum of confusion, they'd left the Wilshire. Juliet could only hope check-in at the airport, then at the hotel in San Francisco would go as well.

She didn't want to think about the *Simpson Show*.

A list of demographics wasn't necessary here. She

knew Carlo had spent enough time in the States off and on to know how important his brief demonstration on the proper way to prepare *biscuit tortoni* and his ten minutes on the air would be. It was the top-rated night-time show in the country and had been for fifteen years. Bob Simpson was an American institution. A few minutes on his show could boost the sale of books even in the most remote areas. Or it could kill it.

And boy, oh boy, she thought, with a fresh gurgle of excitement, did it look impressive to have the *Simpson Show* listed on her itinerary. She offered a last-minute prayer that Carlo wouldn't blow it.

She checked the little freezer backstage to be certain the dessert Carlo had prepared that afternoon was in place and ready. The concoction had to freeze for four hours, so they'd play the before-and-after game for the viewers. He'd make it up on the air, then *voilà,* they'd produce the completed frozen dessert within minutes.

Though Carlo had already gone over the procedure, the tools and ingredients with the production manager and the director, Juliet went over them all again. The whipped cream was chilling and so far none of the crew had pilfered any macaroons. The brand of dry sherry Carlo had insisted on was stored and ready. No one had broken the seal for a quick sample.

Juliet nearly believed she could whip up the fancy frozen dessert herself if necessary and only thanked God she wouldn't have to give a live culinary demonstration in front of millions of television viewers.

He didn't seem to be feeling any pressure, she thought as they settled in the green room. No, he'd already given the little half-dressed blonde on the sofa a big smile and offered her a cup of coffee from the available machine.

Coffee? Even for Hollywood, it took a wild imagination to consider the contents of the pot coffee. Juliet had taken one sip of what tasted like lukewarm mud and set the cup aside.

The little blonde was apparently a new love interest on one of the popular nighttime soaps, and she was jittery with nerves. Carlo sat down on the sofa beside her and began chatting away as though they were old friends. By the time the green room door opened again, she was giggling.

The green room itself was beige—pale, unattractive beige and cramped. The air-conditioning worked, but miserably. Still Juliet knew how many of the famous and near-famous had sat in that dull little room chewing their nails. Or taking quick sips from a flask.

Carlo had exchanged the dubious coffee for plain water and was sprawled on the sofa with one arm tossed over the back. He looked as easy as a man entertaining in his own home. Juliet wondered why she hadn't tossed any antacids in her bag.

She made a pretense of rechecking the schedule while Carlo charmed the rising star and the *Simpson Show* murmured away on the twenty-five-inch color console across the room.

Then the monkey walked in. Juliet glanced up and saw the long-armed, tuxedoed chimpanzee waddle in with his hand caught in that of a tall thin man with harassed eyes and a nervous grin. Feeling a bit nervous herself, Juliet looked over at Carlo. He nodded to both newcomers, then went back to the blonde without missing a beat. Even as Juliet told herself to relax, the chimp grinned, threw back his head and let out a long, loud announcement.

The blonde giggled, but looked as though she'd cut and run if the chimp came one step closer—tux or no tux.

"Behave, Butch." The thin man cleared his throat as he swept his gaze around the room. "Butch just finished a picture last week," he explained to the room in general. "He's feeling a little restless."

With a jiggle of the sequins that covered her, the blonde walked to the door when her name was announced. With some satisfaction, Carlo noted that she wasn't nearly as edgy as she'd been when he'd sat down. She turned and gave him a toothy smile. "Wish me luck, darling."

"The best."

To Juliet's disgust, the blonde blew him a kiss as she sailed out.

The thin man seemed to relax visibly. "That's a relief. Blondes make Butch overexcited."

"I see." Juliet thought of her own hair that could be considered blond or brown depending on the whim. Hopefully Butch would consider it brown and unstimulating.

"But where's the lemonade?" The man's nerves came back in full force. "They know Butch wants lemonade before he goes on the air. Calms him down."

Juliet bit the tip of her tongue to hold back a snicker. Carlo and Butch were eyeing each other with a kind of tolerant understanding. "He seems calm enough," Carlo ventured.

"Bundle of nerves," the man disagreed. "I'll never be able to get him on camera."

"I'm sure it's just an oversight." Because she was used to soothing panic, Juliet smiled. "Maybe you should ask one of the pages."

"I'll do that." The man patted Butch on the head and went back through the door.

"But—" Juliet half rose, then sat again. The chimp stood in the middle of the room, resting his knuckles on the floor. "I'm not sure he should've left Cheetah."

"Butch," Carlo corrected. "I think he's harmless enough." He sent the chimp a quick grin. "He certainly has an excellent tailor."

Juliet looked over to see the chimp grinning and winking. "Is he twitching," she asked Carlo, "or is he flirting with me?"

"Flirting, if he's a male of any taste," he mused. "And, as I said, his tailoring is quite good. What do you say, Butch? You find my Juliet attractive?"

Butch threw back his head and let out a series of sounds Juliet felt could be taken either way.

"See? He appreciates a beautiful woman."

Appreciating the ridiculous, Juliet laughed. Whether he was attracted to the sound or simply felt it was time he made his move, Butch bowlegged his way over to her. Still grinning, he put his hand on Juliet's bare knee. This time, she was certain he winked.

"I never make so obvious a move on first acquaintance," Carlo observed.

"Some women prefer the direct approach." Deciding

he was harmless, Juliet smiled down at Butch. "He reminds me of someone." She sent Carlo a mild look. "It must be that ingratiating grin." Before she'd finished speaking, Butch climbed into her lap and wrapped one of his long arms around her. "He's kind of sweet." With another laugh, she looked down into the chimp's face. "I think he has your eyes, Carlo."

"Ah, Juliet, I think you should—"

"Though his might be more intelligent."

"Oh, I think he's smart, all right." Carlo coughed into his hand as he watched the chimp's busy fingers. "Juliet, if you'd—"

"Of course he's smart, he's in movies." Enjoying herself, Juliet watched the chimp grin up at her. "Have I seen any of your films, Butch?"

"I wouldn't be surprised if they're blue."

She tickled Butch under the chin. "Really, Carlo, how crude."

"Just a guess." He let his gaze run over her. "Tell me Juliet, do you feel a draft?"

"No. I'd say it's entirely too warm in here. This poor thing is all wrapped up in a tux." She clucked at Butch and he clacked his teeth at her.

"Juliet, do you believe people can reveal their personalities by the clothes they wear? Send signals, if you understand what I mean."

"Hmm?" Distracted, she shrugged and helped Butch straighten his tie. "I suppose so."

"I find it interesting that you wear pink silk under such a prim blouse."

"I beg your pardon?"

"An observation, *mi amore*." He let his gaze wander down again. "Just an observation."

Sitting very still, Juliet moved only her head. In a moment, her mouth was as open as her blouse. The monkey with the cute face and excellent tailor had nimbly undone every one of the buttons.

Carlo gave Butch a look of admiration. "I must ask him how he perfected that technique."

"Why you son of a—"

"Not me." Carlo put a hand to his heart. "I'm an innocent bystander."

Juliet rose abruptly, dumping the chimp onto the floor. As she ducked into the adjoining rest room, she heard the laughter of two males—one a chimp, the other a rat.

Juliet took the ride to the airport where they would leave for San Diego in excruciatingly polite silence.

"Come now, *cara,* the show went well. Not only was the title mentioned three times, but there was that nice close-up of the book. My *tortoni* was a triumph, and they liked my anecdote on cooking the long, sensual Italian meal."

"You're a real prince with anecdotes," she murmured.

"*Amore,* it was the monkey who tried to undress you, not I." He gave a long, self-satisfied sigh. He couldn't remember when he'd enjoyed a…demonstration quite so much. "If I had, we'd have missed the show altogether."

"You just had to tell that story on the air, didn't you?" She sent him a cool, killing look. "Do you know how many millions of people watch that show?"

"It was a good story." In the dim light of the limo,

she saw the gleam in his eyes. "Most millions of people like good stories."

"Everyone I work with will have seen that show." She found her jaw was clenched and deliberately relaxed it. "Not only did you just—just *sit* there and let that happy-fingered little creature half strip me, but then you broadcast it on national television."

"*Madonna,* you'll remember I did try to warn you."

"I remember nothing of the kind."

"But you were so enchanted with Butch," he continued. "I confess, it was difficult not to be enchanted myself." He let his gaze roam down to her tidily buttoned blouse. "You've lovely skin, Juliet; perhaps I was momentarily distracted. I throw myself, a simple, weak man, on your mercy."

"Oh, shut up." She folded her arms and stared straight ahead, not speaking again until the driver pulled to the curb at their airline.

Juliet pulled her carry-on bag out of the trunk. She knew the chance was always there that the bags could be lost—sent to San Jose while she went to San Diego—so she always carried her absolute essentials with her. She handed over both her ticket and Carlo's so the check-in could get underway while she paid off the driver. It made her think of her budget. She'd managed to justify limo service in L.A., but it would be cabs and rented cars from here on. Goodbye glamour, she thought as she pocketed her receipt. Hello reality.

"No, this I'll carry."

She turned to see Carlo indicate his leather-bound box of about two feet in length, eight inches in width. "You're better off checking something that bulky."

"I never check my tools." He slung a flight bag over his shoulder and picked up the box by its handle.

"Suit yourself," she said with a shrug and moved through the automatic doors with him. Fatigue was creeping in, she realized, and she hadn't had to prepare any intricate desserts. If he were human, he'd be every bit as weary as she. He might annoy her in a dozen ways, but he didn't gripe. Juliet bit back a sigh. "We've a half hour before they'll begin boarding. Would you like a drink?"

He gave her an easy smile. "A truce?"

She returned it despite herself. "No, a drink."

"Okay."

They found a dark, crowded lounge and worked their way through to a table. She watched Carlo maneuver his box, with some difficulty, around people, over chairs and ultimately under their table. "What's in there?"

"Tools," he said again. "Knives, properly weighted, stainless steel spatulas of the correct size and balance. My own cooking oil and vinegar. Other essentials."

"You're going to lug oil and vinegar through airport terminals from coast to coast?" With a shake of her head, she glanced up at a waitress. "Vodka and grapefruit juice."

"Brandy. Yes," he said, giving his attention back to Juliet after he'd dazzled the waitress with a quick smile. "Because there's no brand on the American market to compare with my own." He picked up a peanut from the bowl on the table. "There's no brand on any market to compare with my own."

"You could still check it," she pointed out. "After all, you check your shirts and ties."

"I don't trust my tools to the hands of baggage carriers." He popped the peanut into his mouth. "A tie is a simple thing to replace, even a thing to become bored with. But an excellent whisk is entirely different. Once I teach you to cook, you'll understand."

"You've got as much chance teaching me to cook as you do flying to San Diego without the plane. Now, you know you'll be giving a demonstration of preparing linguini and clam sauce on *A.M. San Diego*. The show airs at eight, so we'll have to be at the studio at six to get things started."

As far as he could see, the only civilized cooking to be done at that hour would be a champagne breakfast for two. "Why do Americans insist on rising at dawn to watch television?"

"I'll take a poll and find out," she said absently. "In the meantime, you'll make up one dish that we'll set aside, exactly as we did tonight. On the air you'll be going through each stage of preparation, but of course we don't have enough time to finish; that's why we need the first dish. Now, for the good news." She sent a quick smile to the waitress as their drinks were served. "There's been a bit of a mix-up at the studio, so we'll have to bring the ingredients along ourselves. I need you to give me a list of what you'll need. Once I see you settled into the hotel, I'll run out and pick them up. There's bound to be an all-night market."

In his head, he went over the ingredients for his *linguini con vongole biance.* True, the American market would have some of the necessities, but he considered himself fortunate that he had a few of his own in the case at his feet. The clam sauce was his specialty, not to be taken lightly.

"Is shopping for groceries at midnight part of a publicist's job?"

She smiled at him. Carlo thought it was not only lovely, but perhaps the first time she'd smiled at him and meant it. "On the road, anything that needs to be done is the publicist's job. So, if you'll run through the ingredients, I'll write them down."

"Not necessary." He swirled and sipped his brandy. "I'll go with you."

"You need your sleep." She was already rummaging for a pencil. "Even with a quick nap on the plane you're only going to get about five hours."

"So are you," he pointed out. When she started to speak again, he lifted his brow in that strange silent way he had of interrupting. "Perhaps I don't trust an amateur to pick out my clams."

Juliet watched him as she drank. Or perhaps he was a gentleman, she mused. Despite his reputation with women, and a healthy dose of vanity, he was one of that rare breed of men who knew how to be considerate of women without patronizing them. She decided to forgive him for Butch after all.

"Drink up, Franconi." And she toasted him, perhaps in friendship. "We've a plane to catch."

"Salute." He lifted his glass to her.

They didn't argue again until they were on the plane.

Grumbling only a little, Juliet helped him stow his fancy box of tools under the seat. "It's a short flight." She checked her watch and calculated the shopping would indeed go beyond midnight. She'd have to take some of the vile tasting brewer's yeast in the morning. "I'll see you when we land."

He took her wrist when she would have gone past him. "Where are you going?"

"To my seat."

"You don't sit here?" He pointed to the seat beside him.

"No, I'm in coach." Impatient, she had to shift to let another oncoming passenger by.

"Why?"

"Carlo, I'm blocking the aisle."

"Why are you in coach?"

She let out a sigh of a parent instructing a stubborn child. "Because the publisher is more than happy to spring for a first-class ticket for a bestselling author and celebrity. There's a different style for publicists. It's called coach." Someone bumped a briefcase against her hip. Damn if she wouldn't have a bruise. "Now if you'd let me go, I could stop being battered and go sit down."

"First class is almost empty," he pointed out. "It's a simple matter to upgrade your ticket."

She managed to pull her arm away. "Don't buck the system, Franconi."

"I always buck the system," he told her as she walked down the aisle to her seat. Yes, he did like the way she moved.

"Mr. Franconi." A flight attendant beamed at him. "May I get you a drink after take-off?"

"What's your white wine?"

When she told him he settled into his seat. A bit pedestrian, he thought, but not entirely revolting. "You noticed the young woman I was speaking with. The honey-colored hair and the stubborn chin."

Her smile remained bright and helpful though she thought it was a shame that he had his mind on another woman. "Of course, Mr. Franconi."

"She'll have a glass of wine, with my compliments."

Juliet would have considered herself fortunate to have an aisle seat if the man beside her hadn't already been sprawled out and snoring. Travel was so glamorous, she thought wryly as she slipped her toes out of her shoes. Wasn't she lucky to have another flight to look forward to the very next night?

Don't complain, Juliet, she warned herself. When you have your own agency, you can send someone else on the down-and-dirty tours.

The man beside her snored through take-off. On the other side of the aisle a woman held a cigarette in one hand and a lighter in the other in anticipation of the No Smoking sign blinking off. Juliet took out her pad and began to work.

"Miss?"

Stifling a yawn, Juliet glanced up at the flight attendant. "I'm sorry, I didn't order a drink."

"With Mr. Franconi's compliments."

Juliet accepted the wine as she looked up toward first class. He was sneaky, she told herself. Trying to get under her defenses by being nice. She let her notebook close as she sighed and sat back.

It was working.

She barely finished the wine before touchdown, but it had relaxed her. Relaxed her enough, she realized, that all she wanted to do was find a soft bed and a dark room. In an hour—or two, she promised herself and gathered up her flight bag and briefcase.

She found Carlo was waiting for her in first class with a very young, very attractive flight attendant. Neither of them seemed the least bit travel weary.

"Ah, Juliet, Deborah knows of a marvelous twenty-four-hour market where we can find everything we need."

Juliet looked at the willowy brunette and managed a smile. "How convenient."

He took the flight attendant's hand and, inevitably Juliet thought, kissed it. *"Arrivederci."*

"Don't waste time, do you?" Juliet commented the moment they deplaned.

"Every moment lived is a moment to be enjoyed."

"What a quaint little sentiment." She shifted her bag and aimed for baggage claim. "You should have it tattooed."

"Where?"

She didn't bother to look at his grin. "Where it would be most attractive, naturally."

They had to wait longer than she liked for their luggage, and by then the relaxing effects of the wine had worn off. There was business to be seen to. Because he enjoyed watching her in action, Carlo let her see to it.

She secured a cab, tipped the skycap and gave the driver the name of the hotel. Scooting in beside Carlo, she caught his grin. "Something funny?"

"You're so efficient, Juliet."

"Is that a compliment or an insult?"

"I never insult women." He said it so simply, she was absolutely certain it was true. Unlike Juliet, he was completely relaxed and not particularly sleepy. "If this was Rome, we'd go to a dark little café, drink heavy red wine and listen to American music."

She closed her window because the air was damp and chilly. "The tour interfering with your night life?"

"So far I find myself enjoying the stimulating company."

"Tomorrow you're going to find yourself worked to a frazzle."

Carlo thought of his background and smiled. At nine, he'd spent the hours between school and supper washing dishes and mopping up kitchens. At fifteen he'd waited tables and spent his free time learning of spices and sauces. In Paris he'd combined long, hard study with work as an assistant chef. Even now, his restaurant and clients had him keeping twelve-hour days. Not all of his background was in the neatly typed bio Juliet had in her briefcase.

"I don't mind work, as long as it interests me. I think you're the same."

"I have to work," she corrected. "But it's easier when you enjoy it."

"You're more successful when you enjoy it. It shows with you. Ambition, Juliet, without a certain joy, is cold, and when achieved leaves a flat taste."

"But I am ambitious."

"Oh, yes." He turned to look at her, starting off flutters she'd thought herself too wise to experience. "But you're not cold."

For a moment, she thought she'd be better off if he were wrong. "Here's the hotel." She turned from him, relieved to deal with details. "We need you to wait," she instructed the driver. "We'll be going out again as soon as we check in. The hotel has a lovely view of the bay, I'm told." She walked into the lobby with Carlo as the bellboy dealt with their luggage. "It's a shame we won't have time to enjoy it. Franconi and Trent," she told the desk clerk.

The lobby was quiet and empty. Oh, the lucky people who were sleeping in their beds, she thought and pushed at a strand of hair that had come loose.

"We'll be checking out first thing tomorrow, and we won't be able to come back, so be sure you don't leave anything behind in your room."

"But of course you'll check anyway."

She sent him a sidelong look as she signed the form. "Just part of the service." She pocketed her key. "The luggage can be taken straight up." Discreetly, she handed the bellboy a folded bill. "Mr. Franconi and I have an errand."

"Yes, ma'am."

"I like that about you." To Juliet's surprise, Carlo linked arms with her as they walked back outside.

"What?"

"Your generosity. Many people would've slipped out without tipping the bellboy."

She shrugged. "Maybe it's easier to be generous when it's not your money."

"Juliet." He opened the door to the waiting cab and gestured her in. "You're intelligent enough. Couldn't you—how is it—stiff the bellboy then write the tip down on your expense account?"

"Five dollars isn't worth being dishonest."

"Nothing's worth being dishonest." He gave the

driver the name of the market and settled back. "Instinct tells me if you tried to tell a lie—a true lie—your tongue would fall out."

"Mr. Franconi." She planted the tongue in question in her cheek. "You forget, I'm in public relations. If I didn't lie, I'd be out of a job."

"A true lie," he corrected.

"Isn't that a contradiction in terms?"

"Perhaps you're too young to know the variety of truths and lies. Ah, you see? This is why I'm so fond of your country." Carlo leaned out the window as they approached the big, lighted all-night market. "In America, you want cookies at midnight, you can buy cookies at midnight. Such practicality."

"Glad to oblige. Wait here," she instructed the driver, then climbed out opposite Carlo. "I hope you know what you need. I'd hate to get into the studio at dawn and find I had to run out and buy whole peppercorns or something."

"Franconi knows linguini." He swung an arm around her shoulder and drew her close as they walked inside. "Your first lesson, my love."

He led her first to the seafood section where he clucked and muttered and rejected and chose until he had the proper number of clams for two dishes. She'd seen women give as much time and attention to choosing an engagement ring.

Juliet obliged him by pushing the cart as he walked along beside her, looking at everything. And touching. Cans, boxes, bottles—she waited as he picked up, examined and ran his long artist's fingers over the labels as he read every ingredient. Somewhat amused, she watched his diamond wink in the fluorescent light.

"Amazing what they put in this prepackaged garbage," he commented as he dropped a box back on the shelf.

"Careful, Franconi, you're talking about my staple diet."

"You should be sick."

"Prepackaged food's freed the American woman from the kitchen."

"And destroyed a generation of taste buds." He chose his spices carefully and without haste. He opened three brands of oregano and sniffed before he settled on one. "I tell you, Juliet, I admire your American convenience, its practicality, but I would rather shop in Rome where I can walk along the stalls and choose vegetables just out of the ground, fish fresh from the sea. Everything isn't in a can, like the music."

He didn't miss an aisle, but Juliet forgot her fatigue in fascination. She'd never seen anyone shop like Carlo Franconi. It was like strolling through a museum with an art student. He breezed by the flour, scowling at each sack. She was afraid for a moment, he'd rip one open and test the contents. "This is a good brand?"

Juliet figured she bought a two-pound bag of flour about once a year. "Well, my mother always used this, but—"

"Good. Always trust a mother."

"She's a dreadful cook."

Carlo set the flour firmly in the basket. "She's a mother."

"An odd sentiment from a man no mother can trust."

"For mothers, I have the greatest respect. I have one myself. Now, we need garlic, mushrooms, peppers. Fresh."

Carlo walked along the stalls of vegetables, touching, squeezing and sniffing. Cautious, Juliet looked around for clerks, grateful they'd come at midnight rather than midday. "Carlo, you really aren't supposed to handle everything quite so much."

"If I don't handle, how do I know what's good and what's just pretty?" He sent her a quick grin over his shoulder. "I told you, food was much like a woman. They put mushrooms in this box with wrap over it." Disgusted, he tore the wrapping off before Juliet could stop him.

"Carlo! You can't open it."

"I want only what I want. You can see, some are too small, too skimpy." Patiently, he began to pick out the mushrooms that didn't suit him.

"Then we'll throw out what you don't want when we get back to the hotel." Keeping an eye out for the night manager, she began to put the discarded mushrooms back in the box. "Buy two boxes if you need them."

"It's a waste. You'd waste your money?"

"The publisher's money," she said quickly, as she put the broken box into the basket. "He's glad to waste it. Thrilled."

He paused for a moment, then shook his head. "No, no, I can't do it." But when he started to reach into the basket, Juliet moved and blocked his way.

"Carlo, if you break open another package, we're going to be arrested."

"Better to go to jail than to buy mushrooms that will do me no good in the morning."

She grinned at him and stood firm. "No, it's not."

He ran a fingertip over her lips before she could react. "For you then, but against my better judgment."

"*Grazie.* Do you have everything now?"

His gaze followed the path his finger had traced just as slowly. "No."

"Well, what next?"

He stepped closer and because she hadn't expected it, she found herself trapped between him and the grocery cart. "Tonight is for first lessons," he murmured then ran his hands along either side of her face.

She should laugh. Juliet told herself it was ludicrous that he'd make a pass at her under the bright lights of the vegetable section of an all-night market. Carlo Franconi, a man who'd made seduction as much an art as his cooking wouldn't choose such a foolish setting.

But she saw what was in his eyes, and she didn't laugh.

Some women, he thought as he felt her skin soft and warm under his hands, were made to be taught slowly. Very slowly. Some women were born knowing; others were born wondering.

With Juliet, he would take time and care because he understood. Or thought he did.

She didn't resist, but her lips had parted in surprise. He touched his to hers gently, not in question, but with patience. Her eyes had already given him the answer.

He didn't hurry. It didn't matter to him where they were, that the lights were bright and the music manufactured. It only mattered that he explore the tastes that waited for him. So he tasted again, without pressure. And again.

She found she was bracing herself against the cart with her fingers wrapped around the metal. Why didn't she walk away? Why didn't she just brush him aside and stalk out of the store? He wasn't holding her there. On her face his hands were light, clever but not insistent. She could move. She could go. She should.

She didn't.

His thumbs trailed under her chin, tracing there. He felt the pulse, rapid and jerky, and kept his hold easy. He meant to keep it so, but even he hadn't guessed her taste would be so unique.

Neither of them knew who took the next step. Perhaps they took it together. His mouth wasn't so light on hers any longer, nor was hers so passive. They met, triumphantly, and clung.

Her fingers weren't wrapped around the cart now, but gripping his shoulders, holding him closer. Their bodies fit. Perfectly. It should have warned her. Giving without thought was something she never did, until now. In giving, she took, but she never thought to balance the ledger.

His mouth was warm, full. His hands never left her face, but they were firm now. She couldn't have walked away so easily. She wouldn't have walked away at all.

He'd thought he had known everything there was to expect from a woman—fire, ice, temptation. But a lesson was being taught to both. Had he ever felt this warmth before? This kind of sweetness? No, because if he had, he'd remember. No tastes, no sensations ever experienced were forgotten.

He knew what it was to desire a woman—many women—but he hadn't known what it was to crave. For a moment, he filled himself with the sensation. He wouldn't forget.

But he knew that a cautious man takes a step back and a second breath before he steps off a cliff. With a murmur in his own language, he did.

Shaken, Juliet gripped the cart again for balance. Cursing herself for an idiot, she waited for her breath to even out.

"Very nice," Carlo said quietly and ran a finger along her cheek. "Very nice, Juliet."

An eighties woman, she reminded herself as her heart thudded. Strong, independent, sophisticated. "I'm so glad you approve."

He took her hand before she could slam the cart down the aisle. Her skin was still warm, he noted, her pulse still unsteady. If they'd been alone… Perhaps it was best this way. For now. "It isn't a matter of approval, *cara mia,* but of appreciation."

"From now on, just appreciate me for my work, okay?" A jerk, and she freed herself of him and shoved the cart away. Without regard for the care he'd taken in selecting them, Juliet began to drop the contents of the cart on the conveyor belt at checkout.

"You didn't object," he reminded her. He'd needed to find his balance as well, he realized. Now he leaned against the cart and gave her a cocky grin.

"I didn't want a scene."

He took the peppers from the basket himself before she could wound them. "Ah, you're learning about lies."

When her head came up, he was surprised her eyes

didn't bore right through him. "You wouldn't know truth if you fell into it."

"Darling, mind the mushrooms," he warned her as she swung the package onto the belt. "We don't want them bruised. I've a special affection for them now."

She swore at him, loudly enough that the checker's eyes widened. Carlo continued to grin and thought about lesson two.

He thought they should have it soon. Very soon.

Chapter 4

There were times when you knew everything could go wrong, should go wrong, and probably would go wrong, but somehow it didn't. Then there were the other times.

Perhaps Juliet was grouchy because she'd spent another restless night when she couldn't afford to lose any sleep. That little annoyance she could lay smack at Carlo's door, even though it didn't bring any satisfaction. But even if she'd been rested and cheerful, the ordeal at Gallegher's Department Store would have had her steaming. With a good eight hours' sleep, she might have kept things from boiling over.

First, Carlo insisted on coming with her two hours before he was needed. Or wanted. Juliet didn't care to spend the first two hours of what was bound to be a long, hectic day with a smug, self-assured, egocentric chef who looked as though he'd just come back from two sun-washed weeks on the Riviera.

Obviously, *he* didn't need any sleep, she mused as they took the quick, damp cab ride from hotel to mall.

Whatever the tourist bureau had to say about sunny California, it was raining—big, steady drops of it that immediately made the few minutes she'd taken to fuss with her hair worthless.

Prepared to enjoy the ride, Carlo looked out the window. He liked the way the rain plopped in puddles. It didn't matter to him that he'd heard it start that morning, just past four. "It's a nice sound," he decided. "It makes things more quiet, more…subtle, don't you think?"

Breaking away from her own gloomy view of the rain, Juliet turned to him. "What?"

"The rain." Carlo noted she looked a bit hollow-eyed. Good. She hadn't been unaffected. "Rain changes the look of things."

Normally, she would have agreed. Juliet never minded dashing for the subway in a storm or strolling along Fifth Avenue in a drizzle. Today, she considered it her right to look on the dark side. "This one might lower the attendance in your little demonstration by ten percent."

"So?" He gave an easy shrug as the driver swung into the parking lot of the mall.

What she didn't need at that moment was careless acceptance. "Carlo, the purpose of all this is exposure."

He patted her hand. "You're only thinking of numbers. You should think instead of my *pasta con pesto*. In a few hours, everyone else will."

"I don't think about food the way you do," she muttered. It still amazed her that he'd lovingly prepared the first linguini at 6:00 A.M., then the second two hours later for the camera. Both dishes had been an exquisite example of Italian cooking at its finest. He'd looked more like a film star on holiday than a working chef, which was precisely the image Juliet had wanted to project. His spot on the morning show had been perfect. That only made Juliet more pessimistic about the rest of the day. "It's hard to think about food at all on this kind of a schedule."

"That's because you didn't eat anything this morning."

"Linguini for breakfast doesn't suit me."

"My linguini is always suitable."

Juliet gave a mild snort as she stepped from the cab into the rain. Though she made a dash for the doors, Carlo was there ahead of her, opening one. "Thanks." Inside, she ran a hand through her hair and wondered how soon she could come by another cup of coffee. "You don't need to do anything for another two hours." And he'd definitely be in the way while things were being set up on the third floor.

"So, I'll wander." With his hands in his pockets, he looked around. As luck would have it, they'd entered straight into the lingerie department. "I find your American malls fascinating."

"I'm sure." Her voice was dry as he fingered the border of lace on a slinky camisole. "You can come upstairs with me first, if you like."

"No, no." A saleswoman with a face that demanded a second look adjusted two negligees and beamed at him.

"I think I'll just roam around and see what your shops have to offer." He beamed back. "So far, I'm charmed."

She watched the exchange and tried not to clench her teeth. "All right, then, if you'll just be sure to—"

"Be in Special Events on the third floor at eleven-forty-five," he finished. In his friendly, casual way, he kissed her forehead. She wondered why he could touch her like a cousin and make her think of a lover. "Believe me, Juliet, nothing you say to me is forgotten." He took her hand, running his thumb over her knuckles. That was definitely not the touch of a cousin. "I'll buy you a present."

"It isn't necessary."

"A pleasure. Things that are necessary are rarely a pleasure."

Juliet disengaged her hand while trying not to dwell on the pleasure he could offer. "Please, don't be later than eleven-forty-five, Carlo."

"Timing, *mi amore,* is something I excel in."

I'll bet, she thought as she started toward the escalator. She'd have bet a week's pay he was already flirting with the lingerie clerk.

It only took ten minutes in Special Events for Juliet to forget Carlo's penchant for romancing anything feminine.

The little assistant with the squeaky voice was still in charge as her boss continued his battle with the flu. She was young, cheerleader pretty and just as pert. She was also in completely over her head.

"Elise," Juliet began because it was still early on enough for her to have some optimism. "Mr. Franconi's going to need a working area in the kitchen department. Is everything set?"

"Oh, yes." Elise gave Juliet a toothy, amiable grin. "I'm getting a nice folding table from Sporting Goods."

Diplomacy, Juliet reminded herself, was one of the primary rules of PR. "I'm afraid we'll need something a bit sturdier. Perhaps one of the islands where Mr. Franconi could prepare the dish and still face the audience. Your supervisor and I had discussed it."

"Oh, is that what he meant?" Elise looked blank for a moment, then brightened. Juliet began to think dark thoughts about mellow California. "Well, why not?"

"Why not," Juliet agreed. "We've kept the dish Mr. Franconi is to prepare as simple as possible. You do have all the ingredients listed?"

"Oh, yes. It sounds just delicious. I'm a vegetarian, you know."

Of course she was, Juliet thought. Yogurt was probably the high point of her day. "Elise, I'm sorry if it seems I'm rushing you along, but I really need to work out the setup as soon as possible."

"Oh, sure." All cooperation, Elise flashed her straight-toothed smile. "What do you want to know?"

Juliet offered up a prayer. "How sick is Mr. Francis?" she asked, thinking of the levelheaded, business-like man she had dealt with before.

"Just miserable." Elise swung back her straight California-blond hair. "He'll be out the rest of the week."

No help there. Accepting the inevitable, Juliet gave Elise her straight, no-nonsense look. "All right, what have you got so far?"

"Well, we've taken a new blender and some really lovely bowls from Housewares."

Juliet nearly relaxed. "That's fine. And the range?"

Elise smiled. "Range?"

"The range Mr. Franconi needs to cook the spaghetti for this dish. It's on the list."

"Oh. We'd need elecricity for that, wouldn't we?"

"Yes." Juliet folded her hands to keep them from clenching. "We would. For the blender, too."

"I guess I'd better check with maintenance."

"I guess you'd better." Diplomacy, tact, Juliet reminded herself as her fingers itched for Elise's neck. "Maybe I'll just go over to the kitchen layouts and see which one would suit Mr. Franconi best."

"Terrific. He might want to do his interview right there."

Juliet had taken two steps before she stopped and turned back. "Interview?"

"With the food editor of the *Sun*. She'll be here at eleven-thirty."

Calm, controlled, Juliet pulled out her itinerary of the San Diego stop. She skimmed it, though she knew every word by heart. "I don't seem to have anything listed here."

"It came up at the last minute. I called your hotel at nine, but you'd already checked out."

"I see." Should she have expected Elise to phone the television studio and leave a message? Juliet looked into the personality-plus smile. No, she supposed not. Resigned, she checked her watch. The setup could be dealt with in time if she started immediately. Carlo would just have to be paged. "How do I call mall management?"

"Oh, you can call from my office. Can I do anything?"

Juliet thought of and rejected several things, none of which were kind. "I'd like some coffee, two sugars."

She rolled up her sleeves and went to work.

By eleven, Juliet had the range, the island and the ingredients Carlo had specified neatly arranged. It had taken only one call, and some finesse, to acquire two vivid flower arrangements from a shop in the mall.

She was on her third coffee and considering a fourth when Carlo wandered over. "Thank God." She drained the last from the styrofoam cup. "I thought I was going to have to send out a search party."

"Search party?" Idly he began looking around the kitchen set. "I came when I heard the page."

"You've been paged five times in the last hour."

"Yes?" He smiled as he looked back at her. Her hair was beginning to stray out of her neat bun. He might have stepped off the cover of *Gentlemen's Quarterly*. "I only just heard. But then, I spent some time in the most fantastic record store. Such speakers. Quadraphonic."

"That's nice." Juliet dragged a hand through her already frazzled hair.

"There's a problem?"

"Her name's Elise. I've come very close to murdering her half a dozen times. If she smiles at me again, I just might." Juliet gestured with her hand to brush it off. This was no time for fantasies, no matter how satisfying. "It seems things were a bit disorganized here."

"But you've seen to that." He bent over to examine the range as a driver might a car before Le Mans. "Excellent."

"You can be glad you've got electricity rather than your imagination," she muttered. "You have an interview at eleven-thirty with a food editor, Marjorie Ballister, from the *Sun*."

He only moved his shoulders and examined the blender. "All right."

"If I'd known it was coming up, I'd have bought a paper so we could have seen her column and gauged her style. As it is—"

"*Non importante.* You worry too much, Juliet."

She could have kissed him. Strictly in gratitude, but she could have kissed him. Considering that unwise, she smiled instead. "I appreciate your attitude, Carlo. After the last hour of dealing with the inept, the insane and the unbearable, it's a relief to have someone take things in stride."

"Franconi always takes things in stride." Juliet started to sink into a chair for a five-minute break.

"*Dio!* What joke is this?" She was standing again and looking down at the little can he held in his hand. "Who would sabotage my pasta?"

"Sabotage?" Had he found a bomb in the can? "What are you talking about?"

"This!" He shook the can at her. "What do you call this?"

"It's basil," she began, a bit unsteady when she lifted her gaze and caught the dark, furious look in his eyes. "It's on your list."

"Basil!" He went off in a stream of Italian. "You dare call this basil?"

Soothe, Juliet reminded herself. It was part of the job. "Carlo, it says basil right on the can."

"On the can." He said something short and rude as he dropped it into her hand. "Where in your clever notes does it say Franconi uses basil from a can?"

"It just says basil," she said between clenched teeth. "B-a-s-i-l."

"Fresh. On your famous list you'll see fresh. *Accidenti!* Only a philistine uses basil from a can for *pasta con pesto.* Do I look like a philistine?"

She wouldn't tell him what he looked like. Later, she might privately admit that temper was spectacular on him. Dark and unreasonable, but spectacular. "Carlo, I realize things aren't quite as perfect here as both of us would like, but—"

"I don't need perfect," he tossed at her. "I can cook in a sewer if I have to, but not without the proper ingredients."

She swallowed—though it went down hard—pride, temper and opinion. She only had fifteen minutes left until the interview. "I'm sorry, Carlo. If we could just compromise on this—"

"Compromise?" When the word came out like an obscenity, she knew she'd lost the battle. "Would you ask Picasso to compromise on a painting?"

Juliet stuck the can into her pocket. "How much fresh basil do you need?"

"Three ounces."

"You'll have it. Anything else?"

"A mortar and pestle, marble."

Juliet checked her watch. She had forty-five minutes to handle it. "Okay. If you'll do the interview right here, I'll take care of this and we'll be ready for the demonstration at noon." She sent up a quick prayer that there was a gourmet shop within ten miles. "Remember to get in the book title and the next stop on the tour. We'll be hitting another Gallegher's in Portland, so it's a good tie-in. Here." Digging into her bag she brought out an eight-by-ten glossy. "Take the extra publicity shot for her in case I don't get back. Elise didn't mention a photographer."

"You'd like to chop and dice that bouncy little woman," Carlo observed, noting that Juliet was swearing very unprofessionally under her breath.

"You bet I would." She dug in again. "Take a copy of the book. The reporter can keep it if necessary."

"I can handle the reporter," he told her calmly enough. "You handle the basil."

It seemed luck was with her when Juliet only had to make three calls before she found a shop that carried what she needed. The frenzied trip in the rain didn't improve her disposition, nor did the price of a marble pestle. Another glance at her watch reminded her she didn't have time for temperament. Carrying what she considered Carlo's eccentricities, she ran back to the waiting cab.

At exactly ten minutes to twelve, dripping wet, Juliet rode up to the third floor of Gallegher's. The first thing she saw was Carlo, leaning back in a cozy wicker dinette chair laughing with a plump, pretty middle-aged woman with a pad and pencil. He looked dashing, amiable and most of all, dry. She wondered how it would feel to grind the pestle into his ear.

"Ah, Juliet." All good humor, Carlo rose as she walked up to the table. "You must meet Marjorie. She tells me she's eaten my pasta in my restaurant in Rome."

"Loved every sinful bite. How do you do? You must be the Juliet Trent Carlo bragged about."

Bragged about? No, she wouldn't be pleased. But Juliet set her bag on the table and offered her hand. "It's nice to meet you. I hope you can stay for the demonstration."

"Wouldn't miss it." She twinkled at Carlo. "Or a sample of Franconi's pasta."

Juliet felt a little wave of relief. Something would be salvaged out of the disaster. Unless she was way off the mark, Carlo was about to be given a glowing write-up.

Carlo was already taking the little sack of basil out of the bag. "Perfect," he said after one sniff. "Yes, yes, this is excellent." He tested the pestle weight and size. "You'll see over at our little stage a crowd is gathering," he said easily to Juliet. "So we moved here to talk, knowing you'd see us as soon as you stepped off the escalator."

"Very good." They'd both handled things well, she decided. It was best to take satisfaction from that. A quick glance showed her that Elise was busy chatting away with a small group of people. Not a worry in the world, Juliet thought nastily. Well, she'd already resigned herself to that. Five minutes in the rest room for some quick repairs, she calculated, and she could keep everything on schedule.

"You have everything you need now, Carlo?"

He caught the edge of annoyance, and her hand, smiling brilliantly. "*Grazie, cara mia.* You're wonderful."

Perhaps she'd rather have snarled, but she returned the smile. "Just doing my job. You have a few more minutes before we should begin. If you'll excuse me, I'll just take care of some things and be right back."

Juliet kept up a brisk, dignified walk until she was out of sight, then made a mad dash for the rest room, pulling out her brush as she went in.

"What did I tell you?" Carlo held the bag of basil in his palm to judge the weight. "She's fantastic."

"And quite lovely," Marjorie agreed. "Even when she's damp and annoyed."

With a laugh, Carlo leaned forward to grasp both of Marjorie's hands. He was a man who touched, always. "A woman of perception. I knew I liked you."

She gave a quick dry chuckle, and for a moment felt twenty years younger. And twenty pounds lighter. It was a talent of his that he was generous with. "One last question, Carlo, before your fantastic Ms. Trent rushes you off. Are you still likely to fly off to Cairo or Cannes to prepare one of your dishes for an appreciative client and a stunning fee?"

"There was a time this was routine." He was silent a moment, thinking of the early years of his success. There'd been mad, glamorous trips to this country and to that, preparing fettuccine for a prince or cannelloni for a tycoon. It had been a heady, spectacular time.

Then he'd opened his restaurant and had learned that the solid continuity of his own place was so much more fulfilling than the flash of the single dish.

"From time to time I would still make such trips. Two months ago there was Count Lequine's birthday. He's an old client, an old friend, and he's fond of my spaghetti. But my restaurant is more rewarding to me."

He gave her a quizzical look as a thought occurred to him. "Perhaps I'm settling down?"

"A pity you didn't decide to settle in the States." She closed her pad. "I guarantee if you opened a Franconi's right here in San Diego, you'd have clientele flying in from all over the country."

He took the idea, weighed it in much the same way he had the basil, and put it in a corner of his mind. "An interesting thought."

"And a fascinating interview. Thank you." It pleased her that he rose as she did and took her hand. She was a tough outspoken feminist who appreciated genuine manners and genuine charm. "I'm looking forward to a taste of your pasta. I'll just ease over and try to get a good seat. Here comes your Ms. Trent."

Marjorie had never considered herself particularly romantic, but she'd always believed where there was smoke, there was fire. She watched the way Carlo turned his head, saw the change in his eyes and the slight tilt of his mouth. There was fire all right, she mused. You only had to be within five feet to feel the heat.

Between the hand dryer and her brush, Juliet had managed to do something with her hair. A touch here, a dab there, and her makeup was back in shape. Carrying her raincoat over her arm, she looked competent and collected. She was ready to admit she'd had one too many cups of coffee.

"Your interview went well?"

"Yes." He noticed, and approved, that she'd taken the time to dab on her scent. "Perfectly."

"Good. You can fill me in later. We'd better get started."

"In a moment." He reached in his pocket. "I told you I'd buy you a present."

There was a flutter of surprised pleasure she tried to ignore. Just wired from the coffee, she told herself. "Carlo, I told you not to. We don't have time—"

"There's always time." He opened the little box himself and drew out a small gold heart with an arrow of diamonds running through it. She'd been expecting something along the line of a box of chocolates.

"Oh, I—" Words were her business, but she'd lost them. "Carlo, really, you can't—"

"Never say can't to Franconi," he murmured and began to fasten the pin to her lapel. He did so smoothly, with no fumbling. After all, he was a man accustomed to such feminine habits. "It's very delicate, I thought, very elegant. So it suits you." Narrowing his eyes, he stood back, then nodded. "Yes, I was sure it would."

It wasn't possible to remember her crazed search for fresh basil when he was smiling at her in just that way. It was barely possible to remember how furious she was over the lackadaisical setup for the demonstration. Instinctively, she put up her hand and ran a finger over the pin. "It's lovely." Her lips curved, easily, sweetly, as he thought they didn't do often enough. "Thank you."

He couldn't count or even remember the number of presents he'd given, or the different styles of gratitude he'd received. Somehow, he was already sure this would be one he wouldn't forget.

"Prego."

"Ah, Ms. Trent?"

Juliet glanced over to see Elise watching her. Present or no present, it tightened her jaw. "Yes, Elise. You haven't met Mr. Franconi yet."

"Elise directed me from the office to you when I answered the page," Carlo said easily, more than appreciating Juliet's aggravation.

"Yes." She flashed her touchdown smile. "I thought your cookbook looked just super, Mr. Franconi. Everyone's dying to watch you cook something." She opened a little pad of paper with daisies on the cover. "I thought you could spell what it is so I could tell them when I announce you."

"Elise, I have everything." Juliet managed charm and diplomacy to cover a firm nudge out the door. "Why don't I just announce Mr. Franconi?"

"Great." She beamed. Juliet could think of no other word for it. "That'll be a lot easier."

"We'll get started now, Carlo, if you'd just step over there behind those counters, I'll go give the announcements." Without waiting for an assent, she gathered up the basil, mortar and pestle and walked over to the area that she'd prepared. In the most natural of moves, she set everything down and turned to the audience. Three hundred, she judged. Maybe even over. Not bad for a rainy day in a department store.

"Good afternoon." Her voice was pleasant and well pitched. There'd be no need for a microphone in the relatively small space. Thank God, because Elise had botched that minor detail as well. "I want to thank you all for coming here today, and to thank Gallegher's for providing such a lovely setting for the demonstration."

From a few feet away, Carlo leaned on a counter and

watched her. She was, as he'd told the reporter, fantastic. No one would guess she'd been up and on her feet since dawn.

"We all like to eat." This drew the murmured laughter she'd expected. "But I've been told by an expert that eating is more than a basic necessity, it's an experience. Not all of us like to cook, but the same expert told me that cooking is both art and magic. This afternoon, the expert, Carlo Franconi, will share with you the art, the magic and the experience with his own *pasta con pesto.*"

Juliet started the applause herself, but it was picked up instantly. As Carlo stepped out, she melted back. Center stage was his the moment he stepped on it.

"It's a fortunate man," he began, "who has the opportunity to cook for so many beautiful women. Some of you have husbands?" At the question there was a smatter of chuckles and the lifting of hands. "Ah, well." He gave a very European shrug. "Then I must be content to cook."

She knew Carlo had chosen that particular dish because it took little time in preparation. After the first five minutes, Juliet was certain not one member of the audience would have budged if he'd chosen something that took hours. She wasn't yet convinced cooking was magic, but she was certain he was.

His hands were as skilled and certain as a surgeon's, his tongue as glib as a politician's. She watched him measure, grate, chop and blend and found herself just as entertained as she might have been with a well produced one-act play.

One woman was bold enough to ask a question. It

opened the door and dozens of others followed. Juliet needn't have worried that the noise and conversations would disturb him. Obviously he thrived on the interaction. He wasn't, she decided, simply doing his job or fulfilling an obligation. He was enjoying himself.

Calling one woman up with him, Carlo joked about all truly great chefs requiring both inspiration and assistance. He told her to stir the spaghetti, made a fuss out of showing her the proper way to stir by putting his hand over hers and undoubtedly sold another ten books then and there.

Juliet had to grin. He'd done it for fun, not for sales. He was fun, Juliet realized, even if he did take his basil too seriously. He was sweet. Unconsciously, she began to toy with the gold and diamonds on her lapel. Uncommonly considerate and uncommonly demanding. Simply uncommon.

As she watched him laugh with his audience, something began to melt inside of her. She sighed with it, dreaming. There were certain men that prompted a woman, even a practical woman, to dream.

One of the women seated closer to her leaned toward a companion. "Good God, he's the sexiest man I've ever seen. He could keep a dozen lovers patiently waiting."

Juliet caught herself and dropped her hand. Yes, he could keep a dozen lovers patiently waiting. She was sure he did. Deliberately she tucked her hands in the pockets of her skirt. She'd be better off remembering she was encouraging this public image, even exploiting it. She'd be better off remembering that Carlo himself had told her he needed no imagery.

If she started believing half the things he said to

her, she might just find herself patiently waiting. The thought of that was enough to stop the melting. Waiting didn't fit into her schedule.

When every last bite of pasta had been consumed, and every last fan had been spoken with, Carlo allowed himself to think of the pleasures of sitting down with a cool glass of wine.

Juliet already had his jacket.

"Well done, Carlo." As she spoke, she began to help him into it. "You can leave California with the satisfaction of knowing you were a smashing success."

He took her raincoat from her when she would've shrugged into it herself. "The airport."

She smiled at his tone, understanding. "We'll pick up our bags in the holding room at the hotel on the way. Look at it this way. You can sit back and sleep all the way to Portland if you like."

Because the thought had a certain appeal, he cooperated. They rode down to the first floor and went out the west entrance where Juliet had told the cab to wait. She let out a quick sigh of relief when it was actually there.

"We get into Portland early?"

"Seven." Rain splattered against the cab's windshield. Juliet told herself to relax. Planes took off safely in the rain every day. "You have a spot on *People of Interest,* but not until nine-thirty. That means we can have breakfast at a civilized hour and go over the scheduling."

Quickly, efficiently, she checked off her San Diego list and noted everything had been accomplished. She had time for a quick, preliminary glance at her Portland schedule before the cab pulled up to the hotel.

"Just wait here," she ordered both the driver and Carlo. She was up and out of the cab and, because they were running it close, managed to have the bags installed in the trunk within seven minutes. Carlo knew because it amused him to time her.

"You, too, can sleep all the way to Portland."

She settled in beside him again. "No, I've got some work to do. The nice thing about planes is that I can pretend I'm in my office and forget I'm thousands of feet off the ground."

"I didn't realize flying bothered you."

"Only when I'm in the air." Juliet sat back and closed her eyes, thinking to relax for a moment. The next thing she knew, she was being kissed awake.

Disoriented, she sighed and wrapped her arms around Carlo's neck. It was soothing, so sweet. And then the heat began to rise.

"Cara." She'd surprised him, but that had brought its own kind of pleasure. "Such a pity to wake you."

"Hmm?" When she opened her eyes, his face was close, her mouth still warm, her heart still thudding. She jerked back and fumbled with the door handle. "That was uncalled for."

"True enough." Leisurely, Carlo stepped out into the rain. "But it was illuminating. I've already paid the driver, Juliet," he continued when she started to dig into her purse. "The baggage is checked. We board from gate five." Taking her arm, and his big leather case, he led her into the terminal.

"You didn't have to take care of all that." She'd have pulled her arm away if she'd had the energy. Or so she told herself. "The reason I'm here is to—"

"Promote my book," he finished easily. "If it makes you feel better, I've been known to do the same when I traveled with your predecessor."

The very fact that it did, made her feel foolish as well. "I appreciate it, Carlo. It's not that I mind you lending a hand, it's that I'm not used to it. You'd be surprised how many authors are either helpless or careless on the road."

"You'd be surprised how many chefs are temperamental and rude."

She thought of the basil and grinned. "No!"

"Oh, yes." And though he'd read her thoughts perfectly, his tone remained grave. "Always flying off the handle, swearing, throwing things. It leads to a bad reputation for all of us. Here, they're boarding. If only they have a decent Bordeaux."

Juliet stifled a yawn as she followed him through. "I'll need my boarding pass, Carlo."

"I have it." He flashed them both for the flight attendant and nudged Juliet ahead. "Do you want the window or the aisle?"

"I need my pass to see which I've got."

"We have 2A and B. Take your pick."

Someone pushed past her and bumped her solidly. It brought a sinking sensation of déjà vu. "Carlo, I'm in coach, so—"

"No, your tickets are changed. Take the window."

Before she could object, he'd maneuvered her over and slipped in beside her. "What do you mean my ticket's been changed? Carlo, I have to get in the back before I cause a scene."

"Your seat's here." After handing Juliet her boarding pass he stretched out his legs. "*Dio,* what a relief."

Frowning, Juliet studied her stub—2A. "I don't know how they could've made a mistake like this. I'd better see to it right away."

"There's no mistake. You should fasten your belt," he advised, then did so himself. "I changed your tickets for the remaining flights on the tour."

Juliet reached to undo the clasp he'd just secured. "You—but you can't."

"I told you, don't say can't to Franconi." Satisfied with her belt, he dealt with his own. "You work as hard as I do—why should you travel in tourist?"

"Because I'm paid to work. Carlo, let me out so I can fix this before we take off."

"No." For the first time, his voice was blunt and final. "I prefer your company to that of a stranger or an empty seat." When he turned his head, his eyes were like his voice. "I want you here. Leave it."

Juliet opened her mouth and closed it again. Professionally, she was on shaky ground either direction she went. She was supposed to see to his needs and wants within reason. Personally, she'd counted on the distance, at least during flight time, to keep her balanced. With Carlo, even a little distance could help.

He was being kind, she knew. Considerate. But he was also being stubborn. There was always a diplomatic way to handle such things.

She gave him a patient smile. "Carlo—"

He stopped her by simply closing his mouth over hers, quietly, completely and irresistibly. He held her there a moment, one hand on her cheek, the other over the fingers which had frozen in her lap. Juliet felt the floor tilt and her head go light.

We're taking off, she thought dimly, but knew the plane hadn't left the ground.

His tongue touched hers briefly, teasingly; then it was only his lips again. After brushing a hand through her hair, he leaned back. "Now, go back to sleep awhile," he advised. "This isn't the place I'd choose to seduce you."

Sometimes, Juliet decided, silence was the best diplomacy. Without another word, she closed her eyes and slept.

Chapter 5

Colorado. The Rockies, Pike's Peak, Indian ruins, aspens and fast-running streams. It sounded beautiful, exciting. But a hotel room was a hotel room after all.

They'd been busy in Washington State. For most of their three-day stay, Juliet had had to work and think on her feet. But the media had been outstanding. Their schedule had been so full her boss back in New York had probably done handstands. Her report on their run on the coast would be a publicist's dream. Then there was Denver.

What coverage she'd managed to hustle there would barely justify the plane fare. One talk show at the ungodly hour of 7:00 A.M. and one miserly article in the food section of a local paper. No network or local news coverage of the autographing, no print reporter who'd confirm an appearance. Lousy.

It was 6:00 A.M. when Juliet dragged herself out of the shower and began to search through her unpacked garment bag for a suit and a fresh blouse. The cleaners was definitely a priority the minute they moved on to Dallas.

At least Carlo wasn't cooking this morning. She didn't think she could bear to look at food in any form for at least two hours.

With any luck she could come back to the hotel after the show, catch another hour's sleep and then have breakfast in her room while she made her morning calls. The autographing wasn't until noon, and their flight out wasn't until early the next morning.

That was something to hold on to, Juliet told herself as she looked for the right shade of stockings. For the first time in a week, they had an evening free with no one to entertain, no one to be entertained by. A nice, quiet meal somewhere close by and a full night's sleep. With that at the end of the tunnel, she could get through the morning.

With a grimace, she gulped down her daily dose of brewer's yeast.

It wasn't until she was fully dressed that she woke up enough to remember she hadn't dealt with her makeup. With a shrug Juliet slipped out of her little green jacket and headed for the bathroom. She stared at the front door with a combination of suspicion and bad temper when she heard the knock. Peeking through the peephole, she focused on Carlo. He grinned at her, then crossed his eyes. She only swore a little as she pulled open the door.

"You're early," she began, then caught the stirring

aroma of coffee. Looking down, she saw that he carried a tray with a small pot, cups and spoons. "Coffee," she murmured, almost like a prayer.

"Yes." He nodded as he stepped into the room. "I thought you'd be ready, though room service isn't." He walked over to a table, saw that her room could fit into one section of his suite and set down the tray. "So, we deliver."

"Bless you." It was so sincere he grinned again as she crossed the room. "How did you manage it? Room service doesn't open for half an hour."

"There's a small kitchen in my suite. A bit primitive, but adequate to brew coffee."

She took the first sip, black and hot, and she closed her eyes. "It's wonderful. Really wonderful."

"Of course. I fixed it."

She opened her eyes again. No, she decided, she wouldn't spoil gratitude with sarcasm. After all, they'd very nearly gotten along for three days running. With the help of her shower, the yeast and the coffee, she was feeling almost human again.

"Relax," she suggested. "I'll finish getting ready." Expecting him to sit, Juliet took her cup and went into the bathroom to deal with her face and hair. She was dotting on foundation when Carlo leaned on the door-jamb.

"*Mi amore,* doesn't this arrangement strike you as impractical?"

She tried not to feel self-conscious as she smoothed on the thin, translucent base. "Which arrangement is that?"

"You have this—broom closet," he decided as he gestured toward her room. Yes, it was small enough that the subtle, feminine scent from her shower reached all the corners. "While I have a big suite with two baths, a bed big enough for three friends and one of those sofas that unfold."

"You're the star," she murmured as she brushed color over the slant of her cheeks.

"It would save the publisher money if we shared the suite."

She shifted her eyes in the mirror until they met his. She'd have sworn, absolutely sworn, he meant no more than that. That is, if she hadn't known him. "He can afford it," she said lightly. "It just thrills the accounting department at tax time."

Carlo moved his shoulders then sipped from his cup again. He'd known what her answer would be. Of course, he'd enjoy sharing his rooms with her for the obvious reason, but neither did it sit well with him that her accommodations were so far inferior to his.

"You need a touch more blusher on your left cheek," he said idly, not noticing her surprised look. What he'd noticed was the green silk robe that reflected in the mirror from the back of the door. Just how would she look in that? Carlo wondered. How would she look out of it?

After a narrowed-eyed study, Juliet discovered he'd been right. She picked up her brush again and evened the color. "You're a very observant man."

"Hmm?" He was looking at her again, but mentally, he'd changed her neat, high-collared blouse and slim skirt for the provocative little robe.

"Most men wouldn't notice unbalanced blusher." She picked up a grease pencil to shadow her eyes.

"I notice everything when it comes to a woman." There was still a light fog near the top of the mirror from the steam of her shower. Seeing it gave Carlo other, rather pleasant mental images. "What you're doing now gives you a much different look."

Relaxed again, she laughed. "That's the idea."

"But, no." He stepped in closer so he could watch over her shoulder. The small, casual intimacy was as natural for him as it was uncomfortable for her. "Without the pots of paint, your face is younger, more vulnerable, but no less attractive than it is with them. Different..." Easily, he picked up her brush and ran it through her hair. "It's not more, not less, simply different. I like both of your looks."

It wasn't easy to keep her hand steady. Juliet set down the eye-shadow and tried the coffee instead. Better to be cynical than be moved, she reminded herself and gave him a cool smile. "You seem right at home in the bathroom with a woman fixing her face."

He liked the way her hair flowed as he brushed it. "I've done it so often."

Her smile became cooler. "I'm sure."

He caught the tone, but continued to brush as he met her eyes in the glass. "Take it as you like, *cara,* but remember, I grew up in a house with five women. Your powders and bottles hold no secrets from me."

She'd forgotten that, perhaps because she'd chosen to forget anything about him that didn't connect directly with the book. Yet now it made her wonder. Just what sort of insight did a man get into women when he'd been surrounded by them since childhood? Frowning a bit, she picked up her mascara.

"Were you a close family?"

"We are a close family," he corrected. "My mother's a widow who runs a successful dress shop in Rome." It was typical of him not to mention that he'd bought it for her. "My four sisters all live within thirty kilometers. Perhaps I no longer share the bathroom with them, but little else changes."

She thought about it. It sounded cozy and easy and rather sweet. Juliet didn't believe she could relate at all. "Your mother must be proud of you."

"She'd be prouder if I added to her growing horde of grandchildren."

She smiled at that. It sounded more familiar. "I know what you mean."

"You should leave your hair just like this," he told her as he set down the brush. "You have a family?"

"My parents live in Pennsylvania."

He struggled with geography a moment. "Ah, then you'll visit them when we go to Philadelphia."

"No." The word was flat as she recapped the tube of mascara. "There won't be time for that."

"I see." And he thought he was beginning to. "You have brothers, sisters?"

"A sister." Because he was right about her hair, Juliet let it be and slipped out for her jacket. "She married a doctor and produced two children, one of each gender, before she was twenty-five."

Oh yes, he was beginning to see well enough. Though the words had been easy, the muscles in her shoulders had been tight. "She makes an excellent doctor's wife?"

"Carrie makes a perfect doctor's wife."

"Not all of us are meant for the same things."

"I wasn't." She picked up her briefcase and her purse. "We'd better get going. They said it would take about fifteen minutes to drive to the studio."

Strange, he thought, how people always believed their tender spots could go undetected. For now, he'd leave her with the illusion that hers had.

Because the directions were good and the traffic was light, Juliet drove the late model Chevy she'd rented with confidence. Carlo obliged by navigating because he enjoyed the poised, skilled way she handled the wheel.

"You haven't lectured me on today's schedule," he pointed out. "Turn right here at this light."

Juliet glanced in the mirror, switched lanes, then made the turn. She wasn't yet sure what his reaction would be to the fact that there barely was one. "I've decided to give you a break," she said brightly, knowing how some authors snarled and ranted when they had a dip in exposure. "You have this morning spot, then the autographing at World of Books downtown."

He waited, expecting the list to go on. When he turned to her, his brow was lifted. "And?"

"That's all." She heard the apology in her voice as she stopped at a red light. "It happens sometimes, Carlo. Things just don't come through. I knew it was going to be light here, but as it happens they've just started shooting a major film using Denver locations. Every reporter, every news team, every camera crew is covering it this afternoon. The bottom line is we got bumped."

"Bumped? Do you mean there is no radio show, no lunch with a reporter, no dinner engagement?"

"No, I'm sorry. It's just—"

"Fantastico!" Grabbing her face with both hands he kissed her hard. "I'll find out the name of this movie and go to its premiere."

The little knot of tension and guilt vanished. "Don't take it so hard, Carlo."

He felt as though he'd just been paroled. "Juliet, did you think I'd be upset? *Dio,* for a week it's been nothing but go here, rush there."

She spotted the TV tower and turned left. "You've been wonderful," she told him. The best time to admit it, she decided, was when they only had two minutes to spare. "Not everyone I've toured with has been as considerate."

She surprised him. He preferred it when a woman could do so. He twined a lock of the hair he'd brushed around his finger. "So, you've forgiven me for the basil?"

She smiled and had to stop herself from reaching up to touch the heart on her lapel. "I'd forgotten all about it."

He kissed her cheek in a move so casual and friendly she didn't object. "I believe you have. You've a kind heart, Juliet. Such things are beauty in themselves."

He could soften her so effortlessly. She felt it, fought it and, for the moment, surrendered to it. In an impulsive, uncharacteristic move, she brushed the hair on his forehead. "Let's go in. You've got to wake up Denver."

Professionally, Juliet should've been cranky at the lack of obligations and exposure in Denver. It was going to leave a few very obvious blanks on her overall report. Personally, she was thrilled.

According to schedule, she was back in her room by eight. By 8:03, she'd stripped out of her suit and had crawled, naked and happy, into her still-rumpled bed. For exactly an hour she slept deeply, and without any dreams she could remember. By ten-thirty, she'd gone through her list of phone calls and an enormous breakfast. After freshening her makeup, she dressed in her suit then went downstairs to meet Carlo in the lobby.

It shouldn't have surprised her that he was huddled in one of the cozy lounging areas with three women. It shouldn't have irked her. Pretending it did neither, Juliet strolled over. It was then she noticed that all three women were built stupendously. That shouldn't have surprised her, either.

"Ah, Juliet." He smiled, all grace, all charm. She didn't stop to wonder why she'd like to deck him. "Always prompt. Ladies." He turned to bow to all three of them. "It's been a pleasure."

"Bye-bye, Carlo." One of them sent him a look that could have melted lead. "Remember, if you're ever in Tucson…"

"How could I forget?" Hooking his arm with Juliet's, he strolled outside. "Juliet," he murmured, "where is Tucson?"

"Don't you ever quit?" she demanded.

"Quit what?"

"Collecting women."

He lifted a brow as he pulled open the door on the driver's side. "Juliet, one collects matchbooks, not women."

"It would seem there are some who consider them on the same level."

He blocked her way before she could slip inside. "Any who do are too stupid to matter." He walked around the side of the car and opened his own door before she spoke again.

"Who were they anyhow?"

Soberly, Carlo adjusted the brim of the buff-colored fedora he wore. "Female bodybuilders. It seems they're having a convention."

A muffled laugh escaped before she could prevent it. "Figures."

"Indeed yes, but such muscular ones." His expression was still grave as he lowered himself into the car.

Juliet remained quiet a moment, then gave up and laughed out loud. Damn, she'd never had as much fun on tour with anyone. She might as well accept it. "Tucson's in Arizona," she told him with another laugh. "And it's not on the itinerary."

They would have been on time for the autographing if they hadn't run into the detour. Traffic was clogged, rerouted and bad tempered as roads were blocked off for the film being shot. Juliet spent twenty minutes weaving, negotiating and cursing until she found she'd done no more than make a nice big circle.

"We've been here before," Carlo said idly and received a glowering look.

"Oh, really?" Her sweet tone had an undertone of arsenic.

He merely shifted his legs into a less cramped position. "It's an interesting city," he commented. "I think perhaps if you turn right at the next corner, then left two corners beyond, we'll find ourselves on the right track."

Juliet meticulously smoothed her carefully written directions when she'd have preferred to crumple them into a ball. "The book clerk specifically said—"

"I'm sure she's a lovely woman, but things seem a bit confused today." It didn't particularly bother him. The blast of a horn made her jolt. Amused, Carlo merely looked over. "As someone from New York City, you should be used to such things."

Juliet set her teeth. "I never drive in the city."

"I do. Trust me, *innamorata*."

Not on your life, Juliet thought, but turned right. It took nearly ten minutes in the crawling traffic to manage the next two blocks, but when she turned left she found herself, as Carlo had said, on the right track. She waited, resigned, for him to gloat.

"Rome moves faster" was all he said.

How could she anticipate him? she wondered. He didn't rage when you expected, didn't gloat when it was natural. With a sigh, she gave up. "Anything moves faster." She found herself in the right block, but parking space was at a premium. Weighing the ins and outs, Juliet swung over beside a car at the curb. "Look, Carlo, I'm going to have to drop you off. We're already running behind. I'll find a place to park and be back as soon as I can."

"You're the boss," he said, still cheerful after forty-five minutes of teeth-grinding traffic.

"If I'm not there in an hour, send up a flare."

"My money's on you."

Still cautious, she waited until she saw him swing into the bookstore before she fought her way into traffic again.

Twenty frustrating minutes later, Juliet walked into the dignified little bookstore herself. It was, she noted with a sinking stomach, too quiet and too empty. A clerk with a thin-striped tie and shined shoes greeted her.

"Good morning. May I help you?"

"I'm Juliet Trent, Mr. Franconi's publicist."

"Ah yes, right this way." He glided across the carpet to a set of wide steps. "Mr. Franconi's on the second level. It's unfortunate that the traffic and confusion have discouraged people from coming out. Of course, we rarely do these things." He gave her a smile and brushed a piece of lint from the sleeve of his dark blue jacket. "The last time was…let me see, in the fall. J. Jonathan Cooper was on tour. I'm sure you've heard of him. He wrote *Metaphysical Force and You.*"

Juliet bit back a sigh. When you hit dry ground, you just had to wait for the tide.

She spotted Carlo in a lovely little alcove on a curvy love seat. Beside him was a woman of about forty with a neat suit and pretty legs. Such things didn't warrant even a raised brow. But to Juliet's surprise, Carlo wasn't busy charming her. Instead, he was listening intently to a young boy who sat across from him.

"I've worked in the kitchens there for the last three summers. I'm not allowed to actually prepare anything, but I can watch. At home, I cook whenever I can, but with school and the job, it's mostly on weekends."

"Why?"

The boy stopped in midstream and looked blank. "Why?"

"Why do you cook?" Carlo asked. He acknowledged Juliet with a nod, then gave his attention back to the boy.

"Because…" The boy looked at his mother, then back at Carlo. "Well, it's important. I like to take things and put them together. You have to concentrate, you know, and be careful. But you can make something really terrific. It looks good and it smells good. It's…I don't know." His voice lowered in embarrassment. "Satisfying, I guess."

"Yes." Pleased, Carlo smiled at him. "That's a good answer."

"I have both your other books," the boy blurted out. "I've tried all your recipes. I even made your *pasta al tre formaggi* for this dinner party at my aunt's."

"And?"

"They liked it." The boy grinned. "I mean they really liked it."

"You want to study."

"Oh yeah." But the boy dropped his gaze to where his hands rubbed nervously over his knees. "Thing is we can't really afford college right now, so I'm hoping to get some restaurant work."

"In Denver?"

"Any place where I could start cooking instead of wiping up."

"We've taken up enough of Mr. Franconi's time." The boy's mother rose, noting there was now a handful of people milling around on the second level with Carlo's books in hand. "I want to thank you." She offered her hand to Carlo as he rose with her. "It meant a great deal to Steven to talk with you."

"My pleasure." Though he was gracious as always, he turned back to the boy. "Perhaps you'd give me your address. I know of some restaurant owners here in the States. Perhaps one of them needs an apprentice chef."

Stunned, Steven could do nothing but stare. "You're very kind." His mother took out a small pad and wrote on it. Her hand was steady, but when she handed the paper to Carlo and looked at him, he saw the emotion. He thought of his own mother. He took the paper, then her hand.

"You have a fortunate son, Mrs. Hardesty."

Thoughtful, Juliet watched them walk away, noting that Steven looked over his shoulder with the same, blank, baffled expression.

So he has a heart, Juliet decided, touched. A heart that wasn't altogether reserved for *amore.* But she saw Carlo slip the paper into his pocket and wondered if that would be the end of it.

The autographing wasn't a smashing success. Six books by Juliet's count. That had been bad enough, but then there'd been The Incident.

Looking at the all but empty store, Juliet had considered hitting the streets with a sign on her back, then the homey little woman had come along bearing all three of Carlo's books. Good for the ego, Juliet thought. That was before the woman had said something that caused Carlo's eyes to chill and his voice to freeze. All Juliet heard was the name LaBare.

"I beg your pardon, Madame?" Carlo said in a tone Juliet had never heard from him. It could've sliced through steel.

"I said I keep all your books on a shelf in my kitchen, right next to André LaBare's. I love to cook."

"LaBare?" Carlo put his hand over his stack of books

as a protective parent might over a threatened child. "You would dare put my work next to that—that peasant's?"

Thinking fast, Juliet stepped up and broke into the conversation. If ever she'd seen a man ready to murder, it was Carlo. "Oh, I see you have all of Mr. Franconi's books. You must love to cook."

"Well, yes I—"

"Wait until you try some of his new recipes. I had the *pasta con pesto* myself. It's wonderful." Juliet started to take the woman's books from under Carlo's hand and met with resistance and a stubborn look. She gave him one of her own and jerked the books away. "Your family's going to be just thrilled when you serve it," Juliet went on, keeping her voice pleasant as she led the woman out of the line of fire. "And the fettuccine…"

"LaBare is a swine." Carlo's voice was very clear and reached the stairs. The woman glanced back nervously.

"Men." Juliet made her voice a conspiratorial whisper. "Such egos."

"Yes." Gathering up her books, the woman hurried down the stairs and out of the store. Juliet waited until she was out of earshot before she pounced on Carlo.

"How could you?"

"How could I?" He rose, and though he skimmed just under six feet, he looked enormous. "She would *dare* speak that name to me? She would *dare* associate the work of an artist with the work of a jackass? LaBare—"

"At the moment, I don't give a damn who or what this LaBare is." Juliet put a hand on his shoulder and shoved him back onto the love seat. "What I do care about is you scaring off the few customers we have. Now behave yourself."

He sat where he was only because he admired the way she'd ordered him to. Fascinating woman, Carlo decided, finding it wiser to think of her than LaBare. It was wiser to think of flood and famine than of LaBare.

The afternoon had dragged on and on, except for the young boy, Carlo thought and touched the paper in his pocket. He'd call Summer in Philadelphia about young Steven Hardesty.

But other than Steven and the woman who upped his blood pressure by speaking of LaBare, Carlo had found himself perilously close to boredom. Something he considered worse than illness.

He needed some activity, a challenge—even a small one. He glanced over at Juliet as she spoke with a clerk. That was no small challenge. The one thing he'd yet to be in Juliet's company was bored. She kept him interested. Sexually? Yes, that went without saying. Intellectually. That was a plus, a big one.

He understood women. It wasn't a matter of pride, but to Carlo's thinking, a matter of circumstance. He enjoyed women. As lovers, of course, but he also enjoyed them as companions, as friends, as associates. It was a rare thing when a man could find a woman to be all of those things. That's what he wanted from Juliet. He hadn't resolved it yet, only felt it. Convincing her to be his friend would be as challenging, and as rewarding, as it would be to convince her to be his lover.

No, he realized as he studied her profile. With this woman, a lover would come easier than a friend. He had two weeks left to accomplish both. With a smile, he decided to start the campaign in earnest.

Half an hour later, they were walking the three blocks to the parking garage Juliet had found.

"This time I drive," he told Juliet as they stepped inside the echoing gray building. When she started to object, he held out his hand for the keys. "Come, my love, I've just survived two hours of boredom. Why should you have all the fun?"

"Since you put it that way." She dropped the keys in his hand, relieved that whatever had set him off before was forgotten.

"So now we have a free evening."

"That's right." With a sigh she leaned back in her seat and waited for him to start the engine.

"We'll have dinner at seven. Tonight, I make the arrangements."

A hamburger in her room, an old movie and bed. Juliet let the wish come and go. Her job was to pamper and entertain as much as possible. "Whatever you like."

Carlo pulled out of the parking space with a squeal of tires that had Juliet bolting up. "I'll hold you to that, *cara.*"

He zoomed out of the garage and turned right with hardly a pause. "Carlo—"

"We should have champagne to celebrate the end of our first week. You like champagne?"

"Yes, I—Carlo, the light's changing."

He breezed through the amber light, skimmed by the bumper of a battered compact and kept going. "Italian food. You have no objection?"

"No." She gripped the door handle until her knuckles turned white. "That truck!"

"Yes, I see it." He swerved around it, zipped through another light and cut a sharp right. "You have plans for the afternoon?"

Juliet pressed a hand to her throat, thinking she might be able to push out her voice. "I was thinking of making use of the hotel spa. If I live."

"Good. Me, I think I'll go shopping."

Juliet's teeth snapped together as he changed lanes in bumper-to-bumper traffic. "How do I notify next of kin?"

With a laugh, Carlo swung in front of their hotel. "Don't worry, Juliet. Have your whirlpool and your sauna. Knock on my door at seven."

She looked back toward the street. Pamper and entertain, she remembered. Did that include risking your life? Her supervisor would think so. "Maybe I should go with you."

"No, I insist." He leaned over, cupping her neck before she'd recovered enough to evade. "Enjoy," he murmured lightly against her lips. "And think of me as your skin grows warm and your muscles grow lax."

In self-defense, Juliet hurried out of the car. Before she could tell him to drive carefully, he was barreling back out into the street. She offered a prayer for Italian maniacs, then went inside.

By seven, she felt reborn. She'd sweated out fatigue in the sauna, shocked herself awake in the pool and splurged on a massage. Life, she thought as she splashed on her scent, had its good points after all. Tomorrow's flight to Dallas would be soon enough to draft her Denver report. Such as it was. Tonight, all she had to worry about was eating. After pressing a hand to her stomach, Juliet admitted she was more than ready for that.

With a quick check, she approved the simple ivory dress with the high collar and tiny pearly buttons. Unless Carlo had picked a hot dog stand it would suit. Grabbing her evening bag, she slipped across the hall to knock on Carlo's door. She only hoped he'd chosen some place close by. The last thing she wanted to do was fight Denver's downtown traffic again.

The first thing she noticed when Carlo opened his door were the rolled-up sleeves of his shirt. It was cotton, oversized and chic, but her eyes were drawn to the surprising cord of muscles in his forearms. The man did more than lift spoons and spatulas. The next thing she noticed was the erotic scents of spices and sauce.

"Lovely." Carlo took both hands and drew her inside. She pleased him, the smooth, creamy skin, the light, subtle scent, but more, the confused hesitation in her eyes as she glanced over to where the aroma of food was strongest.

"An interesting cologne," she managed after a moment. "But don't you think you've gotten a bit carried away?"

"*Innamorata,* you don't wear Franconi's spaghetti sauce, you absorb it." He kissed the back of her hand. "Anticipate it." Then the other. "Savor it." This time her palm.

A smart woman wasn't aroused by a man who used such flamboyant tactics. Juliet told herself that as the chills raced up her arms and down again. "Spaghetti sauce?" Slipping her hands from his, she linked them behind her back.

"I found a wonderful shop. The spices pleased me very much. The burgundy was excellent. Italian, of course."

"Of course." Cautious, she stepped farther into the suite. "You spent the day cooking?"

"Yes. Though you should remind me to speak to the hotel owner about the quality of this stove. All in all, it went quite well."

She told herself it wasn't wise to encourage him when she had no intention of eating alone with him in his suite. Perhaps if she'd been made out of rock she could have resisted wandering toward the little kitchenette. Her mouth watered. "Oh, God."

Delighted, Carlo slipped an arm around her waist and led her to the stove. The little kitchen itself was in shambles. She'd never seen so many pots and bowls and spoons jammed into a sink before. Counters were splattered and streaked. But the smells. It was heaven, pure and simple.

"The senses, Juliet. There's not one of us who isn't ruled by them. First, you smell, and you begin to imagine." His fingers moved lightly over her waist. "Imagine. You can almost taste it on your tongue from that alone."

"Hmm." Knowing she was making a mistake, she watched him take the lid off the pot on the stove. The tang made her close her eyes and just breathe. "Oh, Carlo."

"Then we look, and the imagination goes one step further." His fingers squeezed lightly at her waist until she opened her eyes and looked into the pot. Thick, red, simmering, the sauce was chunky with meat, peppers and spice. Her stomach growled.

"Beautiful, yes?"

"Yes." She wasn't aware that her tongue slid out over her lips in anticipation. He was.

"And we hear." Beside the sauce a pot of water began to boil. In an expert move, he measured pasta by sight and slid it in. "Some things are destined to be mated." With a slotted spoon, he stirred gently. "Without each other, they are incomplete. But when merged..." he adjusted the flame, "a treasure. Pasta and the sauce. A man and a woman. Come, you'll have some burgundy. The champagne's for later."

It was time to take a stand, even though she took it by the stove. "Carlo, I had no idea this was what you intended. I think—"

"I like surprises." He handed her a glass half filled with dark, red wine. "And I wanted to cook for you."

She wished he hadn't put it quite that way. She wished his voice wasn't so warm, so deep, like his eyes. Like the feelings he could urge out of her. "I appreciate that Carlo, it's just that—"

"You had your sauna?"

"Yes, I did. Now—"

"It relaxed you. It shows."

She sighed, sipping at the wine without thinking. "Yes."

"This relaxes me. We eat together tonight." He tapped his glass to hers. "Men and women have done so for centuries. It has become civilized."

Her chin tilted. "You're making fun of me."

"Yes." Ducking into the refrigerator, he pulled out a small tray. "First you'll try my antipasto. Your palate should be prepared."

Juliet chose a little chunk of zucchini. "I'd think you'd prefer being served in a restaurant."

"Now and then. There are times I prefer privacy." He set down the tray. As he did, she took a small step back. Interested, he lifted a brow. "Juliet, do I make you nervous?"

She swallowed zucchini. "Don't be absurd."

"Am I?" On impulse, he set his wine down as well and took another step toward her. Juliet found her back pressed into the refrigerator.

"Carlo—"

"No, shh. We experiment." Gently, watching her, he brushed his lips over one cheek, then the other. He heard her breath catch then shudder out. Nerves—these he accepted. When a man and woman were attracted and close, there had to be nerves. Without them, passion was bland, like a sauce without spice.

But fear? Wasn't that what he saw in her eyes? Just a trace of it, only briefly. Nerves he'd use, play on, exploit. Fear was something different. It disturbed him, blocked him and, at the same time, moved him.

"I won't hurt you, Juliet."

Her eyes were direct again, level, though her hand was balled into a fist. "Won't you?"

He took her hand, slowly working it open. "No." In that moment, he promised both of them. "I won't. Now we'll eat."

Juliet held off the shudder until he'd turned around to stir and drain his pasta. Perhaps he wouldn't hurt her, she thought and recklessly tossed back her wine. But she might hurt herself.

He didn't fuss. He merely perfected. It occurred to Juliet, as she watched him put the last touches on the meal, that he was no different here in the little hotel kitchen than he'd been before the camera. Juliet added her help in the only way she'd have dared. She set the table.

Yes, it was a mistake, she told herself as she arranged plates. But no one but a fool would walk away from anything that smelled like that sauce. She wasn't a fool. She could handle herself. The moment of weak fear she'd felt in the kitchen was past. She'd enjoy a take-your-shoes-off meal, drink two glasses of really excellent burgundy, then go across the hall and catch eight hours' sleep. The merry-go-round would continue the next day.

She selected a marinated mushroom as Carlo brought in the platter of spaghetti. "Better," he said when she smiled at him. "You're ready to enjoy yourself."

With a shrug, Juliet sat. "If one of the top chefs in the world wants to cook me dinner, why should I complain?"

"*The* top," he corrected and gestured for her to serve herself. She did, barely conquering greed.

"Does it really relax you to stand in a kitchen?"

"It depends. Sometimes it relaxes, sometimes it excites. Always it pleases. No, don't cut." With a shake of his head, he reached over. "Americans. You roll it onto the fork."

"It falls off when I do."

"Like this." With his hands on her wrists, he guided

her. Her pulse was steady, he noted, but not slow. "Now." Still holding her hand, he lifted the fork toward her mouth. "Taste."

As she did, he had the satisfaction of watching her face. Spices exploded on her tongue. Heat seeped through, mellowing to warmth. She savored it, even as she thought of the next bite. "Oh, this is no little sin."

Nothing could have delighted him more. With a laugh, he sat back and started on his own plate. "Small sins are only small pleasures. When Franconi cooks for you, food is not a basic necessity."

She was already rolling the next forkful. "You win that one. Why aren't you fat?"

"Prego?"

"If I could cook like this…" She tasted again and sighed. "I'd look like one of your meatballs."

With a chuckle, he watched her dig in. It pleased him to see someone he cared for enjoying what he'd created. After years of cooking, he'd never tired of it. "So, your mother didn't teach you to cook?"

"She tried." Juliet accepted a piece of the crusty bread he offered but set it aside as she rolled more spaghetti. First things first. "I never seemed to be very good at the things she wanted me to be good at. My sister plays the piano beautifully; I can barely remember the scales."

"So, what did you want to do instead of taking piano lessons?"

"Play third base." It came out so easily, it stunned her. Juliet had thought she'd buried that along with a dozen other childhood frustrations. "It just wasn't done," she said with a shrug. "My mother was determined to raise two well-rounded ladies who would become two well-rounded, successful wives. Win some, lose some."

"You think she's not proud of you?"

The question hit a target she hadn't known was exposed. Juliet reached for her wine. "It's not a matter of pride, but of disappointment, I suppose. I disappointed her; I confused my father. They still wonder what they did wrong."

"What they did wrong was not to accept what you are."

"Maybe," she murmured. "Or maybe I was determined to be something they couldn't accept. I've never worked it out."

"Are you unhappy with your life?"

Surprised, she glanced up. Unhappy? Sometimes frustrated, harassed and pressured. But unhappy? "No. No, I'm not."

"Then perhaps that's your answer."

Juliet took a moment to study him. He was more than gorgeous, more than sexy, more than all those qualities she'd once cynically attributed to him. "Carlo." For the first time she reached out to touch him, just his hand, but he thought it a giant step. "You're a very nice man."

"But of course I am." His fingers curled over hers because he couldn't resist. "I could give you references."

With a laugh, Juliet backed off. "I'm sure you could." With concentration, dedication and just plain greed, she cleared off her plate.

"Time for dessert."

"Carlo!" Moaning, Juliet pressed a hand to her stomach. "Please, don't be cruel."

"You'll like it." He was up and in the kitchen before she found the strength to refuse again. "It's an old, old, Italian tradition. Back to the empire. American cheesecake is sometimes excellent, but this…" He brought out a small, lovely cake with cherries dripping lavishly over it.

"Carlo, I'll die."

"Just a taste with the champagne." He popped the cork with an expert twist and poured two fresh glasses. "Go, sit on the sofa, be comfortable."

As she did, Juliet realized why the Romans traditionally slept after a meal. She could've curled up in a happy little ball and been unconscious in moments. But the champagne was lively, insistent.

"Here." He brought over one plate with a small slice. "We'll share."

"One bite," she told him, prepared to stand firm. Then she tasted. Creamy, smooth, not quite sweet, more nutty. Exquisite. With a sigh of surrender, Juliet took another. "Carlo, you're a magician."

"Artist," he corrected.

"Whatever you want." Using all the willpower she had left, Juliet exchanged the cake for champagne. "I really can't eat another bite."

"Yes, I remember. You don't believe in overindulgence." But he filled her glass again.

"Maybe not." She sipped, enjoying that rich, luxurious aura only champagne could give. "But now I've gotten a different perspective on indulgence." Slipping out of her shoes, she laughed over the rim of her glass. "I'm converted."

"You're lovely." The lights were low, the music soft,

the scents lingering and rich. He thought of resisting.
The fear that had been in her eyes demanded he think
of it. But just now, she was relaxed, smiling. The desire he'd felt tug the moment he'd seen her had never
completely gone away.

Senses were aroused, heightened, by a meal. That
was something he understood perfectly. He also understood that a man and a woman should never ignore
whatever pleasure they could give to each other.

So he didn't resist, but took her face in his hands.
There he could watch her eyes, feel her skin, nearly taste
her. This time he saw desire, not fear but wariness. Perhaps she was ready for lesson two.

She could have refused. The need to do so went
through her mind. But his hands were so strong, so
gentle on her skin. She'd never been touched like that
before. She knew how he'd kiss her and the sense of
anticipation mixed with nerves. She knew, and wanted.

Wasn't she a woman who knew her own mind? She
took her hands to his wrists, but didn't push away. Her
fingers curled around and held as she touched her mouth
to his. For a moment they stayed just so, allowing themselves to savor that first taste, that first sensation. Then
slowly, mutually, they asked for more.

She seemed so small when he held her that a man
could forget how strong and competent she was. He
found himself wanting to treasure. Desire might burn,
but when she was so pliant, so vulnerable, he found
himself compelled to show only gentleness.

Had any man ever shown her such care? Juliet's head
began to swim as his hands moved into her hair. Was
there another man so patient? His heart was pound-

ing against hers. She could feel it, like something wild and desperate. But his mouth was so soft, his hands so gentle. As though they'd been lovers for years, she thought dimly. And had all the time left in the world to continue to love.

No hurry, no rush, no frenzy. Just pleasure. Her heart opened reluctantly, but it opened. He began to pour through. When the phone shrilled, he swore and she sighed. They'd both been prepared to take all the chances.

"Only a moment," he murmured.

Still dreaming, she touched his cheek. "All right."

As he went to answer, she leaned back, determined not to think.

"Cara!" The enthusiasm in his voice, and the endearment had her opening her eyes again. With a warm laugh, Carlo went into a stream of Italian. Juliet had no choice but to think.

Affection. Yes, it was in his voice. She didn't have to understand the words. She looked around to see him smiling as he spoke to the woman on the other end. Resigned, Juliet picked up her champagne. It wasn't easy for her to admit she'd been a fool. Or for her to admit she'd been hurt.

She knew who he was. What he was. She knew how many women he'd seduced. Perhaps she was a woman who knew her own mind, and perhaps she wanted him. But she would never be eased into a long line of *others*. Setting down the champagne, she rose.

"Sì, sì. I love you."

Juliet turned away at the phrase I love you. How

well it slid off his tongue, in any language. How little it meant, in any language.

"Interruptions. I'm sorry."

Juliet turned back and gave him her uncompromising look. "Don't be. The dinner was marvelous, Carlo, thank you. You should be ready to check out by eight."

"A moment," he murmured. Crossing over, he took her by the arms. "What's this? You're angry."

"Of course not." She tried to back away and failed. It was easy to forget just how strong he was. "Why should I be?"

"Reasons aren't always necessary for a woman."

Though he'd said it in a simple tone that offered no insult, her eyes narrowed. "The expert. Well, let me tell you something about *this* woman, Franconi. She doesn't think much of a man who makes love to her one minute then pushes another lover in her face the next."

He held up his hand as he struggled to follow her drift. "I'm not following you. Maybe my English is failing."

"Your English is perfect," she spit at him. "From what I just heard, so's your Italian."

"My…" His grin broke out. "The phone."

"Yes. The phone. Now, if you'll excuse me."

He let her get as far as the door. "Juliet, I admit I'm hopelessly enamored of the woman I was speaking to. She's beautiful, intelligent, interesting and I've never met anyone quite like her."

Furious, Juliet whirled around. "How marvelous."

"I think so. It was my mother."

She walked back to snatch up the purse she'd nearly

forgotten. "I'd think a man of your experience and imagination could do better."

"So I could." He held her again, not so gently, not so patiently. "If it was necessary. I don't make a habit to explain myself, and when I do, I don't lie."

She took a deep breath because she was abruptly certain she was hearing the truth. Either way, she'd been a fool. "I'm sorry. It's none of my business in any case."

"No, it's not." He took her chin in his hand and held it. "I saw fear in your eyes before. It concerned me. Now I think it wasn't me you were afraid of, but yourself."

"That's none of your business."

"No, it's not," he said again. "You appeal to me, Juliet, in many ways, and I intend to take you to bed. But we'll wait until you aren't afraid."

She wanted to rage at him. She wanted to weep. He saw both things clearly. "We have an early flight in the morning, Carlo."

He let her go, but stood where he was for a long time after he'd heard her door shut across the hall.

Chapter 6

Dallas was different. Dallas was Dallas without apology. Texas rich, Texas big and Texas arrogant. If it was the city that epitomized the state, then it did so with flair. Futuristic architecture and mind-twisting freeways abounded in a strange kind of harmony with the more sedate buildings downtown. The air was hot and carried the scents of oil, expensive perfumes and prairie dust. Dallas was Dallas, but it had never forgotten its roots.

Dallas held the excitement of a boomtown that was determined not to stop booming. It was full of downhome American energy that wasn't about to lag. As far as Juliet was concerned they could have been in downtown Timbuktu.

He acted as though nothing had happened—no intimate dinner, no arousal, no surrender, no cross words. Juliet wondered if he did it to drive her crazy.

Carlo was amiable, cooperative and charming. She knew better now. Under the amiability was a shaft of steel that wouldn't bend an inch. She'd seen it. One could say she'd felt it. It would have been a lie to say she didn't admire it.

Cooperative, sure. In his favor, Juliet had to admit that she'd never been on tour with anyone as willing to work without complaint. And touring was hard work, no matter how glamorous it looked on paper. Once you were into your second full week, it became difficult to smile unless you were cued. Carlo never broke his rhythm.

But he expected perfection—spelled his way—and wouldn't budge an inch until he got it.

Charming. No one could enchant a group of people with more style than Franconi. That alone made her job easier. No one would deny his charm unless they'd seen how cold his eyes could become. She had.

He had flaws like any other man, Juliet thought. Remembering that might help her keep an emotional distance. It always helped her to list the pros and cons of a situation, even if the situation was a man. The trouble was, though flawed, he was damn near irresistible.

And he knew it. That was something else she had to remind herself of.

His ego was no small matter. That was something she'd be wise to balance against his unrestricted generosity. Vanity about himself and his work went over the border into arrogance. It didn't hurt her sense of

perspective to weigh that against his innate consider-
ation for others.

But then, there was the way he smiled, the way he
said her name. Even the practical, professional Juliet
Trent had a difficult time finding a flaw to balance
those little details.

The two days in Dallas were busy enough to keep
her driving along on six hours' sleep, plenty of vitamins
and oceans of coffee. They were making up for Denver
all right. She had the leg cramps to prove it.

Four minutes on the national news, an interview with
one of the top magazines in the country, three write-
ups in the Dallas press and two autograph sessions that
sold clean out. There was more, but those headed up
her report. When she went back to New York, she'd go
back in triumph.

She didn't want to think of the dinners with department store executives that started at 10:00 P.M. and lasted
until she was falling asleep in her bananas flambé. She
couldn't bear to count the lunches of poached salmon
or shrimp salad. She'd had to refill her pocket aspirin
bottles and stock up on antacids. But it was worth it.
She should have been thrilled.

She was miserable.

She was driving him mad. Polite, Carlo thought as
they prepared to sit through another luncheon interview.
Yes, she was polite. Her mother had taught her perfect
manners even if she hadn't taught her to cook.

Competent? As far as he was concerned, he'd never
known anyone, male or female, who was as scrupu-
lously competent as Juliet Trent. He'd always admired
that particular quality in a companion, insisted on it

in an associate. Of course, Juliet was both. Precise, prompt, cool in a crisis and unflaggingly energetic. Admirable qualities all.

For the first time in his life he gave serious thought to strangling a woman.

Indifferent. That's what he couldn't abide. She acted as though there was nothing more between them than the next interview, the next television spot, the next plane. She acted as though there'd been no flare of need, of passion, of understanding between them. One would think she didn't want him with the same intensity that he wanted her.

He knew better. Didn't he?

He could remember her ripe, unhesitating response to him. Mouth to mouth, body to body. There'd been no indifference in the way her arms had held him. No, there'd been strength, pliancy, need, demand, but no indifference. Yet now...

They'd spent nearly two days exclusively in each other's company, but he'd seen nothing in her eyes, heard nothing in her voice that indicated more than a polite business association. They ate together, drove together, worked together. They did everything but sleep together.

He'd had his fill of polite. But he hadn't had his fill of Juliet.

He thought of her. It didn't bruise Carlo's pride to admit he thought of her a great deal. He often thought of women, and why not? When a man didn't think of a woman, he was better off dead.

He wanted her. It didn't worry him to admit that he wanted her more every time he thought of her. He'd wanted many women. He'd never believed in self-denial. When a man didn't want a woman, he *was* dead.

But… Carlo found it odd that "buts" so often followed any thoughts he had on Juliet. But he found himself dwelling on her more often than he'd have once considered healthy. Though he didn't mind wanting a woman until he ached, he found Juliet could make him ache more than he'd have once considered comfortable.

He might have been able to rationalize the threat to his health and comfort. But…she was so damn indifferent.

If he did nothing else in the short time they had left in Dallas, he was going to change that.

Lunch was white linen, heavy silver flatware and thin crystal. The room was done in tones of dusty rose and pastel greens. The murmur of conversation was just as quiet.

Carlo thought it a pity they couldn't have met the reporter at one of the little Tex-Mex restaurants over Mexican beer with chili and nachos. Briefly, he promised himself he'd rectify that in Houston.

He barely noticed the reporter was young and running on nerves as they took their seats. He'd decided, no matter what it took, he'd break through Juliet's inflexible shield of politeness before they stood up again. Even if he had to play dirty.

"I'm so happy you included Dallas on your tour, Mr. Franconi," the reporter began, already reaching for her water glass to clear her throat. "Mr. Van Ness sends his apologies. He was looking forward to meeting you."

Carlo smiled at her, but his mind was on Juliet. "Yes?"

"Mr. Van Ness is the food editor for the *Tribune*." Juliet spread her napkin over her lap as she gave Carlo information she'd related less than fifteen minutes before. She sent him the friendliest of smiles and hoped he felt the barbs in it. "Ms. Tribly is filling in for him."

"Of course." Carlo smoothed over the gap of attention. "Charmingly, I'm sure."

As a woman she wasn't immune to that top-cream voice. As a reporter, she was well aware of the importance of her assignment. "It's all pretty confused." Ms. Tribly wiped damp hands on her napkin. "Mr. Van Ness is having a baby. That is, what I mean is, his wife went into labor just a couple of hours ago."

"So, we should drink to them." Carlo signaled a waiter. "Margaritas?" He phrased the question as a statement, earned a cool nod from Juliet and a grateful smile from the reporter.

Determined to pull off her first really big assignment, Ms. Tribly balanced a pad discreetly on her lap. "Have you been enjoying your tour through America, Mr. Franconi?"

"I always enjoy America." Lightly he ran a finger over the back of Juliet's hand before she could move it out of reach. "Especially in the company of a beautiful woman." She started to slide her hand away then felt it pinned under his. For a man who could whip up the most delicate of soufflés, his hands were as strong as a boxer's.

Wills sparked, clashed and fumed. Carlo's voice remained mild, soft and romantic. "I must tell you, Ms. Tribly, Juliet is an extraordinary woman. I couldn't manage without her."

"Mr. Franconi's very kind." Though Juliet's voice was as mild and quiet as his, the nudge she gave him under the table wasn't. "I handle the details; Mr. Franconi's the artist."

"We make an admirable team, wouldn't you say, Ms. Tribly?"

"Yes." Not quite sure how to handle that particular line, she veered off to safer ground. "Mr. Franconi, besides writing cookbooks, you own and run a successful restaurant in Rome and occasionally travel to prepare a special dish. A few months ago, you flew to a yacht in the Aegean to cook minestrone for Dimitri Azares, the shipping magnate."

"His birthday," Carlo recalled. "His daughter arranged a surprise." Again, his gaze skimmed over the woman whose hand he held. "Juliet will tell you, I'm fond of surprises."

"Yes, well." Ms. Tribly reached for her water glass again. "Your schedule's so full and exciting. I wonder if you still enjoy the basics as far as cooking."

"Most people think of cooking as anything from a chore to a hobby. But as I've told Juliet—" His fingers twined possessively with hers "—food is a basic need. Like making love, it should appeal to all the senses. It should excite, arouse, satisfy." He slipped his thumb around to skim over her palm. "You remember, Juliet?"

She'd tried to forget, had told herself she could. Now with that light, insistent brush of thumb, he was bringing it all back. "Mr. Franconi is a strong believer in the sensuality of food. His unusual flair for bringing this out has made him one of the top chefs in the world."

"Grazie, mi amore," he murmured and brought her stiff hand to his lips.

She pressed her shoe down on the soft leather of his loafers and hoped she ground bones. "I think you, and your readers, will find that Mr. Franconi's book, *The Italian Way,* is a really stunning example of his technique, his style and his opinions, written in such a way that the average person following one of his recipes step-by-step can create something very special."

When their drinks were served, Juliet gave another tug on her hand thinking she might catch him off guard. She should have known better.

"To the new baby." He smiled over at Juliet. "It's always a pleasure to drink to life in all its stages."

Ms. Tribly sipped lightly at her margarita in a glass the size of a small birdbath. "Mr. Franconi, have you actually cooked and tasted every recipe that's in your book?"

"Of course." Carlo enjoyed the quick tang of his drink. There was a time for the sweet, and a time for the tart. His laugh came low and smooth as he looked at Juliet. "When something's mine, there's nothing I don't learn about it. A meal, Ms. Tribly, is like a love affair."

She broke the tip of her pencil and hurriedly dug out another. "A love affair?"

"Yes. It begins slowly, almost experimentally. Just a taste, to whet the appetite, to stir the anticipation. Then the flavor changes, perhaps something light, something cool to keep the senses stirred, but not overwhelmed. Then there's the spice, the meat, the variety. The senses are aroused; the mind is focused on the pleasure. It should be lingered over. But finally, there's dessert, the time of indulgence." When he smiled at Juliet, there was no mistaking his meaning. "It should be enjoyed slowly, savored, until the palate is satisfied and the body sated."

Ms. Tribly swallowed. "I'm going to buy a copy of your book for myself."

With a laugh, Carlo picked up his menu. "Suddenly, I have a huge appetite."

Juliet ordered a small fruit salad and picked at it for thirty minutes.

"I've really got to get back." After polishing off her meal and an apricot tart, Ms. Tribly gathered up her pad. "I can't tell you how much I've enjoyed this, Mr. Franconi. I'm never going to sit down to pot roast with the same attitude again."

Amused, Carlo rose. "It was a pleasure."

"I'll be glad to send a clipping of the article to your office, Ms. Trent."

"I'd appreciate that." Juliet offered her hand, surprised when the reporter held it an extra moment.

"You're a lucky woman. Enjoy the rest of your tour, Mr. Franconi."

"Arrivederci." He was still smiling when he sat down to finish his coffee.

"You put on a hell of a show, Franconi."

He'd been expecting the storm. Anticipating it. "Yes, I think I did my—what was it you called it? Ah yes, my spiel very well."

"It was more like a three-act play." With calm, deliberate movements, she signed the check. "But the next time, don't cast me unless you ask first."

"Cast you?"

His innocence was calculated to infuriate. He never

missed his mark. "You gave that woman the very clear impression that we were lovers."

"Juliet, I merely gave her the very correct impression that I respect and admire you. What she takes from that isn't my responsibility."

Juliet rose, placed her napkin very carefully on the table and picked up her briefcase. "Swine."

Carlo watched her walk out of the restaurant. No endearment could have pleased him more. When a woman called a man a swine, she wasn't indifferent. He was whistling when he walked out to join her. It pleased him even more to see her fumbling with the keys of the rented car parked at the curb. When a woman was indifferent, she didn't swear at inanimate objects.

"Would you like me to drive to the airport?"

"No." Swearing again, she jabbed the key into the lock. She'd control her temper. She would control it. Like hell. Slamming both hands down on the roof of the car, she stared at him. "Just what was the point of that little charade?"

Squisito, he thought briefly. Her eyes were a dangerous blade-sharp green. He'd discovered he preferred a woman with temper. "Charade?"

"All that hand-holding, those intimate looks you were giving me?"

"It's not a charade that I enjoy holding your hand, and that I find it impossible not to look at you."

She refused to argue with the car between them. In a few quick steps she was around the hood and toe-to-toe with him. "It was completely unprofessional."

"Yes. It was completely personal."

It was going to be difficult to argue at all if he turned everything she said to his own advantage.

"Don't ever do it again."

"Madonna." His voice was very mild, his move very calculated. Juliet found herself boxed in between him and the car. "Orders I'll take from you when they have to do with schedules and plane flights. When it comes to more personal things, I do as I choose."

It wasn't something she'd expected; that's why she lost her advantage. Juliet would tell herself that again and again—later. He had her by both shoulders and his eyes never left hers as he gave her a quick jerk. It wasn't the smooth, calculated seduction she'd have anticipated from him. It was rough, impulsive and enervating.

His mouth was on hers, all demand. His hands held her still, all power. She had no time to stiffen, to struggle or to think. He took her with him quickly, through a journey of heat and light. She didn't resist. Later, when she would tell herself she had, it would be a lie.

There were people on the sidewalk, cars in the street. Juliet and Carlo were unaware of everything. The heat of a Dallas afternoon soaked into the concrete beneath them. It blasted the air until it hummed. They were concerned with a fire of their own.

Her hands were at his waist, holding on, letting go. A car streaked by, country rock blasting through open windows. She never heard it. Though she'd refused wine at lunch, she tasted it on his tongue and was intoxicated.

Later, much later, he'd take time to think about what was happening. It wasn't the same. Part of him already knew and feared because it wasn't the same. Touching her was different than touching other women. Tasting her—lightly, deeply, teasingly—just tasting her was different than tasting other women. The feelings were new, though he'd have sworn he'd experienced all the feelings that any man was capable of.

He knew about sensations. He incorporated them in his work and in his life. But they'd never had this depth before. A man who found more and didn't reach for it was a fool.

He knew about intimacy. He expected, demanded it in everything he did. But it had never had this strength before.

New experiences were not to be refused, but explored and exploited. If he felt a small, nagging fear, he could ignore it. For now.

Later. They clung to each other and told themselves they'd think later. Time was unimportant after all. Now held all the meaning necessary.

He took his mouth from hers, but his hands held her still. It shocked him to realize they weren't quite steady. Women had made him ache. Women had made him burn. But no woman had ever made him tremble. "We need a place," he murmured. "Quiet, private. It's time to stop pretending this isn't real."

She wanted to nod, to simply put herself completely in his hands. Wasn't that the first step in losing control over your own life? "No, Carlo." Her voice wasn't as strong as she would have liked but she didn't back away. "We've got to stop mixing personal feelings with business. We've got just under two weeks to go on the road."

"I don't give a damn if it's two days or two years. I want to spend it making love with you."

She brought herself back enough to remember they

were standing on a public street in the middle of afternoon traffic. "Carlo, this isn't the time to discuss it."

"Now is always the time. Juliet—" He cupped her face in his hand. "It's not me you're fighting."

He didn't have to finish the thought. She was all too aware that the war was within herself. What she wanted, what was wise. What she needed, what was safe. The tug-of-war threatened to split her apart, and the two halves, put back together, would never equal the whole she understood.

"Carlo, we have a plane to catch."

He said something soft and pungent in Italian. "You'll talk to me."

"No." She lifted her hands to grip his forearms. "Not about this."

"Then we'll stay right here until you change your mind."

They could both be stubborn, and with stubbornness, they could both get nowhere. "We have a schedule."

"We have a great deal more than that."

"No, we don't." His brow lifted. "All right then, we can't. We have a plane to catch."

"We'll catch your plane, Juliet. But we'll talk in Houston."

"Carlo, don't push me into a corner."

"Who pushes?" he murmured. "Me or you?"

She didn't have an easy answer. "What I'll do is arrange for someone else to come out and finish the tour with you."

He only shook his head. "No, you won't. You're too ambitious. Leaving a tour in the middle wouldn't look good for you."

She set her teeth. He knew her too well already. "I'll get sick."

This time he smiled. "You're too proud. Running away isn't possible for you."

"It's not a matter of running." But of survival, she thought and quickly changed the phrase. "It's a matter of priorities."

He kissed her again, lightly. "Whose?"

"Carlo, we have business."

"Yes, of different sorts. One has nothing to do with the other."

"To me they do. Unlike you, I don't go to bed with everyone I'm attracted to."

Unoffended, he grinned. "You flatter me, *cara.*"

She could have sighed. How like him to make her want to laugh while she was still furious. "Purely unintentional."

"I like you when you bare your teeth."

"Then you're going to enjoy the next couple of weeks." She pushed his hands away. "It's a long ride to the airport, Carlo. Let's get going."

Amiable as ever, he pulled his door open. "You're the boss."

A foolish woman might've thought she'd won a victory.

Chapter 7

Juliet was an expert on budgeting time. It was her business every bit as much as promotion. So, if she could budget time, she could just as easily overbudget it when the circumstances warranted. If she did her job well enough, hustled fast enough, she could create a schedule so tight that there could be no time for talk that didn't directly deal with business. She counted on Houston to cooperate.

Juliet had worked with Big Bill Bowers before. He was a brash, warmhearted braggart who handled special events for Books, Etc., one of the biggest chains in the country. Big Bill had Texas sewed up and wasn't ashamed to say so. He was partial to long, exaggerated stories, ornate boots and cold beer.

Juliet liked him because he was sharp and tough and invariably made her job easier. On this trip, she blessed him because he was also long-winded and gregarious. He wouldn't give her or Carlo many private moments.

From the minute they arrived at Houston International, the six-foot-five, two-hundred-and-sixty-pound Texan made it his business to entertain. There was a crowd of people waiting at the end of the breezeway, some already packed together and chatting, but there was no overlooking Big Bill. You only had to look for a Brahma bull in a Stetson.

"Well now, there's little Juliet. Pretty as ever."

Juliet found herself caught in a good-natured, rib-cracking bear hug. "Bill." She tested her lungs gingerly as she drew away. "It's always good to be back in Houston. You look great."

"Just clean living, honey." He let out a boom of a laugh that turned heads. Juliet found her mood lifting automatically.

"Carlo Franconi, Bill Bowers. Be nice to him," she added with a grin. "He's not only big, he's the man who'll promote your books for the largest chain in the state."

"Then I'll be very nice." Carlo offered his hand and met an enormous, meaty paw.

"Glad you could make it." The same meaty hand gave Carlo a friendly pat on the back that could have felled a good-sized sapling. Juliet gave Carlo points for not taking a nosedive.

"It's good to be here" was all he said.

"Never been to Italy myself, but I'm partial to Eye-talian cooking. The wife makes a hell of a pot of spaghetti. Let me take that for you." Before Carlo could object, Bill had hefted his big leather case. Juliet couldn't prevent the smirk when Carlo glanced down at the case as though it were a small child boarding a school bus for the first time.

"Car's outside. We'll just pick up your bags and get going. Airports and hospitals, can't stand 'em." Bill started toward the terminal in his big, yard-long strides. "Hotel's all ready for you; I checked this morning."

Juliet managed to keep up though she still wore three-inch heels. "I knew I could depend on you, Bill. How's Betty?"

"Mean as ever," he said proudly of his wife. "With the kids up and gone, she's only got me to order around."

"But you're still crazy about her."

"A man gets used to mean after a while." He grinned, showing one prominent gold tooth. "No need to go by the hotel straight off. We'll show Carlo here what Houston's all about." As he walked he swung Carlo's case at his side.

"I'd like that." Diplomatically, Carlo moved closer to his side. "I could take that case…"

"No need for that. What you got in here, boy? Weighs like a steer."

"Tools," Juliet put in with an innocent smile. "Carlo's very temperamental."

"Man can't be too temperamental about his tools," Bill said with a nod. He tipped his hat at a young woman with a short skirt and lots of leg. "I've still got the same hammer my old man gave me when I was eight."

"I'm just as sentimental about my spatulas," Carlo murmured. But he hadn't, Juliet noted, missed the legs, either.

"You got a right." A look passed between the two

men that was essential male and pleased. Juliet decided it had more to do with long smooth thighs than tools. "Now, I figured you two must've had your fill of fancy restaurants and creamed chicken by now. Having a little barbecue over at my place. You can take off your shoes, let down your hair and eat real food."

Juliet had been to one of Bill's *little* barbecues before. It meant grilling a whole steer along with several chickens and the better part of a pig, then washing it all down with a couple hundred gallons of beer. It also meant she wouldn't see her hotel room for a good five hours. "Sounds great. Carlo, you haven't lived until you've tasted one of Bill's steaks grilled over mesquite."

Carlo slipped a hand over her elbow. "Then we should live first." The tone made her turn her head and meet the look. "Before we attend to business."

"That's the ticket." Bill stopped in front of the conveyor belt. "Just point 'em out and we'll haul 'em in."

They lived, mingling at Bill's little barbecue with another hundred guests. Music came from a seven-piece band that never seemed to tire. Laughter and splashing rose up from a pool separated from the patio by a spread of red flowering bushes that smelled of spice and heat. Above all was the scent of grilled meat, sauce and smoke. Juliet ate twice as much as she would normally have considered because her host filled her plate then kept an eagle eye on her.

It should have pleased her that Carlo was surrounded by a dozen or so Texas ladies in bathing suits and sundresses who had suddenly developed an avid interest in cooking. But, she thought nastily, most of them wouldn't know a stove from a can opener.

It should have pleased her that she had several men dancing attendance on her. She was barely able to keep the names and faces separate as she watched Carlo laugh with a six-foot brunette in two minuscule ribbons of cloth.

The music was loud, the air heavy and warm. Giving into necessity, Juliet had dug a pair of pleated shorts and a crop top out of her bag and changed. It occurred to her that it was the first time since the start of the tour that she'd been able to sit out in the sun, soak up rays and not have a pad and pencil in her hand.

Though the blonde beside her with the gleaming biceps was in danger of becoming both a bore and a nuisance, she willed herself to enjoy the moment.

It was the first time Carlo had seen her in anything other than her very proper suits. He'd already concluded, by the way she walked, that her legs were longer than one might think from her height. He hadn't been wrong. They seemed to start at her waist and continued down, smooth, slim and New York pale. The statuesque brunette beside him might not have existed for all the attention he paid her.

It wasn't like him to focus on a woman yards away when there was one right beside him. Carlo knew it, but not what to do about it. The woman beside him smelled of heat and musk—heavy and seductive. It made him think that Juliet's scent was lighter, but held just as much punch.

She had no trouble relaxing with other men. Carlo tipped back a beer as he watched her fold those long legs under her and laugh with the two men sitting on either side of her. She didn't stiffen when the young, muscle-bound hunk on her left put his hand on her shoulder and leaned closer.

It wasn't like him to be jealous. As emotional as he was, Carlo had never experienced that particular sensation. He'd also felt that a woman had just as much right to flirt and experiment as he did. He found that particular rule didn't apply to Juliet. If she let that slick-skinned, weight-lifting *buffone* put his hand on her again…

He didn't have time to finish the thought. Juliet laughed again, set aside her plate and rose. Carlo couldn't hear whatever she'd said to the man beside her, but she strolled into the sprawling ranch house. Moments later, the burnished, bare-chested man rose and followed her.

"Maledetto!"

"What?" The brunette stopped in the middle of what she'd thought was an intimate conversation.

Carlo barely spared her a glance. *"Scusi."* Muttering, he strode off in the direction Juliet had taken. There was murder in his eye.

Fed up with fending off the attentions of Big Bill's hotshot young neighbor, Juliet slipped into the house through the kitchen. Her mood might have been foul, but she congratulated herself on keeping her head. She hadn't taken a chunk out of the free-handed, self-appointed Adonis. She hadn't snarled out loud even once in Carlo's direction.

Attending to business always helped steady her temper. With a check of her watch, Juliet decided she could get one collect call through to her assistant at home. She'd no more than picked up the receiver from the kitchen wall phone than she was lifted off her feet.

"Ain't much to you. But it sure is a pleasure to look at what there is."

She barely suppressed the urge to come back with her elbow. "Tim." She managed to keep her voice pleasant while she thought how unfortunate it was that most of his muscle was from the neck up. "You're going to have to put me down so I can make my call."

"It's a party, sweetheart." Shifting her around with a flex of muscle, he set her on the counter. "No need to go calling anybody when you've got me around."

"You know what I think?" Juliet gauged that she could give him a quick kick below the belt, but tapped his shoulder instead. After all, he was Bill's neighbor. "I think you should get back out to the party before all the ladies miss you."

"Got a better idea." He leaned forward, boxing her in with a hand on each side. His teeth gleamed in the style of the best toothpaste ads. "Why don't you and I go have a little party of our own? I imagine you New York ladies know how to have fun."

If she hadn't considered him such a jerk, she'd have been insulted for women in general and New York in particular. Patiently, Juliet considered the source. "We New York ladies," she said calmly, "know how to say no. Now back off, Tim."

"Come on, Juliet." He hooked a finger in the neck of her top. "I've got a nice big water bed down the street."

She put a hand on his wrist. Neighbor or not, she was going to belt him. "Why don't you go take a dive."

He only grinned as his hand slid up her leg. "Just what I had in mind."

"Excuse me." Carlo's voice was soft as a snake from the doorway. "If you don't find something else to do with your hands quickly, you might lose the use of them."

"Carlo." Her voice was sharp, but not with relief. She wasn't in the mood for a knight-in-armor rescue.

"The lady and I're having a private conversation." Tim flexed his pectorals. "Take off."

With his thumbs hooked in his pockets, Carlo strolled over. Juliet noted he looked as furious as he had over the canned basil. In that mood, there was no telling what he'd do. She swore, let out a breath and tried to avoid a scene. "Why don't we all go outside?"

"Excellent." Carlo held out a hand to help her down. Before she could reach for it, Tim blocked her way.

"You go outside, buddy. Juliet and I haven't finished talking."

Carlo inclined his head then shifted his gaze to Juliet. "Have you finished talking?"

"Yes." She'd have slid off the counter, but that would have put her on top of Tim's shoulders. Frustrated, she sat where she was.

"Apparently Juliet is finished." Carlo's smile was all amiability, but his eyes were flat and cold. "You seem to be blocking her way."

"I told you to take off." Big and annoyed, he grabbed Carlo by the lapels.

"Cut it out, both of you." With a vivid picture of Carlo bleeding from the nose and mouth, Juliet grabbed a cookie jar shaped like a ten-gallon hat. Before she could use it, Tim grunted and bent over from the waist. As he gasped, clutching his stomach, Juliet only stared.

"You can put that down now," Carlo said mildly. "It's time we left." When she didn't move, he took the jar himself, set it aside, then lifted her from the counter. "You'll excuse us," he said pleasantly to the groaning Tim, then led Juliet outside.

"What did you do?"

"What was necessary."

Juliet looked back toward the kitchen door. If she hadn't seen it for herself… "You hit him."

"Not very hard." Carlo nodded to a group of sunbathers. "All his muscle is in his chest and his brain."

"But—" She looked down at Carlo's hands. They were lean-fingered and elegant with the flash of a diamond on the pinky. Not hands one associated with self-defense. "He was awfully big."

Carlo lifted a brow as he took his sunglasses back out of his pocket. "Big isn't always an advantage. The neighborhood where I grew up was an education. Are you ready to leave?"

No, his voice wasn't pleasant, she realized. It was cold. Ice cold. Instinctively hers mirrored it. "I suppose I should thank you."

"Unless of course you enjoyed being pawed. Perhaps Tim was just acting on the signals you were sending out."

Juliet stopped in her tracks. "What signals?"

"The ones women send out when they want to be pursued."

Thinking she could bring her temper to order, she

gave herself a moment. It didn't work. "He might have been bigger than you," she said between her teeth. "But I think you're just as much of an ass. You're very much alike."

The lenses of his glasses were smoky, but she saw his eyes narrow. "You compare what's between us with what happened in there?"

"I'm saying some men don't take no for an answer graciously. You might have a smoother style, Carlo, but you're after the same thing, whether it's a roll in the hay or a cruise on a water bed."

He dropped his hand from her arm, then very deliberately tucked both in his pockets. "If I've mistaken your feelings, Juliet, I apologize. I'm not a man who finds it necessary or pleasurable to pressure a woman. Do you wish to leave or stay?"

She felt a great deal of pressure—in her throat, behind her eyes. She couldn't afford the luxury of giving into it. "I'd like to get to the hotel. I still have some work to do tonight."

"Fine." He left her there to find their host.

Three hours later, Juliet admitted working was impossible. She'd tried all the tricks she knew to relax. A half hour in a hot tub, quiet music on the radio while she watched the sun set from her hotel window. When relaxing failed, she went over the Houston schedule twice. They'd be running from 7:00 A.M. to 5:00 P.M., almost nonstop. Their flight to Chicago took off at 6:00.

There'd be no time to discuss, think or worry about anything that had happened within the last twenty-four hours. That's what she wanted. Yet when she tried to work on the two-day Chicago stand, she couldn't. All she could do was think about the man a few steps across the hall.

She hadn't realized he could be so cold. He was always so full of warmth, of life. True, he was often infuriating, but he infuriated with verve. Now, he'd left her in a vacuum.

No. Tossing her notebook aside, Juliet dropped her chin in her hand. No, she'd put herself there. Maybe she could have stood it if she'd been right. She'd been dead wrong. She hadn't sent any signals to the idiot Tim, and Carlo's opinion on that still made her steam, but... But she hadn't even thanked him for helping her when, whether she liked to admit it or not, she'd needed help. It didn't sit well with her to be in debt.

With a shrug, she rose from the table and began to pace the room. It might be better all around if they finished off the tour with him cold and distant. There'd certainly be fewer personal problems that way because there'd be nothing personal between them. There'd be no edge to their relationship because they wouldn't have a relationship. Logically, this little incident was probably the best thing that could have happened. It hardly mattered if she'd been right or wrong as long as the result was workable.

She took a glimpse around the small, tidy, impersonal room where she'd spend little more than eight hours, most of it asleep.

No, she couldn't stand it.

Giving in, Juliet stuck her room key in the pocket of her robe.

* * *

Women had made him furious before. Carlo counted on it to keep life from becoming too tame. Women had frustrated him before. Without frustrations, how could you fully appreciate success?

But hurt. That was something no woman had ever done to him before. He'd never considered the possibility. Frustration, fury, passion, laughter, shouting. No man who'd known so many women—mother, sisters, lovers—expected a relationship without them. Pain was a different matter.

Pain was an intimate emotion. More personal than passion, more elemental than anger. When it went deep, it found places inside you that should have been left alone.

It had never mattered to him to be considered a rogue, a rake, a playboy—whatever term was being used for a man who appreciated women. Affairs came and went, as affairs were supposed to. They lasted no longer than the passion that conceived them. He was a careful man, a caring man. A lover became a friend as desire waned. There might be spats and hard words during the storm of an affair, but he'd never ended one that way.

It occurred to him that he'd had more spats, more hard words with Juliet than with any other woman. Yet they'd never been lovers. Nor would they be. After pouring a glass of wine, he sat back in a deep chair and closed his eyes. He wanted no woman who compared him with a muscle-bound idiot, who confused passion for lust. He wanted no woman who compared the beauty of lovemaking to—what was it?—a cruise on a water bed. *Dio!*

He wanted no woman who could make him ache so—in the middle of the night, in the middle of the day. He wanted no woman who could bring him pain with a few harsh words.

God, he wanted Juliet.

He heard the knock on the door and frowned. By the time he'd set his glass aside and stood, it came again.

If Juliet hadn't been so nervous, she might have thought of something witty to say about the short black robe Carlo wore with two pink flamingos twining up one side. As it was, she stood in her own robe and bare feet with her fingers linked together.

"I'm sorry," she said when he opened the door.

He stepped back. "Come in, Juliet."

"I had to apologize." She let out a deep breath as she walked into the room. "I was awful to you this afternoon, and you'd helped me out of a very tricky situation with a minimum of fuss. I was angry when you insinuated that I'd led that—that idiot on in some way. I had a right to be." She folded her arms under her chest and paced the room. "It was an uncalled for remark, and insulting. Even if by the remotest possibility it had been true, you had no right to talk. After all, you were basking in your own harem."

"Harem?" Carlo poured another glass of wine and offered it.

"With that amazon of a brunette leading the pack." She sipped, gestured with the glass and sipped again. "Everywhere we go, you've got half a dozen women nipping at your ankles, but do I say a word?"

"Well, you—"

"And once, just once, I have a problem with some creep with an overactive libido, and you assume I asked for it. I thought that kind of double standard was outdated even in Italy."

Had he ever known a woman who could change his moods so quickly? Thinking it over, and finding it to his taste, Carlo studied his wine. "Juliet, did you come here to apologize, or demand that I do so?"

She scowled at him. "I don't know why I came, but obviously it was a mistake."

"Wait." He held up a hand before she could storm out again. "Perhaps it would be wise if I simply accepted the apology you came in with."

Juliet sent him a killing look. "You can take the apology I came in with and—"

"And offer you one of my own," he finished. "Then we'll be even."

"I didn't encourage him," she murmured. And pouted. He'd never seen that sulky, utterly feminine look on her face before. It did several interesting things to his system.

"And I'm not looking for the same thing he was." He came to her then, close enough to touch. "But very much more."

"Maybe I know that," she whispered, but took a step away. "Maybe I'd like to believe it. I don't understand affairs, Carlo." With a little laugh, she dragged her hand through her hair and turned away. "I should; my father had plenty of them. Discreet," she added with a lingering taste of bitterness. "My mother could always turn a blind eye as long as they were discreet."

He understood such things, had seen them among both friends and relatives, so he understood the scars and disillusionments that could be left. "Juliet, you're not your mother."

"No." She turned back, head up. "No, I've worked long and hard to be certain I'm not. She's a lovely, intelligent woman who gave up her career, her self-esteem, her independence to be no more than a glorified housekeeper because my father wanted it. He didn't want a wife of his to work. A wife of his," she repeated. "What a phrase. Her job was to take care of him. That meant having dinner on the table at six o'clock every night, and his shirts folded in his drawer. He—damn, he's a good father, attentive, considerate. He simply doesn't believe a man should shout at a woman or a girl. As a husband, he'd never forget a birthday, an anniversary. He's always seen to it that she was provided for in the best material fashion, but he dictated my mother's lifestyle. While he was about it, he enjoyed a very discreet string of women."

"Why does your mother stay his wife?"

"I asked her that a few years ago, before I moved away to New York. She loves him." Juliet stared into her wine. "That's reason enough for her."

"Would you rather she'd have left him?"

"I'd rather she'd have been what she could be. What she might've been."

"The choice was hers, Juliet. Just as your life is yours."

"I don't want to ever be bound to anyone, *anyone* who could humiliate me that way." She lifted her head again. "I won't put myself in my mother's position. Not for anyone."

"Do you see all relationships as being so imbalanced?"

With a shrug, she drank again. "I suppose I haven't seen so many of them."

For a moment he was silent. Carlo understood fidelity, the need for it, and the lack of it. "Perhaps we have something in common. I don't remember my father well, I saw him little. He, too, was unfaithful to my mother."

She looked over at him, but he didn't see any surprise in her face. It was as though she expected such things. "But he committed his adultery with the sea. For months he'd be gone, while she raised us, worked, waited. When he'd come home, she'd welcome him. Then he'd go again, unable to resist. When he died, she mourned. She loved him, and made her choice."

"It's not fair, is it?"

"No. Did you think love was?"

"It's not something I want."

He remembered once another woman, a friend, telling him the same thing when she was in turmoil. "We all want love, Juliet."

"No." She shook her head with the confidence born of desperation. "No, affection, respect, admiration, but not love. It steals something from you."

He looked at her as she stood in the path of the lamplight. "Perhaps it does," he murmured. "But until we love, we can't be sure we needed what was lost."

"Maybe it's easier for you to say that, to think that. You've had many lovers."

It should have amused him. Instead, it seemed to

accent a void he hadn't been aware of. "Yes. But I've never been in love. I have a friend—" again he thought of Summer "—once she told me love was a merry-go-round. Maybe she knew best."

Juliet pressed her lips together. "And an affair?"

Something in her voice had him looking over. For the second time he went to her, but slowly. "Perhaps it's just one ride on the carousel."

Because her fingers weren't steady, Juliet set down the glass. "We understand each other."

"In some ways."

"Carlo—" She hesitated, then admitted the decision had already been made before she crossed the hall. "Carlo, I've never taken much time for carousels, but I do want you."

How should he handle her? Odd, he'd never had to think things through so carefully before. With some women, he'd have been flamboyant, sweeping her up, carrying her off. With another he might have been impulsive, tumbling with her to the carpet. But nothing he'd ever done seemed as important as the first time with Juliet.

Words for a woman had always come easily to him. The right phrase, the right tone had always come as naturally as breathing. He could think of nothing. Even a murmur might spoil the simplicity of what she'd said to him and how she'd said it. So he didn't speak.

He kissed her where they stood, not with the raging passion he knew she could draw from him, not with the hesitation she sometimes made him feel. He kissed her with the truth and the knowledge that longtime lovers often experience. They came to each other with separate needs, separate attitudes, but with this, they locked out the past. Tonight was for the new, and for renewing.

She'd expected the words, the flash and style that seemed so much a part of him. Perhaps she'd even expected something of triumph. Again, he gave her the different and the fresh with no more than the touch of mouth to mouth.

The thought came to her, then was discounted, that he was no more certain of his ground than she. Then he held out his hand. Juliet put hers in it. Together they walked to the bedroom.

If he'd set the scene for a night of romance, Carlo would've added flowers with a touch of spice, music with the throb of passion. He'd have given her the warmth of candlelight and the fun of champagne. Tonight, with Juliet, there was only silence and moonlight. The maid had turned down the bed and left the drapes wide. White light filtered through shadows and onto white sheets.

Standing by the bed, he kissed her palms, one by one. They were cool and carried a hint of her scent. At her wrist her pulse throbbed. Slowly, watching her, he loosened the tie of her robe. With his eyes still on hers, he brought his hands to her shoulders and slipped the material aside. It fell silently to pool at her feet.

He didn't touch her, nor did he yet look at anything but her face. Through nerves, through needs, something like comfort began to move through her. Her lips curved, just slightly, as she reached for the tie of his robe and drew the knot. With her hands light and sure on his shoulders, she pushed the silk aside.

They were both vulnerable, to their needs, to each

other. The light was thin and white and washed with shadows. No other illumination was needed this first time that they looked at each other.

He was lean but not thin. She was slender but soft. Her skin seemed only more pale when he touched her. Her hand seemed only more delicate when she touched him.

They came together slowly. There was no need to rush.

The mattress gave, the sheets rustled. Quietly. Side by side they lay, giving themselves time—all the time needed to discover what pleasures could come from the taste of mouth to mouth, the touch of flesh to flesh.

Should she have known it would be like this? So easy. Inevitable. Her skin was warm, so warm wherever he brushed it. His lips demanded, they took, but with such patience. He loved her gently, slowly, as though it were her first time. As she drifted deeper, Juliet thought dimly that perhaps it was.

Innocence. He felt it from her, not physical, but emotional. Somehow, incredibly, he discovered it was the same for himself. No matter how many had come before, for either of them, they came to each other now in innocence.

Her hands didn't hesitate as they moved over him, but stroked as though she were blind and could only gain her own picture through other senses. He smelled of a shower, water and soap, but he tasted richer, of wine. Then he spoke for the first time, only her name. It was to her more moving, more poetic than any endearment.

Her body moved with his, in rhythm, keeping pace.

She seemed to know, somehow, where he would touch her just before she felt his fingers trace, his palms press. Then his lips began a long, luxurious journey she hoped would never end.

She was so small. Why had he never noticed before how small she was? It was easy to forget her strength, her control, her stamina. He could give her tenderness and wait for the passion.

The line of her neck was slender and so white in the moonlight. Her scent was trapped there, at her throat. Intensified. Arousing. He could linger there while blood heated. His and hers.

He slid his tongue over the subtle curve of her breast to find the peak. When he drew it into his mouth, she moaned his name, giving them both a long, slow nudge to the edge.

But there was more to taste, more to touch. Passion, when heated, makes a mockery of control. Sounds slipped into the room—a catch of breath, a sigh, a moan—all pleasure. Their scents began to mix together—a lover's fragrance. In the moonlight, they were one form. The sheets were hot, twisted. When with tongue and fingertips he drove her over the first peak, Juliet gripped the tousled sheets as her body arched and shuddered with a torrent of sensations.

While she was still weak, still gasping, he slipped into her.

His head was spinning—a deliciously foreign sensation to him. He wanted to bury himself in her, but he wanted to see her. Her eyes were shut; her lips just parted as the breath hurried in and out. She moved with him, slowly, then faster, still faster until her fingers dug into his shoulders.

On a cry of pleasure, her eyes flew open. Looking into them, he saw the dark, astonished excitement he'd wanted to give her.

At last, giving in to the rushing need of his own body, he closed his mouth over hers and let himself go.

Chapter 8

Were there others who understood true passion? Wrapped in Carlo, absorbing and absorbed by Carlo, Juliet knew she hadn't until moments ago. Should it make you weak? She felt weak, but not empty.

Should she feel regret? Yes, logically she should. She'd given more of herself than she'd intended, shared more than she'd imagined, risked more than she should have dared. But she had no regrets. Perhaps later she'd make her list of the whys and why nots. For now, she wanted only to enjoy the soft afterglow of loving.

"You're quiet." His breath whispered across her temple, followed by his lips.

She smiled a little, content to let her eyes close. "So are you."

Nuzzling his cheek against her hair, he looked over to the slant of moonlight through the window. He wasn't sure which words to use. He'd never felt quite like this before with any woman. He'd never expected to. How could he tell her that and expect to be believed? He was having a hard time believing it himself. And yet... perhaps truth was the hardest thing to put into words.

"You feel very small when I hold you like this," he murmured. "It makes me want to hold you like this for a long, long time."

"I like having you hold me." The admission was much easier to make than she'd thought. With a little laugh, she turned her head so that she could see his face. "I like it very much."

"Then you won't object if I go on holding you for the next few hours."

She kissed his chin. "The next few minutes," she corrected. "I have to get back to my room."

"You don't like my bed?"

She stretched and cuddled and thought how wonderful it would be never to move from that one spot. "I think I'm crazy about it, but I've got a little work to do before I call it a night, then I have to be up by six-thirty, and—"

"You work too much." He cut her off, then leaned over her to pick up the phone. "You can get up in the morning just as easily from my bed as yours."

Finding she liked the way his body pressed into hers, she prepared to be convinced. "Maybe. What're you doing?"

"Shh. Yes, this is Franconi in 922. I'd like a wake-up call for six." He replaced the phone and rolled, pulling her on top of him. "There now, everything is taken care of. The phone will ring at dawn and wake us up."

"It certainly will." Juliet folded her hands over his chest and rested her chin on them. "But you told them to call at six. We don't have to get up until six-thirty."

"Yes." He slid his hands down low over her back. "So we have a half hour to—ah—wake up."

With a laugh, she pressed her lips to his shoulder. This once, she told herself, just this once, she'd let someone else do the planning. "Very practical. Do you think we might take a half hour or so to—ah—go to sleep?"

"My thoughts exactly."

When the phone did ring, Juliet merely groaned and slid down under the sheets. For the second time, she found herself buried under Carlo as he rolled over to answer it. Without complaint, she lay still, hoping the ringing of the phone had been part of a dream.

"Come now, Juliet." Shifting most of his weight from her, Carlo began to nibble on her shoulder. "You're playing mole."

She murmured in drowsy excitement as he slid his hand down to her hip. "Mole? I don't have a mole."

"Playing mole." She was so warm and soft and pliant. He'd known she would be. Mornings were made for lazy delights and waking her was a pleasure just begun.

Juliet stretched under the stroke and caress of his hands. Mornings were for a quick shower and a hasty cup of coffee. She'd never known they could be luxurious. "Playing mole?"

"An American expression." The skin over her rib cage was soft as butter. He thought there was no better time to taste it. "You pretend to be dead."

Because her mind was clouded with sleep, her system already churning with passion, it took a moment. "Possum."

"Prego?"

"Playing possum," she repeated and, guided by his hands, shifted. "A mole's different."

"So, they're both little animals."

She opened one eye. His hair was rumpled around his face, his chin darkened with a night's growth of beard. But when he smiled he looked as though he'd been awake for hours. He looked, she admitted, absolutely wonderful.

"You want an animal?" With a sudden burst of energy, she rolled on top of him. Her hands were quick, her mouth avid. In seconds, she'd taken his breath away.

She'd never been aggressive, but found the low, surprised moan and the fast pump of his heart to her liking. Her body reacted like lightning. She didn't mind that his hands weren't as gentle, as patient as they'd been the night before. This new desperation thrilled her.

He was Franconi, known for his wide range of expertise in the kitchen and the bedroom. But she was making him wild and helpless at the same time. With a laugh, she pressed her mouth to his, letting her tongue find all the dark, lavish tastes. When he tried to shift her, to take her because the need had grown too quickly to control, she evaded. His breathless curse whispered into her mouth.

He never lost finesse with a woman. Passion, his passion, had always been melded with style. Now, as she took her frenzied journey over him, he had no style, only needs. He'd never been a man to rush. When he cooked, he went slowly, step-by-step. Enjoy, experience, experiment. He made love the same way. Such things were meant to be savored, to be appreciated by each of the five senses.

It wasn't possible to savor when you were driven beyond the civilized. When your senses were whirling and tangled, it wasn't possible to separate them. Being driven was something new for him, something intoxicating. No, he wouldn't fight it, but pull her with him.

Rough and urgent, he grabbed her hips. Within moments, they were both beyond thought, beyond reason....

His breath was still unsteady, but he held her close and tight. Whatever she'd done, or was doing to him, he didn't want to lose it. The thought flickered briefly that he didn't want to lose her. Carlo pushed it aside. It was a dangerous thought. They had now. It was much wiser to concentrate on that.

"I have to go." Though she wanted nothing more than to curl up against him, Juliet made herself shift away. "We have to be downstairs at checkout in forty minutes."

"To meet Big Bill."

"That's right." Juliet reached onto the floor for her robe, slipping it onto her arms before she stood up. Carlo's lips trembled at the way she turned her back to him to tie it. It was rather endearing to see the unconscious modesty from a woman who'd just exploited every inch of his body. "You don't know how grateful I am that Bill volunteered to play chauffeur. The last thing I want to do is fight the freeway system in this town. I've had to do it before, and it's not a pretty sight."

"I could drive," he murmured, enjoying the way the rich green silk reached the top of her thighs.

"Staying alive is another reason I'm grateful for Bill. I'll call and have a bellman come up for the bags in—thirty-five minutes. Be sure—"

"You check everything because we won't be coming back," he finished. "Juliet, haven't I proven my competency yet?"

"Just a friendly reminder." She checked her watch before she remembered she wasn't wearing it. "The TV spot should be a breeze. Jacky Torrence hosts. It's a jovial sort of show that goes after the fast, funny story rather than nuts and bolts."

"Hmm." He rose, stretching. The publicist was back, he noted with a half smile, but as he reached down for his own robe, he noticed that she'd broken off. Lifting his head, he looked up at her.

Good God, he was beautiful. It was all she could think. Schedules, planning, points of information all went out of her head. In the early morning sun, his skin was more gold than brown, smooth and tight over his rib cage, nipped in at the waist to a narrow line of hip. Letting out a shaky breath, she took a step back.

"I'd better go," she managed. "We can run through today's schedule on the way to the studio."

It pleased him enormously to understand what had broken her concentration. He held the robe loosely in one hand as he took a step closer. "Perhaps we'll get bumped."

"Bite your tongue." Aiming for a light tone, she succeeded with a whisper. "That's an interesting robe."

The tone of her voice was a springboard to an arousal

already begun. "You like the flamingos? My mother has a sense of humor." But he didn't put it on as he stepped closer.

"Carlo, stay right where you are. I mean it." She held up a hand as she walked backward to the doorway.

He grinned, and kept on grinning after he heard the click of the hallway door.

Between Juliet cracking the whip and Bill piloting, their Houston business went like clockwork. TV, radio and print, the media was responsive and energetic. The midafternoon autograph party turned out to be a party in the true sense of the word and was a smashing success. Juliet found herself a spot in a storeroom and ripped open the oversized envelope from her office that had been delivered to the hotel. Settling back, she began to go through the clippings her assistant had air expressed.

L.A. was excellent, as she'd expected. Upbeat and enthusiastic. San Diego might've tried for a little more depth, but they'd given him page one of the *Food* section in one spread and a below-the-fold in the *Style* section in another. No complaints. Portland and Seattle listed a recipe apiece and raved shamelessly. Juliet could've rubbed her hands together with glee if she hadn't been drinking coffee. Then she hit Denver.

Coffee sloshed out of the cup and onto her hand.

"Damn!" Fumbling in her briefcase, she found three crumpled tissues and began to mop up. A gossip column. Who'd have thought it? She gave herself a moment to think then relaxed. Publicity was publicity, after all. And the truth of the matter was, Franconi was gossip. Looking at it logically, the more times his name was in print, the more successful the tour. Resolved, Juliet began to read.

She nodded absently as she skimmed the first paragraph. Chatty, shallow, but certainly not offensive. A lot of people who might not glance at the food or cooking sections would give the gossip columns a working over. All in all, it was probably an excellent break. Then she read the second paragraph.

Juliet was up out of her folding chair. This time the coffee that dripped onto the floor went unnoticed. Her expression changed from surprised astonishment to fury in a matter of seconds. In the same amount of time, she stuffed the clippings back into their envelope. It wasn't easy, but she gave herself five minutes for control before she walked back into the main store.

The schedule called for another fifteen minutes, but Carlo had more than twenty people in line, and that many again just milling around. Fifteen minutes would have to be stretched to thirty. Grinding her teeth, Juliet stalked over to Bill.

"There you are." Friendly as always, he threw his arm over her shoulder and squeezed. "Going great guns out here. Old Carlo knows how to twinkle to the ladies without setting the men off. Damn clever sonofabitch."

"I couldn't have said it better myself." Her knuckles were white on the strap of her briefcase. "Bill, is there a phone I can use? I have to call the office."

"No problem at all. Y'all just come on back with me." He led her through Psychology, into Westerns and around Romances to a door marked Private. "You just help yourself," he invited and showed her into a room with a cluttered metal desk, a goosenecked lamp and stacks upon stacks of books. Juliet headed straight for the phone.

"Thanks, Bill." She didn't even wait until the door closed before she started dialing. "Deborah Mortimor, please," she said to the answering switchboard. Tapping her foot, Juliet waited.

"Ms. Mortimor."

"Deb, it's Juliet."

"Hi. I've been waiting for you to call in. Looks like we've got a strong nibble with the *Times* when you come back to New York. I just—"

"Later." Juliet reached into her briefcase for a roll of antacids. "I got the clippings today."

"Great, aren't they?"

"Oh sure. They're just dandy."

"Uh-huh." Deb waited only a beat. "It's the little number in Denver, isn't it?"

She gave the rolling chair a quick kick. "Of course it is."

"Sit down, Juliet." Deb didn't have to see to know her boss was pacing.

"Sit down? I'm tempted to fly back to Denver and ring Chatty Cathy's neck."

"Killing columnists isn't good for PR, Juliet."

"It was garbage."

"No, no, it wasn't that bad. Trash maybe, but not garbage."

She struggled for control and managed to get a very slippery rein on her temper. Popping the first antacid into her mouth, she crunched down. "Don't be cute, Deb. I didn't like the insinuations about Carlo and me. *Carlo Franconi's lovely American traveling compan-*

ion," she quoted between her teeth. "Traveling companion. It makes me sound as though I'm just along for the ride. And then—"

"I read it," Deb interrupted. "So did Hal," she added, referring to the head of publicity.

Juliet closed her eyes a moment. "And?"

"Well, he went through about six different reactions. In the end, he decided a few comments like that were bound to come up and only added to Franconi's—well, mystique might be the best term."

"I see." Her jaw clenched, her fingers tight around the little roll of stomach pills. "That's fine then, isn't it? I'm just thrilled to add to a client's mystique."

"Now, Juliet—"

"Look, just tell dear old Hal that Houston went perfectly." She was definitely going to need two pills. Juliet popped another out of the roll with her thumb. "I don't even want you to mention to him that I called about this—this tripe in Denver."

"Whatever you say."

Taking a pen, she sat down and made space on the desk. "Now, give me what you have with the *Times*."

A half hour later, Juliet was just finishing up her last call when Carlo poked his head in the office. Seeing she was on the phone, he rolled his eyes, closed the door and leaned against it. His brow lifted when he spotted the half-eaten roll of antacids.

"Yes, thank you, Ed, Mr. Franconi will bring all the necessary ingredients and be in the studio at 8:00. Yes." She laughed, though her foot was tapping out a rhythm on the floor. "It's absolutely delicious. Guaranteed. See you in two days."

When she hung up the receiver, Carlo stepped forward. "You didn't come to save me."

She gave him a long, slow look. "You seemed to be handling the situation without me."

He knew the tone, and the expression. Now all he had to do was find the reason for them. Strolling over, he picked up the roll of pills. "You're much too young to need these."

"I've never heard that ulcers had an age barrier."

His brows drew together as he sat on the edge of the desk. "Juliet, if I believed you had an ulcer, I'd pack you off to my home in Rome and keep you in bed on bland foods for the next month. Now…" He slipped the roll into his pocket. "What problem is there?"

"Several," she said briskly as she began to gather up her notes. "But they're fairly well smoothed out now. We'll need to go shopping again in Chicago for that chicken dish you'd planned to cook. So, if you've finished up here, we can just—"

"No." He put a hand on her shoulder and held her in the chair. "We're not finished. Shopping for chicken in Chicago isn't what had you reaching for pills. What?"

The best defense was always ice. Her voice chilled. "Carlo, I've been very busy."

"You think after two weeks I don't know you?" Impatient, he gave her a little shake. "You dig in that briefcase for your aspirin or your little mints only when you feel too much pressure. I don't like to see it."

"It comes with the territory." She tried to shrug off his hand and failed. "Carlo, we've got to get to the airport."

"We have more than enough time. Tell me what's wrong."

"All right then." In two sharp moves, she pulled the clipping out of her case and pushed it into his hands.

"What's this?" He skimmed it first without really reading it. "One of those little columns about who is seen with whom and what they wear while they're seen?"

"More or less."

"Ah." As he began to read from the top, he nodded. "And you were seen with me."

Closing her notebook, she slipped it neatly into her briefcase. Twice she reminded herself that losing her temper would accomplish nothing. "As your publicist, that could hardly be avoided."

Because he'd come to expect logic from her, he only nodded again. "But you feel this intimates something else."

"It *says* something else," she tossed back. "Something that isn't true."

"It calls you my traveling companion." He glanced up, knowing that wouldn't sit well with her. "It's perhaps not the full story, but not untrue. Does it upset you to be known as my companion?"

She didn't want him to be reasonable. She had no intention of emulating him. "When companion takes on this shade of meaning, it isn't professional or innocent. I'm not here to have my name linked with you this way, Carlo."

"In what way, Juliet?"

"It gives my name and goes on to say that I'm never out of arm's length, that I guard you as though you were my own personal property. And that you—"

"That I kiss your hand in public restaurants as though

I couldn't wait for privacy," Carlo read at a glance. "So? What difference does it make what it says here?"

She dragged both hands through her hair. "Carlo, I'm here, with you, to do a job. This clipping came through my office, through my supervisor. Don't you know something like this could ruin my credibility?"

"No," he said simply enough. "This is no more than gossip. Your supervisor, he's upset by this?"

She laughed, but it had little to do with humor. "No, actually, it seems he's decided it's just fine. Good for your image."

"Well, then?"

"I don't want to be good for your image," she threw back with such passion, it shocked both of them. "I won't be one of the dozens of names and faces linked with you."

"So," he murmured. "Now, we push away to the truth. You're angry with me, for this." He set the clipping down. "You're angry because there's more truth in it now than there was when it was written."

"I don't want to be on anyone's list, Carlo." Her voice had lowered, calmed. She dug balled fists into the pockets of her skirt. "Not yours, not anyone's. I haven't come this far in my life to let that happen now."

He stood, wondering if she understood how insulting her words were. No, she'd see them as facts, not as darts. "I haven't put you on a list. If you have one in your own mind, it has nothing to do with me."

"A few weeks ago it was the French actress, a month before that a widowed countess."

He didn't shout, but it was only force of will that kept his voice even. "I never pretended you were the first woman in my bed. I never expected I was the first man in yours."

"That's entirely different."

"Ah, now you find the double standard convenient." He picked up the clipping, balled it in his fist then dropped it into the wastebasket. "I've no patience for this, Juliet."

He was to the door again before she spoke. "Carlo, wait." With a polite veneer stretched thinly over fury he turned. "Damn." Hands still in her pockets, she paced from one stack of books to the other. "I never intended to take this out on you. It's totally out of line and I'm sorry, really. You might guess I'm not thinking very clearly right now."

"So it would seem."

Juliet let out a sigh, knowing she observed the cutting edge of his voice. "I don't know how to explain, except to say that my career's very important to me."

"I understand that."

"But it's no more important to me than my privacy. I don't want my personal life discussed around the office water cooler."

"People talk, Juliet. It's natural and it's meaningless."

"I can't brush it off the way you do." She picked up her briefcase by the strap then set it down again. "I'm used to staying in the background. I set things up, handle the details, do the legwork, and someone else's picture gets in the paper. That's the way I want it."

"You don't always get what you want." With his thumbs hooked in his pockets, he leaned back against the door and watched her. "Your anger goes deeper than a few lines in a paper people will have forgotten tomorrow."

She closed her eyes a moment, then turned back to him. "All right, yes, but it's not a matter of being angry. Carlo, I've put myself in a delicate position with you."

Carefully, he weighed the phrase, tested it, judged it. "Delicate position?"

"Please, don't misunderstand. I'm here, with you, because of my job. It's very important to me that that's handled in the best, the most professional manner I can manage. What's happened between us…"

"What has happened between us?" he prompted when she trailed off.

"Don't make it difficult."

"All right, we'll make it easy. We're lovers."

She let out a long, unsteady breath, wondering if he really believed that was easy. For him it might be just another stroll through the moonlight. For her, it was a race through a hurricane. "I want to keep that aspect of our relationship completely separate from the professional area."

It surprised him he could find such a statement endearing. Perhaps the fact that she was half romanticist and half businesswoman was part of her appeal to him. "Juliet, my love, you sound as though you're negotiating a contract."

"Maybe I do." Nerves were beginning to run through her too quickly again. "Maybe I am, in a way."

His own anger had disappeared. Her eyes weren't nearly as certain as her voice. Her hands, he noted, were twisting together. Slowly, he walked toward her, pleased that though she didn't back away, the wariness was back. "Juliet…" He lifted a hand to brush through her hair. "You can negotiate terms and times, but not emotion."

"You can—regulate it."

He took both her hands, kissing them. "No."

"Carlo, please—"

"You like me to touch you," he murmured. "Whether we stand here alone, or we stand in a group of strangers. If I touch your hand, like this, you know what's in my mind. It's not always passion. There are times, I see you, I touch you, and I think only of being with you—talking, or sitting silently. Will you negotiate now how I am to touch your hand, how many times a day it's permitted?"

"Don't make me sound like a fool."

His fingers tightened on hers. "Don't make what I feel for you sound foolish."

"I—" No, she couldn't touch that. She didn't dare. "Carlo, I just want to keep things simple."

"Impossible."

"No, it's not."

"Then tell me, is this simple?" With just his fingertips on her shoulder, he leaned down to kiss her. So softly, so lightly, it was hardly a kiss at all. She felt her legs dissolve from the knees down.

"Carlo, we're not staying on the point."

He slipped his arms around her. "I like this point much better. When we get to Chicago…" His fingers slipped up and down her spine as he began to brush his lips over her face. "I want to spend the evening alone with you."

"We—have an appointment for drinks at ten with—"

"Cancel it."

"Carlo, you know I can't."

"Very well." He caught the lobe of her ear between his teeth. "I'll plead fatigue and make certain we have a very quick, very early evening. Then, I'll spend the rest of the night doing little things, like this."

His tongue darted inside her ear, then retreated to the vulnerable spot just below. The shudder that went through her was enough to arouse both of them. "Carlo, you don't understand."

"I understand that I want you." In a swift mood swing, he had her by the shoulders. "If I told you now that I want you more than I've wanted any other woman, you wouldn't believe me."

She backed away from that, but was caught close again. "No, I wouldn't. It isn't necessary to say so."

"You're afraid to hear it, afraid to believe it. You won't get simple with me, Juliet. But you'll get a lover you'll never forget."

She steadied a bit, meeting his look levelly. "I've already resigned myself to that, Carlo. I don't apologize to myself, and I don't pretend to have any regrets about coming to you last night."

"Then resign yourself to this." The temper was back in his eyes, hot and volatile. "I don't care what's written in the paper, what's whispered about in offices in New York. You, this moment, are all I care about."

Something shattered quietly inside her. A defense built instinctively through years. She knew she shouldn't take him literally. He was Franconi after all. If he cared about her, it was only in his way, and in his time. But something had shattered, and she couldn't rebuild it so quickly. Instead, she chose to be blunt.

"Carlo, I don't know how to handle you. I haven't the experience."

"Then don't handle me." Again, he took her by the shoulders. "Trust me."

She put her hands on his, held them a moment, then drew them away. "It's too soon, and too much."

There were times, in his work, where he had to be very, very patient. As a man, it happened much more rarely. Yet he knew if he pushed now, as for some inexplicable reason he wanted to, he'd only create more distance between them. "Then, for now, we just enjoy each other."

That's what she wanted. Juliet told herself that was exactly what she wanted—no more, no less. But she felt like weeping.

"We'll enjoy each other," she agreed. Letting out a sigh, she framed his face with her hands as he so often did with her. "Very much."

He wondered, when he lowered his brow to hers, why it didn't quite satisfy.

Chapter 9

Burned out from traveling, ready for a drink and elevated feet, Juliet walked up to the front desk of their Chicago hotel. Taking a quick glimpse around the lobby, she was pleased with the marble floors, sculpture and elegant potted palms. Such places usually lent themselves to big, stylish bathrooms. She intended to spend her first hour in Chicago with everything from the neck down submerged.

"May I help you?"

"You have a reservation for Franconi and Trent."

With a few punches on the keyboard, the clerk brought up their reservations on the screen. "You'll both be staying for two nights, Miss Trent?"

"Yes, that's right."

"It's direct bill. Everything's set. If you and Mr.

Franconi will just fill out these forms, I'll ring for a bellman."

As he scrawled the information on the form, Carlo glanced over. From the profile, she looked lovely, though perhaps a bit tired. Her hair was pinned up in the back, fluffed out on the sides and barely mussed from traveling. She looked as though she could head a three-hour business meeting without a whimper. But then she arched her back, closing her eyes briefly as she stretched her shoulders. He wanted to take care of her.

"Juliet, there's no need for two rooms."

She shifted her shoulder bag and signed her name. "Carlo, don't start. Arrangements have already been made."

"But it's absurd. You'll be staying in my suite, so the extra room is simply extra."

The desk clerk stood at a discreet distance and listened to every word.

Juliet pulled her credit card out of her wallet and set it down on the counter with a snap. Carlo noted, with some amusement, that she no longer looked the least bit tired. He wanted to make love with her for hours.

"You'll need the imprint on this for my incidentals," she told the clerk calmly enough. "All Mr. Franconi's charges will be picked up."

Carlo pushed his form toward the clerk then leaned on the counter. "Juliet, won't you feel foolish running back and forth across the hall? It's ridiculous, even for a publisher, to pay for a bed that won't be slept in."

With her jaw clenched, she picked up her credit card again. "I'll tell you what's ridiculous," she said under her breath. "It's ridiculous for you to be standing here deliberately embarrassing me."

"You have rooms 1102 and 1108." The clerk pushed the keys toward them. "I'm afraid they're just down the hall from each other rather than across."

"That's fine." Juliet turned to find the bellman had their luggage packed on the cart and his ears open. Without a word, she strode toward the bank of elevators.

Strolling along beside her, Carlo noted that the cashier had a stunning smile. "Juliet, I find it odd that you'd be embarrassed over something so simple."

"I don't think it's simple." She jabbed the up button on the elevator.

"Forgive me." Carlo put his tongue in his cheek. "It's only that I recall you specifically saying you wanted our relationship to be simple."

"Don't tell me what I said. What I said has nothing to do with what I meant."

"Of course not," he murmured and waited for her to step inside the car.

Seeing the look on Juliet's face, the bellman began to worry about his tip. He put on a hospitality-plus smile. "So, you in Chicago long?"

"Two days," Carlo said genially enough.

"You can see a lot in a couple of days. You'll want to get down to the lake—"

"We're here on business," Juliet interrupted. "Only business."

"Yes, ma'am." With a smile, the bellman pushed his cart into the hall. "1108's the first stop."

"That's mine." Juliet dug out her wallet again and pulled out bills as the bellman unlocked her door.

"Those two bags," she pointed out then turned to Carlo. "We'll meet Dave Lockwell in the bar for drinks at 10:00. You can do as you like until then."

"I have some ideas on that," he began but Juliet moved past him. After stuffing the bills in the bellman's hand, she shut the door with a quick click.

Thirty minutes, to Carlo's thinking, was long enough for anyone to cool down. Juliet's stiff-backed attitude toward their room situation had caused him more exasperation than annoyance. But then, he expected to be exasperated by women. On one hand, he found her reaction rather sweet and naive. Did she really think the fact that they were lovers would make the desk clerk or a bellman blink twice?

The fact that she did, and probably always would, was just another aspect of her nature that appealed to him. In whatever she did, Juliet Trent would always remain proper. Simmering passion beneath a tidy, clean-lined business suit. Carlo found her irresistible.

He'd known so many kinds of women—the bright young ingenue greedy to her fingertips, the wealthy aristocrat bored both by wealth and tradition, the successful career woman who both looked for and was wary of marriage. He'd known so many—the happy, the secure, the desperate and seeking, the fulfilled and the grasping. Juliet Trent with the cool green eyes and quiet voice left him uncertain as to what pigeonhole she'd fit into. It seemed she had all and none of the feminine qualities he understood. The only thing he was certain of was that he wanted her to fit, somehow, into his life.

The best way, the only way, he knew to accomplish

that was to distract her with charm until she was already caught. After that, they'd negotiate the next step.

Carlo lifted the rose he'd had sent up from the hotel florist out of its bud vase, sniffed its petals once, then walked down the hall to Juliet's room.

She was just drying off from a hot, steamy bath. If she'd heard the knock five minutes before, she'd have growled. As it was, she pulled on her robe and went to answer.

She'd been expecting him. Juliet wasn't foolish enough to believe a man like Carlo would take a door in the face as final. It had given her satisfaction to close it, just as it gave her satisfaction to open it again. When she was ready.

She hadn't been expecting the rose. Though she knew it wasn't wise to be moved by a single long-stemmed flower with a bud the color of sunshine, she was moved nonetheless. Her plans to have a calm, serious discussion with him faltered.

"You look rested." Rather than giving her the rose, he took her hand. Before she could decide whether or not to let him in, he was there.

A stand, Juliet reminded herself even as she closed the door behind him. If she didn't take a stand now, she'd never find her footing. "Since you're here, we'll talk. We have an hour."

"Of course." As was his habit, he took a survey of her room. Her suitcase sat on a stand, still packed, but with its top thrown open. It wasn't practical to unpack and repack when you were bouncing around from city to city. Though they were starting their third week on the road, the contents of the case were still neat and organized. He'd have expected no less from her. Her note-book and two pens were already beside the phone. The only things remotely out of place in the tidy, impersonal room were the Italian heels that sat in the middle of the rug where she'd stepped out of them. The inconsistency suited her perfectly.

"I can discuss things better," she began, "if you weren't wandering around."

"Yes?" All cooperation, Carlo sat and waved the rose under his nose. "You want to talk about our schedule here in Chicago?"

"No—yes." She had at least a dozen things to go over with him. For once she let business take a back seat. "Later." Deciding to take any advantage, Juliet remained standing. "First, I want to talk about that business down at the desk."

"Ah." The sound was distinctly European and as friendly as a smile. She could have murdered him.

"It was totally uncalled for."

"Was it?" He'd learned that strategy was best plotted with friendly questions or simple agreement. That way, you could swing the final result to your own ends without too much blood being shed.

"Of course it was." Forgetting her own strategy, Juliet dropped down on the edge of the bed. "Carlo, you had no right discussing our personal business in public."

"You're quite right."

"I—" His calm agreement threw her off. The firm, moderately angry speech she'd prepared in the tub went out the window.

"I must apologize," he continued before she could balance herself. "It was thoughtless of me."

"Well, no." As he'd planned, she came to his defense. "It wasn't thoughtless, just inappropriate."

With the rose, he waved her defense away. "You're too kind, Juliet. You see, I was thinking only of how practical you are. It's one of the things I most admire about you." In getting his way, Carlo had always felt it best to use as much truth as possible. "You see, besides my own family, I've known very few truly practical women. This trait in you appeals to me, as much as the color of your eyes, the texture of your skin."

Because she sensed she was losing ground, Juliet sat up straighter. "You don't have to flatter me, Carlo. It's simply a matter of establishing ground rules."

"You see." As if she'd made his point, he sat forward to touch her fingertips. "You're too practical to expect flattery or to be swayed by it. Is it any wonder I'm enchanted by you?"

"Carlo—"

"I haven't made my point." He retreated just enough to keep his attack in full gear. "You see, knowing you, I thought you would agree that it was foolish and impractical to book separate rooms when we want to be together. You do want to be with me, don't you, Juliet?"

Frustrated, she stared at him. He was turning the entire situation around. Certain of it, Juliet groped for a handhold. "Carlo, it has nothing to do with my wanting to be with you."

His brow lifted. "No?"

"No. It has to do with the line that separates our business and our personal lives."

"A line that's difficult to draw. Perhaps impossible for me." The truth came out again, though this time unplanned. "I want to be with you, Juliet, every moment we have. I find myself resenting even the hour that you're here and I'm there. A few hours at night isn't enough for me. I want more, much more for us."

Saying it left him stunned. It hadn't been one of his clever moves, one of his easy catch-phrases. That little jewel had come from somewhere inside where it had quietly hidden until it could take him by surprise.

He rose, and to give himself a moment, stood by the window to watch a stream of Chicago traffic. It rushed, then came to fitful stops, wound and swung then sped on again. Life was like this, he realized. You could speed right along but you never knew when something was going to stop you dead in your tracks.

Juliet was silent behind him, torn between what he'd said, what he'd meant and what she felt about it. From the very beginning, she'd kept Carlo's definition of an affair in the front of her mind. Just one ride on the carousel. When the music stopped, you got off and knew you'd gotten your money's worth. Now, with a few words he was changing the scope. She wondered if either of them was ready.

"Carlo, since you say I am, I'll be practical." Drawing together her resources, she rose. "We have a week left on tour. During that time, we've got Chicago and four other cities to deal with. To be honest, I'd rather if our only business right now was with each other."

He turned, and though she thought the smile was a bit odd, at least he smiled. "That's the nicest thing you've said to me in all these days and all these cities, Juliet."

She took a step toward him. It seemed foolish to

think about risks when they had such little time. "Being with you isn't something I'll ever forget, no matter how much I might want to in years to come."

"Juliet—"

"No, wait. I want to be with you, and part of me hates the time we lose with other people, in separate rooms, in all the demands that brought us to each other in the first place. But another part of me knows that all of those things are completely necessary. Those things will still be around after we're each back in our separate places."

No, don't think about that now, she warned herself. If she did, her voice wouldn't be steady.

"No matter how much time I spend with you in your suite, I need a room of my own if for no other reason than to know it's there. Maybe that's the practical side of me, Carlo."

Or the vulnerable one, he mused. But hadn't he just discovered he had a vulnerability of his own? Her name was Juliet. "So, it will be as you want in this." And for the best perhaps. He might just need a bit of time to himself to think things through.

"No arguing?"

"Do we argue ever, *cara?*"

Her lips curved. "Never." Giving in to herself as much as him, she stepped forward and linked her arms around his neck. "Did I ever tell you that when I first started setting up this tour I looked at your publicity shot and thought you were gorgeous?"

"No." He brushed his lips over hers. "Why don't you tell me now?"

"And sexy," she murmured as she drew him closer to the bed. "Very, very sexy."

"Is that so?" He allowed himself to be persuaded onto the bed. "So you decided in your office in New York that we'd be lovers?"

"I decided in my office in New York that we'd never be lovers." Slowly, she began to unbutton his shirt. "I decided that the last thing I wanted was to be romanced and seduced by some gorgeous, sexy Italian chef who had a string of women longer than a trail of his own pasta, but—"

"Yes." He nuzzled at her neck. "I think I'll prefer the 'but.'"

"But it seems to me that you can't make definitive decisions without all the facts being in."

"Have I ever told you that your practicality arouses me to the point of madness?"

She sighed as he slipped undone the knot in her robe. "Have I ever told you that I'm a sucker for a man who brings me flowers?"

"Flowers." He lifted his head then picked up the rose-bud he'd dropped on the pillow beside them. "Darling, did you want one, too?"

With a laugh, she pulled him back to her.

Juliet decided she'd seen more of Chicago in the flight into O'Hare than during the day and a half she'd been there. Cab drives from hotel to television station, from television station to department store, from department store to bookstore and back to the hotel again weren't exactly leisurely sight-seeing tours. Then and there she decided that when she took her vacation at the end of the month, she'd go somewhere steamy with sun and do nothing more energetic than laze by a pool from dawn to dusk.

The only hour remotely resembling fun was another shopping expedition where she watched Carlo select a plump three-pound chicken for his cacciatore.

He was to prepare his *pollastro alla cacciatora* from simmer to serve during a live broadcast of one of the country's top-rated morning shows. Next to the *Simpson Show* in L.A., Juliet considered this her biggest coup for the tour. *Let's Discuss It* was the hottest hour on daytime TV, and remained both popular and controversial after five consecutive seasons.

Despite the fact that she knew Carlo's showmanship abilities, Juliet was nervous as a cat. The show would air live in New York. She had no doubt that everyone in her department would be watching. If Carlo was a smash, it would be his triumph. If he bombed, the bomb was all hers. Such was the rationale in public relations.

It never occurred to Carlo to be nervous. He could make cacciatore in the dark, from memory with the use of only one hand. After watching Juliet pace the little green room for the fifth time, he shook his head. "Relax, my love, it's only chicken."

"Don't forget to bring up the dates we'll be in the rest of the cities. This show reaches all of them."

"You've already told me."

"And the title of the book."

"I won't forget."

"You should remember to mention you prepared this dish for the President when he visited Rome last year."

"I'll try to keep it in mind. Juliet, wouldn't you like some coffee?"

She shook her head and kept pacing. What else?

"I could use some," he decided on the spot.

She glanced toward the pot on a hot plate. "Help yourself."

He knew if she had something to do, she'd stop worrying, even for a few moments. And she'd stop pacing up and down in front of him. "Juliet, no one with a heart would ask a man to drink that poison that's been simmering since dawn."

"Oh." Without hesitation, she assumed the role of pamperer. "I'll see about it."

"Grazie."

At the door, she hesitated. "The reporter for the *Sun* might drop back before the show."

"Yes, you told me. I'll be charming."

Muttering to herself, she went to find a page.

Carlo leaned back and stretched his legs. He'd have to drink the coffee when she brought it back, though he didn't want any. He didn't want to board the plane for Detroit that afternoon, but such things were inevitable. In any case, he and Juliet would have the evening free in Detroit—what American state was that in?

They wouldn't be there long enough to worry about it.

In any case, he would soon be in Philadelphia and there, see Summer. He needed to. Though he'd always had friends and was close to many of them, he'd never needed one as he felt he needed one now. He could talk to Summer and know what he said would be listened to carefully and not be repeated. Gossip had never bothered him in the past, but when it came to Juliet… When it came to Juliet, nothing was as it had been in the past.

None of his previous relationships with women had ever become a habit. Waking up in the morning beside a woman had always been pleasant, but never necessary. Every day, Juliet was changing that. He couldn't imagine his bedroom back in Rome without her, yet she'd never been there. He'd long since stopped imagining other women in his bed.

Rising, he began to pace as Juliet had.

When the door opened, he turned, expecting her. The tall, willowy blonde who entered wasn't Juliet, but she was familiar.

"Carlo! How wonderful to see you again."

"Lydia." He smiled, cursing himself for not putting the name of the *Sun*'s reporter with the face of the woman he'd spent two interesting days in Chicago with only eighteen months before. "You look lovely."

Of course she did. Lydia Dickerson refused to look anything less. She was sharp, sexy and uninhibited. She was also, in his memory, an excellent cook and critic of gourmet foods.

"Carlo, I was just thrilled when I heard you were coming into town. We'll do the interview after the show, but I just had to drop back and see you." She swirled toward him with the scent of spring lilacs and the swish of a wide-flared skirt. "You don't mind?"

"Of course not." Smiling, he took her outstretched hand. "It's always good to see an old friend."

With a laugh, she put her hands on his shoulders. "I should be angry with you, *caro*. You do have my number, and my phone didn't ring last night."

"Ah." He put his hands to her wrists, wondering just how to untangle himself. "You'll have to forgive us,

Lydia. The schedule is brutal. And there's a...complication." He winced, thinking how Juliet would take being labeled a complication.

"Carlo." She edged closer. "You can't tell me you haven't got a few free hours for...an old friend. I've a tremendous recipe for *vitèllo tonnato*." She murmured the words and made the dish sound like something to be eaten in the moonlight. "Who else should I cook it for but the best chef in Italy?"

"I'm honored." He put his hands on her hips hoping to draw her away with the least amount of insult. It wouldn't occur to him until later that he'd felt none, absolutely none, of the casual desire he should have. "I haven't forgotten what a superb cook you are, Lydia."

Her laugh was low and full of memories. "I hope you haven't forgotten more than that."

"No." He let out a breath and opted to be blunt. "But you see I'm—"

Before he could finish being honest, the door opened again. With a cup of coffee in her hand, Juliet walked in, then came to a dead stop. She looked at the blonde wound around Carlo like an exotic vine. Her brow lifted as she took her gaze to Carlo's face. If only she had a camera.

Her voice was as cool and dry as her eyes. "I see you've met."

"Juliet, I—"

"I'll give you a few moments for the...pre-interview," she said blandly. "Try to wrap it up by eight-fifty, Carlo. You'll want to check the kitchen set." Without another word, she shut the door behind her.

Though her arms were still around Carlo's neck,

Lydia looked toward the closed door. "Oops," she said lightly.

Carlo let out a long breath as they separated. "You couldn't have put it better."

At nine o'clock, Juliet had a comfortable seat midway back in the audience. When Lydia slipped into the seat beside her, she gave the reporter an easy nod, then looked back to the set. As far as she could tell, and she'd gone over every inch of it, it was perfect.

When Carlo was introduced to cheerful applause she began to relax, just a little. But when he began preparations on the chicken, moving like a surgeon and talking to his host, his studio and television audience like a seasoned performer, her relaxation was complete. He was going to be fantastic.

"He's really something, isn't he?" Lydia murmured during the first break.

"Something," Juliet agreed.

"Carlo and I met the last time he was in Chicago."

"Yes, I gathered. I'm glad you could make it by this morning. You did get the press kit I sent in?"

She's a cool one, Lydia thought and shifted in her seat. "Yes. The feature should be out by the end of the week. I'll send you a clipping."

"I'd appreciate it."

"Miss Trent—"

"Juliet, please." For the first time, Juliet turned and smiled at her fully. "No need for formality."

"All right, Juliet, I feel like a fool."

"I'm sorry. You shouldn't."

"I'm very fond of Carlo, but I don't poach."

"Lydia, I'm sure there isn't a woman alive who

wouldn't be fond of Carlo." She crossed her legs as the countdown for taping began again. "If I thought you'd even consider poaching, you wouldn't be able to pick up your pencil."

Lydia sat still for a moment, then leaned back with a laugh. Carlo had picked himself quite a handful. Served him right. "Is it all right to wish you luck?"

Juliet shot her another smile. "I'd appreciate it."

The two women might've come to amicable terms, but it wasn't easy for Carlo to concentrate on his job while they sat cozily together in the audience. His experience with Lydia had been a quick and energetic two days. He knew little more of her than her preference for peanut oil for cooking and blue bed linen. He understood how easy it was for a man to be executed without trial. He thought he could almost feel the prickle of the noose around his throat.

But he was innocent. Carlo poured the mixture of tomatoes, sauce and spices over the browned chicken and set the cover. If he had to bind and gag her, Juliet would listen to him.

He cooked his dish with the finesse of an artist completing a royal portrait. He performed for the audience like a veteran thespian. He thought the dark thoughts of a man already at the dock.

When the show was over, he spent a few obligatory moments with his host, then left the crew to devour one of his best cacciatores.

But when he went back to the green room, Juliet was nowhere in sight. Lydia was waiting. He had no choice but to deal with her, and the interview, first.

She didn't make it easy for him. But then, to his

knowledge, women seldom did. Lydia chatted away as though nothing had happened. She asked her questions, noted down his answers, all the while with mischief gleaming in her eyes. At length, he'd had enough.

"All right, Lydia, what did you say to her?"

"To whom?" All innocence, Lydia blinked at him. "Oh, your publicist. A lovely woman. But then I'd hardly be one to fault your taste, darling."

He rose, swore and wondered what a desperate man should do with his hands. "Lydia, we had a few enjoyable hours together. No more."

"I know." Something in her tone made him pause and glance back. "I don't imagine either of us could count the number of few enjoyable hours we've had." With a shrug, she rose. Perhaps she understood him, even envied what she thought she'd read in his eyes, but it wasn't any reason to let him off the hook. "Your Juliet and I just chatted, darling." She dropped her pad and pencil in her bag. "Girl talk, you know. Just girl talk. Thanks for the interview, Carlo." At the door, she paused and turned back. "If you're ever back in town without a…complication, give me a ring. *Ciao*."

When she left he considered breaking something. Before he could decide what would be the most satisfying and destructive, Juliet bustled in. "Let's get moving, Carlo. The cab's waiting. It looks like we'll have enough time to get back to the hotel, check out and catch the earlier plane."

"I want to speak with you."

"Yes, fine. We'll talk in the cab." Because she was already heading down the winding corridor he had no choice but to follow.

"When you told me the name of the reporter, I simply didn't put it together."

"Put what together?" Juliet pulled open the heavy metal door and stepped out on the back lot. If it had been much hotter, she noted, Carlo could've browned his chicken on the asphalt. "Oh, that you'd known her. Well, it's so hard to remember everyone we've met, isn't it?" She slipped into the cab and gave the driver the name of the hotel.

"We've come halfway across the country." Annoyed, he climbed in beside her. "Things begin to blur."

"They certainly do." Sympathetic, she patted his hand. "Detroit and Boston'll be down and dirty. You'll be lucky to remember your own name." She pulled out her compact to give her make-up a quick check. "But then I can help out in Philadelphia. You've already told me you have a...friend there."

"Summer's different." He took the compact from her. "I've known her for years. We were students together. We never— Friends, we're only friends," he ended on a mutter. "I don't enjoy explaining myself."

"I can see that." She pulled out bills and calculated the tip as the cab drew up to the hotel. As she started to slide out, she gave Carlo a long look. "No one asked you to."

"Ridiculous." He had her by the arm before she'd reached the revolving doors. "You ask. It isn't necessary to ask with words to ask."

"Guilt makes you imagine all sorts of things." She swung through the doors and into the lobby.

"Guilt?" Incensed, he caught up with her at the elevators. "I've nothing to be guilty for. A man has to commit some crime, some sin, for guilt."

She listened calmly as she stepped into the elevator car and pushed the button for their floor. "That's true, Carlo. You seem to me to be a man bent on making a confession."

He went off on a fiery stream of Italian that had the other two occupants of the car edging into the corners. Juliet folded her hands serenely and decided she'd never enjoyed herself more. The other passengers gave Carlo a wide berth as the elevator stopped on their floor.

"Did you want to grab something quick to eat at the airport or wait until we land?"

"I'm not interested in food."

"An odd statement from a chef." She breezed into the hall. "Take ten minutes to pack and I'll call for a bellman." The key was in her hand and into the lock before his fingers circled her wrist. When she looked up at him, she thought she'd never seen him truly frustrated before. Good. It was about time.

"I pack nothing until this is settled."

"Until what's settled?" she countered.

"When I commit a crime or a sin, I do so with complete honesty." It was the closest he'd come to an explosion. Juliet lifted a brow and listened attentively. "It was Lydia who had her arms around me."

Juliet smiled. "Yes, I saw quite clearly how you were struggling. A woman should be locked up for taking advantage of a man that way."

His eyes, already dark, went nearly black. "You're sarcastic. But you don't understand the circumstances."

"On the contrary." She leaned against the door.

"Carlo, I believe I understood the circumstances perfectly. I don't believe I've asked you to explain anything. Now, you'd better pack if we're going to catch that early plane." For the second time, she shut the door in his face.

He stood where he was for a moment, torn. A man expected a certain amount of jealousy from a woman he was involved with. He even, well, enjoyed it to a point. What he didn't expect was a smile, a pat on the head and breezy understanding when he'd been caught in another woman's arms. However innocently.

No, he didn't expect it, Carlo decided. He wouldn't tolerate it.

When the sharp knock came on the door, Juliet was still standing with a hand on the knob. Wisely, she counted to ten before she opened it.

"Did you need something?"

Carefully, he studied her face for a trap. "You're not angry."

She lifted her brows. "No, why?"

"Lydia's very beautiful."

"She certainly is."

He stepped inside. "You're not jealous?"

"Don't be absurd." She brushed a speck of lint from her sleeve. "If you found me with another man, under similar circumstances, you'd understand, I'm sure."

"No." He closed the door behind him. "I'd break his face."

"Oh?" Rather pleased, she turned away to gather a few things from her dresser. "That's the Italian temperament, I suppose. Most of my ancestors were rather staid. Hand me that brush, will you?"

Carlo picked it up and dropped it into her hand. "Staid—this means?"

"Calm and sturdy, I suppose. Though there was one—my great-great-grandmother, I think. She found her husband tickling the scullery maid. In her staid sort of way, she knocked him flat with a cast-iron skillet. I don't think he ever tickled any of the other servants." Securing the brush in a plastic case, she arranged it in the bag. "I'm said to take after her."

Taking her by the shoulders, he turned her to face him. "There were no skillets available."

"True enough, but I'm inventive. Carlo…" Still smiling, she slipped her arms around his neck. "If I hadn't understood exactly what was going on, the coffee I'd fetched for you would've been dumped over your head. *Capice?*"

"Sì." He grinned as he rubbed his nose against hers. But he didn't really understand her. Perhaps that was why he was enchanted by her. Lowering his mouth to hers, he let the enchantment grow. "Juliet," he murmured. "There's a later plane for Detroit, yes?"

She had wondered if he would ever think of it. "Yes, this afternoon."

"Did you know it's unhealthy for the system to rush." As he spoke, he slipped the jacket from her arms so that it slid to the floor.

"I've heard something about that."

"Very true. It's much better, medically speaking, to take one's time. To keep a steady pace, but not a fast one. And, of course, to give the system time to relax at regular intervals. It could be very unhealthy for us to pack now and race to the airport." He unhooked her skirt so that it followed her jacket.

"You're probably right."

"Of course I'm right," he murmured in her ear. "It would never do for either of us to be ill on the tour."

"Disastrous," she agreed. "In fact, it might be best if we both just lay down for a little while."

"The very best. One must guard one's health."

"I couldn't agree more," she told him as his shirt joined her skirt and jacket.

She was laughing as they tumbled onto the bed.

He liked her this way. Free, easy, enthusiastic. Just as he liked her cooler, more enigmatic moods. He could enjoy her in a hundred different ways because she wasn't always the same woman. Yet she was always the same.

Soft, as she was now. Warm wherever he touched, luxurious wherever he tasted. She might be submissive one moment, aggressive the next, and he never tired of the swings.

They made love in laughter now, something he knew more than most was precious and rare. Even when the passion began to dominate, there was an underlying sense of enjoyment that didn't cloud the fire. She gave him more in a moment than he'd thought he'd ever find with a woman in a lifetime.

She'd never known she could be this way—laughing, churning, happy, desperate. There were so many things she hadn't known. Every time he touched her it was something new, though it was somehow as if his touch was all she'd ever known. He made her feel fresh and desirable, wild and weepy all at once. In the space of minutes, he could bring her a sense of contentment and a frantic range of excitements.

The more he brought, the more he gave, and the easier it became for her to give. She wasn't aware yet, nor was he, that every time they made love, the intimacy grew and spread. It was gaining a strength and weight that wouldn't break with simply walking away. Perhaps if they'd known, they would have fought it.

Instead, they loved each other through the morning with the verve of youth and the depth of familiarity.

Chapter 10

Juliet hung up the phone, dragged a hand through her hair and swore. Rising, she swore again then moved toward the wide spread of window in Carlo's suite. For a few moments she muttered at nothing and no one in particular. Across the room, Carlo lay sprawled on the sofa. Wisely, he waited until she'd lapsed into silence.

"Problems?"

"We're fogged in." Swearing again, she stared out the window. She could see the mist, thick and still hanging outside the glass. Detroit was obliterated. "All flights are cancelled. The only way we're going to get to Boston is to stick out our thumbs."

"Thumbs?"

"Never mind." She turned and paced around the suite.

Detroit had been a solid round of media and events,

and the Renaissance Center a beautiful place to stay, but now it was time to move on. Boston was just a hop away by air, so that the evening could be devoted to drafting out reports and a good night's sleep. Except for the fact that fog had driven in from the lake and put the whole city under wraps.

Stuck, Juliet thought as she glared out the window again. Stuck when they had an 8:00 A.M. live demonstration on a well-established morning show in Boston.

He shifted a bit, but didn't sit up. If it hadn't been too much trouble, he could've counted off the number of times he'd been grounded for one reason or another. One, he recalled, had been a flamenco dancer in Madrid who'd distracted him into missing the last flight out. Better not to mention it. Still, when such things happened, Carlo reflected, it was best to relax and enjoy the moment. He knew Juliet better.

"You're worried about the TV in the morning."

"Of course I am." As she paced, she went over every possibility. Rent a car and drive—no, even in clear weather it was simply too far. They could charter a plane and hope the fog cleared by dawn. She took another glance outside. They were sixty-five floors up, but they might as well have been sixty-five feet under. No, she decided, no television spot was worth the risk. They'd have to cancel. That was that.

She dropped down on a chair and stuck her stockinged feet up by Carlo's. "I'm sorry, Carlo, there's no way around it. We'll have to scrub Boston."

"Scrub Boston?" Lazily he folded his arms behind his head. "Juliet, Franconi scrubs nothing. Cook, yes, scrub, no."

It took her a moment to realize he was serious. "I mean cancel."

"You didn't say cancel."

She heaved out a long breath. "I'm saying it now." She wiggled her toes, finding them a bit stiff after a ten-hour day. "There's no way we can make the television spot, and that's the biggest thing we have going in Boston. There're a couple of print interviews and an autographing. We didn't expect much to move there, and we were depending on the TV spot for that. Without it…" She shrugged and resigned herself. "It's a wash."

Letting his eyes half close, Carlo decided the sofa was an excellent place to spend an hour or so. "I don't wash."

She shot him a level look. "You're not going to have to do anything but lie on your—back," she decided after a moment, "for the next twenty-four hours."

"Nothing?"

"Nothing."

He grinned. Moving faster than he looked capable of, he sat up, grabbed her by the arms and pulled her down with him. "Good, you lie with me. Two backs, *madonna,* are better than one."

"Carlo." She couldn't avoid the first kiss. Or perhaps she didn't put her best effort into it, but she knew it was essential to avoid the second. "Wait a minute."

"Only twenty-four hours," he reminded her as he moved to her ear. "No time to waste."

"I've got to— Stop that," she ordered when her thoughts started to cloud. "There're arrangements to be made."

"What arrangements?"

She made a quick mental sketch. True, she'd already checked out of her room. They'd only kept the suite for convenience, and until six. She could book another separate room for the night, but—she might as well admit in this case it was foolish. Moving her shoulders, she gave in to innate practicality. "Like keeping the suite overnight."

"That's important." He lifted his head a moment. Her face was already flushed, her eyes already soft. Almost as if she'd spoken aloud, he followed the train of thought. He couldn't help but admire the way her mind worked from one point to the next in such straight lines.

"I have to call New York and let them know our status. I have to call Boston and cancel, then the airport and change our flight. Then I—"

"I think you have a love affair with the phone. It's difficult for a man to be jealous of an inanimate object."

"Phones are my life." She tried to slip out from under him, but got nowhere. "Carlo."

"I like it when you say my name with just a touch of exasperation."

"It's going to be more than a touch in a minute."

He'd thought he'd enjoy that as well. "But you haven't told me yet how fantastic I was today."

"You were fantastic." It was so easy to relax when he held her like this. The phone calls could wait, just a bit. After all, they weren't going anywhere. "You mesmerized them with your linguini."

"My linguini is hypnotic," he agreed. "I charmed the reporter from the *Free Press*."

"You left him stupefied. Detroit'll never be the same."

"That's true." He kissed her nose. "Boston won't know what it's missing."

"Don't remind me," she began, then broke off. Carlo could almost hear the wheels turning.

"An idea." Resigned, he rolled her on top of him and watched her think.

"It might work," she murmured. "If everyone co-operates, it might work very well. In fact, it might just be terrific."

"What?"

"You claim to be a magician as well as an artist."

"Modesty prevents me from—"

"Save it." She scrambled up until she stradled him. "You told me once you could cook in a sewer."

Frowning, he toyed with the little gold hoop she wore in her ear. "Yes, perhaps I did. But this is only an expression—"

"How about cooking by remote control?"

His brows drew together, but he ran his hand idly to the hem of her skirt that had ridden high on her thigh. "You have extraordinary legs," he said in passing, then gave her his attention. "What do you mean by remote control?"

"Just that." Wound up with the idea, Juliet rose and grabbed her pad and pencil. "You give me all the ingredients—it's linguini again tomorrow, right?"

"Yes, my specialty."

"Good, I have all that in the file anyway. We can set up a phone session between Detroit and the studio in Boston. You can be on the air there while we're here."

"Juliet, you ask for a lot of magic."

"No, it's just basic electronics. The host of the

show—Paul O'Hara—can put the dish together on the air while you talk him through it. It's like talking a plane in, you know. Forty degrees to the left—a cup of flour."

"No."

"Carlo."

Taking his time, he pried off his shoes. "You want him, this O'Hara who smiles for the camera, to cook my linguini?"

"Don't get temperamental on me," she warned, while her mind leaped ahead to possibilities. "Look, you write cookbooks so the average person can cook one of your dishes."

"Cook them, yes." He examined his nails. "Not like Franconi."

She opened her mouth, then closed it again. Tread softly on the ego, Juliet reminded herself. At least until you get your way. "Of course not, Carlo. No one expects that. But we could turn this inconvenience into a real event. Using your cookbook on the air, and some personal coaching from you via phone, O'Hara can prepare the linguini. He's not a chef or a gourmet, but an average person. Therefore, he'll be giving the audience the average person's reactions. He'll make the average person's mistakes that you can correct. If we pull it off, the sales of your cookbook are going to soar. You know you can do it." She smiled winningly. "Why you even said you could teach me to cook, and I'm helpless in the kitchen. Certainly you can talk O'Hara through one dish."

"Of course I can." Folding his arms again, he stared up at the ceiling. Her logic was infallible, her idea creative. To be truthful, he liked it—almost as much as he liked the idea of not having to fly to Boston. Still, it hardly seemed fair to give without getting. "I'll do it—on one condition."

"Which is?"

"Tomorrow morning, I talk this O'Hara through linguini. Tonight…" And he smiled at her. "We have a dress rehearsal. I talk you through it."

Juliet stopped tapping the end of her pencil on the pad. "You want me to cook linguini?"

"With my guidance, *cara mia,* you could cook anything."

Juliet thought it over and decided it didn't matter. The suite didn't have a kitchen this time, so he'd be counting on using the hotel's. That may or may not work. If it did, once she'd botched it, they could order room service. The bottom line was saving what she could of Boston. "I'd love to. Now, I've got to make those calls."

Carlo closed his eyes and opted for a nap. If he was going to teach two amateurs the secrets of linguini within twelve hours, he'd need his strength. "Wake me when you've finished," he told her. "We have to inspect the kitchen of the hotel."

It took her the best part of two hours, and when she hung up for the last time, Juliet's neck was stiff and her fingers numb. But she had what she wanted. Hal told her she was a genius and O'Hara said it sounded like fun. Arrangements were already in the works.

This time Juliet grinned at the stubborn fog swirling outside the window. Neither rain nor storm nor dark of night, she thought, pleased with herself. Nothing was going to stop Juliet Trent.

Then she looked over at Carlo. Something tilted inside her that had both her confidence and self-satisfaction wavering. Emotion, she reflected. It was something she hadn't written into the itinerary.

Well, maybe there was one catastrophe that wasn't in the books. Maybe it was one she couldn't work her way through with a creative idea and hustle. She simply had to take her feelings for Carlo one step at a time.

Four more days, she mused, and the ride would be over. The music would stop and it would be time to get off the carousel.

It wasn't any use trying to see beyond that yet; it was all blank pages. She had to hold on to the belief that life was built one day at a time. Carlo would go, then she would pick up the pieces and begin her life again from that point.

She wasn't fool enough to tell herself she wouldn't cry. Tears would be shed over him, but they'd be shed quietly and privately. Schedule in a day for mourning, she thought then tossed her pad away.

It wasn't healthy to think of it now. There were only four days left. For a moment, she looked down at her empty hands and wondered if she'd have taken the steps she'd taken if she'd known where they would lead her. Then she looked over at him and simply watched him sleep.

Even with his eyes closed and that irrepressible inner life he had on hold, he could draw her. It wasn't simply a matter of his looks, she realized. She wasn't a woman who'd turn her life sideways for simple physical attraction. It was a matter of style. Smiling, she rose and walked closer to him as he slept. No matter how practical she was, how much common sense she possessed, she couldn't have resisted his style.

There'd be no regrets, she reaffirmed. Not now, nor in five days' time when an ocean and priorities separated them. As years passed, and their lives flowed and altered, she'd remember a handful of days when she'd had something special.

No time to waste, he'd said. Catching her tongue in her teeth Juliet decided she couldn't agree more. Reaching up, she began to unbutton her blouse. As a matter of habit, she draped it carefully over the back of a chair before she unhooked her skirt. When that fell, she lifted it, smoothed it out and folded it. The pins were drawn out of her hair, one by one, then set aside.

Dressed in a very impractical lace camisole and string bikini she moved closer.

Carlo awoke with his blood pumping and his head whirling. He could smell her scent lightly in her hair, more heady on her skin as her mouth took command of his. Her body was already heated as she lay full length on him. Before he could draw his first thoughts together, his own body followed suit.

She was all lace and flesh and passion. There wasn't time to steady his control or polish his style. Urgent and desperate, he reached for her and found silk and delicacy, strength and demand wherever he touched.

She unbuttoned his shirt and drew it aside so that their skin could meet and arouse. Beneath hers, she felt his heartbeat race and pound until power made her dizzy. Capturing his lips once again, she thought only of driving him to madness. She could feel it spread through him, growing, building, so that it would dominate both of them.

When he rolled so that she was trapped between the back of the sofa and his body, she was ready to relinquish control. With a moan, dark and liquid, she let herself enjoy what she'd begun.

No woman had ever done this to him. He understood that as his only thoughts were to devour everything she had. His fingers, so clever, so skilled, so gentle, pulled at the lace until the thin strap tore with hardly a sound.

He found her—small soft breasts that fit so perfectly in his hands, the strong narrow rib cage and slender waist. His. The word nearly drove him mad. She was his now, as she'd been in the dream she'd woken him from. Perhaps he was still dreaming.

She smelled of secrets, small, feminine secrets no man ever fully understood. She tasted of passion, ripe, shivering passion every man craved. With his tongue he tasted that sweet subtle valley between her breasts and felt her tremble. She was strong; he'd never doubted it. In her strength, she was surrendering completely to him, for the pleasure of each.

The lace smelled of her. He could have wallowed in it, but her skin was irresistible. He drew the camisole down to her waist and feasted on her.

With her hands tangled in his hair, her body on fire, she thought only of him. No tomorrows, no yesterdays. However much she might deny it in an hour, they'd become a single unit. One depended on the other for pleasure, for comfort, for excitement. For so much more she didn't dare think of it. She yearned for him; nothing would ever stop it. But now, he was taking her, fast and furious, through doors they'd opened together. Neither of them had gone there before with another, nor would again.

Juliet gave herself over to the dark, the heat, and to Carlo.

He drew the thin strings riding on her hips, craving the essence of her. When he'd driven her over the first peak, he knew and reveled in it. With endless waves of desire, he whipped her up again, and yet again, until they were both trembling. She called out his name as he ran his lips down her leg. All of her was the thought paramount in his mind. He'd have all of her until she was willing, ready to have all of him.

"Juliet, I want you." His face was above hers again, his breath straining. "Look at me."

She was staggering on that razor's edge between reason and madness. When she opened her eyes, his face filled her vision. It was all she wanted.

"I want you," he repeated while the blood raged in his head. "Only you."

She was wrapped around him, her head arched back. For an instant, their eyes met and held. What coursed through them wasn't something they could try to explain. It was both danger and security.

"Only," she murmured and took him into her.

They were both stunned, both shaken, both content. Naked, damp and warm, they lay tangled together in silence. Words had been spoken, Juliet thought. Words that were part of the madness of the moment. She would have to take care not to repeat them when passion was spent. They didn't need words; they had four days. Yet she ached to hear them again, to say them again.

She could set the tone between them, she thought. She had only to begin now and continue. No pressure. She kept her eyes closed a moment longer. No regrets. The extra moment she took to draw back her strength went unnoticed.

"I could stay just like this for a week," she murmured. Though she meant it, the words were said lazily. Turning her head, she looked at him, smiled. "Are you ready for another nap?"

There was so much he wanted to say. So much, he thought, she didn't want to hear. They'd set the rules; he had only to follow them. Nothing was as easy as it should've been.

"No." He kissed her forehead. "Though I've never found waking from a nap more delightful. Now, I think it's time for your next lesson."

"Really?" She caught her bottom lip between her teeth. "I thought I'd graduated."

"Cooking," he told her, giving her a quick pinch where Italian males were prone to.

Juliet tossed back her hair and pinched him back. "I thought you'd forget about that."

"Franconi never forgets. A quick shower, a change of clothes and down to the kitchen."

Agreeable, Juliet shrugged. She didn't think for one minute the management would allow him to give a cooking lesson in their kitchen.

Thirty minutes later, she was proven wrong.

Carlo merely bypassed management. He saw no reason to go through a chain of command. With very little fuss, he steered her through the hotel's elegant dining room and into the big, lofty kitchen. It smelled exotic and sounded like a subway station.

They'd stop him here, Juliet decided, still certain they'd be dining outside or through room service within the hour. Though she'd changed into comfortable jeans, she had no plans to cook. After one look at the big room with its oversized appliances and acres of counter, she was positive she wouldn't.

It shouldn't have surprised her to be proven wrong again.

"Franconi!" The name boomed out and echoed off the walls. Juliet jumped back three inches.

"Carlo, I think we should—" But as she spoke, she looked up at his face. He was grinning from ear to ear.

"Pierre!"

As she looked on, Carlo was enveloped by a wide, white-aproned man with a drooping moustache and a face as big and round as a frying pan. His skin glistened with sweat, but he smelt inoffensively of tomatoes.

"You Italian lecher, what do you do in my kitchen?"

"Honor it," Carlo said as they drew apart. "I thought you were in Montreal, poisoning the tourists."

"They beg me to take the kitchen here." The big man with the heavy French accent shrugged tanklike shoulders. "I feel sorry for them. Americans have so little finesse in the kitchen."

"They offered to pay you by the pound," Carlo said dryly. "Your pounds."

Pierre held both hands to his abundant middle and laughed. "We understand each other, old friend. Still,

I find America to my liking. You, why aren't you in Rome pinching ladies?"

"I'm finishing up a tour for my book."

"But yes, you and your cookbooks." A noise behind him had him glancing around and bellowing in French. Juliet was certain the walls trembled. With a smile, he adjusted his hat and turned back to them. "That goes well?"

"Well enough." Carlo drew Juliet up. "This is Juliet Trent, my publicist."

"So it goes very well," Pierre murmured as he took Juliet's hand and brushed his lips over it. "Perhaps I will write a cookbook. Welcome to my kitchen, *mademoiselle*. I'm at your service."

Charmed, Juliet smiled. "Thank you, Pierre."

"Don't let this one fool you," Carlo warned. "He has a daughter your age."

"Bah!" Pierre gave him a lowered brow look. "She's but sixteen. If she were a day older I'd call my wife and tell her to lock the doors while Franconi is in town."

Carlo grinned. "Such flattery, Pierre." With his hands hooked in his back pockets, he looked around the room. "Very nice," he mused. Lifting his head, he scented the air. "Duck. Is that duck I smell?"

Pierre preened. "The specialty. *Canard au Pierre.*"

"Fantastico." Carlo swung an arm around Juliet as he led her closer to the scent. "No one, absolutely no one, does to duck what Pierre can do."

The black eyes in the frying-pan face gleamed. "No, you flatter me, *mon ami.*"

"There's no flattery in truth." Carlo looked on while an assistant carved Pierre's duck. With the ease of experience, he took a small sliver and popped it into Juliet's mouth. It dissolved there, leaving behind an elusive flavor that begged for more. Carlo merely laid his tongue on his thumb to test. "Exquisite, as always. Do you remember, Pierre, when we prepared the Shah's engagement feast? Five, six years ago."

"Seven," Pierre corrected and sighed.

"Your duck and my cannelloni."

"Magnificent. Not so much paprika on that fish," he boomed out. "We are not in Budapest. Those were the days," he continued easily. "But..." The shrug was essentially Gallic. "When a man has his third child, he has to settle down, *oui?*"

Carlo gave another look at the kitchen, and with an expert's eye approved. "You've picked an excellent spot. Perhaps you'd let me have a corner of it for a short time."

"A corner?"

"A favor," Carlo said with a smile that would have charmed the pearls from oysters. "I've promised my Juliet to teach her how to prepare linguini."

"Linguini con vongole biance?" Pierre's eyes glittered.

"Naturally. It is my specialty."

"You can have a corner of my kitchen, *mon ami,* in exchange for a plate."

Carlo laughed and patted Pierre's stomach. "For you, *amico,* two plates."

Pierre clasped him by the shoulders and kissed both cheeks. "I feel my youth coming back to me. Tell me what you need."

In no time at all, Juliet found herself covered in a

white apron with her hair tucked into a chef's hat. She might have felt ridiculous if she'd been given the chance.

"First you mince the clams."

Juliet looked at Carlo, then down at the mess of clams on the cutting board. "Mince them?"

"Like so." Carlo took the knife and with a few quick moves had half of the clams in small, perfect pieces. "Try."

Feeling a bit like an executioner, Juliet brought the knife down. "They're not…well, alive, are they?"

"*Madonna,* any clam considers himself honored to be part of Franconi's linguini. A bit smaller there. Yes." Satisfied, he passed her an onion. "Chopped, not too fine." Again, he demonstrated, but this time Juliet felt more at home. Accepting the knife, she hacked again until the onion was in pieces and her eyes were streaming.

"I hate to cook," she muttered but Carlo only pushed a clove of garlic at her.

"This is chopped very fine. Its essence is what we need, not so much texture." He stood over her shoulder, watching until he approved. "You've good hands, Juliet. Now here, melt the butter."

Following instructions, she cooked the onion and garlic in the simmering butter, stirring until Carlo pronounced it ready.

"Now, it's tender, you see. We add just a bit of flour." He held her hand to direct it as she stirred it in. "So it thickens. We add the clams. Gently," he warned before she could dump them in. "We don't want them bruised. Ah…" He nodded with approval. "Spice," he told her. "It's the secret and the strength."

Bending over her, he showed her how to take a pinch of this, a touch of that and create. As the scent became more pleasing, her confidence grew. She'd never remember the amounts or the ingredients, but found it didn't matter.

"How about that?" she asked, pointing to a few sprigs of parsley.

"No, that comes just at the end. We don't want to drown it. Turn the heat down, just a little more. There." Satisfied, he nodded. "The cover goes on snug, then you let it simmer while the spices wake up."

Juliet wiped the back of her hand over her damp brow. "Carlo, you talk about the sauce as though it lived and breathed."

"My sauces do," he said simply. "While this simmers, you grate the cheese." He picked up a hunk and with his eyes closed, sniffed. *"Squisito."*

He had her grate and stir while the rest of the kitchen staff worked around them. Juliet thought of her mother's kitchen with its tidy counters and homey smells. She'd never seen anything like this. It certainly wasn't quiet. Pans were dropped, people and dishes were cursed, and fast was the order of the day. Busboys hustled in and out, weighed down with trays, waiters and waitresses breezed through demanding their orders. While she watched wide-eyed, Carlo ignored. It was time to create his pasta.

Unless it was already cooked and in a meal, Juliet thought of pasta as something you got off the shelf in a cardboard box. She learned differently, after her hands were white to the wrists with flour. He had her measure and knead and roll and spread until her elbows creaked. It was nothing like the five-minute throw-it-together kind she was used to.

As she worked, she began to realize why he had such stamina. He had to. In cooking for a living the way Franconi cooked for a living, he used as much energy as any athlete did. By the time the pasta had passed his inspection, her shoulder muscles ached the way they did after a brisk set of tennis.

Blowing the hair out of her eyes and mopping away sweat, Juliet turned to him. "What now?"

"Now you cook the pasta."

She tried not to grumble as she poured water into a Dutch oven and set it on to boil.

"One tablespoon salt," Carlo instructed.

"One tablespoon salt," she muttered and poured it in. When she turned around, he handed her a glass of wine.

"Until it boils, you relax."

"Can I turn down the heat?"

He laughed and kissed her, then decided it was only right to kiss her again. She smelled like heaven. "I like you in white." He dusted flour from her nose. "You're a messy cook, my love, but a stunning one."

It was easy to forget the noisy, bustling kitchen. "Cook?" A bit primly, she adjusted her hat. "Isn't it chef?"

He kissed her again. "Don't get cocky. One linguini doesn't make a chef."

She barely finished her wine when he put her back to work. "Put one end of the linguini in the water. Yes, just so. Now, as it softens coil them in. Careful. Yes,

yes, you have a nice touch. A bit more patience and I might take you on in my restaurant."

"No, thanks," Juliet said definitely as the steam rose in her face. She was almost certain she felt each separate pore opening.

"Stir easily. Seven minutes only, not a moment more." He refilled her glass and kissed her cheek.

She stirred, and drained, measured parsley, poured and sprinkled cheese. By the time she was finished, Juliet didn't think she could eat a thing. Nerves, she discovered with astonishment. She was as nervous as a new bride on her first day in the kitchen.

With her hands clasped together, she watched Carlo take a fork and dip in. Eyes closed, he breathed in the aroma. She swallowed. His eyes remained closed as he took the first sample. Juliet bit her lip. Until then, she hadn't noticed that the kitchen had become as quiet as a cathedral. A quick glimpse around showed her all activity had stopped and all eyes were on Carlo. She felt as though she were waiting to be sentenced or acquitted.

"Well?" she demanded when she couldn't stand it any longer.

"Patience," Carlo reminded her without opening his eyes. A busboy rushed in and was immediately shushed. Carlo opened his eyes and carefully set down the fork. *"Fantastico!"* He took Juliet by the shoulders and gave her the ceremonial kiss on each cheek as applause broke out.

Laughing, she pulled off her hat with a flourish. "I feel like I won a Gold Medal in the decathlon."

"You've created." As Pierre boomed orders for

plates, Carlo took both her hands. "We make a good team, Juliet Trent."

She felt something creeping too close to the heart. It just didn't seem possible to stop it. "Yes, we make a good team, Franconi."

Chapter 11

By twelve the next day, there was absolutely nothing left to be done. Carlo's remote control demonstration on the proper way to prepare linguini had gone far beyond Juliet's hopes for success. She'd stayed glued to the television, listening to Carlo's voice beside her and through the speakers. When her supervisor called personally to congratulate her, Juliet knew she had a winner. Relaxed and satisfied, she lay back on the bed.

"Wonderful." She folded her arms, crossed her ankles and grinned. "Absolutely wonderful."

"Did you ever doubt it?"

Still grinning, she shot a look at Carlo as he finished off the last of both shares of the late breakfast they'd ordered. "Let's just say I'm glad it's over."

"You worry too much, *mi amore*." But he hadn't seen her dig for her little roll of pills in three days. It pleased him enormously to know that he relaxed her so that she didn't need them. "When it comes to Franconi's linguini, you have always a success."

"After this I'll never doubt it. Now we have five hours before flight time. Five full, completely unscheduled hours."

Rising he sat on the end of the bed and ran his fingers along the arch of her foot. She looked so lovely when she smiled, so lovely when she let her mind rest. "Such a bonus," he murmured.

"It's like a vacation." With a sigh, she let herself enjoy the little tingles of pleasure.

"What would you like to do with our vacation of five full, unscheduled hours?"

She lifted a brow at him. "You really want to know?"

Slowly, he kissed each one of her toes. "Of course. The day is yours." He brushed his lips over her ankle. "I'm at your service."

Springing up, she threw her arms around his neck and kissed him, hard. "Let's go shopping."

Fifteen minutes later, Juliet strolled with Carlo through the first tower of the enormous circular shopping center attached to the hotel. People huddled around the maps of the complex, but she breezed around the curve and bypassed one. No maps, no schedules, no routes. Today, it didn't matter where they went.

"Do you know," she began, "with all the department stores, malls and cities we've been through, I haven't had a chance to shop?"

"You don't give yourself time."

"Same thing. Oh, look." She stopped at a window

display and studied a long evening dress covered with tiny silver bangles.

"Very dashing," Carlo decided.

"Dashing," Juliet agreed. "If I were six inches taller it might not make me look like a scaled-down pillar. Shoes." She pulled him along to the next shop.

In short order, Carlo discovered Juliet's biggest weakness. The way to her heart wasn't through food, nor was it paved with furs and diamonds. Jewelry displays barely earned her glance. Evening clothes brought a brief survey while day wear and sports clothes won mild interest. But shoes were something different. Within an hour, she'd studied, fondled and critiqued at least fifty pairs. She found a pair of sneakers at 30 percent off and bought them to add to an already substantial collection. Then with a careful maneuver to pick and choose, she weeded her selection down to three pair of heels, all Italian.

"You show excellent taste." With the patience of a man accustomed to shopping expeditions, Carlo lounged in a chair and watched her vacillate between one pair then the other. Idly, he picked up one shoe and glanced at the signature inside. "He makes an elegant shoe and prefers my lasagna."

Wide-eyed, Juliet pivoted on the thin heels. "You know him?"

"Of course. Once a week he eats in Franconi's."

"He's my hero." When Carlo gave her his lifted brow look, she laughed. "I know I can put on a pair of his shoes and go eight hours without needing emergency surgery. I'll take all three," she said on impulse, then sat down to exchange the heels for her newly bought sneakers.

"You make me surprised," he commented. "So many shoes when you have only two feet. This is not my practical Juliet."

"I'm entitled to a vice." Juliet pushed the Velcro closed. "Besides, I've always known Italians make the best shoes." She leaned closer to kiss his cheek. "Now I know they make the best…pasta." Without a blink at the total, she charged the shoes and pocketed the receipt.

Swinging the bag between them, they wandered from tower to tower. A group of women strolled by, earning Carlo's appreciation. Shopping during lunch hour, he gauged as he tossed an extra look over his shoulder. One had to admire the American workforce.

"You'll strain your neck that way," Juliet commented easily. She couldn't help but be amused by his blatant pleasure in anything female. He merely grinned.

"It's simply a matter of knowing just how far to go."

Comfortable, Juliet enjoyed the feel of his fingers laced with hers. "I'd never argue with the expert."

Carlo stopped once, intrigued by a choker in amethysts and diamonds. "This is lovely," he decided. "My sister, Teresa, always preferred purple."

Juliet leaned closer to the glass. The small, delicate jewels glimmered, hot and cold. "Who wouldn't? It's fabulous."

"She has a baby in a few weeks," he murmured, then nodded to the discreetly anxious clerk. "I'll see this."

"Of course, a lovely piece, isn't it?" After taking it out of the locked case, he placed it reverently in Carlo's hand. "The diamonds are all superior grade, naturally, and consist of one point three carat. The amethyst—"

"I'll have it."

Thrown off in the middle of his pitch, the clerk blinked. "Yes, sir, an excellent choice." Trying not to show surprise, he took the credit card Carlo handed him along with the choker and moved farther down the counter.

"Carlo." Juliet edged closer and lowered her voice. "You didn't even ask the price."

He merely patted her hand as he skimmed the other contents in the case. "My sister's about to make me an uncle again," he said simply. "The choker suits her. Now emeralds," he began, "would be your stone."

She glanced down at a pair of earrings with stones the color of dark, wet summer grass. The momentary longing was purely feminine and easily controlled. Shoes she could justify; emeralds, no. She shook her head and laughed at him. "I'll just stick with pampering my feet."

When Carlo had his present nicely boxed and his receipt in hand they wandered back out. "I love to shop," Juliet confessed. "Sometimes I'll spend an entire Saturday just roaming. It's one of the things I like best about New York."

"Then you'd love Rome." He'd like to see her there, he discovered. By the fountains, laughing, strolling through the markets and cathedrals, dancing in the clubs that smelled of wine and humanity. He wanted to have her there, with him. Going back alone was going back to nothing. He brought her hand to his lips as he thought of it, holding it there until she paused, uncertain.

"Carlo?" People brushed by them, and as his look became more intense, she swallowed and repeated his name. This wasn't the mild masculine appreciation she'd seen him send passing women, but something deep and dangerous. When a man looked at a woman this way, the woman was wise to run. But Juliet didn't know if it were toward him or away.

He shook off the mood, warning himself to tread carefully with her, and himself. "If you came," he said lightly, "I could introduce you to your hero. Enough of my lasagna and you'd have your shoes at cost."

Relieved, she tucked her arm through his again. "You tempt me to start saving for the airfare immediately. Oh, Carlo, look at this!" Delighted, she stopped in front of a window and pointed. In the midst of the ornate display was a three-foot Indian elephant done in high-gloss ceramic. Its blanket was a kaleidoscope of gilt and glitter and color. Opulent and regal, its head was lifted, its trunk curled high. Juliet fell in love. "It's wonderful, so unnecessarily ornate and totally useless."

He could see it easily in his living room along with the other ornate and useless pieces he'd collected over the years. But he'd never have imagined Juliet's taste running along the same path. "You surprise me again."

A bit embarrassed, she moved her shoulders. "Oh, I know it's awful, really, but I love things that don't belong anywhere at all."

"Then you must come to Rome and see my house." At her puzzled look, he laughed. "The last piece I acquired is an owl, this high." He demonstrated by holding out a palm. "It's caught a small, unfortunate rodent in its talons."

"Dreadful." With something close to a giggle, she kissed him. "I'm sure I'd love it."

"Perhaps you would at that," he murmured. "In any case, I believe the elephant should have a good home."

"You're going to buy it?" Thrilled, she clasped his hand as they went inside. The shop smelled of sandalwood and carried the tinkle of glass from wind chimes set swaying by a fan. She left him to make arrangements for shipping while she poked around, toying with long strings of brass bells, alabaster lions and ornamental tea services.

All in all, Juliet mused, it had been the easiest, most relaxing day she'd had in weeks, maybe longer. She'd remember it, that she promised herself, when she was alone again and life wound down to schedules and the next demand.

Turning, she looked at Carlo as he said something to make the clerk laugh. She hadn't thought there were men like him—secure, utterly masculine and yet sensitive to female moods and needs. Arrogant, he was certainly that, but generous as well. Passionate but gentle, vain but intelligent.

If she could have conjured up a man to fall in love with…oh no, Juliet warned herself with something like desperation. It wouldn't be Carlo Franconi. Couldn't be. He wasn't a man for one woman, and she wasn't a woman for any man. They both needed their freedom. To forget that would be to forget the plans she'd made and had been working toward for ten years. It was best to remember that Carlo was a ride on a carousel, and that the music only played so long.

She took a deep breath and waited for her own advice to sink in. It took longer than it should have. Determined, she smiled and walked to him. "Finished?"

"Our friend will be home soon, very soon after we are."

"Then we'll wish him bon voyage. We'd better start thinking airport ourselves."

With his arm around her shoulders, they walked out. "You'll give me our Philadelphia schedule on the plane."

"You're going to be a smash," she told him. "Though you might want to try my brewer's yeast before it's done."

"I can't believe it." At eight o'clock, Juliet dropped down into a chair outside customer service. Behind her, the conveyor belt of baggage was stopped. "The luggage went to Atlanta."

"Not so hard to believe," Carlo returned. He'd lost his luggage more times than he cared to remember. He gave his leather case a pat. His spatulas were safe. "So, when do we expect our underwear?"

"Maybe by ten tomorrow morning." Disgusted, Juliet looked down at the jeans and T-shirt she'd worn on the flight. She carried her toiletries and a few odds and ends in her shoulder bag, but nothing remotely resembling a business suit. No matter, she decided. She'd be in the background. Then she took a look at Carlo.

He wore a short-sleeved sweatshirt with the word *Sorbonne* dashed across it, jeans white at the stress points and a pair of sneakers that weren't nearly as new as hers. How the hell, she wondered, was he supposed to go on the air at 8:00 A.M. dressed like that?

"Carlo, we've got to get you some clothes."

"I have clothes," he reminded her, "in my bags."

"You're on *Hello, Philadelphia* in the morning at eight, from there we go directly to breakfast with reporters from the *Herald* and the *Inquirer*. At ten, when our bags may or may not be back, you're on *Midmorning Report*. After that—"

"You've already given me the schedule, my love. What's wrong with this?"

When he gestured toward what he wore, Juliet stood up. "Don't be cute, Carlo. We're heading for the closest department store."

"Department store?" Carlo allowed himself to be pulled outside. "Franconi doesn't wear department store."

"This time you do. No time to be choosey. What's in Philadelphia?" she muttered as she hailed a cab. "Wannamaker's." Holding the door open for him, she checked her watch. "We might just make it."

They arrived a half hour before closing. Though he grumbled, Carlo let her drag him through the old, respected Philadelphia institution. Knowing time was against them, Juliet pushed through a rack of slacks. "What size?"

"Thirty-one, thirty-three," he told her with his brow lifted. "Do I choose my own clothes?"

"Try this." Juliet held out a pair of dun-colored pleated slacks.

"I prefer the buff," he began.

"This is better for the camera. Now shirts." Leaving him holding the hanger, she pounced on the next rack. "Size?"

"What do I know from American sizes?" he grumbled.

"This should be right." She chose an elegant shade

of salmon in a thin silk that Carlo was forced to admit he'd have looked twice at himself. "Go put these on while I look at the jackets."

"It's like shopping with your mother," he said under his breath as he headed for the dressing rooms.

She found a belt, thin and supple with a fancy little buckle she knew he wouldn't object to. After rejecting a half dozen jackets she came across one in linen with a casual, unstructured fit in a shade between cream and brown.

When Carlo stepped out, she thrust them at him, then stood back to take in the entire view. "It's good," she decided as he shrugged the jacket on. "Yes, it's really good. The color of the shirt keeps the rest from being drab and the jacket keeps it just casual enough without being careless."

"The day Franconi wears clothes off the rack—"

"Only Franconi could wear clothes off the rack and make them look custom-tailored."

He stopped, meeting the laughter in her eyes. "You flatter me."

"Whatever it takes." Turning him around, she gave him a quick push toward the dressing room. "Strip it off, Franconi. I'll get you some shorts."

The look he sent her was cool, with very little patience. "There's a limit, Juliet."

"Don't worry about a thing," she said breezily. "The publisher'll pick up the tab. Make it fast; we've got just enough time to buy your shoes."

She signed the last receipt five minutes after the PA system announced closing. "You're set." Before he could do so himself, she bundled up his packages. "Now, if we can just get a cab to the hotel, we're in business."

"I wear your American shoes in protest."

"I don't blame you," she said sincerely. "Emergency measures, *caro*."

Foolishly, he was moved by the endearment. She'd never lowered her guard enough to use one before. Because of it, Carlo decided to be generous and forgive her for cracking the whip. "My mother would admire you."

"Oh?" Distracted, Juliet stood at the curb and held out her hand for a cab. "Why?"

"She's the only one who's ever poked and prodded me through a store and picked out my clothes. She hasn't done so in twenty years."

"All publicists are mothers," she told him and switched to her other arm. "We have to be."

He leaned closer and caught her earlobe between his teeth. "I prefer you as a lover."

A cab screeched to a halt at the curb. Juliet wondered if it was that which had stolen her breath. Steadying, she bundled Carlo and the packages inside. "For the next few days, I'll be both."

It was nearly ten before they checked into the Cocharan House. Carlo managed to say nothing about the separate rooms, but he made up his mind on the spot that she'd spend no time in her own. They had three days and most of that time would be eaten up with business. Not a moment that was left would be wasted.

He said nothing as they got into the elevator ahead of the bellman. As they rode up, he hummed to himself as Juliet chatted idly. At the door of his suite, he took her arm.

"Put all the bags in here, please," he instructed the bellman. "Ms. Trent and I have some business to see to immediately. We'll sort them out." Before she could say a word, he took out several bills and tipped the bellman himself. She remained silent only until they were alone again.

"Carlo, just what do you think you're doing? I told you before—"

"That you wanted a room of your own. You still have it," he pointed out. "Two doors down. But you're staying here, with me. Now, we'll order a bottle of wine and relax." He took the packages she still carried out of her hands and tossed them on a long, low sofa. "Would you prefer something light?"

"I'd prefer not to be hustled around."

"So would I." With a grin, he glanced over at his new clothes. "Emergency measures."

Hopeless, she thought. He was hopeless. "Carlo, if you'd just try to understand—"

The knock on the door stopped her. She only muttered a little as he went to answer.

"Summer!" She heard the delight in his voice and turned to see him wrapped close with a stunning brunette.

"Carlo, I thought you'd be here an hour ago."

The voice was exotic, hints of France, a slight touch of British discipline. As she stepped away from Carlo, Juliet saw elegance, flash and style all at once. She saw Carlo take the exquisite face in his hands, as he had so often with hers, and kiss the woman long and hard.

"Ah, my little puff pastry, you're as beautiful as ever."

"And you, Franconi, are as full of..." Summer broke off as she spotted the woman standing in the center of the room. She smiled, and though it was friendly enough, she didn't attempt to hide the survey. "Hello. You must be Carlo's publicist."

"Juliet Trent." Odd, Carlo felt as nervous as a boy introducing his first heartthrob to his mother. "This is Summer Cocharan, the finest pastry chef on either side of the Atlantic."

Summer held out a hand as she crossed into the room. "He's flattering me because he hopes I'll fix him an éclair."

"A dozen of them," Carlo corrected. "Beautiful, isn't she, Summer?"

While Juliet struggled for the proper thing to say, Summer smiled again. She'd heard something in Carlo's voice she'd never expected to. "Yes, she is. Horrid to work with, isn't he, Juliet?"

Juliet felt the laugh come easily. "Yes, he is."

"But never dull." Angling her head, she gave Carlo a quick, intimate look. Yes, there was something here other than business. About time, too. "By the way, Carlo, I should thank you for sending young Steven to me."

Interested, Carlo set down his leather case. "He's working out then?"

"Wonderfully."

"The young boy who wanted to be a chef," Juliet murmured and found herself incredibly moved. He hadn't forgotten.

"Yes, did you meet him? He's very dedicated," Summer went on when Juliet nodded. "I think your idea of sending him to Paris for training will pay off. He's going to be excellent."

"Good." Satisfied, Carlo patted her hand. "I'll speak with his mother and make the arrangements."

Brows knit, Juliet stared at him. "You're going to send him to Paris?"

"It's the only place to study cordon bleu properly." Carlo gave a shrug as though the matter were everyday. "Then, when he's fully trained, I'll simply steal him away from Summer for my own restaurant."

"Perhaps you will," Summer smiled. "Then again, perhaps you won't."

He was going to pay for the education and training of a boy he'd met only once, Juliet thought, baffled. What sort of a man was it who could fuss for twenty minutes over the knot of his tie and give with such total generosity to a stranger? How foolish she'd been to think, even for a minute, that she really knew him.

"It's very kind of you, Carlo," she murmured after a moment.

He gave her an odd look, then shrugged it off. "Dues are meant to be paid, Juliet. I was young once and had only a mother to provide for me. Speaking of mothers," he went on smoothly, changing the topic. "How is Monique?"

"Gloriously happy still," Summer told him, and smiled thinking of her mother. "Keil was obviously the man she'd been looking for." With a laugh, she turned back to Juliet. "I'm sorry, Carlo and I go back a long way."

"Don't be. Carlo tells me you and he were students together."

"A hundred years ago, in Paris."

"Now Summer's married her big American. Where's Blake, *cara*? Does he trust you with me?"

"Not for long." Blake came through the open doorway, still elegant after a twelve-hour day. He was taller than Carlo, broader, but Juliet thought she recognized a similarity. Power, both sexual and intellectual.

"This is Juliet Trent," Summer began. "She's keeping Carlo in line on his American tour."

"Not an easy job." A waiter rolled in a bucket of champagne and glasses. Blake dismissed him with a nod. "Summer tells me your schedule in Philadelphia's very tight."

"She holds the whip," Carlo told him with a gesture toward Juliet. But when his hand came down, it brushed her shoulder in a gesture of casual and unmistakable intimacy.

"I thought I might run over to the studio in the morning and watch your demonstration." Summer accepted the glass of champagne from her husband. "It's been a long time since I've seen you cook."

"Good." Carlo relaxed with the first sip of frosty wine. "Perhaps I'll have time to give your kitchen an inspection. Summer came here to remodel and expand Blake's kitchen, then stayed on because she'd grown attached to it."

"Quite right." Summer sent her husband an amused look. "In fact, I've grown so attached I've decided to expand again."

"Yes?" Interested, Carlo lifted his brow. "Another Cocharan House?"

"Another Cocharan," Summer corrected.

It took him a moment, but Juliet saw the moment the words had sunk in. Emotion she'd always expected from him, and it was there now, in his eyes as he set down his glass. "You're having a child."

"In the winter." Summer smiled and stretched out her hand. "I haven't figured out how I'm going to reach the stove for Christmas dinner."

He took her hand and kissed it, then kissed her cheeks, one by one. "We've come a long way, *cara mia.*"

"A very long way."

"Do you remember the merry-go-round?"

She remembered well her desperate flight to Rome to flee from Blake and her feelings. "You told me I was afraid to grab the brass ring, and so you made me try. I won't forget it."

He murmured something in Italian that made Summer's eyes fill. "And I've always loved you. Now make a toast or something before I disgrace myself."

"A toast." Carlo picked up his glass and slipped his free arm around Juliet. "To the carousel that doesn't end."

Juliet lifted her glass and, sipping, let the champagne wash away the ache.

Cooking before the camera was something Summer understood well. She spent several hours a year doing just that while handling the management of the kitchen in the Philadelphia Cocharan House, satisfying her own select clients with a few trips a year if the price and the occasion were important enough, and, most important of all, learning to enjoy her marriage.

Though she'd often cooked with Carlo, in the kitchen

of a palace, in the less expensive area of the flat she still kept in Paris and dozens of other places, she never tired of watching him in action. While she was said to create with the intensity of a brain surgeon, Carlo had the flair of an artist. She'd always admired his expansiveness, his ease of manner, and especially his theatrics.

When he'd put the finishing touches on the pasta dish he'd named, not immodestly, after himself, she applauded with the rest of the audience. But she'd hitched a ride to the studio with him and Juliet for more reason than to feed an old friend's ego. If Summer knew anyone in the world as well as she did herself, it was Carlo. She'd often thought, in many ways, they'd risen from the same dough.

"*Bravo,* Franconi." As the crew began to serve his dish to the audience, Summer went up to give him a formal kiss on the cheek.

"Yes." He kissed her back. "I was magnificent."

"Where's Juliet?"

"On the phone." Carlo rolled his eyes to the ceiling. "*Dio,* that woman spends more time on the phone than a new bride spends in bed."

Summer checked her watch. She'd noted Carlo's schedule herself. "I don't imagine she'll be long. I know you're having a late breakfast at the hotel with reporters."

"You promised to make crêpes," he reminded her, thinking unapologetically of his own pleasure.

"So I did. In return, do you think you could find a small, quiet room for the two of us?"

He grinned and wiggled his brows. "My love, when

Franconi can't oblige a lady with a quiet room, the world stops."

"My thoughts exactly." She hooked her arm through his and let him lead her down a corridor and into what turned out to be a storage room with an overhead light. "You've never lacked class, *caro*."

"So." He made himself comfortable on a stack of boxes. "Since I know you don't want my body, superb as it is, what's on your mind?"

"You, of course, *chérie*."

"Of course."

"I love you, Carlo."

Her abrupt seriousness made him smile and take her hands. "And I you, always."

"You remember, not so long ago when you came through Philadelphia on tour for another book?"

"You were wondering how to take the job redoing the American's kitchen when you were attracted to him and determined not to be."

"In love with him and determined not to be," she corrected. "You gave me some good advice here, and when I visited you in Rome. I want to return the favor."

"Advice?"

"Grab the brass ring, Carlo, and hold on to it."

"Summer—"

"Who knows you better?" she interrupted.

He moved his shoulders. "No one."

"I saw you were in love with her the moment I stepped into the room, the moment you said her name. We understand each other too well to pretend."

He sat a moment, saying nothing. He'd been skirting around the word, and its consequences, very carefully for days. "Juliet is special," he said slowly. "I've thought perhaps what I feel for her is different."

"Thought?"

He let out a small sound and gave up. "Known. But the kind of love we're speaking of leads to commitment, marriage, children."

Instinctively Summer touched a hand to her stomach. Carlo would understand that she still had small fears. She didn't have to speak of them. "Yes. You told me once, when I asked you why you'd never married, that no woman had made your heart tremble. Do you remember what you told me you'd do if you met her?"

"Run for a license and a priest." Rising, he slipped his hands into the pockets of the slacks Juliet had selected for him. "Easy words *before* the heart trembles. I don't want to lose her." Once said, he sighed. "It's never mattered before, but now it matters too much to make the wrong move. She's elusive, Summer. There are times I hold her and feel part of her pull away. I understand her independence, her ambition, and even admire them."

"I have Blake, but I still have my independence and my ambition."

"Yes." He smiled at her. "Do you know, she's so like you. Stubborn." When Summer lifted a brow, he grinned. "Hard in the head and so determined to be the best. Qualities I've always found strangely appealing in a beautiful woman."

"Merci, mon cher ami," Summer said dryly. "Then where's your problem?"

"You'd trust me."

She looked surprised, then moved her shoulders as though he'd said something foolish. "Of course."

"She can't—won't," Carlo corrected. "Juliet would find it easier to give me her body, even part of her heart than her trust. I need it, Summer, as much as I need what she's already given me."

Thoughtful, Summer leaned against a crate. "Does she love you?"

"I don't know." A difficult admission for a man who'd always thought he understood women so well. He smiled a little as he realized a man never fully understood the woman most important to him. With any other woman he'd have been confident he could guide and mold the emotions to his own preference. With Juliet, he was confident of nothing.

"There are times she seems very close and times she seems very detached. Until yesterday I hadn't fully begun to know my own mind."

"Which is?"

"I want her with me," he said simply. "When I'm an old man sitting by the fountains watching the young girls, I'll still want her with me."

Summer moved over to put her hands on his shoulders. "Frightening, isn't it?"

"Terrifying." Yet somehow, he thought, easier now that he'd admitted it. "I'd always thought it would be easy. There'd be love, romance, marriage and children. How could I know the woman would be a stubborn American?"

Summer laughed and dropped her forehead to his. "No more than I could know the man would be a stubborn American. But he was right for me. Your Juliet is right for you."

"So." He kissed Summer's temple. "How do I convince her?"

Summer frowned a moment, thinking. With a quick smile, she walked over to a corner. Picking up a broom, she held it out to him. "Sweep her off her feet."

Juliet was close to panic when she spotted Carlo strolling down the corridor with Summer on his arm. They might've been taking in the afternoon sun on the Left Bank. The first wave of relief evaporated into annoyance. "Carlo, I've turned this place upside down looking for you."

He merely smiled and touched a finger to her cheek. "You were on the phone."

Telling herself not to swear, she dragged a hand through her hair. "Next time you wander off, leave a trail of bread crumbs. In the meantime, I've got a very cranky cab driver waiting outside." As she pulled him along, she struggled to remember her manners. "Did you enjoy the show?" she asked Summer.

"I always enjoy watching Carlo cook. I only wish the two of you had more time in town. As it is, your timing's very wise."

"Yes?" Carlo pushed open the door and held it for both women.

"The French swine comes through next week."

The door shut with the punch of a bullet. "LaBare?"

Juliet turned back. She'd heard him snarl that name before. "Carlo—"

He held up a hand, silencing any interruption. "What does the Gallic slug do here?"

"Precisely what you've done," Summer returned. Tossing back her hair, she scowled at nothing. "He's written another book."

"Peasant. He's fit to cook only for hyenas."

"For rabid hyenas," Summer corrected.

Seeing that both of her charges were firing up, Juliet took an arm of each. "I think we can talk in the cab."

"He will not speak to you," Carlo announced, ignoring Juliet. "I will dice him into very small pieces."

Though she relished the image, Summer shook her head. "Don't worry. I can handle him. Besides, Blake finds it amusing."

Carlo made a sound like a snake. Juliet felt her nerves fraying. "Americans. Perhaps I'll come back to Philadelphia and murder him."

Trying her best, Juliet nudged him toward the cab. "Come now, Carlo, you know you don't want to murder Blake."

"LaBare," he corrected with something close to an explosion.

"Who is LaBare?" Juliet demanded in exasperation.

"Swine," Carlo answered.

"Pig," Summer confirmed. "But I have plans of my own for him. He's going to stay at the Cocharan House." Summer spread her hands and examined her nails. "I'm going to prepare his meals personally."

With a laugh, Carlo lifted her from the ground and kissed her. "Revenge, my love, is sweeter than even your meringue." Satisfied, he set her down again. "We were students with this slug." Carlo explained to Juliet. "His crimes are too numerous to mention." With a snap, Carlo adjusted his jacket. "I refuse to be on the same continent as he."

Running out of patience, Juliet glanced at the scowling cab driver. "You won't be," she reminded him. "You'll be back in Italy when he's here."

Carlo brightened and nodded. "You're right. Summer, you'll call me and tell me how he fell on his face?"

"Naturally."

"Then it's settled." His mood altered completely, he smiled and picked up the conversation as it ended before the mention of the Frenchman's name. "Next time we come to Philadelphia," Carlo promised. "You and I will make a meal for Blake and Juliet. My veal, your bombe. You haven't sinned, Juliet, until you've tasted Summer's bombe."

There wouldn't be a next time, Juliet knew, but she managed to smile. "I'll look forward to it."

Carlo paused as Juliet opened the door of the cab. "But tonight, we leave for New York."

Summer smiled as she stepped inside. "Don't forget to pack your broom."

Juliet started to climb into the front seat. "Broom?"

Carlo took Summer's hand in his and smiled. "An old French expression."

Chapter 12

Nₑw York hadn't changed. Perhaps it was hotter than when Juliet had left it, but the traffic still pushed, the people still rushed and the noise still rang. As she stood at her window at the Harley, she absorbed it.

No, New York hadn't changed, but she had.

Three weeks before, she'd looked out her office window at not so different a view. Her primary thought then had been the tour, to make a success of it. For herself, she admitted. She'd wanted the splash.

She realized she'd gotten it. At that moment, Carlo was in his suite, giving an interview to a reporter for the *Times*. She'd made a half-dozen excuses why she didn't have time to sit in on it. He'd accepted her usual list of phone calls and details, but the truth had been, she'd needed to be alone.

Later, there'd be another reporter and a photographer

from one of the top magazines on the stands. They had network coverage of his demonstration at Bloomingdale's. *The Italian Way* had just climbed to number five on the bestsellers list. Her boss was ready to canonize her.

Juliet tried to remember when she'd ever been more miserable.

Time was running out. The next evening, Carlo would board a plane and she'd take the short cab ride back to her apartment. While she unpacked, he'd be thousands of miles above the Atlantic. She'd be thinking of him while he flirted with a flight attendant or a pretty seat companion. That was his way; she'd always known it.

It wasn't possible to bask in success, to begin plans on her next assignment when she couldn't see beyond the next twenty-four hours.

Wasn't this exactly what she'd always promised herself wouldn't happen? Hadn't she always picked her way carefully through life so that she could keep everything in perfect focus? She'd made a career for herself from the ground up, and everything she had, she'd earned. She'd never considered it ungenerous not to share it, but simply practical. After all, Juliet had what she considered the perfect example before her of what happened when you let go of the reins long enough to let someone else pick them up.

Her mother had blindly handed over control and had never guided her own life again. Her promising career in nursing had dwindled down to doctoring the scraped knees of her children. She'd sacrificed hunks of herself for a man who'd cared for her but could never be faithful. How close had she come to doing precisely the same thing?

If she was still certain of anything, Juliet was certain she couldn't live that way. Exist, she thought, but not live.

So whether she wanted to or not, whether she thought she could or not, she had to think beyond the next twenty-four hours. Picking up her pad, she went to the phone. There were always calls to be made.

Before she could push the first button, Carlo strolled in. "I took your key," he said before she could ask. "So I wouldn't disturb you if you were napping. But I should've known." He nodded toward the phone, then dropped into a chair. He looked so pleased with himself she had to smile.

"How'd the interview go?"

"Perfectly." With a sigh, Carlo stretched out his legs. "The reporter had prepared my ravioli only last night. He thinks, correctly, that I'm a genius."

She checked her watch. "Very good. You've another reporter on the way. If you can convince him you're a genius—"

"He has only to be perceptive."

She grinned, then on impulse rose and went to kneel in front of him. "Don't change, Carlo."

Leaning down, he caught her face in his hands. "What I am now, I'll be tomorrow."

Tomorrow he'd be gone. But she wouldn't think of it. Juliet kissed him quickly then made herself draw away. "Is that what you're wearing?"

Carlo glanced down at his casual linen shirt and

trim black jeans. "Of course it's what I'm wearing. If I wasn't wearing this, I'd be wearing something else."

"Hmm." She studied him, trying to judge him with a camera's eye. "Actually, I think it might be just right for this article. Something informal and relaxed for a magazine that's generally starched collars and ties. It should be a unique angle."

"Grazie," he said dryly as he rose. "Now when do we talk about something other than reporters?"

"After you've earned it."

"You're a hard woman, Juliet."

"Solid steel." But she couldn't resist putting her arms around him and proving otherwise. "After you've finished being a hit across the hall, we'll head down to Bloomingdale's."

He nudged her closer, until their bodies fit. "And then?"

"Then you have drinks with your editor."

He ran the tip of his tongue down her neck. "Then?"

"Then you have the evening free."

"A late supper in my suite." Their lips met, clung, then parted.

"It could be arranged."

"Champagne?"

"You're the star. Whatever you want."

"You?"

She pressed her cheek against his. Tonight, this last night, there'd be no restriction. "Me."

It was ten before they walked down the hall to his suite again. Juliet had long since lost the urge to eat, but her enthusiasm in the evening hadn't waned.

"Carlo, it never ceases to amaze me how you perform. If you'd chosen show business, you'd have a wall full of Oscars."

"Timing, *innamorata*. It all has to do with timing."

"You had them eating your pasta out of your hand."

"I found it difficult," he confessed and stopped at the door to take her into his arms. "When I could think of nothing but coming back here tonight with you."

"Then you do deserve an Oscar. Every woman in the audience was certain you were thinking only of her."

"I did receive two interesting offers."

Her brow lifted. "Oh, really?"

Hopeful, he nuzzled her chin. "Are you jealous?"

She linked her fingers behind his neck. "I'm here and they're not."

"Such arrogance. I believe I still have one of the phone numbers in my pocket."

"Reach for it, Franconi, and I'll break your wrist."

He grinned at her. He liked the flare of aggression in a woman with skin the texture of rose petals. "Perhaps I'll just get my key then."

"A better idea." Amused, Juliet stood back as he opened the door. She stepped inside and stared.

The room was filled with roses. Hundreds of them in every color she'd ever imagined flowed out of baskets, tangled out of vases, spilled out of bowls. The room smelled like an English garden on a summer afternoon.

"Carlo, where did you get all these?"

"I ordered them."

She stopped as she leaned over to sniff at a bud. "Ordered them, for yourself?"

He plucked the bud out of its vase and handed it to her. "For you."

Overwhelmed, she stared around the room. "For me?"

"You should always have flowers." He kissed her wrist. "Roses suit Juliet best."

A single rose, a hundred roses, there was no in-between with Carlo. Again, he moved her unbearably. "I don't know what to say."

"You like them."

"Like them? Yes, of course, I love them, but—"

"Then you have to say nothing. You promised to share a late supper and champagne." Taking her hand, he led her across the room to the table already set by the wide uncurtained window. A magnum of champagne was chilling in a silver bucket, white tapers were waiting to be lit. Carlo lifted a cover to show delicately broiled lobster tails. It was, Juliet thought, the most beautiful spot in the world.

"How did you manage to have all this here, waiting?"

"I told room service to have it here at ten." He pulled out her chair. "I, too, can keep a schedule, my love." When he'd seated her, Carlo lit the candles, then dimmed the lights so that the silver glinted. At another touch, music flowed out toward her.

Juliet ran her fingertip down the slim white column of a candle then looked at him when he joined her. He drew the cork on the champagne. As it frothed to the lip, he filled two glasses.

He'd make their last night special, she thought. It was so like him. Sweet, generous, romantic. When they parted ways, they'd each have something memorable to take with them. No regrets, Juliet thought again and smiled at him.

"Thank you."

"To happiness, Juliet. Yours and mine."

She touched her glass to his, watching him as she sipped. "You know, some women might suspect a seduction when they're dined with champagne and candlelight."

"Yes. Do you?"

She laughed and sipped again. "I'm counting on it."

God, she excited him, just watching her laugh, hearing her speak. He wondered if such a thing would mellow and settle after years of being together. How would it feel, he wondered, to wake comfortably every morning beside the woman you loved?

Sometimes, he thought, you would come together at dawn with mutual need and sleepy passion. Other times you would simply lie together, secure in the night's warmth. He'd always considered marriage sacred, almost mysterious. Now he thought it would be an adventure—one he intended to share with no one but Juliet.

"This is wonderful." Juliet let the buttery lobster dissolve on her tongue. "I've been completely spoiled."

Carlo filled her glass again. "Spoiled. How?"

"This champagne's a far cry from the little Reisling I splurge on from time to time. And the food." She took another bite of lobster and closed her eyes. "In three weeks my entire attitude toward food has changed. I'm going to end up fat and penniless supporting my habit."

"So, you've learned to relax and enjoy. Is it so bad?"

"If I continue to relax and enjoy I'm going to have to learn how to cook."

"I said I'd teach you."

"I managed the linguini," she reminded him as she drew out the last bite.

"One lesson only. It takes many years to learn properly."

"Then I guess I'll have to make do with the little boxes that say complete meal inside."

"Sacrilege, *caro,* now that your palate is educated." He touched her fingers across the table. "Juliet, I still want to teach you."

She felt her pulse skid, and though she concentrated, she couldn't level it. She tried to smile. "You'll have to write another cookbook. Next time you tour, you can show me how to make spaghetti." Ramble, she told herself. When you rambled, you couldn't think. "If you write one book a year, I should be able to handle it. When you come around this time next year, I could manage the next lesson. By then, maybe I'll have my own firm and you can hire me. After three bestsellers, you should think about a personal publicist."

"A personal publicist?" His fingers tightened on hers then released. "Perhaps you're right." He reached in his pocket and drew out an envelope. "I have something for you."

Juliet recognized the airline folder and took it with a frown. "Is there trouble on your return flight? I thought I'd…" She trailed off when she saw her own name on a departing flight for Rome.

"Come with me, Juliet." He waited until her gaze lifted to his. "Come home with me."

More time, she thought as she gripped the ticket. He was offering her more time. And more pain. It was time she accepted there'd be pain. She waited until she was certain she could control her voice, and her words. "I can't, Carlo. We both knew the tour would end."

"The tour, yes. But not us." He'd thought he'd feel confident, assured, even cheerful. He hadn't counted on desperation. "I want you with me, Juliet."

Very carefully, she set the ticket aside. It hurt, she discovered, to take her hand from it. "It's impossible."

"Nothing's impossible. We belong with each other."

She had to deflect the words, somehow. She had to pretend they didn't run deep inside her and swell until her heart was ready to burst. "Carlo, we both have obligations, and they're thousands of miles apart. On Monday, we'll both be back at work."

"That isn't something that must be," he corrected. "It's you and I who must be. If you need a few days to tidy your business here in New York, we'll wait. Next week, the week after, we fly to Rome."

"Tidy my business?" She rose and found her knees were shaking. "Do you hear what you're saying?"

He did, and didn't know what had happened to the words he'd planned. Demands were coming from him where he'd wanted to show her need and emotion. He was stumbling over himself where he'd always been surefooted. Even now, cursing himself, he couldn't find solid ground.

"I'm saying I want you with me." He stood and grabbed her arms. The candlelight flickered over two confused faces. "Schedules and plans mean nothing, don't you see? I love you."

She went stiff and cold, as though he'd slapped her. A hundred aches, a multitude of needs moved through her, and with them the knowledge that he'd said those words too many times to count to women he couldn't even remember.

"You won't use that on me, Carlo." Her voice wasn't strong, but he saw fury in her eyes. "I've stayed with you until now because you never insulted me with that."

"Insult?" Astonished, then enraged, he shook her. "Insult you by loving you?"

"By using a phrase that comes much too easily to a man like you and doesn't mean any more than the breath it takes to say it."

His fingers loosened slowly until he'd dropped her arms. "After this, after what we've had together, you'd throw yesterdays at me? You didn't come to me untouched, Juliet."

"We both know there's a difference. I hadn't made my success as a lover a career." She knew it was a filthy thing to say but thought only of defense. "I told you before how I felt about love, Carlo. I won't have it churning up my life and pulling me away from every goal I've ever set. You—you hand me a ticket and say come to Rome, then expect me to run off with you for a fling, leaving my work and my life behind until we've had our fill."

His eyes frosted. "I have knowledge of flings, Juliet, of where they begin and where they end. I was asking you to be my wife."

Stunned, she took a step back, again as if he'd struck her. His wife? She felt panic bubble hot in her throat. "No." It came out in a whisper, terrified. Juliet ran to the door and across the hall without looking back.

It took her three days before she'd gathered enough strength to go back to her office. It hadn't been difficult to convince her supervisor she was ill and needed a replacement for the last day of Carlo's tour. As it was, the first thing he told her when she returned to the office days later was that she belonged in bed.

She knew how she looked—pale, hollow-eyed. But she was determined to do as she'd once promised herself. Pick up the pieces and go on. She'd never do it huddled in her apartment staring at the walls.

"Deb, I want to start cleaning up the schedule for Lia Barrister's tour in August."

"You look like hell."

Juliet glanced up from her desk, already cluttered with schedules to be photocopied. "Thanks."

"If you want my advice, you'll move your vacation by a few weeks and get out of town. You need some sun, Juliet."

"I need a list of approved hotels in Albuquerque for the Barrister tour."

With a shrug, Deb gave up. "You'll have them. In the meantime, look over these clippings that just came in on Franconi." Looking up, she noted that Juliet had knocked her container of paperclips on the floor. "Coordination's the first thing to go."

"Let's have the clippings."

"Well, there's one I'm not sure how to deal with." Deb slipped a clipping out of the folder and frowned at it. "It's not one of ours, actually, but some French chef who's just starting a tour."

"LaBare?"

Impressed, Deb looked up. "Yeah. How'd you know?"

"Just a sick feeling."

"Anyway, Franconi's name was brought up in the interview because the reporter had done a feature on him. This LaBare made some—well, unpleasant comments."

Taking the clipping, Juliet read what her assistant had highlighted. "Cooking for peasants by a peasant," she read in a mumble. "Oil, starch and no substance…" There was more, but Juliet just lifted a brow. She hoped Summer's plan of revenge went perfectly. "We're better off ignoring this," she decided, and dropped the clipping in the trash. "If we passed it on to Carlo, he might challenge LaBare to a duel."

"Skewers at ten paces?"

Juliet merely sent her a cool look. "What else have you got?"

"There might be a problem with the Dallas feature," she said as she gave Juliet a folder. "The reporter got carried away and listed ten of the recipes straight out of the book."

Juliet's head flew back. "Did you say ten?"

"Count 'em. I imagine Franconi's going to blow when he sees them."

Juliet flipped through the clippings until she came to it. The feature was enthusiastic and flattering. The timid Ms. Tribly had used the angle of preparing an entire meal from antipasto to dessert. Carlo's recipes from *The Italian Way* were quoted verbatim. "What was she thinking of?" Juliet muttered. "She could've used one or two without making a ripple. But this…"

"Think Franconi's going to kick up a storm?"

"I think our Ms. Tribly's lucky she's a few thousand miles away. You'd better get me legal. If he wants to sue, we'll be better off having all the facts."

After nearly two hours on the phone, Juliet felt almost normal. If there was a hollowness, she told herself it was a skipped lunch—and breakfast. If she tended to miss whole phrases that were recited to her, she told herself it was hard to keep up with legalese.

They could sue, or put Ms. Tribly's neck in a sling, both of which would create a miserable mess when she had two other authors scheduled for Dallas that summer.

Carlo would have to be told, she reflected as she hung up. It wouldn't be possible, or at least ethical, to crumple up the clipping and pretend it didn't exist as she had with the one from LaBare. The problem was whether to let legal inform him, pass it off through his editor or bite the bullet and write him herself.

It wouldn't hurt to write him, she told herself as she toyed with her pen. She'd made her decision, said her piece and stepped off the carousel. They were both adults, both professionals. Dictating his name on a letter couldn't cause her any pain.

Thinking his name caused her pain.

Swearing, Juliet rose and paced to the window. He hadn't meant it. As she had consistently for days, Juliet went over and over their last evening together.

It was all romance to him. Just flowers and candlelight. He could get carried away with the moment and not suffer any consequences. I love you—such a simple phrase. Careless and calculating. He hadn't meant it the way it had to be meant.

Marriage? It was absurd. He'd slipped and slid his way out of marriage all of his adult life. He'd known exactly how she'd felt about it. That's why he'd said it, Juliet decided. He'd known it was safe and she'd never agree. She couldn't even think about marriage for years. There was her firm to think of. Her goals, her obligations.

Why couldn't she forget the way he'd made her laugh, the way he'd made her burn? Memories, sensations didn't fade even a little with the days that had passed. Somehow they gained in intensity, haunted her. Taunted her. Sometimes—too often—she'd remember just the way he'd looked as he'd taken her face in his hand.

She touched the little heart of gold and diamonds she hadn't been able to make herself put away. More time, she told herself. She just needed more time. Perhaps she'd have legal contact him after all.

"Juliet?"

Turning from the window, Juliet saw her assistant at the door. "Yes?"

"I rang you twice."

"I'm sorry."

"There's a delivery for you. Do you want them to bring it in here?"

An odd question, Juliet thought and returned to her desk. "Of course."

Deb opened the door wider. "In here."

A uniformed man wheeled a dolly into the room. Confused, Juliet stared at the wooden crate nearly as big as her desk. "Where do you want this, Miss?"

"Ah—there. There's fine."

With an expert move, he drew the dolly free. "Just sign here." He held out a clipboard as Juliet continued to stare at the crate. "Have a nice day."

"Oh—yes, thank you." She was still staring at it when Deb came back in with a small crowbar.

"What'd you order?"

"Nothing."

"Come on, open it." Impatient, Deb handed her the crowbar. "I'm dying."

"I can't think what it might be." Slipping the crowbar under the lid, Juliet began to pry. "Unless my mother sent on my grandmother's china like she's been threatening for the last couple of years."

"This is big enough to hold a set for an army."

"Probably all packing," Juliet muttered as she put her back into it. When the lid came off, she began to push at the heaps of Styrofoam.

"Does your grandmother's china have a trunk?"

"A what?"

"A trunk." Unable to wait, Deb shoved through the styrofoam herself. "Good God, Juliet, it looks like an elephant."

Juliet saw the first foolish glitter and stopped thinking. "Help me get it out."

Between the two of them, they managed to lift the big, bulky piece of ceramic out of the crate and onto her desk. "That's the most ridiculous thing I've ever seen," Deb said when she caught her breath. "It's ugly, ostentatious and ridiculous."

"Yes," Juliet murmured, "I know."

"What kind of madman would send you an elephant?"

"Only one kind," Juliet said to herself and ran her hand lovingly down the trunk.

"My two-year-old could ride on it," Deb commented and spotted the card that had come out with the packing.

"Here you are. Now you'll know who to press charges against."

She wouldn't take the card. Juliet told herself she wouldn't look at it. She'd simply pack the elephant back up and ship it away. No sensible woman became emotional about a useless piece of glass three feet high.

She took the card and ripped it open.

Don't forget.

She started to laugh. As the first tears fell, Deb stood beside her without a clue. "Juliet—are you all right?"

"No." She pressed her cheek against the elephant and kept laughing. "I've just lost my mind."

When she arrived in Rome, Juliet knew it was too late for sanity. She carried one bag which she'd packed in a frenzy. If it'd been lost en route, she wouldn't have been able to identify the contents. Practicality? She'd left it behind in New York. What happened next would determine whether she returned for it.

She gave the cab driver Carlo's address and settled back for her first whirlwind ride through Rome. Perhaps she'd see it all before she went home. Perhaps she was home. Decisions had to be made, but she hoped she wouldn't make them alone.

She saw the fountains Carlo had spoken of. They rose and fell, never ending and full of dreams. On impulse she made the driver stop and wait while she dashed over to one she couldn't even name. With a wish, she flung in a coin. She watched it hit and fall to join thousands of other wishes. Some came true, she told herself. That gave her hope.

When the driver barreled up to the curb and jerked to a halt she began to fumble with bills. He took pity on her and counted out the fare himself. Because she was young and in love, he added only a moderate tip.

Not daring to let herself stop her forward progress, Juliet ran up to the door and knocked. The dozens of things she wanted to say, had planned to say, jumbled in her mind until she knew she'd never be able to guarantee what would come out first. But when the door opened, she was ready.

The woman was lovely, dark, curvy and young. Juliet felt the impetus slip away from her as she stared. So soon, was all she could think. He already had another woman in his home. For a moment, she thought only to turn and walk away as quickly as she could. Then her shoulders straightened and she met the other woman's eyes straight on.

"I've come to see Carlo."

The other woman hesitated only a moment, then smiled beautifully. "You're English."

Juliet inclined her head. She hadn't come so far, risked so much to turn tail and run. "American."

"Come in. I'm Angelina Tuchina."

"Juliet Trent."

The moment she offered her hand, it was gripped. "Ah, yes, Carlo spoke of you."

Juliet nearly laughed. "How like him."

"But he never said you would visit. Come this way. We're just having some tea. I missed him when he was in America, you see, so I've kept him home from the restaurant today to catch up."

It amazed her that she could find it amusing. It ran through her mind that Angelina, and many others, were going to be disappointed from now on. The only woman who was going to catch up with Carlo was herself.

When she stepped into the salon, amusement became surprise. Carlo sat in a high-backed satin chair, having an intense conversation with another female. This one sat on his lap and was no more than five.

"Carlo, you have company."

He glanced up, and the smile he'd used to charm the child on his lap vanished. So did every coherent thought in his mind. "Juliet."

"Here, let me take this." Angelina slipped Juliet's bag from her hand while she gave Carlo a speculative look. She'd never seen him dazed by a woman before. "Rosa, come say good morning to Signorina Trent. Rosa is my daughter."

Rosa slipped off Carlo's lap and, staring all the way, came to Juliet. "Good morning, Signorina Trent." Pleased with her English, she turned to her mother with a spate of Italian.

With a laugh, Angelina picked her up. "She says you have green eyes like the princess Carlo told her of. Carlo, aren't you going to ask Miss Trent to sit down?" With a sigh, Angelina indicated a chair. "Please, be comfortable. You must forgive my brother, Miss Trent. Sometimes he loses himself in the stories he tells Rosa."

Brother? Juliet looked at Angelina and saw Carlo's warm, dark eyes. Over the quick elation, she wondered how many different ways you could feel like a fool.

"We must be on our way." Angelina walked over to kiss her still silent brother's cheek. As she did, she was already planning to drop by her mother's shop and relate the story of the American who'd made Carlo lose his voice. "I hope we meet again while you're in Rome, Miss Trent."

"Thank you." Juliet took her hand and met the smile, and all its implications, with an acknowledging nod. "I'm sure we will."

"We'll let ourselves out, Carlo. *Ciao.*"

He was still silent as Juliet began to wander around the room, stopping here to admire this, there to study that. Art of every culture was represented at its most opulent. It should've been overwhelming, museumlike. Instead it was friendly and lighthearted, just a bit vain and utterly suited to him.

"You told me I'd like your home," she said at length. "I do."

He managed to rise but not to go to her. He'd left part of himself back in New York, but he still had his pride. "You said you wouldn't come."

She moved one shoulder and decided it was best not to throw herself at his feet as she'd intended. "You know women, Franconi. They change their minds. You know me." She turned then and managed to face him. "I like to keep business in order."

"Business?"

Grateful she'd had the foresight, Juliet reached in her purse and drew out the Dallas clipping. "This is something you'll want to look over."

When she came no farther, he was forced to go over and take it from her. Her scent was there, as always. It reminded him of too much, too quickly. His voice was flat and brisk as he looked at her. "You came to Rome to bring me a piece of paper?"

"Perhaps you'd better look at it before we discuss anything else."

He kept his eyes on hers for a long, silent minute before he lowered them to the paper. "So, more clippings," he began, then stopped. "What's this?"

She felt her lips curve at the change of tone. "What I thought you'd want to see."

She thought she understood the names he called the unfortunate Ms. Tribly though they were all in fast, furious Italian. He said something about a knife in the back, balled the clipping up and heaved it in a scrubbed hearth across the room. Juliet noted, as a matter of interest, that his aim was perfect.

"What does she try to do?" he demanded.

"Her job. A bit too enthusiastically."

"Job? Is it her job to quote all my recipes? And wrong!" Incensed, he whirled around the room. "She has too much oregano in my veal."

"I'm afraid I didn't notice," Juliet murmured. "In any case, you're entitled to retribution."

"Retribution." He relished the word and made a circle of his hands. "I'll fly to Dallas and squeeze my retribution from her skinny throat."

"There's that, of course." Juliet pressed her lips together to keep the laughter in. How had she ever thought she'd convince herself she could do without him? "Or a legal suit. I've given it a lot of thought, however, and feel the best way might be a very firm letter of disapproval."

"Disapproval?" He spun back to her. "Do you simply disapprove of murder in your country? She over-spiced my veal."

After clearing her throat, Juliet managed to soothe. "I understand, Carlo, but I believe it was an honest mistake all around. If you remember the interview, she was nervous and insecure. It appears to be you just overwhelmed her."

Muttering something nasty, he stuck his hands in his pockets. "I'll write to her myself."

"That might be just the right touch—if you let legal take a look at it first."

He scowled, then looked at her carefully from head to foot. She hadn't changed. He'd known she wouldn't. Somehow that fact comforted and distressed all at once. "You came to Rome to discuss lawsuits with me?"

She took her life in her hands. "I came to Rome," she said simply.

He wasn't sure he could go any closer without having to touch, and touching, take. The hurt hadn't faded. He wasn't certain it ever would. "Why?"

"Because I didn't forget." Since he wouldn't come to her, she went to him. "Because I couldn't forget, Carlo. You asked me to come and I was afraid. You said you loved me and I didn't believe you."

He curled his fingers to keep them still. "And now?"

"Now I'm still afraid. The moment I was alone, the moment I knew you'd gone, I had to stop pretending. Even when I had to admit I was in love with you, I thought I could work around it. I thought I had to work around it."

"Juliet." He reached for her, but she stepped back quickly.

"I think you'd better wait until I finish. Please," she added when he only came closer.

"Then finish quickly. I need to hold you."

"Oh, Carlo." She closed her eyes and tried to hang on. "I want to believe I can have a life with you without giving up what I am, what I need to be. But you see, I love you so much I'm afraid I'd give up everything the moment you asked me."

"*Dio,* what a woman!" Because she wasn't certain if it was a compliment or an insult, Juliet remained silent as he took a quick turn around the room. "Don't you understand that I love you too much to ask? If you weren't who you are, I wouldn't be in love with you? If I love Juliet Trent, why would I want to change her into that Juliet Trent?"

"I don't know, Carlo. I just—"

"I was clumsy." When she lifted her hands, he caught them in his to quiet her. "The night I asked you to marry me, I was clumsy. There were things I wanted to say, ways I'd wanted to say them, but it was too important. What comes easily with every woman becomes impossible with the only woman."

"I didn't think you'd meant—"

"No." Before she could resist, he'd brought her hands to his lips. "I've thought back on what I said to you. You thought I was asking you to give up your job, your home, and come to Rome to live with me. I was asking less, and much more. I should have said—Juliet, you've become my life and without you, I'm only half of what I was. Share with me."

"Carlo, I want to." She shook her head and went into his arms. "I want to. I can start over, learn Italian. There must be a publisher in Rome who could use an American."

Drawing her back by the shoulders, he stared at her. "What are you talking about, starting over? You're starting your own firm. You told me."

"It doesn't matter. I can—"

"No." He took her more firmly. "It matters a great deal, to both of us. So you'll have your own firm one day in New York. Who knows better than I how successful you'll be? I can have a wife to brag about as much as I brag about myself."

"But you have your restaurant here."

"Yes. I think perhaps you'd consider having a branch of your public relations company in Rome. Learning Italian is an excellent decision. I'll teach you myself. Who better?"

"I don't understand you. How can we share our lives if I'm in New York and you're in Rome?"

He kissed her because it had been much too long. He drew her closer because she was willing to give something he'd never have asked. "I never told you my plans that night. I've been considering opening another restaurant. Franconi's in Rome is, of course, the best. Incomparable."

She found his mouth again, dismissing any plans but that. "Of course."

"So, a Franconi's in New York would be twice the best."

"In New York?" She tilted her head back just enough

to see him. "You're thinking of opening a restaurant in New York?"

"My lawyers are already looking for the right property. You see, Juliet, you wouldn't have escaped me for long."

"You were coming back."

"Once I could be certain I wouldn't murder you. We have our roots in two countries. We have our business in two countries. We'll have our lives in two countries."

Things were so simple. She'd forgotten his unending generosity. Now she remembered everything they'd already shared, thought of everything they'd yet to share. She blinked at tears. "I should've trusted you."

"And yourself, Juliet." He framed her face until his fingers slid into her hair. *"Dio,* how I've missed you. I want my ring on your finger, and yours on mine."

"How long does it take to get a license in Rome?"

Grinning, he whirled her in his arms. "I have connections. By the end of the week you'll be—what is it?—stuck with me."

"And you with me. Take me to bed, Carlo." She pressed against him, knowing she had to get still closer. "I want you to show me again what the rest of our lives will be like."

"I've thought of you, here, with me." He pressed his lips against her temple as he remembered the words she'd hurled at him on that last night. "Juliet." Troubled, he drew away, touching only her hands. "You know what I am, how I've lived. I can't take it back, nor would I if I could. There've been other women in my bed."

"Carlo." Her fingers tightened on his. "Perhaps I said foolish things once, but I'm not a fool. I don't want to be the first woman in your bed. I want to be the last. The only."

"Juliet, *mi amore,* from this moment there is only you."

She pressed his hand to her cheek. "Can you hear it?"

"What?"

"The carousel." Smiling, she held out her arms. "It's never stopped."

* * * * *

REQUEST YOUR FREE BOOKS!

2 FREE NOVELS
FROM THE ROMANCE COLLECTION
PLUS 2 FREE GIFTS!

YES! Please send me 2 FREE novels from the Romance Collection and my 2 FREE gifts (gifts are worth about $10). After receiving them, if I don't wish to receive any more books, I can return the shipping statement marked "cancel." If I don't cancel, I will receive 4 brand-new novels every month and be billed just $6.24 per book in the U.S. or $6.74 per book in Canada. That's a savings of at least 22% off the cover price. It's quite a bargain! Shipping and handling is just 50¢ per book in the U.S. and 75¢ per book in Canada.* I understand that accepting the 2 free books and gifts places me under no obligation to buy anything. I can always return a shipment and cancel at any time. Even if I never buy another book, the two free books and gifts are mine to keep forever.

194/394 MDN F4XY

Name _____ (PLEASE PRINT) _____

Address _____ Apt. # _____

City _____ State/Prov. _____ Zip/Postal Code _____

Signature (if under 18, a parent or guardian must sign)

Mail to the Harlequin® Reader Service:
IN U.S.A.: P.O. Box 1867, Buffalo, NY 14240-1867
IN CANADA: P.O. Box 609, Fort Erie, Ontario L2A 5X3

Want to try two free books from another line?
Call 1-800-873-8635 or visit www.ReaderService.com.

* Terms and prices subject to change without notice. Prices do not include applicable taxes. Sales tax applicable in N.Y. Canadian residents will be charged applicable taxes. Offer not valid in Quebec. This offer is limited to one order per household. Not valid for current subscribers to the Romance Collection or the Romance/Suspense Collection. All orders subject to credit approval. Credit or debit balances in a customer's account(s) may be offset by any other outstanding balance owed by or to the customer. Please allow 4 to 6 weeks for delivery. Offer available while quantities last.

Your Privacy—The Harlequin® Reader Service is committed to protecting your privacy. Our Privacy Policy is available online at www.ReaderService.com or upon request from the Harlequin Reader Service.

We make a portion of our mailing list available to reputable third parties that offer products we believe may interest you. If you prefer that we not exchange your name with third parties, or if you wish to clarify or modify your communication preferences, please visit us at www.ReaderService.com/consumerschoice or write to us at Harlequin Reader Service Preference Service, P.O. Box 9062, Buffalo, NY 14269. Include your complete name and address.

ROM13R

ANOUSKA KNIGHT

How do you learn to love again?

In one tragic moment, Holly Jefferson's life as she knew it changed forever. Now—to the external world, at least—she's finally getting back on her feet, running her bakery. But inside, she's still going through the motions befitting a twenty-seven-year-old widow.

Then she meets Ciaran Argyll. His privileged and charmed life feels a million miles from her own. However, there's more to Ciaran than the superficial world that surrounds him, and he, too, is wrestling with his own ghosts. Will Holly find the missing ingredient that allows her to live again—and embrace an unknown and unexpected tomorrow?

Available now wherever books are sold.

Be sure to connect with us at:
Harlequin.com/Newsletters
Facebook.com/HarlequinBooks
Twitter.com/HarlequinBooks

HARLEQUIN® HQN™
www.Harlequin.com

PHAK928

NORA ROBERTS